Reviews from readers like you. . . .

"Amazing, thoroughly gripping, and terrifically exciting...A big thumbs up for a must read book. It's hard to put the book down once you've started to read this magnificent story."
Bella Hoadley, Fresno, California

"All the ingredients one loves to see in a novel. In addition to the many historical facts was romance, secrets, suspense and intrigue, all of which leaves you anxious to see what happens next...A well written tale."
Sandy Swanson, Tulsa, Oklahoma

"A very descriptive and entertaining storyline that makes you feel you're right there in the action with the characters, seeing the story unfold...Hard book to put down, with an unexpected twist at the end...Definitely worth reading."
Bobby Fena, Fresno, California

"A sensational...riveting tale of an era that still haunts us today."
Linda Starr, Sacramento, California

"The Camburin Seed has all the elements of a great drama. I wouldn't be surprised if we see this on the big screen some day. I would recommend this book to men and women alike. . ."
Jocelyn Fuller, Fresno Magazine

THE CAMBURIN SEED

Mitch Taylor

ISBN 0-9765475-0-3

♣ Simba's Publishing

Mailing Address:
P.O. Box 27634
Fresno, CA 93729-7634
website: SimbasPublishing.com
Toll Free: 1-877-274-6227

Printed in the United States Of America

INTRODUCTION

The sole purpose of this book is to tell the story of a
dangerous time when the best and the worst in man
battled. To capture the heart of the story, I have taken
certain liberties with descriptions of some of the
locations for continuity. Yet, I have tried to remain
faithful to the historical events. It is not a travel log,
but a story of love, courage and betrayal during a war
that was measured in the number of lives lost. It is not
my intention that upon completing this book the
reader travel to the Far East, rather, it is my hope that
the reader will appreciate more, those they love, and
realize that all extraordinary accomplishments are
achieved by ordinary people.

This book is dedicated to my lovely wife, Marsha, who has believed in me every step of the way and gave me the courage to make this book a reality.

AND

Special thanks to Bill Donohue for editing this book.

CHAPTER ONE

The engine of the jet droned on in the night as they moved across the China Sea toward Southeast Asia. Brian was unable to sleep on airplanes; his long legs were always uncomfortably curled and stuffed between the seats. Jealously, he glanced at his fellow passengers who were sleeping comfortably, and he wondered why they were going to Thailand. A few of the passengers were wearing American military uniforms, but most were dressed as businessmen. Again Brian complained to himself that his luck should have been better. Since American troops had left Vietnam, the world ignored that part of the globe. It was 1975, and there was even a peaceful co-existence between North and South Vietnam, although it was an uneasy peace and did not appear likely to last. Brian was convinced that the world was tired of reading about Asians killing one another. So the trouble in Cambodia was of little interest to him, and it was just an inconvenience to the world. His plan to work for a news service had been made with the assumption that he would be stationed in the Mid-East and eventually Europe. Having to start in Bangkok had come as a disappointment, and he intended to make it a short stay. After working for one of the largest papers in America for four years, he was secure in his talent. He was determined that he would quickly find the means to showcase his writing and immediately demand reassignment. Asia was no place for him. America was finally free of Vietnam, and he was not going to be ensnared into a back page region where he would be forgotten.

Brian felt the stare of someone, and looking around he found a stewardess watching him. When she realized he had caught her staring she hurriedly approached him.

"Can I get you something? Another pillow perhaps?" She wore too much makeup to actually be attractive, but her smile was warm and her figure was full.

"I'm fine," he replied with a smile. Brian was used to being shown attention from women and he handled it with ease.

"Is this your first trip to Thailand?"

"Yes, I'm afraid it's my first trip out of the United States," he smiled.

"What brings you so far from home?"

"My work. I'm a journalist." Brian's voice lacked enthusiasm.

"I think you'll find it interesting," She said as she began to straighten his pillow. "But it's terribly hot. We have a layover there for two days, and I'll spend it in a pool or air-conditioned hotel room." An overhead call light turned on several rows ahead of Brian's seat. "I better see what they need." The stewardess turned and moved away. As she did she glanced back over her shoulder and smiled at Brian.

Brian returned the gesture and then decided to act as if he were trying to sleep. He didn't want to visit with her any longer. Turning in his seat he tried to find a more comfortable position and reminded himself of his promise. He would do whatever it took to be re-assigned to the Mid-East or Europe. Then he would return home within a few years to write his own ticket. He had no interest in the stewardess so he closed his eyes and pretended to fall asleep.

     With a surprising jolt, Brian awoke when the jet touched down. Still half asleep, he glanced around the cabin unsure of his surroundings until he found the smile of the stewardess and realized where he was. He was tired and uncomfortable. For what seemed like a long time, the airplane taxied about the airport. Watching out the window Brian found the airport facilities to be nearly non-existent for an international airport. There were few airplanes, and the buildings looked old and in need of maintenance. There were no jet ways being extended to the few planes that were there. Instead, pick-up trucks with steps welded to their backs chased after the awkward slow moving aircraft like autograph hunters.
     When the airplane finally came to a full stop, the passengers jumped up from their seats to swiftly gather their belongings only to find themselves in long lines that were not moving. Without leaving his seat, Brian watched the exercise in futility with a superior smile.
     Then with great anticipation the doors of the jumbo jet were opened. Those closest to the doors let out an uncomfortable sigh that Brian understood when the wave of hot air from outside the jet reached his seat. Never before had he felt anything quite like it, the air was steamy and instantly terribly uncomfortable.
     "Oh God, what have I done?" he said aloud to himself. At that moment his only ambition was to reach the air-conditioned terminal. Brian grabbed his carry-on bag from the overhead storage bin and forced

his way into the line of slowly deplaning passengers. When he reached the door the stewardesses were thanking everyone for traveling on their airline and wishing them well. As Brian passed the stewardess that had spoke to him, she discreetly placed a small piece of paper in his hand.

"Thank you for flying with us," she smiled.

Brian promptly returned the smile and hurried down the portable staircase. When he reached the ground, he opened his hand and saw the name of a hotel written on the paper. Without hesitating he dropped the paper and hurried towards the terminal doors. When he stepped inside the terminal Brian paused in anticipation of relief from the air conditioning, but it did not come. Looking around in confusion, he realized that all the doors in the terminal were open, and there was no air conditioning. Miserably hot, he began to make his way through the crowd to find the reception he had been promised. Disappointedly, he looked up and down the row of little Thai men holding signs with passengers' names. All the men wore the same type of thin rubber sandals. Their shirt tales were un-tucked, and exaggerated smiles exposed bad teeth, but none of them held a sign with his name.

"Brian Trask," an American voice called.

"That's me," Brian answered looking over the crowd. Behind several rows of people waiting and greeting the arrivals stood an odd combination of two men. One was a rough looking American about 45 years old. He was of medium height and built as though at one time he had a good physique. His hair was thinning but his bright blue eyes were alert. Next to him stood an extraordinarily tall Asian dressed in a brown suit, white shirt and thin dark tie. He looked more like an American Indian than an Asian and towered above his countryman.

Brian made his way through the crowd. "I'm Brian Trask," he said again when he reached them. The American did not reply or appear friendly. Instead he watched Brian closely for a moment until he realized he was making Brian uncomfortable and only then held out his hand with a smile.

"I'm Sheldon Harris, your new boss." They shook hands firmly. "And this is Prince Kriangsak. Welcome to Bangkok."

Taken by surprise by the introduction, Brian left his hand half extended. "Prince?" He looked at Sheldon not knowing what to do next. Prince Kriangsak nobly grasped Brian's hand in his massive hand and shook it vigorously.

"Don't worry," laughed Sheldon. "Princes are one thing Thailand has more of than they know what to do with. You'll meet more than one prince while you're here." Brian mispronounced the prince's name as he responded to the handshake, which caused Sheldon to laugh again. "Call him Prince. Everyone else does."

The tall Asian smiled at Brian in a warm, almost childish manner. "Sheldon is not the most respectful person, but it's ok."

"Thank you," replied Brian, wanting to laugh but still unsure if it was a joke. "I have another bag to pick up, Mr. Harris."

"Call me Sheldon. The baggage claim is this way." Sheldon turned and started down a hallway. As he followed, Brian couldn't keep himself from repeatedly turning to look back at the prince, as if he would observe something royal.

"Are you really a prince?" he finally had to ask.

The tall figure nodded proudly and then smiled, exposing long, yellow teeth that needed a dentist.

"He probably is," answered Sheldon glancing back. "But then again, I once met a prince driving a cab."

Watching the prince, Brian expected to see insult spread across his face, but instead he continued to smile.

"There is some connection somewhere, or at least he insists there is," Sheldon continued. "And to be truthful, people treat him as if he's important."

They reached the baggage claim area, and Brian quickly retrieved his second bag.

"Are you hungry?" asked Sheldon.

"Not really. I ate on the plane."

"Well, you're going to eat again. There's a restaurant across the street I like, and there's someone there I want to see."

"Certainly," replied Brian.

They all started for the main doors of the terminal. Brian watched the prince as he walked. When the Thai noticed Brian was still staring, he turned to face Brian and smiled.

"Are you really a prince?" Brian asked.

The yellow teeth grinned at him again, while the Prince nodded proudly.

Stepping outside, Brian expected to see a building on the opposite side of the road. Instead there was a roof of corrugated, rusty metal held up by wooden poles. Rickety wooden tables were pushed close together in the shade, and at one end a cook stood over a wood-burning stove built out of bricks.

"That's your restaurant?" Brian asked disbelievingly.

"You're in Asia now," Sheldon said, as he stepped between two parked cars and timed his crossing of the street. "No better place to eat than where the locals prefer," he added over his shoulder as he and the Prince speedily started across the street.

Reluctantly, Brian stood on the sidewalk and watched the Thais enjoy their meals.

By the time Brian managed the traffic with his two bags, the Prince and Sheldon sat comfortably at a table. Dropping his bags, Brian pulled a rickety chair to him and sat down. "I can't believe the heat!"

"You'll get used to it," said Sheldon in an uninterested tone. He was busy watching someone in the crowd. "Order the soup. You'll enjoy that, but only eat the shrimp at the bottom."

"I'm really not hungry."

A waitress appeared over his shoulder, and Sheldon ordered in Thai. From his gestures Brian realized Sheldon had ignored him and ordered for the three of them. Almost instantly, a brown bottle was placed in front of each of them. The bottle was cold and wet from the ice bucket it had been stored in.

"That's the largest bottle of beer I've ever seen," said Brian. Filling his glass, he took a large drink. It was bitter with a terribly sharp after-taste, and his lips went numb from the first sip. "What's in this?" he said shaking his head. The waitress set three large bowls of soup down. Thinking it would get rid of the beer's taste, Brain took a large spoonful. As he did, Sheldon's eyes grew wide. Instantly Brian's mouth was on fire.

"I told you to eat the shrimp at the bottom," said Sheldon with a laugh.

Brian's eyes were watering. He reached out and quickly finished the glass of beer and then re-ordered and drank two more.

Sheldon slowly ate the shrimp from the bottom of his bowl. He was clearly preoccupied with watching someone in the crowd, and the Prince was preoccupied with watching Sheldon. When Brian had enough of the silence, he leaned back and tried to pick out who it was that held Sheldon's attention. "Who are we watching?" he asked still wiping his tears.

Sheldon was surprised by his question as though he had forgotten Brian was even there. "You see that young man sitting at the table near the end? The table with two other men and one woman?"

"I can't see ... Oh yes, I see him now. The unshaven one with messy hair?"

"Yeah, that's him," replied Sheldon. The Prince did not turn to look.

"Why is he of such interest?"

"Oh, I don't know." Sheldon tried to turn his attention to Brian but he promptly returned to watching the young man. "He's a student activist, or at least he used to be. You know, Yankee-go-home type. His name came up with something I've been working on with one of our guys in Cambodia."

"Cambodia!" Brian's laugh turned Sheldon's attention to him.

"Yeah. You've heard of it?" mocked Sheldon.

The Prince had finished his soup without any effect from the spice and leaned forward into the conversation. "Sheldon suspects everyone these days. The boy is a fairly well known peace activist, just as you have in your universities."

"Chovat hasn't been at the university in over a year!" exclaimed Sheldon. "If anything, he's a criminal, a black marketer. But any time I put someone on him, we come up empty." Sheldon turned his attention back to Brian. "But now I've a good correspondent in Cambodia named Godfrey, and

Chovat's name has been connected with a big story from there. That's not just some harmless student!"

"Put me on Chovat!" Brian enthusiastically leaned back for another look at Chovat.

"You?" said Sheldon disbelievingly. "You couldn't find your way across town yet," Sheldon laughed. "No, you're going to be busy just trying to figure out what country you're in for awhile."

"I can do it!" demanded Brian.

Sheldon ignored him and went back to eating his soup.

CHAPTER TWO

Even on a late Sunday afternoon the streets of the city were busy. As had become his habit, Brian had gone into the office when he knew Sheldon was absent to see the latest report on Cambodia. Unfortunately, he had not been able to convince Sheldon to allow him to independently cover anything of real importance.   The war in Cambodia was growing from a province dispute to a question of survival for the pro-US Regime. He told himself that sooner or later he would be in the office when something big happened and Sheldon's absence would be the beginning of his career. Brian hadn't grown particularly fond of any of the Thai staff; in fact, he found them a damned nuisance. Indeed, the interior city was a nuisance and he was anxious to transfer to the Mid-East.

Disappointed that today was not going to bring any important breaking story, Brian set out walking for the Cho Phia Hotel. There was no major downtown or central district to the city. Rather hotels, businesses and homes were mixed together with clubs and bars sprinkled throughout.

Like most other Americans in the city, he had adopted Tiger's Bar as his socializing spot. It was a natural gathering place, and every ex-patriot ended up there sooner or later. There was an interesting assortment of American businessmen and retired military that had made Bangkok their home to avoid retiring to the confines of American society. But today being Sunday, the Hotel Cho Phia would be the place to go. The hotel would be showing films of sporting events, sometimes football, sometimes baseball or basketball. You never knew which it would be until the lights were dimmed and the old projector flickered to life. It didn't matter that the films were of games played years ago. Everyone enjoyed the slice of home and became excited as if they were watching the game live. The fact was that it was very American and attracted Americans from all over the city to eat popcorn and enjoy the company of their own kind. Besides, the hotel was one of the exceptions to the local law that forbade the selling of liquor and beer in the afternoon between the hours of two and five. Like anyplace else, Bangkok had laws, but unlike anywhere else, there were clearly defined exceptions.

When he came to the last corner that required crossing, the traffic was too thick to venture into. Glancing over his shoulder, he noticed a Buddhist monk sitting out of the way with his legs folded beneath his thin orange robe. For some reason they made Brian feel a little uneasy, probably because of the memory of seeing T.V. news reports of monks in Vietnam pouring gasoline on themselves and lighting themselves on fire to protest the war. Any sort of fanaticism made Brian uneasy, and when a young man, regardless of social status would shave his head, dress in an orange robe and spend three months living in the streets off the un-requested generosity of passers-by, Brian thought it safe to say you were dealing with a fanatic.

The air was hideous with the smell of gasoline and diesel exhaust. He shook his head at the thought of the monk picking such a place to beg. A city bus passed very close to the curb and its black smoke made Brian choke. Buses were loud noisy gray things with every side window broken out. The busses moved through the city so packed with people that some of the passengers hung partially out the broken windows. During rush hour it was not unusual to see them so overloaded on one side that they traveled along at a tilt.

Bangkok was a disorganized city that had collided with modern times. The truck and car drivers constantly blew their horns and changed lanes any time the impulse struck them. On occasion, Brian had seen cabs slip through a traffic jam by driving onto a sidewalk and chasing the pedestrians into building doorways. Crossing a street was a perilous task and not to be taken lightly. It required a cunning ability to anticipate which direction every approaching vehicle might go. The only redeeming feature of the motoring public was the unspoken rule to never become upset with someone blowing his horn or cutting you off. It was simply to be expected.

At just the right moment Brian dashed across the boulevard and into the crowd on the far sidewalk. There he was caught up in a human obstacle course where he was frequently forced to step around, or over the black-clothed peasants that were peppered among the otherwise modern crowd. On the peasants shoulders rested bamboo poles with baskets on each end filled with fruits, vegetables, and large spiny melons of some sort. They wandered along at a slow pace, and blocked the flow of pedestrians to stare up at a tall building. Then they would stop, sometimes in front of small-westernized grocery stores and sit down and open up shop. They didn't speak to the passers-by; they just waited. Most of them were old, prune-faced women that watched from under pointed coolie hats with tired and lonely expressions. Brian was certain their sad looks were as intentional as neon signs, so he ignored them. No matter where you were in the city, they were there and invariably with the same expression.

There was an opening in the crowd so he slipped through and picked up his pace. Over the sidewalk, mingling with the car exhaust, came the smell of Kobe beef being barbecued on a hibachi. Every other block or so, some modern-dressed Thai had a Kobe concession. It was a smoky, delicious smell, and the brown sauce they put over the meat gave it a sweet aroma. Every time Brian managed to control his appetite with three or four of the small wooden spears wrapped with thin slices of meat. The cook's hands were always dirty, and clouds of flies hovered just above the puffs of smoke. Brian moved to the edge of the sidewalk closest to the street where he could avoid every stop and start of the crowd. One after another motorbikes buzzed by him like angry bees. The bikers used the gutter for their own private lane, and the bikes blew dirty water and litter up at him as they passed. Remembering how, once as a boy, he had ridden his bicycle in the gutters until he hit something slimy that made him fall and break his arm, he watched them speed down the block hoping it would happen to them.

Passing a demolished building, Brian watched a family of workers loading debris into wheelbarrows by hand. Everyone in the family was struggling, even a small shirtless boy of four or five years. He was barely as large as the broken bricks he carried and he was dirty and very tired. His steady pace and inattentive parents made it obvious that he was used to the work and that he understood that by filling the wheelbarrows, he was filling his rice bowl.

Near the river, the old north side of the city had been designed after the cities of Europe. Wide boulevards like spokes of a wheel dumped into circular drives that had monuments as hubs. The buildings were made of stone, and both the streets and the buildings were well kept and clean. However, at some point in its history, the blueprint of Bangkok had been distorted. As it had grown south towards the Gulf of Siam, the city had hurriedly erected offices and hotels fashioned after those in America. These hasty acts had created large dirty areas lined with broken-window apartment buildings, now suited only for use as warehouses. They had overlooked the fact that with nowhere to go, the poor would stay. Their presence would keep out foreign business, and the newborn city would be strangled with the old impoverished filth and streets that flooded when it rained. He hated this section of town and tried to avoid it, but crossing through it was the shortest route to the hotel and therefore the fastest way out of the sun. The heat was draining and sticky, and the streets smelled hot and musty like some large sweaty animal.

Brian tried to think about something besides the heat. The fact that it was Sunday was in and of itself a small cause for celebration. Next week he might be assigned to a newsworthy story, rather than one covering the arrival of a minor foreign diplomat or some export show. The assignments Sheldon had given him were hardly of interest to the English newspaper of this city and of no interest to anyone outside Bangkok.

Over the period of time that he had been in the city, he and Sheldon had almost become friends. He didn't think Sheldon had any real friends. However, Sheldon did have a select few people he spent his time with, and Brian and the Prince were among the first to be included.

Brian had liked the Prince immediately. He was just one of those people you couldn't help but like. He was simple, and anxious to please his American friends. The Prince didn't know anything about politics and only cared about enjoying life and making everything an event. Although the Prince never had a dime, he was completely comfortable spending other people's money. And he did so generously. Sheldon defined Thais as better friends than Americans because they expected everything and gave little, so you knew where you stood.

With the passing of his first four weeks had come the increasingly disconcerting reports and endless photos of the situation in Cambodia. It was no longer just attacks by guerrillas unexpectedly appearing to over-run remote government outposts. The Khmer Rouge were boldly taking the battle to the government and doing so in daylight. The provinces were now lost and retaken on a daily basis. Yet the world merely watched with the weary eye of a tired policeman.

Although the reports from Cambodia tried to explain all that was happening, they were outdated before transmitted. Cambodia was covered by a blanket that restlessly tossed and turned with the ever-changing developments of war. In the last week, the fighting had three times slipped over the border at a high cost of Thai lives, and the people of Bangkok began to nervously glance at Americans for reassurance of old promises. It was never asked, but the question was, without fail, there: Would America protect them as promised?

If only he could get Sheldon to send him. Brian was sure he could make a name for himself, and that would move him to a better job. He knew he could go to and survive whatever happened. All but a few journalists did, and he was sure those that didn't had made mistakes that he wouldn't. Experience was their excuse. Brian knew he could prove himself if given the chance. Experience was merely the gathering of mistakes. It was the way people justified their own mistakes, mistakes he wouldn't make.

Brian smiled at the thought of the adage; "There's no fool like an old fool." He was sure of his ability and that he could do a better job than most simply by relying on his talents. Experience was the excuse for those that didn't have the heart.

The thought of Sheldon trying to teach him anything was infuriating. Sheldon was a fence sitter, ready to jump on whatever side was the most popular. He didn't have an honest opinion on any issue, just a cat's nimbleness to land on all fours. Even without experience, Brian knew he was a better journalist than Sheldon had ever been.

The Cho Phia was a very modern and very Western hotel. It was one of the more exclusive in the city and its immediate area was kept clean, but as usual, there was an unmistakable feature of Thailand close at hand. Somewhere near the steps that led up to the revolving glass doors were one or two street dogs tired and half asleep. They had undoubtedly learned that Westerners were a safe and easy touch for handouts. Anytime Brian saw a dog in the city, it was shorthaired and beat-up looking. There weren't many of them because they led hard lives. Until recently, Thais had eaten dogs, and although it was now illegal to butcher and sell them, some people still saw them as a staple. Brian smirked with the thought that the only dogs he had ever seen looked lean and fast. Maybe the short fat ones had been too slow and ended up in someone's pot.

Hurrying past the doorman Brian pushed his way through the doors and into the cool and busy lobby. It was packed with American tourists. The men usually wore loud Bermuda shorts and dark socks and dress shoes. They were totally out of place and under the mistaken belief that they were in charge. The tiny gift shop on the ground floor was the center of attraction as Americans leaving for the airport and the next country on their itinerary hurriedly purchased a memento for someone they had forgotten. Bellhops rushed by carrying luggage in both hands and under both arms, or pulling carts loaded with small mountains of luggage closely followed by jabbering overweight American women.

The bar was already dark, but there was no sound of a projector, only the mixture of many male voices. Walking into the darkness, he waited for his eyes to adjust. The long bar was vaguely visible with its dim overhead lights. As soon as his eyes could make out more than shadows, Brian began searching for Sheldon and the Prince, he was sure they would be there. Sheldon was a regular and would never miss Sunday afternoon films.

The room was large and could have been in any well-kept hotel in the States. A large wood parquet dance floor was now covered with small tables with red tablecloths and small red glass candleholders. The light from the flames flickered on the mysterious faces of the men sitting around each table.

"Brian!" He heard the friendly sound of the Prince's voice from far in the back. Brian started winding his way through the tables towards the sound.

Many of those that showed up regularly were retired military men that had not returned to America. They gave the place the atmosphere of intrigue and the sadness of lost patriots. Unlike the tourists in the lobby they were discussing the conditions in Cambodia.

"Brian!" the Prince called again, standing this time. Sheldon was sitting at the table and unenthusiastically raised his arm in contribution to the effort of flagging Brian.

Passing two empty tables closer to the screen, Brian made mental note of their location.

"*Sawadee*," said the Prince when Brian reached the table.

"Hello, Prince," smiled Brian.

"Brian. What have you been up to today?" asked Sheldon without interest.

"There are empty tables closer. Why are you back here?" Brian asked as he took a seat.

"They're showing the first game of the '63 World Series," replied Sheldon, attracting the cocktail waitress's attention. "I'm not interested."

"*Singha?*" Sheldon asked Brian with a glance.

"That's fine."

Sheldon nodded to the waitress and held up three fingers.

Sheldon was wearing a blue polo shirt and looked very comfortable and cool. Away from the office he was a different man. His sense of humor flowered, and he liked to tease. He had a calm self-confident look about him.

"How many places have you been stationed?" Brian asked.

Sheldon looked at him while tilting his bottle of beer high and finishing it. "Why?"

"I was just wondering. How 'bout you, Prince? How many countries have you visited?" Brian asked, knowing the answer but wanting to tease him.

"I've never left my home," said the Prince, tapping the table with his finger. "Why should I, when everything I could ever want is right here?" He was very proud of his country, and his voice emphasized his enthusiasm.

"Somehow this travelogue is going to end up in Cambodia!" Sheldon laughed, "You're not ready, and I have everyone I need there."

Three beers were set down on the table from behind Brian, and Sheldon pushed money from a pile in front of him towards the waitress.

"Why does my young friend want to go to such a place?" the Prince asked with sincerity.

Brian drank from his beer and it made his lips numb. Sheldon swore that Thai beer had formaldehyde in it that caused the sensation.

"I'm not sure if I can make you understand," Brian said to the Prince. "Ambition I suppose."

"But why would you allow a dangerous trip to be important. Why take a trip like that if you don't have to?"

"Because I have to. I'm a reporter, it's my job."

The Prince nodded as if he understood but it was clear that he was confused. Brian was grateful for the opportunity to once again express his desire in front of Sheldon.

The Prince's expression grew puzzled, and he glanced between Brian and the beer bottle in front of him. "All you want is to go and see it, so you can write about it?"

Sheldon roared with laughter and slapped the edge of the table while tilting his chair back.

"The people in the States need to know what's happening," said Brian quietly.

"Why?" the Prince asked sincerely, "Do they want to get involved?"

"No."

The Prince hesitated with the thought. "If they have no desire to get involved, then why are they so curious?"

The candlelight waved across his questioning face.

Brian glanced at Sheldon, but it was clear from his expression that he was amused with Brian's predicament and didn't intend to help.

"I don't understand," continued the Prince. "It seems ugly that your people would be so concerned with the grief of others when they do not want to help. If you want to supply them with stories of other countries, then why not tell them about the pleasurable things in my country?"

Sheldon's renewed laughter interrupted the Prince. "Now this really sounds like a travelogue!"

Brian laughed along with Sheldon, and he hoped that with the distraction the Prince would drop the subject.

The projector was turned on and with the flickering sound, the announcers introduced themselves. So he wouldn't block Sheldon's view of the screen, and to escape the Prince, Brian pulled his chair around the table and placed it next to Sheldon.

"Thanks," Sheldon said without looking at him.

The Prince was not really interested in the film and glanced around the room comparing the looks of the waitresses.

"There were a handful of reports from Cambodia this morning," said Brian.

Sheldon nodded, uninterested.

"One of them was from your friend Godfrey."

"What did it say?" Sheldon turned his chair towards him in an unexpected degree of interest.

"Oh. Something about refugees accumulating in Poipet, or somewhere like that."

"What else?" asked Sheldon.

The Prince had decided which of the waitresses was the most attractive and watched her every move without concern for the conversation.

"Something about 'crossings.'" Brian shook his head and sipped his beer. "I really couldn't make much out of that part. Besides, I didn't pay that much attention."

"Think. What did it say?" Sheldon was irritated and the tone of his voice attracted the Prince's attention.

"I really don't remember. Let me think." Brian paused. "I put the report on your desk."

"What did it say, just basically?" Sheldon persisted.

The Prince glanced back and forth between them, and the Star Spangled Banner began to play out of the projector.

"Something about moveable organized destination," Brian shook his head. "I really don't remember. It may not have been anything like that."

Sheldon settled back in his chair consumed with his own thoughts. Brian and the Prince glanced at each other, confused by Sheldon's mood. He was no longer relaxed, and in the candlelight his blue eyes were far away.

Sheldon looked up with a serious expression. "I know this has something to do with that boy at the airport. Chovat. I can feel it!"

"What boy?" asked the Prince.

For an instant Sheldon's eyes flashed surprise. Then he looked at his two companions as if deciding whether or not to tell them.

"Godfrey and I have been through a lot together. We started out together. He's a good journalist, but he's screwed up his career a couple of times by filing reports before checking the accuracy of his sources." Sheldon paused and lit a cigarette. "About six weeks ago he wrote me and told me about a man he had met there. Evidently he had convinced Godfrey that there was some sort of organized group helping people get across the border into Thailand."

"You mean helping refugees?" Brian asked.

"Well not just refugees."

"Insurgents?" exclaimed the Prince.

"No, not really." Sheldon drank from his beer. "What these people are supposed to be, are communists, but they are not insurgents." He leaned forward as if to explain a complicated problem. "You see, Godfrey believes that the Khmer Rouge is purging itself even now."

"That doesn't make any sense!" said Brian, looking over his shoulder for the waitress.

"No, not at all," added the Prince.

"Well, logically you're both right," said Sheldon. "The Khmer Rouge is busy fighting a war against the government. It would be the worst time for it." Sheldon paused to smoke, and when he looked up he had a sparkle in his eyes. "But, it would also be the best time for it, maybe the only chance for it."

"I don't understand," said Brian.

"The Khmer Rouge isn't one body fighting for one leader or one ideology. It's made up of a lot of splinter groups, all coming under the present leadership of two men, Yeng Sary and Khiev Samphen, both of whom answer to Popot."

The Prince was uncomfortable but listened with an intent that gave authority to Sheldon.

"Yeng Sary is older, and most people believe he is merely a figurehead, but Khiev Samphen is another story. He was educated in France. He is young, aggressive, and smart! It's Samphen that holds the Khmer Rouge together."

"What's all this have to do with Godfrey's story?" Brian asked while digging into his pocket for money to pay the waitress. She placed three new bottles of beer down and removed the empties. The Prince put on his most dignified but friendly smile and pushed some of the bills on the table towards her. Thinking that the Prince was a generous man she returned the flirtatious grin before walking away.

"You're awfully free with my money!" snorted Sheldon.

Boyishly, the Prince smiled and then chuckled. His eyes lit up with an idea, and he leaned over and grabbed Sheldon's shoulder in one of his large hands. "Let's go to the Sea Palace and take a massage."

"Go on with your story," Brian insisted, only to hesitate and look at the Prince. "Palace?"

"It's a whorehouse!" exclaimed Sheldon, glancing at the Prince irritatedly.

"Massage parlor!" insisted the Prince.

"What they rub depends on how much you pay them! It's a cat house!" exclaimed Sheldon.

"Go on with your story!" Brian insisted.

"Where was I?"

"Samphen holds …"

"Oh yes," interrupted Sheldon, glancing back at the Prince and shaking his head. "He was the Minister of Economy in the Sihanouk regime. Then in 1967, it was rumored that Sihanouk had him executed. In March 1970, Sihanouk was ousted and Lon Nol became President. Not having any central leadership the Khmer Rouge was more of a nuisance than a real threat. Then out of the blue Samphen reappears very much alive to the misfortune of the government. Behind him the splinter groups fell in line."

"But what's all this have to do with border crossing?" asked Brian.

"Well, assume for a minute you're Samphen or Sary, or maybe even Popot. While your fighters are busy winning your war, it makes sense to prepare to get rid of any of them that might challenge you at the end of the war."

The Prince seemed uncomfortable again.

"A coup before there's even a government," said Brian.

"Exactly."

Brian sat quietly for a moment lost in all the implications. "Let's hope America doesn't get caught up in this part of the world again." He was speaking more to himself than to his companions. When he looked up, he found the Prince was watching him with a surprised and serious expression.

"There's been a lot of a promises made to this country," Sheldon said quietly. "They supported our venture in Vietnam."

"Of course," Brian said as he looked at the Prince. "Do you think your government will allow communist refugees in?"

"No, no. It will never chance that!" said the Prince.

"That's what I'm talking about. Some incident on the border escalating into a clash between the Khmer Rouge and this country and the United States being pulled into it." said Brian, shaking his head.

"The Khmer Rouge is busy trying to win a war in their own country," replied Sheldon.

"Right now, but do you think the Thai army could stand on its own?" argued Brian.

Sheldon now looked surprised and stared at him. Brian was a little shocked to find Sheldon would be in favor of U.S. involvement of any kind. He had spent so much time in this part of the world that Brian had assumed he knew better.

"The interesting thing," Sheldon continued, "is that they're crossing into this country with evidently the help of someone. That's what Godfrey is doing. He's trying to find out how, and who."

"Then you're looking for confirmation?" Brian asked eagerly.

"Yes. Cambodia's only the mouth on the funnel." Sheldon tapped the table with his finger. "The organization, if there is one, has to be on this side of the border." Sheldon settled back in his chair.

Brian hesitated as long as he could, "Send me to the border. With Godfrey on one side and me on the other …"

"No!" Sheldon said cutting short a drink of his beer. The tone of his voice was forceful. Reluctantly, Brian let the idea fade away. The Prince was concerned with his own thoughts, and they were all quiet.

"I'll tell you what," said Sheldon, "you know the facts now. So I want you to keep a special watch on the reports, messages, whatever comes in from Godfrey." Sheldon's voice had the sound of someone doing a favor.

"All right." Brian tried to sound interested, but it really wasn't the type of break he had hoped for. "But what are we really talking about? What's supposed to be happening and to whom?"

"Since this war started five years ago, one million people have died. How much of that is involved with the purge is unknown, but we know that it appears to be in the thousands and that it's spread throughout the social structure. From mayors of provinces to rice farmers. If you do or did support Sihanouk, you are in danger. If you're educated or wealthy, you're in danger. If you're poor and uneducated, you're in danger. In short, everyone is expendable. It doesn't seem to make any difference or any sense. It appears to be a killing frenzy, but no one really knows what's happening. It's more rumor than fact."

"What about the boy at the airport? How's he fit into this?" Brian asked.

"I'm not sure that he does." Sheldon hesitated and watched them. "But Godfrey was also given his name from inside Cambodia."

Brian tried to imagine what Godfrey was doing right then.

"No!" The Prince exclaimed in interruption. "We have some university students who are anti-American, but there are no real communists in my country. No more than in your country!"

The men at the tables around them turned and watched. Brian was intimidated and surprised by the Prince's anger.

"No!" continued the Prince. "All of our problems come from outside. Our neighbors cause us grief."

"Let's talk about something else," interjected Sheldon.

"Yes, let's talk about where to have dinner," said Brian.

"My country will never be communist," the Prince grumbled. "We have our king and the people love and respect him."

"Certainly, but what about dinner? Brian's buying," Sheldon said, raising his eyebrows to Brian.

"Never, we'll never," insisted the Prince.

"You're right. But what about dinner?" persisted Sheldon.

For a moment the Prince sat quietly, and Brian was sure he was going to grumble on.

"I know!" The Prince said excitedly with the unexpected return of his lighthearted smile. "There is to be a royal tea this evening at ..."

"Oh no!" Sheldon interrupted while emphatically shaking his head.

"What the hell, Sheldon. I've never been to anything royal. Let's give it a try." Brian turned to the Prince, trying not to appear too eager. "Can we go dressed like this?"

"Certainly."

Sheldon's steel blue eyes glued to Brian with determination. "You don't understand what a tea is."

"It will be a fine time!" interrupted the Prince.

"I'd rather go to the Sea Palace!" complained Sheldon.

"Come on," prodded Brian.

"Yes, it's settled!" The Prince jumped to his feet. "I don't do enough for my friends and this we will enjoy!" He hurried towards the door. Brian stood and waited for his reluctant companion. Looking up at Brian, Sheldon's expression unenthusiastically surrendered as he stood.

"I suppose seeing you at this thing will be worth my going," Sheldon said, starting for the door. "But I'd rather watch the game."

"Oh come on. This is an old game, who cares, besides he's trying to pick up the tab this time!"

They had reached a point where two of the tables were too close together for them to slip through at the same time. Sheldon speedily cut Brian off so he could pass first.

"It's free, Brian," Sheldon said over his shoulder.

CHAPTER THREE

What Sheldon had balked at about the invitation was his knowledge that, as far as the Prince was concerned, the government was run by the Royal Family. Therefore, any government agency putting on a tea was in fact participating in a royal tea. Brian's image of a grand event based on royal traditions had been crushed with the realization that what they were really at was sponsored by the Cultural Bureau and held on the front lawn and garden of the Agency's building.

The air was filled with the chatter of overly polite confusion. Sheldon and the Prince had at first moved Brian through the crowd under the excuse of introducing him to governmental officials that could be sources of information in the future, friends to be put upon for favors, or at least people that could be bribed. However, other than merely giving quick introductions to people glancing over their shoulders as Sheldon drove him along, they had introduced him only to three or four uninterested and arrogant minor officials. What they had really been doing was following a white-coated waiter like a bee to a hive, while he aimlessly pollinated his way through the crowd, serving glasses of warm wine.

Eventually, making the mistake of confusing their quarry with a guest wearing a white jacket, they had lost the waiter. Sheldon and the Prince were forced to bravely set out on their own to find one of the temporary bars in the garden.

"Royal tea!" Brian said aloud. What a disappointment he thought, remembering the enthusiasm he had shown at the invitation. He was sure that the only royalty there was the Prince, if he really was royalty.

It was especially hot for that time of day and jammed into the crowd he was constantly bumped. Wishing he had never left the cool, dark bar of the hotel, Brian decided to make his way to the far side of the garden where there were trees and shade. Impatiently, he maneuvered his way through the crowd until he could slip with gratitude under the shadows of the trees.

Brian had been standing there for a long time when a Thai Army officer approached him and struck up a short conversation. The officer had already had too much to drink, and learning that Brian was a correspondent, he had all of a sudden become iron willed with his ability to handle the growing threat on the border. Unfortunately, the sight of his soft belly straining the buttons of his khaki brown shirt kept him from being reassuring, and out of boredom Brian had slipped away.

Many of the guests were the powerful or near powerful. Although the men were well dressed, you could tell their true positions in life by the material of the dresses the ladies accompanying them wore. Thai silk with a lavish sash slung over one shoulder adorned the women of the wealthy or truly powerful. The rest wore dresses of brightly colored cotton. Although Thai cotton was exotic, it still lacked the sheen and glamour of the more elegant attire and caused the ladies in cotton to jealously glance at those in silk. Many of the women carried bright colored parasols over their shoulders for shade. The important men were constantly surrounded by small cackling circles of the less powerful competing for attention, and somewhere close at hand there would be a woman dressed in silk quietly waiting with a hint of a smile and always with her long black hair pulled tightly into a bun. The Thai women were more delicate and feminine looking than Western women and infinitely more patient.

Thinking that he had been absent too long, Brian was about to plunge back into the swarm when the Prince appeared. He waved at Brian with a hand clasping a cocktail while he reached back into the crowd to pull someone from the mass.

Suddenly, Brian's eyes were pulled to a Western woman that laughingly escaped the crowd with the Prince. Brian couldn't take his eyes off of her. Mixed with the brown Thai women with their black tight hair she was like a pearl on a black sand beach. The Asian sun had bleached her hair to a soft blonde mane that freely broke over her shoulders. She was wearing a delicate white lace blouse open to her cleavage and it fit tightly around her small waist. A white skirt layered its way to below her knees, its material so thin that the sunlight behind her allowed the faintest silhouette of her body to pass through. Her face was gently sculptured and held large sleepy brown eyes like those of a small animal watching rain through a window.

As they moved closer, he could see a gold necklace and crucifix resting on her milky skin above her small breasts. She was captivating and although it made him feel foolish he couldn't help but be excited. She was truly beautiful.

"Brian!" exclaimed the Prince as they reached him. "I have brought someone I want you to meet.

This is Callie." Laughingly, the Prince gently put an arm around her shoulder.

Smiling immodestly she looked up at Brian with confident eyes that locked to his.

"A beauty that can make any man forget about the heat!" The Prince grinned boyishly at Brian. "Brian is unaccustomed to our sun and, it seems, to our women!" the Prince roared, delighted in his own humor. "Maybe he will be more comfortable with you."

For an instant she appeared embarrassed. Then the slightest smile pulled at her lips. "I'm quite sure with you around he'll become accustomed to both." Her voice was soft and extremely feminine and held a quality of refinement, but her stare remained boldly locked to Brian's eyes.

"He will! He will!" laughed the Prince. "He's a good man. I'm a good judge of people and he's someone I wanted you to meet."

Her stare became steady and then she quickly glanced at the crowd and then back at Brian. Instantly, he was afraid she would leave, and his thoughts raced for a way to keep her there. "How long have you been in Thailand?" she asked to Brian's relief.

"Four weeks. Just over four weeks," said Brian, more off balance than she. He returned her stare until the Prince slapped Brian on the shoulder.

"Not long enough to adjust to the heat, or to find that our capital is a wonderful place. He's a writer, a journalist, and he wants to leave the land of smiles to go to Cambodia where the fools kill each other."

Her eyes flashed curiosity. "Another journalist. We seem to have more of them every day."

Her voice held a faint challenge. "Have you lived abroad before?"

"This is the first time," he said as he paused somewhat embarrassed, his eyes moving to the Prince and then back to her. "I've never been out of the states before." The admission surprised him.

She smiled and somehow became even more beautiful. Her eyes warmed and released the challenge.

Erratically, from the edge of the crowd, an overweight woman began to shout in a friendly voice something towards them. She was round and dressed beautifully in a traditional Thai dress made of cotton. Too rapidly for Brian to understand, the Prince responded in his native tongue and nodded to the woman happily.

"I must leave you," he explained, turning back to them and putting an arm around each of their shoulders. "*Sawadee!*"

Brian's mind scrambled with the hope of finding something he might say to keep Callie from also leaving. But before he could, the Prince had turned and was making his way into the crowd with the woman. Turning back to Callie, he was relieved to find that she appeared comfortable and without intention of leaving. Looking at her, he told himself not to stare but her eyes were intense and would not allow him to look away. For a moment they simply stared at each other.

"He does have a wide variety of women," said Brian trying to sound charming.

"You haven't been here long!" Callie was trying not to laugh. "That's his wife."

Brian's head jerked to the crowd, but the Prince had already vanished. The Prince had already introduced Brian to his wife and it was not this woman.

"You've met Nakron," Callie laughed.

He liked the sound of her laugh. It was a light, infectious sound and very feminine, but he was uncomfortable with his confusion and could only smile feebly.

"Don't feel bad. What you have to understand is that here everyone is a combination of both the old and the new." She paused, still smiling. "Traditionally, men have a wife, and one, sometimes several, minor wives. Concubines."

"How many does he have?" Brian asked, nearly speechless with his own surprise.

"Look at it this way, Nakron is his wife. The lady you just saw is his mistress."

"I'll be damned," Brian said aloud to himself glancing back into the crowd. Callie turned and began to slowly walk, one hand holding the other behind her back. Without thinking about it, he moved along with her. Walking through the shadows an occasional ray of sunlight would flicker and dance in her blond hair. It was an awkward and over-used word, but she really was lovely.

"The Prince likes to think of himself as some-sort of Asian Casanova." She smiled up at him.

"I'd say he's doing fairly well at it."

"Oh. I'm afraid he is too dear for that. He loves Nakorn, but like a schoolboy he needs attention. He's a good husband."

"It confuses me," laughed Brian. "I suppose I haven't been here long enough to see a man with concubines as a good husband."

She glanced at him and her expression became questioning. "Does that bother you?"

"No," he replied unconvincingly. "It's just that a lot of things are so …" he paused, looking for the right word, "odd."

She gently took hold of his arm, "Brian, you and I are the odd ones. This is their country and their way of life." She was not lecturing but neither was she merely explaining. He liked the feel of her touch.

"I suppose I am still out of place," he smiled.

"It will come to you," she released his arm. "Before you know it you'll be as at home here as you were in the States. Maybe more."

"That wouldn't be difficult. I'm not sure I ever felt at home."

Callie tilted her head in curiosity but didn't say anything. The question in her expression made Brian wish he hadn't said that; he hadn't meant to.

"What do you mean?" she finally asked.

"Nothing."

"No," she insisted politely. "Why did you leave? Was it just the job?"

He didn't know how to answer her or even if there was any one answer, but he did know that she wasn't going to be satisfied with any lighthearted remark. Her eyes intensified with his delay. "Nothing made me come. There was just nothing there to hold me," he said casually while he wondered what could make a woman like her come to such a country. He tried to guess her age. It was somewhere in the late 20's or early 30's. "There was just nothing there holding me." It sounded cumbersome to his own ear, but he wanted her to know he was available, and he wanted to leave the awkward subject.

Her expression was still curious, but a faint smile appeared at the corner of her mouth that embarrassed Brian.

"Maybe I just wanted to see some of the world, not just read about it in the morning paper," he added in an effort to unhook himself. "What about you? How did you end up here?"

She seemed reluctant to give up her inquiries, and he expected another question.

"I wanted to travel. Originally I intended to go around the world with the idea of ending up in Paris and living there for awhile."

Europe. That's where she belonged. In a city like Paris walking along the Seine in the evening, watching the river barges glide under the old stone bridges. In the City of Lights, not the sweltering heat of Bangkok.

"I studied French. I speak it fluently. So when I ran low on money I took a job requiring a French speaking person."

"Where do you work? At an Embassy?"

"No. Shortly after I arrived, friends found me a position at the University. Now I also work in conjunction with the Cultural Bureau."

"What's the Cultural Bureau's function anyway?" Brian asked. He didn't really care. He was just happy to keep her talking.

"No one is really sure what it is, or what it is supposed to accomplish," she laughed. "But foreign aid provides the funds for cultural development, and the government tries to find productive ways to spend it. More than anything we travel to the provinces and attempt to modernize the countryside." She paused and watched him for a moment. "Trying to talk the traditional into seeking out modern medical treatment. Show them how to use new farm equipment. Try to convince them to grow different crops. Whatever has to be done to improve their conditions."

Brian's smile had been growing with each description until he was now ready to laugh.

"What?" she wanted to laugh also. "What's so funny?"

"I just can't see you knee-deep in a rice paddy surrounded by generations of water buffalo farmers scratching their heads and wondering how their buffalo are going to pull your tractor."

"No." They both laughed. "They really are a remarkable people," she defended. "You shouldn't be so judgmental."

When their laughter stopped, she continued to stare at him with a faint smile. Then she spoke with the air of a confession. "Once, in the North, we tried to talk a small hill tribe into giving up the cultivation of opium in exchange for growing strawberries." The delight in her voice was now contagious and Brian began to laugh. "The elders were so very patient with us, but when they realized you could only eat strawberries we lost all credibility!"

"Would they even grow here?" Brian asked under his laugh.

"No one knows!" she exclaimed.

Even though she had seemed easy to talk to, Brian had at first felt a little awkward and self-conscious, but their laughter now carried all that away. He stopped walking and gestured to the crowd. "It looks as if the Cultural Bureau is convincing some. What could be more modern?"

"Oh, they are a wonderful people." Her voice was full and warm, and her eyes were distant as they danced in the crowd. "Make no mistake. Under all that Western façade is a distinct pride and love for who they are and what their country is." She turned to him with a happy and subtle excitement. "Do you know what Thailand means?"

"No."

"Thai means 'free,' free land." Her voice caressed the phrase. "It's the only country in the region that successfully defied European colonization. Burma, Cambodia, Laos, Vietnam, all of them fell victim, but not Thailand. They would ride huge angry elephants into battle, and fight wildly for their freedom." Lovingly she looked back at the crowd. "They are wonderfully their own."

Brian was almost jealous of the country and everyone in it. Then for a moment their eyes fixed, hers sparkling with intensity. Impulsively, she glanced away as if she were about to say something and changed her mind. She resumed walking under the shade of the last tree.

"Have you had a chance to see the city or meet many people?" The sound of her voice was casual, and she didn't look at him.

"Not really. Sheldon, that's ..."

"Sheldon Harris," she interrupted. "I know who he is."

"He and the Prince are about the only two I've gotten to know."

They had reached the end of the shadows and they stopped. She looked up at him and again she appeared to want to say something. "I have to be getting back." She rushed the words out and purposely avoided his eyes.

From inside himself Brian could hear his voice asking to see her again, but nothing passed his lips. He only nodded.

"It was nice meeting you," she said hurriedly, starting for the crowd. "I hope you'll like it in Bangkok."

Without hesitation he replied, "Yes, it was nice meeting you." He turned and started back to where he had last seen the Prince, angry with himself for letting the chance slip away. He was certain that he would never see her again and just as certain that he would demand the Prince to tell him everything he knew about her and arrange another meeting.

"Brian," she called.

Turning he found that she had stopped. The light that had so quickly vanished from her eyes returned. She paused, and anxious that he would have another opportunity, Brian was about to speak.

"I'm having some friends over next Friday," she paused as if unsure of herself. "Would you like to come? It would give you a chance to meet ..."

"Yes," he interrupted, "I would like that very much."

"I live at 214 Songwat Road. Can you find it?"

"I'll find it," he said assertively.

"Good. Then I'll see you about 6:00." She smiled and then hurriedly turned and disappeared into the crowd.

Hurriedly, and with a million questions, Brian set out to find the Prince.

CHAPTER FOUR

In the last week, the news had been bad. The war in Cambodia kept gathering momentum. The government's Mekong River stronghold had been overrun and the U.S. Congress had placed severe limitations on aid. Sheldon had been outraged, and the city had taken on a somber mood and looked distrusting at Americans. The communist countries throughout the region hovered over Thailand like vicious dogs eagerly waiting for the slightest move. Its alliance with the United States in allowing American bombers to fly from Thailand during the Vietnam War had not been forgotten, and had made it clear that it would soon be time to pay for its misplaced loyalty.

For Brian, the more immediate danger was the cab ride through 5:20 p.m. traffic. He rocked from side to side as the driver erratically zigzagged in and out of any small opening in the congestion.

"Slow down! Slow down! *Cha!*" he ordered, trying to sound Thai. Brian was more concerned with a possible delay due to an accident than with an injury. It wouldn't have been so bad if it were merely his driver, but it was every car on the road. They all darted about like confused, ugly little bugs hiding when a light is turned on. The driver glanced in his rearview mirror but ignored Brian's instructions.

"Slow down!" Brian demanded once more. The driver turned his attention elsewhere.

Frustrated, Brian tried to accept the situation. Undoubtedly, they would cause an accident but hopefully they would avoid the impact. "You'd make more money if you would slow down!" The driver didn't bother to look this time.

For the last week the Prince had been very pleased and self-congratulatory with Brian's invitation to Callie's, but he hadn't told him much more than Brian had already learned about her. Sheldon at first had been his unimpressed self, but as the week had rolled by he had mentioned that he had met her once, and that he knew several men that had unsuccessfully attempted to be more than an acquaintance to her. By Thursday morning Brian noticed that Sheldon occasionally stopped what he was doing and watched him, and by late that afternoon he had made it quite clear that these other men were considerably more prominent than Brian and that he didn't understand her preference.

At first Brian had wondered if Sheldon might not be one of those she had kept at a distance, but he had dismissed the thought with the image of Sheldon being enthusiastic about anything other than his job or a cold drink at the end of the day. In any case, he was sure that although Sheldon had not said anything to him when he left the office, he would conveniently call early tomorrow morning to satisfy himself that Brian had not stayed away all night.

Unexpectedly, the cab jerked over to the side of the road and made a quick stop.

"200 *baht*," the driver said turning around with an open palm.

They were stopped in front of a bridge. Outside Brian's window was a small road just slightly wider than an alley running alongside the river.

"This your soi," said the driver gesturing to the small road.

The area was chaotic, as it was swollen with docking fishing canoes. A haphazard wharf ran parallel to the soi and was overrun with noisy buyers and sellers of fish. Teak wood canoes banged into one another as they were being unloaded. So many canoes had jammed into the dock that one could have stepped from one to another until he was 15 feet from the shore.

Multitudes of wicker baskets were being passed out over the heads of the fishermen to those farthest out to be filled with fish and passed back into shore.

"214 Songwat Road?" Brian insisted.

The driver's hand pumped toward the soi. "200 baht. Songwat down," he urged, jabbing at the air with his upturned palm. "Fisherman in way. Easy you walk."

Brian glanced at the soi. There was no way to get the car beyond that point.

"214 Songwat?" Brian asked, turning both of his palms up and shaking his head. "*Tee-nai*? Where?"

The driver shook his head, grinning. Brian was sure the humor was for his awkward Thai and probable misuse of the word. "Where?!" he demanded.

"200 baht." The driver's grin disappeared and he twisted his arm in a snaking motion leaving the impression that Brian was to walk down the soi and turn right somewhere.

Giving up Brian slid over and opened the door.

"I know I have to turn right," he mumbled to himself. "I'm not going to walk into the river."

He slammed the door and reached into his pocket. The driver's hand now thrust out the window.

Reluctantly, Brian pulled out a wad of crumpled Thai bills, each denomination a different color and depicting a different scene. Without fail, the paper was crisp like new American bills and hard to separate. Preoccupied with the prospect of wandering around the dock, Brian mistakenly peeled off a tan and blue 400 baht bill and placed it in the driver's palm.

"*Kopkun!*" the driver squealed, hitting the accelerator. At the same instant Brian realized his mistake, but it was too late to do anything but watch the beat-up Japanese compact dart into traffic in a cloud of blue, smelly smoke. For a moment he stood there feeling ridiculously foreign. Then starting down the soi, Brian unconvincingly tried to console himself that it was only twenty dollars and would have been reasonable in the States.

Once into the steaming soi he found it a carnival atmosphere. Only noticed when in the way he walked along enjoying the hectic atmosphere. Small people most of them dressed in black-scrambled about in all directions. One old man dashed about shouting orders while marking something down in a dog-eared tablet. He seemed to be everywhere all at once, pointing his pencil at a particular fisherman and shouting above the noise. His authority made it clear he was a broker buying the catch.

Large baskets filled with silver fish of all shapes and sizes, some of them with their gills still flickering, were being lifted and carried by old women with wrinkled and weathered faces. Some of the women balanced the baskets on their heads, but most strapped them to their backs and peered out from under pointed coolie hats. Amazingly, some carried two baskets, one on each end of a bamboo pole, and still they managed to weave in and out of the crowd without striking anyone with either end. The baskets bounced along at a trot, the air smelled fishy, and the noise sounded happy.

"Ride?" shouted a young boy powering a pedicab alongside Brian, his bony knees rhythmically pushing at the pedals. He couldn't have been more than eight, but like so many of the children Brian had seen he already had the serious face of a businessman. The three-wheeled bicycle was an enterprise, not the toy Brian remembered from his childhood.

"*Mai chai plao*," Brian said, shaking his head and smiling guiltily. He would have enjoyed a scenic ride on the waterfront, and the boy might have known exactly where Songwat Road was but Brian was ashamed of the image of a large man lazily gliding along in a covered basket seat while a small boy with skinny knees struggled with the pedals. Without any change in his expression the boy pedaled on. He was a businessman and he had a living to make.

In exploration, Brian moved on to the wood planks of the dock, where he had to continuously dodge to stay out of the way of the crowd. Fishermen are fishermen wherever you go, he thought, watching the good-natured heckling between boats, each two-man crew out-describing, if not out-fishing, the other. Looking down to the water, Brian saw the canoes were a deep, brownish red where wet, and white and crusty where dry. In the bottom of each were piles of fish not yet transferred to baskets. The sides of the canoes clattered into each other like happy teasing between old friends.

The far shore looked green and lush. The
bright sun blindingly reflected off the water and the
strong wind off the river brushed his face, slipped
under his sunglasses in small jets, and tickled his
cheeks like wings of tiny insects. In front of him a
young muscular fisherman squatted on the dock. With
lightening hands, he was cleaning and filleting fat,
ugly fish. Brian stopped to watch like a young boy
hypnotized with the intrigue of danger. He was
certain the fisherman would miscalculate a flick of his
knife and remove one of his flat broad toes. The
fisherman glanced up with a smile exposing long and
spotted yellow teeth. It was a happy smile and one
that fit the river. He wore only a headband and shorts,
both dirty from wiping the fish entrails from his
hands. His brown body was lean and strong but
chapped and crusty like the canoes below him. He
was the first Thai in days that hadn't looked at Brian
with suspicion. Jabbing the point of his knife into the
largest chunk of fish he held it up for Brian to take.
"*Dee horm*," he insisted, bobbing his head.

Brian took the fish and the man grabbed a
piece for himself and popped it into his mouth. "*Dee
horm,*" he reassured Brian joyously.

Brian stared at him with a smile just as warm
and unassuming and placed the fish in his mouth. It
was juicy and clean tasting.

The fisherman's smile widened and then he
went back to work.

Wherever fishermen are, there are certainties
thought Brian. Flocks of seagulls will noisily dive
about fighting for scraps. Both laughter and arguing
will bark in the air. The water will smell a little dirty
but rich and thick. The world will seem young and
energetic, and people will gather to watch and buy.
It's hard work, but simple and honest, and whatever

else they might be, these people had the river, and the catch had been good!

The first soi that turned to the right was shaded on both sides by large umbrella trees. Only fifty feet long it dead-ended in a small-gated courtyard of a two-story house. The house itself was western in design but it was flavored Thai with a steep A-frame roof decorated with yellow, wavy trim. At the tip of the roof's frame, a curl pointed up into the air, making it look like the bow of a boat the river had left aground. The courtyard was clean and empty except for a black and white cat that sat methodically watching Brian. Even though it was right behind him, the noise of the docks seemed distant.

The house had a small balcony, which held a number of large Australian ferns and white wicker chairs. He imagined Callie sitting there watching the river. It was mellow and just looked like a place where she would be.

Glancing at his watch he started towards the gate. Being twenty minutes early instantly seemed uncomfortable. She might not be ready for a guest. She might even be in the shower. The heat encouraged showers. People took three or four a day just to escape the heat. Embarrassed, he realized that the back of his shirt was wet and clinging to him. He scolded himself for taking a cab with plastic seat covers. He knew better.

The cat had watched him approach as far as it would allow. It turned and cautiously retreated. At a safer distance from Brian, it stopped and glanced back at him, but Brian's continued approach was too much for the cat's courage, so it turned and disappeared under a fence.

All of a sudden he had the terrible thought that his memory of her might be mistaken, that she wouldn't be all he remembered.

Reaching the gate, he hesitated and glanced at the four homes that made up the cul-de-sac. They were all the same except for size and amount of carving in the trim. Each had a small courtyard, and in each courtyard was an ornate, miniature house sitting on a pedestal, each kept very clean but without any apparent purpose. The larger the house, the larger the miniature house. He had seen them scattered all over the city more often in front of houses, but only rarely in front of commercial buildings and banks.

He reached into his shirt pocket and removed a folded piece of paper.

"214 Songwat Road," he said aloud before looking at it. The paper read the same.

The first house had 214 painted in small numbers on the eave, but glancing around he couldn't find a road sign. He felt he was at Callie's, but he nervously wanted confirmation before opening the gate.

"You're right. You found it." Callie's voice came from the balcony.

Looking up, he found that she was smiling and obviously entertained by his talking to himself, and that, if anything, his memory had been conservative. Everything about her was captivating. She had that mysterious, sultry look about her that all women like to think they have but very few do, the type that makes men want them and at the same time intimidates them all just a little.

"I'll be right down and let you in," she said, disappearing into the house.

Brian unlatched the gate and crossed the courtyard to the front door. He waited only a moment, when the door opened, and she was standing in front of him.

"You're early," she said with a smile. Brian was embarrassed. "But I'm glad," she added politely. "You can help me." Taking him by the hand Callie led him through the door and up a flight of stairs.

The building wasn't a house at all but an apartment. The front door was actually an entry into the interior where you either went straight to enter the ground floor quarters or up a staircase to her apartment.

Callie led him up the stairs without looking back. She was wearing a turquoise cotton dress that fit tightly around her waist and exposed most of her back. She seemed smaller than Brian remembered. Her perfume was clean and fresh.

As she opened the door to her apartment she glanced back with a smile. "Make yourself comfortable," she said, as she closed the door behind them and disappeared into the kitchen.

Her apartment was furnished with two large over-stuffed chairs and a couch. Small tables with two or three neatly stacked magazines were placed by each of the chairs. A watercolor painting hung above the couch, and a very large and out of date radio sat in the corner. The room was cooled by a slow and silent ceiling fan. French doors opened onto the balcony and filled the room with cheerful sunlight and made the room perfect for growing the many plants in it. It was warm and distinctively personal.

From the kitchen came the sound of ice being hurriedly dropped into glasses. Brian moved to the balcony door for the view of the river. As he looked down on the dock, it moved with people like ants on an anthill that had been stirred with a stick, and he wondered if the fisherman had cut himself yet.

"Here you are," Callie said, coming up behind him and handing him a glass.

"Thank you."

"I'm afraid the others aren't going to be able to make it," she announced.

"Really? That's too bad," he said, trying to sound disappointed.

"Oh, it's fine. I'll introduce you some other time."

"That would be nice." He liked the thought that she was already planning other times. "You have a wonderful view of the river."

She moved up alongside him and watched the dock. "It's the nicest thing about this place," she smiled.

"How long have you lived here?"

"In this apartment or Bangkok?" she asked, turning to him.

She was only inches away, and again he could smell the clean scent of soap and a light perfume.

"Both," he smiled.

"I've been in Bangkok a little over three years, but I've only lived here about nine months."

For the first time he raised the glass to drink and realized that it was iced tea. Almost without thinking, he glanced from the glass to her.

"I think you'll like it," she said with a mischievous half-smile.

"What else is in here?" he grinned.

"Try it." Her smile widened.

It was tea, but it was laced with some type of herb and orange flavor and the taste of something else he couldn't make out.

"It's good, but what is it?" he asked distrusting.

She laughed, and, with a tilt of her head, raised her eyebrows as if it were a secret.

"Is there alcohol … rum or something?" He couldn't quite tell.

"Something." She said as she took his hand. "Come along. You can keep me company while I make dinner."

She led him into the kitchen and positioned him out of the way but where she could see him while she cooked.

The kitchen was westernized with at least the basic modern conveniences. Their dinner of chopped vegetables and meats was pushed into separate little piles on a wood chopping board.

"What did you think of our dock?" she asked, turning on the gas stove to heat four small pots already placed on the burners.

"It reminded me of a carnival. An oriental carnival," he said, thinking of the bicycle boy. "They were all so busy, so caught up with what they were doing that you'd think the war in Cambodia was on the other side of the world."

"*Mia pen rai*," she said to herself, smiling.

"What?" Brian asked.

She began to stir the popping oil as it heated. "It's Thai. You might say it's the unofficial motto of Thailand. It means, 'never mind,' or 'let it be.'"

Sipping his tea he thought how applicable it was to the dock and how fishermen must live a slower life than the merchants of the city. "The city people certainly haven't been so relaxed this week," he said.

"No. They wouldn't be. The more Westernized they become, the more distrusting they are," she explained.

"So much for modernization." The tea kept tasting better to him. "A lot of the fishermen looked more Chinese than Thai," he said, not really able to tell the difference, but searching for something to say.

She smiled to herself as if she knew he could not, and filled each pot with food. "Some of them are." With a mocking intensity she added, "The Mongols were the cause of that."

"Not really?" he asked, drinking more of the tea.

She laughed and stirred one of the pots. The air filled with a steamy, delicious smell.

"Actually, yes, or at least partially." She glanced at him as if to see if he was truly interested. "The majesty of old Siam had its roots in China." She glanced at him again. "Southeastern Chinese came here and formed the kingdom Nanchoa hundreds of years ago."

"Is that right?" he tried to sound interested even though he wasn't.

"Yes." She laughed knowing he was more interested in the tea. She seemed comfortable and happy that he was there. She was warm and genuine and was generous with her smile.

"What smells so wonderful? What are you making?" he asked. All the pots were now angry little engines exploding with sizzles and crackles.

"*Khao pad*," she said, politely pronouncing slowly and tapping one of the pots with the chopsticks she used for stirring. "Fried rice with shrimp. *Hoy mok*, fish in a chili sauce." Her expression abruptly seemed worried. "You do like hot, spicy food?"

"Yes. It's fine."

"*Nua pat khing*, Ginger Beef," she continued, obviously relieved, "and *Mee krob*, fried noodles with anything the cook has on hand."

They laughed and Brian finished the last of his drink and set in on the counter.

"Here, try a little of this," she said, pinching a piece of fish in the chopsticks and bringing it to his mouth. "There's no fishy taste to it. In fact, it's smoky tasting, if anything."

Brian took the bite, and while he was chewing, she stood in front of him, anxiously waiting for approval. Then biting into something with a crunch his eyes began to widen and instantly filled with tears.

"Oh, no! There was a pepper in it, wasn't there!" she exclaimed.

He opened his mouth to speak but nothing came out. He could only nod his head as the fire spread up his sinuses and down into his lungs.

She grabbed his glass and was handing it to him when she realized it was empty. In a near panic she rushed to the pitcher of ice tea and hurriedly poured. Choking, Brian grabbed it from her and drank it all in gulps only to thrust it back for a refill. The second glass began to help.

"I'm sorry, I'm so sorry!" she repeated embarrassedly.

Brian shook his head and bent over to breathe. "It's good," he rattled out in a breathless voice. Then, facing her and wiping the tears from his eyes, "But let's not have it again for awhile." He said with a raspy laugh that relaxed her worried expression.

Dinner had been delicious, but Callie had spent most of it apologizing while Brian, as discreetly as possible, searched his food for anything that remotely looked like peppers, and drank a lot of tea.

By the time they had finished, there was no doubt that the disguised flavor in the tea was some type of liquor. He was not drunk, but his legs had that relaxed, heavy feeling one gets just before it hits.

Without thinking to offer help he had watched her place one bowl into another until she had one tilting stack she could carry to the sink. Then, along with a half empty-pitcher of tea, they moved onto the balcony and lowered a green canvas canopy for shade from the setting sun.

It was very relaxing watching the river, and they were soon lost in a conversation about the States. The idea that he could have met her in America didn't feel right. Even if the Royal Tea hadn't been too royal, he liked the fact that they had met there while in an exotic country.

Talking about Thailand was something she loved. Her enthusiasm for the country seemed misplaced, but she had so much of it that he couldn't help wondering if he wasn't giving their relationship a chance. For a long time she told one funny or touching story after another. He liked listening to her. Her voice was rich and confident, her laughter real and contagious.

"You'll love it here!" she said.

At that moment he wanted nothing else but to be where he was. He was comfortable and happy, and even if she was wrong about Thailand she had been right about the tea. With every glass it became more delicious and intoxicating.

The river glistened now with the last of the sunset, and the dock was nearly empty. The slow moving figures of the last two fishermen seemed lonely, like men sweeping up after a circus. Content to watch the day end, they didn't speak. On the horizon large purple clouds blocked the sun as it set and distorted its shape until it was no longer round but a wavy band that stretched across the sky in an explosion of gold and orange. The glow hiding behind the clouds became more intense and the clouds became violet and then pink. Only to be drained away when the sun dropped and left the world weak and washed out for that period of time in which it is still light but not day. It would be hours before the sun rolled to the side of the world he had left. He thought of the people he knew there and what they would do with the approaching day. For the first time, since he arrived, he realized how far away he really was. He glanced at his watch and found it was eight thirty. "I'm still not used to the late sunsets."

The fishermen started home.

"It's like summertime in the States year round." Her voice was quiet and happy. The last of the light was fading, and, like a blanket being unrolled, a dark shadow moved up the river.

"You're friends missed it. They should have come," he said, still watching the river.

She didn't say anything and her silence made him look at her. She hadn't been watching the sunset; rather, her eyes were fixed on him. She didn't smile or speak; she just watched. Brian stood and picked up the pitcher from in front of her. Her glass was full, so he poured the last of the tea into his. Then he raised his eyebrows and nodded in recognition of the empty pitcher. "They would have liked this." He started for the balcony's railing, carefully putting the pitcher down as he moved.

"I never invited anyone else," she said from behind him.

He stopped and looked back to her. She was staring and serious. Through a puzzled but pleased expression, a smile played off and on at the corners of his mouth. "I'm glad," he said staring at her for a moment longer and then moving to the railing.

The river was a dark, quiet mass, its slow current apparent in the long lines that slowly crawled across its surface. Lights blinked on from the other shore, and a few street lamps scattered around the dock turned on a pale blue light.

"What are those?" he quietly asked, pointing to one of the miniature houses. She stood up and moved beside him. The wind from the river moved through her hair and rearranged it; yet it still looked soft and inviting to the touch.

"It's a spirit house, a temple," she answered, standing very close to him. "Wherein rests the lord of peace and love." Her voice was warm and surrounded him.

"Why are they all facing North?" said Brian, glancing around the small neighborhood, thinking how clean her perfume smelled.

"Because they aren't to be overshadowed," she replied, not really interested in the conversation.

"Why?" Brian turned to her.

"So there will be no gloom. That's why mine's up here."

Glancing behind him, he found that a small but very ornate one rested on a pedestal tucked among the ferns.

"Do you believe in that?" he asked, turning to her. His eyes now refused to leave her.

She stared at him, almost smiling. "What do you believe in?" she said carefully. "What brought you to this world?" Her voice was soft.

"Your tea," he said, not allowing her question to distract him.

"Don't tease." She spoke quietly, her eyes now fixed to his.

He reached out and brushed her hair back. "Do you know ..." he hesitated, memorizing her face, "how beautiful you are?"   She reached up and gently touched his cheek with her fingertips.   He slipped his arms around her waist.   "You belong here," he said, gently pulling her towards him.   "But you mustn't think I do."

"I won't. I won't," she whispered.

CHAPTER FIVE

Brian awoke to the sound of the shower. The sunlight squeezing between the curtains and the coolness of the bedroom reassured him that it was still early. Rolling onto his back, he felt content and comfortable. Getting up seemed unimportant, and he immediately dismissed the impulse. The breeze from an oscillating fan on her dresser passed over the sheet and across his chest. Remembering the night he smiled. What had started as passion had become something else. He wasn't sure what, but it had never been that way before. Questioning it now seemed only to make it more vague as a frost covered window becomes foggier if you stand too close. More than anything, he was pleased with himself.

The fan's air passed over him again, and he realized he was daydreaming. In a moment she would appear and it would be just another day. Undoubtedly, she would be preparing to go somewhere and politely and anticlimactically it would be over and time for him to thank her for dinner and leave.

Soberly he pulled back the sheet, stepped from the bed, and began to dress. Sheldon's story of her inapproachability had been wrong, but why should this be any different than any other day. It had been a romantic night. Two ex-patriots in a strange land had found each other and spent an evening together. He told himself it was time to go.

Brian moved down the hall buttoning the middle button of his shirt, but with the rich dark smell of coffee meeting him he left his shirt open. It was hard to find good coffee in Bangkok. Following the aroma into the kitchen, he found two cups placed in front of a small but full pot waiting on a warmer. The white china cups looked alert with the morning. Filling and drinking from one, the hot liquid moved through and opened his lungs. It was his first real cup in weeks, and he wanted to drink it slowly and take some time starting the day. The shower turned off and disappointedly he told himself he would have to hurry.

"Brian?" he heard her say as she walked into the bedroom, not finding him there. After a few moments of silence, she called his name again as she entered the kitchen. "There's coffee. Oh, good, you've found it." Without hesitating she walked to him placed her arms around his neck and kissed him. "I don't drink much of it myself, but I was sure you'd like it." Then half filling the other cup, she said, "It feels like it's not going to be as warm today." She was wearing a white and violet silk robe.

She looked at him with an expression that made him think she was remembering last night. Amazingly, he felt embarrassed. "That's a beautiful robe." Brian spoke to change an awkward moment.

"Thank you," she said with an amused smile.

"How'd you sleep?" Brian asked, moving to the balcony doors.

"Fine," she replied with caution. "How'd you sleep?"

"Fine. Like a rock." Brian opened the door.

From behind him she sighed. "Brian, what's going on?"

"What do you mean?" he said, without looking at her. "Nothing." He couldn't explain it, but he was uncomfortable. "I should be going," he said, turning and putting the empty cup on one of the small tables. "Thanks for dinner and the wonderful evening," he said, quickly buttoning his shirt. She looked very clean and fresh after her shower. The hair about her shoulders was wet and shiny. She was beautiful even in the morning, thought Brian as he resisted the impulse to embrace her.

"Is something bothering you? Is something wrong?" She sounded confused and a little sad. "I thought we might spend the morning together. We could go to Saturday Market. It's wonderful!" she moved towards him. "You haven't seen much of the city. You said it yourself. Or we could do something you want." Her voice gained urgency. "It's going to be a mild day. Not too hot! We could go to the rose garden at Chaisri. It's a short trip." Brian was surprised by her insistence and instinctively stepped back. "Or lunch at ..." she stopped at once and looked away embarrassed by her own effort and obvious disappointment.

He watched her wanting to help her but not knowing how. The noise from outside and the movement of the ceiling fan now seemed loud. She combed her hair back with her fingers and glanced at him. Her expression was that of a scolded child.

"Let's try the Market," he said casually. Callie looked up at him in surprise. Then her body slowly relaxed and the embarrassment that had filled the room evaporated with her smile.

When they left the apartment they were met by a pale, blue sky spotted with cotton clouds. It was cooler this morning, but Brian knew it would be hot before long. He was envious of Callie who looked cool and eager for the day. She was wearing khaki shorts with a blue cotton shirt tied in a knot at her stomach and rubber sandals. She was used to the approaching heat that would soon melt him.

When they reached the soi paralleling the river, Brian turned in the direction of the main street.

"This way!" Callie had stopped and was facing the dock. "We have to take a boat."

"Boat?!"

"Yes. Hurry, there's a particular one I want to hire."

Brian followed her quick pace onto and then down the dock. She kept stopping and standing on her tiptoes to see over the other customers who were hiring canoes only to speedily move on when she didn't find what she was looking for. When she had stopped once to try and see over the crowd, Brian noticed there were no other foreigners on the dock. He then noticed a young boy in a canoe with what had to be his grandfather. He was looking in their direction and yelling something. Their boat was a long way down the line of canoes, and Brian couldn't make out what he was saying. The boy started waving his arms in the air and continued calling.

"Is that who you're looking for?" Brian turned Callie in the direction of the boy.

"Oh. Wonderful! They haven't gone," Callie said with excitement.

Taking Brian's hand she led him down the line of canoes ignoring the invitations of the other would-be paddlers.

"I always try to get this particular one," she said, glancing back at him with a smile. "Song Per Song is a happy little boy, and I have great luck when I'm with him."

When they reached the boat, the little boy stood up and placed his palms together as if he were praying. "*S bai dee roo*," he said, bowing.

Callie released Brian's hand and placed her palms together in the same gesture. "*S bai dee kop kun*," she said, returning the bow. The man in the boat was smiling.

Taking Brian's hand again she hung one leg over the dock and carefully lowered herself into the canoe. The boy wrapped his arms around her and affectionately hugged her. "And how is your English coming?" she asked, returning his squeeze.

"O.K., American!"

"Well!" she laughed, "it's improving!"

Callie moved to the center of the canoe and sat down. "Behind me darling," she said gesturing to Brian.

The little boy's expression became serious as he watched Brian lower himself into the canoe.

He was a funny looking little boy. His black hair was short and parted on the side. Boyishly, a strand fell across his forehead, but his ears were growing faster than the rest of him and were too large for his head. Brian was sure Song Per Song had an all-encompassing crush on Callie, and, remembering the one he had suffered through at that age, he couldn't help but smile at the menacing little face, and rub his head understandingly as he passed.

Song Per Song jerked away and stared angrily at Brian while the old man and Callie laughed.

"Don't be offended Song Per Song," she said, extending her hand to Brian and pulling him towards her.

When Brian was in place behind Callie, the boy pushed off from the dock and then dropped to his knees and fell into rhythm with the strokes of his grandfather's paddle.

"What was that all about?" asked Brian.

"You touched his head." She twisted sideways so she could see Brian.

Brian stared at her, not understanding the explanation. Callie's eyes brightened. She laughingly continued.   "Thais consider the head the most important part of the body. Never touch a Thai on the head unless you intend to strongly insult him. And never, never, point your feet directly at a Thai when sitting in public. Feet are ..."

"The least important part of the body," Brian interrupted. "These people!"

"And never, under any circumstances, display in public any affection to someone of the opposite sex!" She leaned back into him so that he would have to wrap his arms around her. "We're showing very poor taste darling," she said with a laugh.

The calm river reflected the sky and the clouds as it wandered away from the city and cut into a green horizon like a flat brown ribbon. Riding high in the water, three giant barges with shiny corrugated sheet-metal roofs lumbered along in a string. Their unpainted wooden hulls and rounded roofs reminded Brian of Noah's Ark.

The river was wide, and in the current their small canoe glided across the water with only the sound of its paddles to keep them company. It was lazy and peaceful, and Brian was glad Callie had insisted on spending the day together. He knew Sheldon would expect him in the office, but he didn't care.

The boy looked back, and, seeing Brian's arms wrapped around Callie and his hands resting on her bare legs, his concern became disapproval. He craned his neck as if measuring the canoe in reassurance that the arrangement was unnecessary. Then he began speaking Thai very rapidly to Callie. When she answered she was somehow able to speak the language without it sounding like piano cords breaking. She was pleasant to listen to with the affectionate tone of her voice muffling the twangs and pings of the language. With one last glance at Brian, the boy reluctantly turned around.

"I believe he's a little jealous. What were you talking about?" asked Brian.

"Song Per Song wanted to know about you."

"Wanted to know what?"

"If we were lovers," she laughed.

"You must have told him no, or he would have already put me in the river."

She laughed and the boy glanced back.

"He may yet!" she added.

They both laughed, but the boy didn't turn this time.

By the time they reached the middle of the river the canoe had drifted far downstream. Their starting point was a dot over Brian's shoulder and a place from which all complications watched.

"I could live on the river," Brian announced in comfort. She laid her head back on his chest. "Do all fishermen become water taxis on Saturday?" he asked, putting his hand in the river.

"Many do. Saturday Market is very special."

From behind them came the high-pitched buzz of a speedboat approaching. When it sounded as though it was too close, Brian turned. The old man under the coolie hat was unconcerned and smiled. The noise came from a very long, sleek craft that was cutting its way up river. It was not wide enough for two to sit abreast, but ten or twelve could sit one behind the other. The first half of the boat was raised out of the water causing those in front to hold tight to the sides. A bright red and yellow canvas top covered it to shade its passengers. In the back, a man wearing a white shirt was standing, holding onto a long pole that had the screaming little engine fastened to it. Ten or fifteen feet behind the boat, the pole eagerly entered the water and sprayed it up in a high arch.

The old man didn't bother to look as the boat sped by. He simply continued to smile at Brian and shrugged his shoulders aimlessly. The modern world was of no temptation to him.

"What are those?" Brian asked Callie.

"Tourists boats. I call them rooster trails."

"They're too loud," Brian said, turning back. "Are they going to this market?"

The old man laughed.

"He speaks English!" Brian exclaimed. "Why hasn't he said anything?"

"Because you haven't said anything to him." Callie gently squeezed Brian's hand.

Brian looked back at him and found that the old man was still smiling. "Good morning."

"Good morning," the old man said in near perfect English.

Brian could feel Callie laughing even though she made no sound.

When they were nearly to the far side of the river, their canoe turned and started paralleling the bank. Looking back at the shoreline they had left, they saw the skyline of a modern city, but the shore closest to them had only rusty tin roof structures built on pilings. Circling each was a flimsy catwalk three or four feet above the water. The residents moved over them with the skill and ease of generations of practice. Thin old men wearing brightly colored skirts sat bare-chested on the catwalks and waved as they passed. Each home had long bamboo poles anchored into the river bottom, some with fishing nets stretched between them waiting repair. One of the homes had a small wooden patio built out over the water, and all of them had a platform built two or three inches below the surface. On these watery sidewalks mothers were washing clothes or bathing their infants. Delighted by the feel of the lapping river, the babies slapped at it with laughter, while playful, naked brown children with black eyes swam around the canoe like happy young seals barking at the morning.

Callie raised her arm and pointed out three boys standing fifteen feet above the water on pilings that had not yet been completely driven into the river bottom. Laughing, the first jumped twirling his arms until he hit with a splash that sprinkled into the canoe. Then the second leaped and splashed them again. The last boy was small, and now alone he looked hesitantly down at his calling friends. His body jerked with several false starts.

"He's going to shimmy back down," Brian chuckled.

"Poor thing."

Unexpectedly, the boy's face lost its fear to a smile, and, with a scream of glee, he stepped off. Like a stiff, little arrow, he kept his hands at his sides and pierced the water with a small splash that didn't reach the canoe. Callie craned forward to look at him, but he was already on the surface, his expression glowing with excitement. The three boys laughingly splashed each other and swam back towards the poles.

Brian looked at Song Per Song, expecting to find him jealously watching the boys. Surprisingly, he gave the boys only a glance.

On the catwalk of one house, a boy about the age of Song Per Song was gazing out over the river. He was wearing only shorts and was enjoying the mild morning unaware of their approach. When the canoe was nearly past him, he finally looked at its passengers. Instantly, he sprang to his feet and ran into the house only to reappear holding something in his hand, and then dive into the water. Although he used only his free hand, he was swiftly to the canoe and hooked his arm over the side. He was smiling and speaking, but before Brian could try to decipher what he was saying, Callie began to shake her head. In the boy's hand, he held an elephant carved out of teakwood. Its base was as large as a brick, and it was beautifully sculptured and looked heavy. Callie reached over and pried the boy's arm free just as Song Per Song appeared over them shouting at the boy and raising his paddle threateningly. Floating away the boy stared at Song Per Song menacingly.

"Jesus, I thought you like these people?" said Brian.

Callie was quiet for a moment, and Song Per Song returned to the front of the boat. "I couldn't let him try to peddle that to you and neither could Song Per Song." She leaned back into him. "Fishermen pass their craft from one generation to another. They are very proud and protective."

"I don't need Song Per Song to crack another kid in the head to protect me!" announced Brian.

Callie was silent for a moment, and then she turned so she could see him. "He wasn't protecting you, he was protecting himself." She paused and glanced at the shore. "And that boy."

"From what?" Brian asked knowing her answer and resenting it.

"You." She spoke gently trying not to offend. "You've seen the street children in the city, poor little things, begging every chance they see a Westerner. But that boy was a fisherman's son."

Brian's resentment disappeared with the image of the profane little children that wandered around the streets of the city selling whatever they could to any foreigner they could find. Watching the industrious little Song Per Song paddling the canoe, he decided she was right.

As they continued down the river, the homes continued with them, and the laughter of the children playing in the water was joyfully about them.

"How much farther?"

"Not much. Look to your left!" said Callie quickly.

They had been so involved watching the families and homes that they hadn't noticed the soundless vessel approaching them.

"What the hell is that?" He said aloud to himself.

"The Royal Barge. Isn't it beautiful?" she answered.

The old man and boy stopped paddling to bow as it passed, and the laughter of the children stopped.

Well over two hundred feet long and built low in the water, it majestically moved with the perfect rhythm of its one hundred oars. It was decorated in gold and carved like a serpent. The head towered to the sky. Its mouth was held shut by a huge gold ring. From the ring hung a gold sash, and halfway down the sash was a large cluster of crystals. At the end of the sash, nearly to the water, was an even larger cluster of crystals. They looked like chandeliers that would light the monster's course at night. As it moved alongside them, the sunlight reflected from its gold scales into the water and blindingly into Brian and Callie's eyes. It was perfectly carved, with each scale fitting up over the next. The gills of the giant were flared, as if it was exhaling, and its dark eyes seemed to watch their small craft with disdain.

Although they were close enough to hear it cut through the water, not one of the oarsmen glanced in their direction. They were dressed in red silk helmets and uniforms, which gave the beast a spiny red back. In the middle of the boat was the Royal Pavilion which was shaded by red and gold silk that waved with the movement of the ship. In the pavilion was a large, empty, gold throne. As it passed, you could almost see the image of an ancient emperor, piously overseeing the silent efforts of his crew. On the tail stood three men, their arms wrapped around the rudder with the royal banner fluttering above them.

Brian watched it quietly until the swimming children began laughing again and the old man and boy resumed their paddling. Their efforts seemed feeble now, and Song Per Song appeared embarrassed at their slow pace.

"Don't worry, Song," said Brian. "I doubt if they can fish."

The boy glanced back and gave him a somewhat friendly smile.

"Does the King still use that?" Brian asked Callie.

"I've never seen it out before. I told you Song Per Song brings me luck!" She was excited and proud of their good fortune. "You really do love it here," said Brian.

Callie hesitated. "Of course."

As they started around a bend in the river and passed the last piling house, the laughter of the children faded away. Wild greenery ran down the bank and out into the first few feet of the water. The old man and boy corrected their course only enough to keep them from grounding the canoe. Branches slowly moved past Brian's head like bony fingers reaching for him. They were unable to see around the bend, but the sound of voices came from the other side and Brian assumed it was another dock.

"We must be getting closer," he said.

Callie leaned her head back and smiled at him with an excited expression.

As they pulled around the bend, Brian was disappointed to find that the noises and voices had come from houseboats. Like tired old women, three of the boats were grounded in the mouth of an inlet. Rusty, corrugated sheet-metal bowed over them for roofs, each piece hammered and bent to fit into the next. The walls were constructed of old, wormy woods of all types, obviously scavenged from any available source. Their living compartments looked too heavy for the boats and pushed them down into the mud. There were too many people on all of them, and the people were dirty and as tired as their boats.

"*Rua buk kon*," said the old man to Brian.

Brian was confused and struggled with the interpretation. "*Buk kon*, person, boat person, boatpeople!" The old man smiled and nodded approvingly.

"Do they live on those things all the time?" Brian asked the old man.

"No come off."

"They fish for a living?"

The old man's face wrinkled up, and he nodded, disheartened. "Poor fishermen. Just to eat. They no sell."

Their canoe turned and started into another inlet. The greenery thickened, and trees loomed up their branches, tangling together and forming a high green roof above their heads. It was an emerald tunnel that twisted and turned its way inland towards a secret place. Occasionally, the water splashed from an unseen animal taking refuge from their advance. Song Per Song kept glancing back at them, the excitement in his eyes growing with every stroke of his paddle. On their left, the jungle thinned, and the ghostly remains of a temple appeared, its once proud, pointed dome now broken and chipped to rubble. Creeping vines hung from the ledges and cracks, as the jungle methodically reclaimed its space.

Coming towards them was a woman paddling a canoe. In it were fruits and vegetables of every color. She smiled happily as they passed one another and waved a bright yellow mango at Song Per Song. "We're almost there!" Callie's voice was excited, and she squeezed his hand hard. The growing sound of a great many voices and Thai music pulled their canoe around the last bend, and the Market exploded before them.

"I don't believe it!" said Brian in amazement. Hundreds of canoes stretched down the waterway and around the next bend. There were so many canoes packed together that paddles could not be put into the water. Instead the boatmen moved their canoes by pulling on the side of the boat next to them. A long, flat raft had been pushed close to the shore, and six men sat on it playing musical instruments, their music cheerfully encouraging the excitement about them. The canoes were filled to their brims with everything imaginable. Silk flashed in the sunlight as an end of the roll was thrown from a seller's canoe to a buyer's. Bunches of bananas, mangoes, and every other kind of fruit flew through the air like juggling props. Large bags of rice were bounced over the heads of those separating buyer from seller. Artists held their watercolor paintings above their heads and called to the crowd like auctioneers. Jade jewelry fastened to paddles was held out for inspection. Mounds of sandals threatened to avalanche into adjacent canoes. Brightly colored cotton shirts were displayed by using crossed sticks which disguised canoes as sailing ships. From strings extending between poles hung rainbows made of flower leis. Buyers haggled with their arms waving only to finalize a purchase and turn to another boat and start again as the seller. It was like a marvelous barrel that had been dropped and crashed open with wonderful things flying in every direction.

"This is madness!" Brian happily exclaimed, disbelieving his own eyes.

"Isn't it wonderful!" she wheeled around to him, her eyes brilliant with excitement.

"Yes!" He was amazed and paused not knowing what to call it. "It really is wonderful. It's like a pirates' market!"

Her expression toyed with an idea, and then her attention melted over him. Her eyes sparkled and she smiled. "I'm so glad I brought you."

Only by sheer ingenuity had Song Per Song managed to maneuver the canoe into the wildness.

The bottom of their boat was now filled with fruit and vegetables. Mangoes and pineapples rolled about with every movement of their canoe. To be protected from the fruit, the flower leis Callie had bought hung over the side of the canoe, and several of the bright cotton shirts were tucked beside Brian. Around his neck were still more leis that smelled sweet.

The pleasure that comes from discovering that particular piece of fruit which surely will be most delicious or the most perfect flower lei for her had overpowered Brian and made him a haggler with anyone willing to sell, and they were all willing.

"Brian you have to slow down!" Callie laughed and placed her hand on his shoulder. "You're buying long before you should."

He tried to look at her, but he was arguing with an old woman over a melon.

"You don't even know what that is!" Callie insisted playfully. When you cut those things open they smell terrible!"

He stopped and turned to her with a serious expression. "What do they taste like?" he said.

She shook her head, trying not to laugh. "They're delicious!"

Instantly, Brian was hammering the old woman with an offer. He enjoyed haggling. He had never done it before, and it was fun.

When he finally turned around with the melon, Callie was sitting with her back resting on the side of the boat. The canoe next to them was filled with watercolor paintings, and she was staring at one of them. The art peddler's back was to them, as he feverishly argued with someone on the other side. From his position, Brian was unable to determine which one of the paintings Callie was so enthralled with. So systematically he began to look at each in a process of elimination. Most depicted villages with coolies working in the paddies or the river with the sun rising or setting. They were all poorly painted, and he couldn't imagine which had attracted her attention. Then, checking a second time, he saw one he hadn't noticed. Unlike the others, it was an oil painting, but instead of canvas the artist had pressed a leaf of some sort flat and allowed it to dry. On the coarse, brown texture of the leaf was painted two small birds perched on a branch. The painter's hand had so delicately created each feather that it looked soft to the touch and made Callie watch the birds as if she expected them to fly away.

Brian set the melon on the bottom of their canoe and reached over and picked up the painting. The peddler glanced protectively over his shoulder and finished the other sale. Brian could feel her watching him, and he felt almost ashamed as if he had peeked through a keyhole.

"*Tou-rai?*" he asked already knowing he would buy it, whatever the price.

"One thousand baht," smiled the peddler.

"Brian, that's too much!" Callie demanded.

Brian reached into his pocket and pulled out a wad of crumpled bills.

"It's not worth fifty dollars!"

Brian counted six hundred.

"We still have to pay for the boat." She raised up on her knees.

"Song, how much for the boat?" Brian asked digging into his other pocket. Song was laying with his chest on the front of the canoe reaching into another boat that sold dried fruit and Kobe beef.

"Song, the boat?" How much?"

"One hundred ten baht," he replied, without looking back.

There were several bills at the bottom of his pocket. Pulling them out he counted a total of 1200 baht.

"I'll take it." Brian handed the peddler his demand.

"Taxi fare! You won't even have enough for that!" She was upset with him.

"They owe me a ride from yesterday." Brian leaned past her and pulled on Song Per Song's leg to get his attention. The boy sat up chewing on an orange piece of dried fruit he had liberated. "Here you go Song." Brian placed the last 200 baht in the boy's hand.

Song Per Song glanced excitedly back at the old man who craned forward to count it for himself. "You come next week!" Song said without looking at Brian.

Turning to her, Brian set the painting in her lap. For a moment her face was expressionless while she glanced several times between the painting and Brian. Then, looking down, she stared at the painting. When she looked up at him, it was with large soft eyes that seemed to see into him. She looked fragile and almost sad. She was amazingly beautiful without any effort to be so, and she was unaware of it. "That was very sweet of you." She spoke quietly, with her eyes intensely fixed to his. The feeling he'd enjoyed in bed this morning returned, and Brian promised himself he would not fall in love with her.

"*Mai pen rai,*" he smiled.

CHAPTER SIX

Setting the bottled water down, Brian caught sight of a manila folder. The thick beige packet lay on his desk as if patiently awaiting his attention. He had used the day searching the office files and old headlines collecting notes and photographs to put together a chronology of the war in Cambodia. Glancing at his watch he knew that Sheldon would be ready to leave the office soon, but he was eager and opened the file and began to read the dates, thinking of just how to frame an article that could distinguish the problems of Cambodia from Vietnam and bring the difference home to American readers.

1941

Nordam Shinouk Becomes King

1949

Cambodia Granted Independence as Associate State
Of French Union

1953

Military Power Is Transferred By France to
Cambodian Government,
Giving It Sovereign Independence

Ho Chi Minh's Viet Minh Communists Invade
Cambodia

1954

Fighting Between Viet Minh and Cambodia Ends
With Geneva Agreement

1955

Cambodia Financially and Economically
Independent of France and Other Former French

Indochina States of Vietnam And Laos

Sihanouk Abdicates In Favor Of His Father,
King Norodom Suramarit

1960

Suramarit Dies; Sihanouk Refused To Become King

Prince Sihanouk Elected Head of State

Brian shook his head. "Sounds like a Shakespeare
play," he said aloud to himself.

1965

Sihanouk Breaks Diplomatic Relations With The U.S.
After South Vietnamese Planes Attack Viet Cong

Forces Fleeing Into Cambodia

1969

August – Cambodian People Stage
Pro-American Demonstrations
To Avert Overthrow of Their Government

Sihanouk Establishes Diplomatic Relations With U.S.

October – U.S. Opens Embassy

1970

March – A Series of Demonstrations Against North
Vietnam Rocks The Capital

North Vietnam's Embassies Sacked
Sihanouk Overthrown

March 18 – Lon Nol Becomes Head Of Government
And Acting President

North Vietnamese Missions Evacuate Diplomats

Civil War Breaks Out With Anti-Lon Nol Forces
Attacking Government Positions in Northeast

April – North Vietnamese Forces Attack Cambodian
Outposts in Northeastern Border Area Which
Communists Views as Sanctuary for War in Vietnam

May – U.S. And South Vietnamese Forces
Launch 60 Day Incursion into Cambodia

North Vietnamese Seize
Famed Angkor Wat Complex in Northwest

June – U.S. Ends Incursion

October – Monarchy Abolished By Legislature

Cambodia's Name Officially Changed to
Khmer Republic

1971

U.S. Military and Economic Aid
Totaled $260 Million Dollars

Communist Forces Make Gains

Lon Nol Suffers Stroke

1972

January – South Vietnamese Forces Withdraw

March – Lon Nol Assumes Total Power

Khmer Rouge Forces Launch Heaviest Attack
On Capital

Since Start Of War Hitting Phnom Penh With
200 Rockets and Shells
Killing More Than Fifty People and Wounding 120

1973

January – Khmer Rouge Rebels Launch
First Military Effort

Reportedly to Cut Phnom Penh's Land
And Sea Links With Outside Worlds

6,000 to 7,000 Troops Occupied Portions of
Mekong River,
But Retreat In Face Of U.S. Air Attacks

U.S. Economic Aid $93.1 Million Dollars;
Military Aid, $138 Million Dollars

"No one is paying attention," said Brian. "As long as
there are no boots on the ground, America thinks
we're not there." He shook his head. There had to be
a big story in all of this.

1974

Communists Launch New Offensive,
Strengthen Forces and Modify Tactics
And Build Logistical Bases

U.S. Economic Aid $275.5 Million Dollars
Military Aid, $381.3 Million Dollars

1975

January 1 – Khmer Rouge Launch New Offensive
With Coordinated Attacks Closing Mekong River
to Supply Convoys and Taking Control of
Any Major Highways

Over the years the news media in the United
States hadn't troubled the American people by going
into any definition of what was taking place in
Cambodia. Television and newspapers simply pointed
out that young American soldiers were being killed in
Vietnam by marauding guerilla forces that escaped
across the border into Cambodia only to regroup and
attack again. The Cambodian people were thought of

as condoning the Viet Cong's use of their country
when in fact they did not.   Their small and ill-
equipped army was incapable of entering the war on
either side, so they were forced to ignore the entries
and exits of their stronger neighbor and to protest to
the United States when the bombing spilled over their
border.   Sihanouk's friendly attitude towards North
Vietnam may have been nothing more than the
pragmatic realization of a leader that it was safer to
anger the South and the United States than it was to
anger the bold and aggressive North.   Or he may have
been a man that hoped to one day have unquestionable
power over the lives of his people, which he expected
to establish through debts owed to him by the North.
Brian drank from the bottled water and wondered
which it was. The long, troubled history of the region
had been written in simple paragraphs that put people
in countries on one side or the other of a straight line.
There was no room for noncommittal or un-
involvement, yet that was the only hope Cambodia
had.

The image of the country as a safe haven for
America's enemies had been carefully painted by
politicians that avoided the complex in order to pacify
a questioning public. It was seen as a dark land where
communist forces imprisoned captured American
fliers and housed their supplies for waging war. Both
images were true, yet they were not the complete
truth. Cambodia was a country of few cities and many
remote villages. The Cambodians that participated in
the war effort against South Vietnam were a minority
that either believed in the ultimate goal or had been
forced into taking sides by the concentrated air strikes

from U.S. forces. A story was there, but Brian knew that unless he could find a hook, it would be an unpopular one in the States and doubted that it would be worth the effort. He needed something that would touch the American public and force them to care about the welfare of a backward country of rural rice farmers that had no impact on their daily lives and no connection to their heartstrings.

"Americans will never hear a bell for thee," he said aloud to himself sarcastically.

In the folder was a stack of several black and white photographs. The first had been taken of Sihanouk and Samphen years before the alleged attempt by Sihanouk to have Samphen killed. They were standing side by side, and Sihanouk had a fatherly arm wrapped around Samphen's shoulder. Like every successful politician, Sihanouk knew how to work the camera and posed with the puckered smile of a happy and proud parent. The young man's face looked into the camera with an innocent expression that showed he was unaccustomed to attention from the press. He was dressed very plainly in the dark uniform that lower government officials wore. The photograph had been taken when Samphen was in his mid-thirties, but he looked very young with the hair above his ears clipped boyishly short. He was nice looking and appeared more Western than oriental. A small portion of the article which accompanied the photograph described the young man seen with Sihanouk as the Minister of Economy, a dedicated servant of the people who was ostentatiously honest. The article went on to briefly add that Samphen was well known in the Capital as a bachelor who rode to and from work on a bicycle and lived in a small room. Nothing foretold that he would one day be attacking the Capital as a Khmer Rouge leader.

The next photograph was taken in March 1974 in Hanoi at a military parade. It was of Yeng Sary and Khiev Samphen, now leaders of the Khmer Rouge forces in Cambodia. The years that had passed between the two photographs showed in Samphen's face. He still looked young and even more Western with his hair longer and conservatively parted on the side, but there was no trace of the innocence. The 44 year old stood watching the Vietnamese army march by with a stern and committed expression. The boyish look had become a handsome and charismatic face of a strong leader, which even in a photograph made the viewer feel the power of the individual. Even though he was merely one of the recognized leaders of a rag-tag guerilla army, Samphen stood proudly erect while his older comrade humbly watched the strength of his neighbor pass. There was no intimidation in Samphen. If anything, he appeared to be watching for fault. He was there on business to obtain the necessary weaponry to win in his own country, and if necessary, in the future the resolve on his face left no doubt, that Samphen would turn it against the North Vietnamese.

"Destiny," Brian said aloud. "That's what you look like."

The determination about Samphen was riveting. It cast its own shadow, and Brian couldn't help feeling a strange type of admiration for the man. Reluctantly, he set the picture aside and picked up the photograph of the man in Cambodia that Sheldon had such great faith would break a deep secret. Although Godfrey was an impressive and handsome figure, he didn't have any of the charisma of Samphen. Instead he looked independent and even rather cocky. The only photograph Brian had found of Godfrey was taken when he and several other journalists had arrived in Vietnam to cover the war back in 1970. Godfrey stepped onto the runway of Denang from a U.S. Marine helicopter with an expression that seemed to say "Start up the war, I'm here." Around his neck were four cameras, and as luggage he carried a single bag over his shoulder. The blades of the helicopter were still spinning, so he held a wide brim hat to his head with one hand which made him look like he was saluting the camera that had caught his image. Brian could have immediately disliked him just from the photograph for he reeked of overconfidence to the point of conceit. Shuffling his way through the rest of the photographs, Brian put the ones Godfrey had taken together. Each had an unmistakable mark to it for they all were carefully taken to catch more than merely an image. Godfrey knew angles and he used them well. He gave shots taken in combat careful attention so as to capture the atmosphere along with the visual image. One of Brian's favorites had been taken when the United States was still fighting in Vietnam. It was a company of American infantrymen crossing a stream. Some of them were fording the fast-moving water by wading in waist high, while the less aggressive tried like cats to cross by jumping from one bolder to the next. They all looked awkward and out of place and their young faces held expressions confused by the explanations they had been given for their presence in a country that didn't want them. They were alone in a land that breathed with the desire to kill them, and their only hope was to return home to a country that scorned them. They were a small group of a lost generation.

The most impressive photograph was a recent one Godfrey had taken after a rocket attack on a town in Cambodia. A small boy of five or six squatted in the middle of a road looking into a four foot wide crater. His arms braced between his knees, and his chin supported a face that was both stunned and frightened with the power of war. It wasn't that this child brought out the feeling of pity, for his wonder had an adult expression that questioned the value of anything that could be worth such destruction. From the photographs Brian felt as though he was getting to know Godfrey. The war in Cambodia was a newsworthy event that could provide him with countless bylines, and Brian was jealous.

Brian had also discovered that Godfrey was an egotist that didn't want to bother confirming a story. He made a fool of himself and lost his credibility trying to be as big as the news. It had happened last summer when the war in Cambodia was still small news. Godfrey had been put into contact with a man that claimed to be a deserter from the North Vietnamese army. The man convinced Godfrey that he had stolen secret papers from his superiors that outlined both an attack by the North into South Vietnam and theorized that once victory was achieved the ultimate objective of controlling all of Asia. Without waiting to check thoroughly into the man's story Godfrey purchased the documents and wrote the story as fact. Although it had been ignored by most American newspapers, the European and English papers throughout Asia had run the story. The embarrassment had come two days later when the man was arrested by the Thai police, and it was proven that the entire matter had been a fabrication aimed at any newspaper man silly enough to pay for the fairytale. By the third day the same newspapers not only informed their readers, but the explanation they provided chastised Godfrey for unprofessional reporting. He needed a big story to put him back where he believed his talent deserved, and he believed

Kiev Samphen was the key. All other reasons being forgotten, Godfrey was determined to vindicate himself to prove the crossings were taking place under the nose of every other reporter.

The one other photograph Brian was taking home with him was of the university student Sheldon had suspected might know something. There was nothing remarkable about the image. In fact, it looked like any other except for the fact that it was taken of an anti-American protest staged by students in front of the American Embassy. One of the figures in it was the young man, but the thought that he could be involved in anything that would attract such strong characters as Samphen and Godfrey didn't feel right. Looking again at the last photograph of Samphen, Brian doubted that the college student could provide the type of big lead that Sheldon hoped. Brian glanced over the notes and photographs spread across the table with the uncomfortable feeling that he was missing something. Then he rearranged them as if they were pieces of a puzzle that would fall into place. There was nothing that even remotely could be construed as a clue, but he had the feeling that the first, even if it was a small one, was right in front of him.

"Brian, let's go!" Sheldon's voice startled Brian. "Let's get out of here."

Turning around Brian could see that Sheldon was anxious to leave the office which was out of character. It had grown to be a habit for them to leave together and walk down to the corner where they would flag separate cabs. "I'll be right with you," replied Brian, as he discreetly pushed the photos and notes into the file.

"What are you working on?" questioned Sheldon.

"Just some background." Brian tried to sound uninterested. He didn't want to share his thoughts, knowing that Sheldon would either discourage the article or take control of it. "I'm ready. Let's go." As discreetly as possible Brian took the folder and followed Sheldon out of the office.

As they stepped onto the street, Sheldon lit a cigarette. "What's in the file?"

"Don't you and the Prince have plans?" answered Brian.

"He'll undoubtedly be at Tiger's." Sheldon glanced down the street in the opposite direction as they turned towards the corner. "I'll meet him later, but first I want to stop at home. How about you and Callie?"

"I don't know what we'll do. Maybe she has something planned." Since their first dinner together, unless she was in the Provinces, Brian had spent every night at Callie's except one, and that one had been a mistake. He hadn't seen the Prince in a few days so he had stopped off to have one or two quick cocktails with him and Sheldon. Unfortunately, Sheldon's dry humor had been in top form and when Brian stood up to leave, he found himself besieged with jokes of how well Callie had trained him. At first, only to prove Sheldon wrong Brian had sat down for one more drink, but somehow it had gotten out of control and taken on what had seemed at the time to be a matter of pride. The one cocktail turned into a long line with Brian beating off Sheldon's attacks by ordering still another and saying that Callie could wait. When they finally did leave it had been too late to wake her so he had walked home to his apartment scolding himself for not doing what he really wanted. Remembering the wasted evening Brian changed hands and carried the file in the one farthest from Sheldon.

"Are you going directly to Callie's?"

"No. I'll stop at home and clean up."

"If she hasn't anything special planned why don't the two of you meet us?" Sheldon glanced at the folder. "We'll have a few laughs and go somewhere for dinner."

"We'll see," Brian said, while trying to think of an excuse. Once or twice during the week he and Callie would go out with Sheldon and the Prince, but on the weekends if Brian did not work they guarded their privacy and spent the time alone. They passed the days exploring the city and the evenings enjoying the sound of each other's laughter. It was their time, and he didn't want to share it.

"If it's easier, just give me a time and I'll catch a cab to your place and we'll pick up Callie," offered Sheldon.

"It would be easier just to meet you."

"We'll have dinner at that German place she likes so much. Isn't that her favorite?"

"Yes," Brian lied. Her favorite restaurant was Salanorasingh where you sat at low tables and watched Siamese dancers perform.

"If she has made plans just tell her you want to go with us. She'll do whatever you want," insisted Sheldon.

"Yeah, but I hate to do that. With us working most of the weekends, she has to do everything around my schedule."

"Oh, she's a good sport. Besides she'll have a good time," Sheldon glanced at the folder. "You're not going to work tonight?"

Brian was a little surprised at Sheldon's insistence. After the last evening of drinking with Sheldon and the Prince, Brian had made it a rule to include Callie even when the Prince and Sheldon wanted to stop for one drink after work. The Prince loved to see Callie and usually insisted that she sit in between him and Brian. Her sense of humor sparked the Prince, and in no time they were all very happy and filled wherever they were with a party atmosphere. Yet, sometimes Sheldon seemed uncomfortable with her presence, not as though she were intruding but rather with her attitude towards Brian. Although it was discreet, so as not to embarrass herself or offend any Thais, Callie was very affectionate in public. Even if it were nothing more than keeping a hand on Brian's leg or touching his hair.

It was obvious to Brian that Sheldon was a little infatuated with Callie.

"I can't make any promises, but it may work out," Brian said, smiling to himself and thinking of her. Callie really was a good sport. Other than her spiced tea, she really didn't like the taste of liquor and never drank more than one or two, but she was consistently charming and never complained about where the four of them went or how long they stayed. At night, Bangkok was a chameleon that changed from a serious, overcrowded capital to an exotic magic store where the mysteries of Asia collided with the neon of the West and everything was for sale. Patpong Road was a small area packed with restaurants and clubs with names like the Bad Apple, Neil's Tavern and Madrid. It was like a splendid train wreck where both the West and the East tangled together until neither could be separated and restored to its original shape. It was wild and bright.

Usually they began and ended at Tigers where occasionally the Prince or Sheldon would catch a second wind and they would energetically attempt to infect the others. If they were at a table and Brian started to go along with the current, Callie would lean against him as a hint that she was tired, and if they were standing she would laughingly put herself between Brian and the bar. If either of these hints did not work, she was quick to distract him with a conversation meant just for his ears. Amazingly, she could at the same time manage to follow whatever else was being said so that if interrupted by the Prince or Sheldon she could usher them out of her and Brian's conversation without their realizing that she was trying to leave. If conversation didn't work she looked at him with eyes as sultry as the hot night, and he was ready to leave.

"What's with the smile?" Sheldon asked in a serious voice.

Realizing that he had been day dreaming, Brian erased the smile. "You know, Sheldon, one thing I don't believe any of the media has done very well is to distinguish the different countries of Asia," said Brian to change the subject.

"What do you mean?"

"Just that America had one gigantic problem in this area of the world. The war in Vietnam. It overpowered Americans and they began to think of the whole region as Vietnam. They hear the words 'Cambodia,' 'Laos,' or even 'Thailand,' and they think it is merely semantics, all meaning the same thing: Vietnam. When any one of those countries is reported to be having problems, most Americans simply think it is more of the same. It's just like Central America." Brian stepped from the curb to look for a cab. "I bet 90% of the Americans can't name the countries of Central America."

"I've never thought of it that way. You may be right, but what does that have to do with anything?" Sheldon smirked.

"I'd like to try a series of articles aimed at just that!" Brian announced defiantly.

"Getting a little ambitious, aren't we!" Sheldon's voice was patronizing.

"I'm better than you think and certainly better than the assignments you give me."

Sheldon stopped and looked intensely at Brian until the atmosphere was uneasy. "I'll tell you what I'll do. Since you're so sure of yourself, you and I will work Godfrey's story of these crossings from this side of the border." Sheldon resumed walking before Brian could reply. "We'll go together to the border, and we'll find out how good you are."

Stunned, Brian could only watch Sheldon for a moment and then he hurried after him. "How?" Brian excitedly asked, only to hate himself for it.

Looking back over his shoulder, Sheldon stepped off the curb to wave down a cab. "I thought you'd have that figured out." He was patronizing again. "I'm in the mood for Tigers." A cab pulled in front of Brian and interrupted Sheldon. "This one's mine," Sheldon said, taking hold of the door handle. Sheldon hesitated and looked at Brian seriously. "We'll talk more about "how" later. I'll see you after awhile."

"That will depend on Callie."

"You'll be there," Sheldon said as he opened the door and stepped halfway in. "Hell, the only place she wouldn't go with you was the cockfights."

Brian nodded in recalling how inhumane Callie had thought even the invitation was and how she had lectured them for just thinking about going. Thai boxing was bad enough with the fighters being allowed to use both their hands and their feet. She had sat through that, cringing with every blow.

Making two animals fight to the death was barbaric and inexcusable.

"She's too good for you kid," Sheldon said, leaning out the window. Brian smiled and the cab sped away. Excitedly Brian started off for Callie's with the news.

CHAPTER SEVEN

Brian had arrived at Callie's before her, so he let himself in with a key she kept hidden under a potted fern and made himself comfortable on the balcony. The first swallow of a potent Thai beer slightly numbed his lips.

Below on the docks, he saw the excited wave of Song Per Song who was running towards him. "Little wharf rat," Brian said aloud to himself with a smile. Undoubtedly, Son Per Song was rushing through the growing crowd to collect on last night's bet.

In an effort to soften the blow to Song Per Song's puppy love for Callie, Brian had attempted to win his friendship by teaching him poker, the result of which was a tenuous friendship at best, and the persistent gambling frenzy of an eight-year-old Asian. Without glancing at Brian again, Song Per Song ran down the soi through the courtyard and into the building and up the stairs. There was a hesitation after knocking before he rushed into the apartment.

"You have my money?" asked Song Per Song as he appeared on the balcony. His little face was serious.

"Yes, but how about a chance to win it back?" asked Brian as he poured a little of the beer into a plastic cup and handed it to Song Per Song.

"Pay first." Song Per Song took the cup with wide eyes and a smile.

"What?" Don't you trust me?"

"I trust you pay."

"Song," Brian hesitated as he pulled folded bills and a deck of cards from his shirt pocket. "You're a distrusting soul."

With a wide grin and one motion, the boy took the money, pulled up a chair, placed a small wicker table between them, and began to shuffle the cards. "Now Play."

"You're too serious about money Song," Brian reached behind him where another cold beer waited. "Today's my lucky day. Today I got the assignment I wanted, and I'll win back my money from you."

"You be going away?" Song Per Song's hands froze and he looked up at Brian with his most serious expression. "You take Callie?"

For a moment Brian considered teasing the boy with a yes. "I'll be gone for a little while, but she'll be here," Brian replied mercifully.

Satisfied the boy began to deal the cards.

The card game had not been going on very long when Brian heard Callie opening the door. Both he and Song Per Song had been so involved with the game that neither had noticed her walking through the courtyard. "Hello Darling," she said opening the door. Her voice sounded happy, and before he could turn to face her, Callie was on the balcony. "And who's winning this evening?" She bent down and kissed his cheek.

"Who else," Brian said nodding towards Song Per Song.

"Oh, what a shame," she laughed, "because I know someone's grandfather is looking for him, and he certainly won't approve of gambling." She spoke slowly to emphasize importance.

The boy quickly dropped his cards and stood. Then with an even quicker bow to Callie he disappeared out the door.

"You certainly know how to break up a game," said Brian.

"You don't really want him to become one of those fanatics gambling over everything and playing the numbers downtown." Callie brushed her hand through his hair. "He likes gambling too much, I'm afraid, even more than fishing."

"I thought we might go out for dinner this evening," said Brian as he relaxed. "Sheldon and I need to discuss something so I thought he could join us."

"I was hoping we could go to Sananorasingh for dinner," she said with a glance. Her voice no longer sounded happy.

"You want to take Sheldon there?" teased Brian.

"No. I wanted us to be alone so that we could discuss something."

"What's wrong?" asked Brian as he reached out and touched her arm.

"Nothing," she insisted, trying to smile.

Brian watched her disbelievingly. When she realized he was watching her, Callie all of a sudden seemed very happy and she began to laugh. "Really darling, everything is fine."

"I know what it is! You want me to take you somewhere special this weekend," said Brian.

"I never said that."

"You're thinking it, though." Brian's face lit up. "Payata Beach! That's it, isn't it?"

Callie's smile grew with the mention of the little resort town, and she looked past him as if remembering the three days they had spent there. It being the off-season, they had enjoyed the long, white beaches and sidewalk cafes by themselves. Without the tourists, the hotel staff and waiters had treated them like personal friends and gone out of their way to insure everything was perfect and their privacy well protected. The townspeople had been warm and friendly, and the driver of one of the overly decorated mini busses had even abandoned his normal route and cruised them along the waterfront and anywhere else in the town they had wanted to go for half fare. Callie hated to leave, and on their last day there had made him promise to take her back before the European tourist season began.

"That was a lovely weekend. Someday we'll go back." Her eyes focused on him again. "But that has nothing to do with it, and nothing is wrong." She turned her attention to the river, and Brian decided to leave the subject for the time being.

"I think we should go with Sheldon tonight," said Brian. "There is something ..."

"Can't you talk to him about your new assignment tomorrow?" she interrupted. She no longer tried to sound or appear happy. Brian was shocked that she knew anything about the matter and could not answer for a moment. Callie watched him with anticipation. "Were you going to have Sheldon tell me?"

"Of course not," said Brian shaking his head. "How did you know? Sheldon just told me!"

"The Prince told me," answered Callie nonchalantly.

"Prince!" How in the hell did he ..." he paused. "Sheldon must have told him, and the gossip couldn't wait to tell you," Brian said hesitantly. "Really it's not a big deal. We're simply going to the border for a few days."

"It's about breaking a story on the refugees crossing into Thailand," Callie announced with certainty. "Sheldon believes he can break the story by following a university student named Chovat who is supposed to be involved."

Brian watched her in disbelief. "Where did you hear all this? What else do you know?"

She stared at him for a moment. "I know you're both making a mistake. The story isn't how people are getting into this country, but why they are coming."

"There is a war in Cambodia." Brian stood up. His voice sounded lighthearted, causing her to pause.

"There is more than a war."

"More rumors," said Brian with a sigh. "This isn't 1943, and we're not dealing with Nazi Germany." He stared at her for a moment. "What exactly is it that's bothering you?" He couldn't prevent his voice from sounding a little angry.

Callie hesitated, then said "Just your attitude." Her expression intensified. She moved closer to Brian. "Please don't think that I'm interfering, or that I expect you to make me an active part of your career, but I just don't want to see us make a mistake." She stopped and looked vulnerable.

"All right," he said, caught up in her serious mood.

"Brian you could be one of the best in the business," she hesitated, then went on "but you might turn out to be only a run of the mill, and if you're not careful, you'll never reach your potential." Brian tried not to look surprised, but her frankness caught him off guard, and he felt himself step backwards. Callie looked tense as if she regretted saying anything.

"Really? Just what is it you think can make me a run of the mill?"

"Your style is fine. There is nothing wrong with your style, but you hold back," she said without hesitation.

"What do you mean?" he asked quietly, as he began to fill his anger.

She watched him for a moment, and then her face became strong. "You're cold. Sometimes I'm not certain that you care about anyone including me."

Something inside of him collapsed. He would have been truly angry if he weren't so disarmed. "That's honest. Is this what you wanted to talk to me about tonight?" asked Brian.

"Partly." She tried to smile. "Most journalists supply facts, but you write. You make the readers feel like they're there. But, as a person, just as a person, not as a writer, you resent the fact that you're here, and that shows in your writing."

"Of course I do," he said defensively. "Cambodia is the biggest story in the region right now. It's not wrong for me to want to write about it, and here I sit with the silly things Sheldon hands down to me."

"Why can't you find your own story? You have the talent. Why do you have to take the approach Sheldon wants, and believe what Sheldon believes? Why can't you open up to these people?"

Brian hesitated, not wanting to be angry. "As far as wishing I could cover the war, I can't change that. Callie, in a few months it won't just be over. It will be forgotten. But right now, it's the story worth covering. I want the chance."

"I know you do. I just don't know why you want it, or what you want with me. Sometimes I think you feel I'm in the way and that you wished you hadn't met me, at least not now." She paused. "Oh, Brian I don't mean to sound foolish. I've been happy with you, but things are beginning to seem so complicated and I really don't know how you feel. Then I learn it's about to start, that you'll soon be …"

"It will only be for a few days," interrupted Brian. "I'm going to be in Thailand. It's no different than when you go to the provinces."

"No Brian." She spoke with certainty. "Things are about to start that could separate us."

"What are you talking about? It has nothing to do with us."

"Believe me, I know. We have to take steps or it will all crumble." She moved to him and wrapped her arms around him. "That's what I wanted to talk to you about tonight. There is no reason for you to rent an apartment you're never at." She was self-conscious and spoke hastily. "I've been thinking about it for a long time, and I want you to move in with me."

Although he tried to hide it, Brian could feel the surprise escape through his expression. He should have seen it coming, but he hadn't, and he realized that without meaning to, he had misled her. He assumed that one day he would be leaving and it would end. Actually living together would only make it more difficult on both of them when the time came.

"We're always together anyway," she added, "And if you're going to be spending time away from me in a dangerous place I want us together every possible moment. If we're not careful, they'll take you away from me. They'll destroy us."

"Who will destroy us, who are you talking about?" asked Brian.

"You're job, the people, the world. There really isn't much room for happiness. They don't want people to be happy."

Brian hesitated. His mind was racing with all the changes, and he didn't know what to do. "You're sure that's what you want?"

"Of course." She tightened her hug affectionately. "You're such a silly dear. For all intents and purposes we live together now." She had a faint smile of anticipation.

He didn't want to do it. He felt trapped. "I don't think it's a good idea." He had to force the words out, and he felt guilty as soon as he did.

Her smile vanished and the confidence in her eyes disappeared.

"Callie, we have to remember that we don't know how long I'll be here."

"Even if you are sent across the border, it wouldn't be permanent." She bit her lower lip and looked shocked. "You would still be a part of this bureau and would return here when it was over."

"I don't want to hurt you."

"You're not."

"It's just that it is really not as simple as you make it sound."

"What's so difficult about it? Our lives would be the same," she insisted.

"Not really. Things would be different."

For a moment she stared at him, the shock becoming pain, and then her expression changed and she looked at him as if seeing something she didn't like. "If that's the way you want it Brian," she said walking away from him. She kept her back to him and the balcony filled with her embarrassment, and

Brian's anger at himself for not having realized what she wanted before it became an issue. He could have handled it differently if he had been ready for it.

"It has nothing to do with how I feel about you."

"It has everything to do with it." Her voice was strong and composed. She turned around and her eyes angrily watched him.

"You're not like this, Callie. It's not like you to be angry and pushy."

"Pushy!" she exclaimed. "I can't think of anyone that needs a good push as much as you do!"

"We've never fought before. Let's not start over this."

"I can't think of anything better to start over. You're so frustrating!"

"I'm only thinking about later. What will happen when ..."

"You're always thinking about later," she interrupted. "You've put everything into neat little compartments, this for now, that for later. God help us if something doesn't fit into your plans, because if it doesn't, you just don't have anyplace for it at all! We do live together. Your apartment is just a closet for things. Not living here only gives you the feeling that you're really not committed. That your plans haven't been changed!"

"That isn't true." Brian said becoming defensive.

"It is true." She stepped towards him and tried to compose herself. "Brian, I'm not angry because of your decision. I'm angry with why you made it." She shook her head and closed her eyes as the emotions swept over her again. "It's such a waste. It's just such a waste!"

She glanced out the window and when her eyes came back to him they glistened with tears. "I know how important it is to you to be recognized as capable of covering something as important as the war. But I can't help but think its wrong for you to want to go for that reason. I won't ask you not to. I understand that you're afraid that if we live together I'll try to stop you, which will make it harder on you. I suppose I should be flattered because if you didn't care for me it would be easy for you to say yes. You've planned this for a long time. I've known that from the beginning and I know that you will go." She began to lose control of her voice. "But can't we stop waiting for it? Does everything else in your life have to hang in the balance? You hide from your feelings, and without your feelings, there is no point in sending you. You'd only be another hack."

"I'm not holding back. I could be gone for a long time. We don't know what is going to happen. Or what it would be like when I came back," he said defensively.

"That's an excuse!" she exploded. "I know you care for me, and I know you could care for the people right here! Don't you realize that the only thing that has held you back is your own ambition? You want to be the first with the story, but you really don't want to care about the people!"

"That's not true. It's not ambition. Not the way you make it sound. It's not like I've made up my mind to get there at any cost."

"Sheldon is aware that you can write and I know you can! It's just that you don't see what's around you. You wouldn't hurt anyone intentionally, but you're hurting yourself. You're hurting us!"

"What have I done that is so wrong?" he demanded.

"You watch, Brian. You stand back and you watch people as if they're not part of your world. As if they're not real."

"That's ridiculous. I've ..."

"It's true! That's why you feel exposed after you've written something that you know is good. You don't like to deal with your own feelings. Because after you have, you can't deny their existence. They don't want to be put back in a dark compartment to be brought out and dusted off when it's more convenient."

"Callie I don't have to care about this country or the people as much as you do to write about it!" said Brian, not knowing how else to respond to her.

"No, not to just write. To just be another journalist saying where and when, but you could be so much more!" She stepped in front of him. "Brian you have something special. You can capture people! Not just what they look like or what they say but how they feel and what they think. No one will ever believe in you as much as me!"

Her commitment and uncompromising belief in him strangled both his breath and his anger. He stood there watching her as if he were hearing about someone else.

"We could be happy together, and you could make an area of the world come alive for people who have no idea what it really is! I know you have the talent and the feelings, but you step away from them because you think it's premature and that it's the wrong place or the wrong people! But Brian, there is no right place or right people. There are only people, just people!" Her anger made her face flush, and the tears she refused to release made her eyes sparkle. She had never been more beautiful. "I hate you for the waste. Not only because you put it between us but because it will keep you from being what you could be, should be, already are if you would just give it a chance. Give me a chance!"

"Callie..." Brian didn't know what to say. It was all swirling around him.

"I'm not going tonight," she said starting for the balcony door.

"I can't wait to be what you want! I can't be you and feel about these people the way you do!" he said in an angry voice. "In my business, you can't allow yourself to become personally involved. You have to stay apart from the story!"

"They're not a story!" she yelled. "They're people, and if you would accept that you'd be a better writer. Be different than all those other men chasing about trying to be the first one at the fire. Don't be Sheldon! The point is you could do better!"

"Why are you doing all this?" demanded Brian.

The anger poured from her eyes, "We're not here for your amusement! And you're no better than us!" she stepped towards him. "You have to be more, or be less!"

"What do you mean?" Brian's voice was cold.

"I mean exactly what I'm saying." She said without hesitation. "You're using them for your own ends," she paused. "And evidently me as well."

"I didn't come here in the peace corp." Brian shouted. "And have I made you any promises? Have I misled you in anyway?" he demanded.

She stared at him, "No Brian, you haven't." Her voice was very calm and strong. "I just thought more of you." She stared at him in disappointment, and it made him even more angry.

"Damn it, Callie. Feel anyway you want about these people, but don't tell me how to feel! You don't' have that right."

"Of course not." She was aloof.

"Now get ready and let's go!"

"No, Brian."

"What?" The strength in her voice made him pause. "Don't do this, you'll regret it!"

She stared at him for a moment, "I think I already do." She turned and walked into the apartment.

"Just wait a minute!" he called after her from the doorway, but she ignored him and rushed down the hall and slammed the bedroom door behind her.

Frustrated and angry, he started for the door hoping she would call after him, and then unpredictably he was alone on the other side of the door.

The thought that the past 3 hours might not have been long enough caused Brian to hesitate at Callie's front door. He told himself that she wouldn't be angry, that she would be calm, but he wasn't convinced. He thought about walking around the wharf to give her more time. When he knocked, it sounded too loud and hollow, and he reminded himself that he was doing the right thing. He thought about using the hidden key to let himself in, but just then the door opened and Callie stood quietly in front of him. She had changed into casual clothes, but she looked uncomfortable and tense, her eyes red and swollen.

"I didn't mean to make you angry," he said not knowing how else to start.

"Neither did I," she stopped herself from saying anymore.

For what seemed like a very long time, he waited for her to say something, but she only watched him with crystal eyes that were ready to break under the tension. "I hope you didn't come here to just end things," she finally said with a shallow voice. "I shouldn't have talked to you like that. I won't ever do it again. I just want things to be the way they were!" She looked frightened.

"I don't see how they can be," he said shaking his head. Her eyes pleaded with his. Brian glanced past her into the plant-filled room. He leaned to his side and grasped the handle of the large suitcase he had brought. Looking at her again, he watched a tear roll down her cheek towards a warm smile.

CHAPTER EIGHT

Although the apartment was homey, it was empty without Callie, and the nights passed slowly. Two days after he had moved in with her, Callie had left for the Province leaving Brian with quiet resentment. It was unfair that she would cause such a battle over the thought of him going to the border only to immediately go herself. It made him feel a little foolish and brow-beaten, but to protest her going would have made it only more difficult for him when his turn came. Brian hadn't paid much attention to the Cultural Bureau because he suspected it was a bureaucratic farce aimed at collecting aid from America, not changing Thailand. Now he was envious of Callie. She was out of the city visiting villages along the border while he sat and waited for Sheldon. Sheldon's plan to follow Chovat had changed. He simply refused to let go of the suspicion that there was a connection between the crossings and the angry young man. They had lost all contact with him, and it was beginning to appear hopeless that Brian would ever leave the city.

Spread across Brian's desk were reports and radio photos of Cambodia. The general staff of the Cambodian Army had made an announcement to the international press. A general had delivered the message in front of a war weary group of soldiers and civilians of the capital. He was wearing dark sunglasses and khaki fatigues without any insignias to identify his rank. The general admitted that the government forces in the North were lost, and that at this time the remaining army was not capable of reclaiming the provinces that had been lost to the Khmer Rouge. All government forces were being pulled back to form a defensive ring around the capital. The only other concern would be the defense of the highway that led from the capital through the town of Poipet and into Thailand. This supply route would be kept open at all costs. The general promised that from this defensive ring victory would spring. The rainy season would bog down and demoralize the Khmer Rouge and provide the government forces with the opportunity to reorganize and obtain the necessary equipment from the United States. Fresh armies would then strike out into the delta and crush Samphen's thugs in an iron claw. The faces of those around the general didn't find any comfort in the plan. It was February, and the rainy season wouldn't start until July.

"Brian!" called Sheldon as he approached from behind. "You and I are going to Poipet." Sheldon spoke matter of factly and Brian thought he must have misunderstood and hesitated. "That is unless you have something you can't tear yourself away from! There are 30,000 refugees in Poipet. We have to find something!" Sheldon was determined.

Brian immediately came to his feet and started for the door. "It's about time. I'll hurry home and pack."

"Wait a minute." Sheldon held the palm of his hand up at Brian. "We're not going off half-cocked." He spoke slowly and emphatically. "We don't want to screw this up."

"Damn, we're not going to screw anything up. I'm telling you right now, Godfrey is not getting anywhere. He needs us to help!" insisted Brian.

"Go home and pick up a change of clothes and your passport."

"I'm on my way," Brian said, starting for the door.

"Meet me at the train station in 45 minutes," Sheldon called after him.

"I'll be there in half an hour," Brian shouted over his shoulder as he hurried out.

Bangkok was over 150 miles from the border of Cambodia so they caught the train to Prachinbury where they rented a car and connected with a highway that led into Cambodia. The highway was only one lane going in each direction but it was well-made and easy to drive. It seemed strange to Brian that only miles away from the border it held a normal flow of traffic. Unlike the city, the motorists leisurely traveled through the countryside and extended courtesies to one another. Whenever possible the slower traffic would pull to the side and allow Sheldon to pass. He was the only driver that seemed concerned with time and sped down the lush jungle-lined road. The rental car's air conditioning did not work and the wind came through the window like blasts through an oven door.

"With the mood of Bangkok, I expected the roads to be jammed with army vehicles," said Brian glancing at Sheldon.

"We're not there yet," Sheldon smiled. He was excited to be in the field again. "Besides, the capital is like a spider web. Hundreds of silk lines string out to the provinces. Most of the time a vibration at the end of one is ignored." Sheldon paused to adjust the rearview mirror. "But, a jerk the size of 30,000 refugees pouring into the border will send everyone scrambling at the other end." He paused and raised his eyebrows in thought. "But the countryside looks peaceful."

"You really like it here don't you?" asked Brian.

"It's one of the better places I've been stationed."

"Do you ever think about giving it up, retiring and going home to the States?" Brian had to talk above the sound of the wind rushing through the window.

"Oh, I think of the States," Sheldon paused and shrugged his shoulders. "But not seriously. The only thing I don't like here is the music. Thailand and Iran have the worst music." He started laughing. "The singers sound like a woman in high heels just stepped on their toes!" Sheldon mocked the sound and they both laughed.

When they had been quiet for a while Sheldon inquisitively glanced over at Brian. "How attached are you to Callie?"

"What brought that up?" Brian asked taken by surprise.

"I don't know. She certainly is to you."

"Yes."

"Women and this business never seem to work well together," Sheldon warned.

"She doesn't get in the way."

Sheldon quickly looked at him. "I didn't mean that." The tone of his voice was apologetic. "Besides if you were ever reassigned Callie would pack up and go without complaining."

"I don't think so. She loves it here."

Sheldon looked at him and smiled. "She would go."

"One of these days the Khmer Rouge will roll down this highway," said Brian to change the subject.

Sheldon looked out his window and watched the green countryside move past. Everywhere there was a break in the jungle, there was a rice paddy. "The coolies agree with you," Sheldon said, still looking out the window. "They're waiting for the worst."

"I haven't noticed anything," said Brian.

Sheldon looked at Brian. "How many rice paddies have we passed?"

Brian was silent.

"How many?" repeated Sheldon.

"I have no idea," answered Brian, uninterested in being lectured.

"Well, a lot. Right?"

"Thousands," Brian exaggerated and looked out the window.

"How many water buffalo did you see?"

"What?" Brian laughed at the absurdity of the question.

"There were plenty of farmers in the paddies, weren't there?" Sheldon persisted. He was obviously trying to make a point.

"Yeah, so it's just another day to them."

"But how many water buffalo did you see?"

"None. Not one."

"In Asia when a farmer doesn't have his water buffalo out with him in the field, it's because it's either already dead, or he is worried about its safety."

"There were children out there!" exclaimed Brian.

"Buffalo can't be risked," Sheldon answered.

"But their kids can?" Brian questioned with disbelief.

"Water buffalo are the family's tractor, harvester, plow," said Sheldon as he glanced at Brian. His voice lost its argumentative tone. "They'll pull your crop to market, carry sick family members to help. They're the family pet, and their milk feeds the children. Without the water buffalo, there would be no family. That's why they're not out. They can't be risked."

"That's an interesting way to predict a war," Brian smiled.

"As far as the rice farmers are concerned, the war is already here. Thousands of refugees are only miles away, and if allowed in, they're not going to run off with your child. That would only give them another mouth to feed," Sheldon glanced at Brian. "But they might take your buffalo."

Ahead of them was a truck moving very slowly. Sheldon slowed and nosed the car over the divider line to see if he could pass. "Life here is much harder, so the answers have to be much simpler. You protect your family by first protecting your animal," he said while passing the truck.

There was no traffic in the opposite direction, but far ahead of them was a roadblock. "The border," said Sheldon.

Brian watched the roadblock grow closer with excitement.

Sheldon slowed and then stopped the car. The army trucks that blocked the road were large troop carriers with high canvas tops that blocked their view of what was beyond. Thai soldiers approached both sides of the car holding their weapons ready at their waists.

"At least they're not pointing them at us," said Sheldon, barely loud enough for Brian to hear as he turned off the engine. The soldiers had stern distrusting expressions and watched their every move. They would have been intimidating if they weren't peering out from under American-supplied helmets that looked too big for their heads. In fact, everything from their boots to their weapons looked too big. They looked more like children playing in their father's clothes than a serious first line defense.

An officer approached Sheldon's side of the car, so Sheldon stepped out and met him half way. They began talking and Sheldon reached back into his back pocket and removed his papers. Brian opened his door and as he stepped out the guard's attention focused on his hands. The mid-afternoon sun sweltered in a white sky, but the air was clean and fresh and was a nice change from the smells of the city. The sound of anger and confusion from a large crowd came from far beyond the trucks. On both sides of the road there were long trenches filled with soldiers. Scattered in front of the trenches were holes with two soldiers in each. Most of the men in the holes in the trenches had their helmets off and were resting with their backs against the dirt. Parked off to one side there were U.S. built tanks. Their crews were sitting on them with their shirts off and smoking cigarettes.

Brian moved past the guards towards the trucks, and as he did they turned to watch him. Looking through the small gap between the front of one truck and the back of another, he could see another set of trucks blocking the road 100 yards farther down the highway. The scattered holes stretched all the way to the second barricade, but those soldiers had their helmets on and watched ahead of them intensely.

"Brian," Sheldon called. "Your papers?"

Brian walked to the front of the car where the officer and Sheldon waited. The guards had the trunk of the car open, and one was searching the passenger compartment. Brian handed the officers his papers and waited while the guard suspiciously glanced several times at the photograph and Brian. Handing them back, the officer gave an order to the guards who stopped searching and closed everything up.

"Get back in the car," Sheldon said, holding a hand out to the officer.

The guards' suspicions had not been relieved by the paper check. They watched Brian open the door with the same distrusting expressions.

"They mean business," Brian said, as Sheldon opened his door and climbed in behind the wheel.

Sheldon nodded and started the engine and backed up so that they could pull off the road and drive around the blockading trucks. "Don't they. They're pumped up."

When they were around the first blockade and back on the road Brian took one of the cameras they brought and started photographing the holes passing outside his window. From over the car came a wap,wap,wap ... Brian stuck his head out the window just as a helicopter gun ship passed over them. It was so low that the displaced air from its blades pushed the car to one side and Brian could see the boots of the pilot through the tinted green glass nose. "That guy had blue eyes," said Brian excitedly, snapping a photo. When the helicopter reached the second set of trucks it bore a hole up into the sky, turned left, and flew away paralleling the border.

As their car approached the second set of trucks, soldiers ran out in front of the car, pointing their guns at the windshield.

"Just hold your papers out the window," Sheldon said, doing so with his and stopping the car. "These guys are nervous."

"Listen to the noise!" said Brian. The crowd on the other side of the truck sounded like a riot. "*Nang sue pin*, newspaper," Brian said to the guard approaching his window. The guard waved them around while the other lowered their rifles just as another helicopter passed overhead.

Sheldon drove the car off the road and around the trucks. "My God," exclaimed Sheldon. "We'll never get around this."

On the other side of the trucks was a countless sea of people. The road was lined with soldiers in a V formation, and by pushing the crowd together they created a funnel, which compressed it until only individuals stood in front of a row of tables. The tables were shaded by green, canvas tarps, and under the tarps, sat Thai army officers and government personnel. The people standing at the tables begged, cried, and waved papers at those in the shade. Families held hands and pulled one another close. Seeing foreigners, people waved papers at the car and called to them from the other side of the blockading soldiers. When they had traveled a few hundred feet, the line of soldiers and the crowd swarmed around them. A tangled knot of people poured over the car and pressed money on the windows in an effort to bribe their way across the border. Taking up the entire highway, a long string of desperation wound its way to the horizon. There were trucks, busses, and cars. Tied to the trucks and cars were chickens and ducks in makeshift wooden cages. Motorcycles and pushcarts wedged between the smallest of gaps. Everything was at a standstill, only those on foot filtering through. A yellow school bus overloaded with people inside was also covered with still more sitting on its roof and hood. On the edge of the bus roof, a young girl sat holding onto the side with one hand while she clung to the neck of a small white goat jammed into her lap. The goat's mouth continuously moved, but it could not be heard above the panic of the crowd. Dogs with ropes around their necks darted between the people searching for their lost masters. Some had already given up and lay panting under the carts.

Straddled over one small motorcycle were a man, woman and three young children. Brian had been shooting pictures as fast as he could. Outside his window a wailing little girl squatted along side the road while people pushed around her. The back of small Japanese trucks sagged to the ground under the weight of too many people. A small boy wearing an army cap struggled along with a gunny sack around his shoulder, while an infant brother or sister stuck its head out the top and screamed in his ear. One man on a motorcycle had strapped large wicker baskets to its side and carried two children in each basket. A mother and young son sat side by side, each holding their knees to their chests for security. The son was trying to console his mother but was unable to control his own tears. Some people just hunkered down staring out into nothing. All the children were crying and grabbing at their parents' legs as they rushed about in confusion. Like a flock of blackbirds, a covey of Catholic sisters stood quietly in a small group. Jammed into the backs of trucks and sticking out of windows of cars were lamps, mattresses, bird cages, farming tools, and every other odd assortment of belongings hastily chosen not to be left behind.

Disarmed soldiers with the drawn expression of deserters dragged along in the crowd. What had to be hundreds of water buffaloes pulled carts filled with families and belongings or simply carried the old or the young on their backs. The animals' bellowing moos were mournful and frightened, and children on the backs patted their thick necks to comfort them.

"We have to get off this road or we won't get anywhere," said Sheldon, glancing at Brian for a suggestion.

Brian was only half listening as he continued to watch the hot and thirsty exodus. Two things were shared by everyone in the crowd, confusion and despair, and it had a language of its own.

CHAPTER NINE

Although they had been on the Cambodian side for over an hour they had managed to travel only a few miles. Ironically, the farther they moved from the border, the calmer the crowd became. Aimlessly waiting in line, the refugees knew there was trouble ahead, but they were still too far away from safety to allow panic to overtake them. Hope was all they had, and they clung to it silently with a tight fist.

"Over there. That must be it!" Sheldon said, pointing to a small but empty side road. "That's what I've been looking for."

The side road was not paved and led off into the jungle. At its intersection with the highway, a taxi from the city lay shattered and burned from an explosion. The bodies of the occupants had been taken away.

"Are you sure?" asked Brian.

"No," answered Sheldon with a concerned glance. His voice held a nervous tone which Brian had never heard before. Sheldon turned the car down the road and picked up speed. It was wide enough for only one small vehicle and was full of pot-holes. Moving as fast as it could, the front and rear of the car see-sawed from one hole to the next. Clouds of dust blew into the car so Brian rolled his window up. They were speedily into the jungle where branches and limbs cracked and scraped against the side of the car, but Sheldon did not slow down. In minutes, they had traveled farther than they had managed in over an hour on the highway. The road began to twist and turn, but still Sheldon drove as fast as possible. He was concentrating on the road so Brian didn't distract him by talking.

After ten or fifteen miles, the road became worse. Brian began to wonder if they hadn't made a mistake. Then the jungle thinned and the road began to wind down a hill. At the bottom of the hill was a small town with fifteen to twenty wood and concrete buildings circling a green square. A canal edged the side of the town, and a small bridge carried the road over the waterway and beyond. On the far side of the bridge thatch roof huts lined the shore.

"This is the right road. I've been here before!" There was relief in Sheldon's voice and as they drove into the town, Sheldon slowed and glanced around in recognition of the surroundings. Ringing around the square was a sturdy bamboo frame with a rusted corrugated metal roof. It was made for an open air market, but the rows of wooden tables were now deserted.

"It's a clean little place," said Brian, as he glanced around the tidy village.

"We're not far from Poipet." announced Sheldon with a happy voice.

The town was deserted except for six or seven children playing on the lawn of the square, and there was one store-restaurant combination that was open. The rest of the residents were undoubtedly among the refugees back on the highway.

"Why aren't they leaving?" Brian asked, nodding to the children.

"Maybe their side's winning," Sheldon jokingly answered.

There was only one other vehicle on the street, and that was a clumsy looking half-Jeep, half-truck army vehicle parked off to one side of the dirt road. As they approached it, a soldier appeared in front of them and held a hand up instructing them to halt. When they stopped Brian noticed a group of soldiers standing in the doorway. Although they were Cambodian soldiers and had actually been fighting a war they looked just as out of place in their American made uniforms as the Thais had on the other side of the border.

Sheldon began to rattle away in broken Cambodian as the soldier bent down to look in the window. Unlike the guards at the border, the soldier was relaxed and scratched his face unconcerned with them. When Sheldon used the word "Poipet," the soldier began to shake his head, and the tone of his voice became authoritative.

"What's wrong?" asked Brian.

"I don't know yet," answered Sheldon. The soldier continued to shake his head, and his voice became stronger. "We have to wait," Sheldon announced with irritation, as he pulled the car over. "There's some trouble ahead. Khmer Rouge may be just down the road, or something. I'm not sure I understand him."

They waited in the car until it was clear that it was not going to be a short delay. Sheldon impatiently told Brian to follow him, and they walked back down the street to the restaurant that was still open for business. It faced the square and had a bamboo shade built over two wooden tables. Sheldon knew exactly where he was going and hurried along as he angrily complained about the delay and how hungry he was. The soldiers suspiciously watched them when Brian and Sheldon sat down at one of the tables. An old man dressed in black with a white apron instantly appeared and hovered over their shoulders. He was somewhere in his mid-sixties with thick, gray hair laid back across his head in large wet looking tubes. The old man had a round face that looked Chinese and smiled at them with a friendly expression. Sheldon ordered something in Cambodian which caused the old man to break into an excited dialogue.

"Damn. He doesn't have any food. The town's people bought it from him and then took what he wouldn't sell." Sheldon was disgusted.

"Well, that's all right. My stomach is bothering me a little anyway. But he must have something for you," said Brian staring back at the soldiers down the street.

Sheldon looked up to the old man and they spoke again.

"Nothing," he said glancing at Brian. Then he spoke to the old man once more which caused him to hurry back into the building. "He can give us something cold to drink."

"Sheldon!" called someone from behind him. "What are you doing here in the rough?" The voice had an Australian accent.

Looking over his shoulder through one of the windows, Brian saw two foreigners sitting inside the building. It was shadowy inside, but he recognized them both as journalists that had been pointed out to him somewhere in Bangkok by Sheldon.

"We're headed for Poipet," Sheldon answered nodding towards Brian. His voice was cold and held a trace of dislike.

Both of the men nodded recognition at Brian, but they didn't speak to him. "Have your own gun bearer I see," one Australian laughed, pointing a finger at the three cameras around Brian's neck. Not trusting the soldiers that were losing a war, Brian had taken the cameras out of the car. "You're going to be here for awhile. They had some trouble a few miles up the road."

"How long ago?" asked Sheldon.

"Noise just stopped."

Sheldon craned his neck to look down the road and over the bridge.

"Don't bother," the Australian continued. "We're out here with the soldiers. Tagged along to pick up a line, but their officer's a son of a bitch and only allows you to cover what the fucking monkey wants!" he said, with a nod down the road. "Not even you could get around this monkey." Both the Australians laughed loudly. There was something unlikable about them so Brian ignored them.

The old man reappeared and placed two brown bottles on the table. It seemed indecent that children could play in the square and an old man could serve beer to Westerners while fifteen miles away in one direction thousands crawled towards the border, and only a short distance away in the opposite direction, a battle had just been fought. But it had been a long, hot trip and Brian's mouth tasted chalky from the dusty road. Thankful, he picked up the bottle. It was cold, but its thick musty taste actually made him more thirsty. The old man waited between Brian and Sheldon. With the war so close, the only credit he was going to allow was the time between delivery of the beers and the time it took for Sheldon to dig the money out of his pocket. Two women walked up and sat at the next table. One was a young and pretty woman, holding a baby, and the other was an old woman that dotingly reached over and stroked the baby's head with an ancient hand. Brian watched the child. Asian babies were pretty little things with fat cheeks and big black eyes. This one smiled and laughed as it rested its head on its mother's chest. Distracted by their arrival, the old man stepped over to them and the three of them talked happily. Even though Brian could not understand what they said, he was sure it was the old man's grandchild by the way he lovingly cooed over the baby. When the old man turned to collect his money from Sheldon, he had a happy grin and pointed back and forth between himself and the baby.

"Come here you old monkey," demanded one of the Australians.

With a humble shuffle the old man hurried back inside. Brian watched as the Australians ordered again in English by gesturing as if the old man was stupid.   Brian felt ashamed and angry as he remembered the miles of refugees. The Australians must have also passed them, but it obviously hadn't made an impression on them.

"I don't have the ability to cover the war, but they do," said Brian defiantly.

Sheldon glanced over his shoulder. The old man was bowing in an effort to show the Australians he understood, but they kept up their harassment. When Sheldon looked back at Brian, he had a sober expression. "They don't work for me."

"I think I'll go for a walk," Brian said quietly.

Sheldon nodded and turned around to look back down the road towards the highway. "Don't go too far. If they give us the go ahead I don't want to have to come looking for you."

Brian walked past the army vehicle and out onto the bridge. Off to one side in the canal, nosed into the far bank, were three large houseboats. They were much cleaner and built better than the ones he had seen with Callie on their first trip to Saturday Market. He wondered if she was home yet, and he tried to imagine what she would be doing. She had probably been disappointed when she found his note and had showered and changed into shorts brooding over a night without him. She did that when she was upset with him. She would become very quiet and busy herself with caring for her plants. Brian liked the thought that it bothered her that he was not there, and for a moment he wished he was. "You're here," he reminded himself. "You're finally here." Then he wondered if Sheldon was right, if Callie would go with him after all this was over and he was reassigned. She loved Thailand so much she might not. He imagined them living in a bleached out village overlooking the Mediterranean. Brian could see her walking up a small winding road with a warm Grecian wind blowing her hair and her white dress. "Yes," he told himself. "That would be perfect. She would love it there."

The houseboats were empty, and he realized that their apartment was also. Callie would not be home for hours, even if she did get home tonight. Beyond the boats was a large field covered in six-foot tule grass that swayed back and forth with the breeze. One hundred yards beyond was the dark, thick jungle. For a moment Brian had the feeling of dread as if something was watching him from the shadows of the jungle. He peered into it but could see nothing, yet the feeling grew until he shook it off telling himself he was imagining things.

On the bank below him, was a circular cement wall. Inside the wall was a miniature, elaborate hut. It was another of those things that had taken time and experience to build but had no apparent purpose. He was about to look away when he thought he saw the mud inside the wall moving. Looking closer, he could see that it was undulating in two tubular bands. The mud closed together like waves rolling towards each other. When they touched, the surface erupted and the heads of two hissing cobras sprang out. The snakes flared their hoods and defiantly stared at each other hissing their hatred. The undersides of their hoods were striped with blue scales. Brian remembered reading that the shiny blue stripes were to hold the attention of the snake's prey until it could position itself to strike. Now he noticed that there were many waves under the mud and he realized it was a snake pit. Sheldon had told him that if a town or village would provide the venom, the government would refine it into anti-venom without charge. Each year a large number of people were bitten and since the countryside was so remote, unless the anti-venom was close at hand many died.

Snakes made him cringe, and although these were kept like dairy cows for milking, the fierce sound coming from their deadly mouths made his skin crawl and he decided he shouldn't have left Sheldon and started back.

"What the hell is worth fighting over?" Brian said aloud to himself. It was disgusting to him that people would kill one another for anything in this land. Neither the country, nor the people were worth dying for.

When Brian returned to the table, an army officer was sitting with Sheldon. At first, Brian thought it was a friendly conversation, but stepping to the table he could tell by Sheldon's tone of voice that it was not. The mother and grandmother sat quietly at the next table and looked nervous. Brian thought they were going out of their way not to attract the officer's attention, but their timidness seemed unnatural, if not in fact suspicious.

"This is your companion," the officer asked holding his palm out for Brian's papers while he looked Brian up and down.

"Yes. As I was saying we're on our way to Poipet...."

"You cannot travel this road," the officer interrupted, the tone of his voice making it clear that he enjoyed talking down to Sheldon in English.

Sheldon took a deep breath, "We're journalists and ..."

"Why?" Brian interrupted. The officer quickly turned to stare at Brian. He was angry with the blunt tone Brian used. "Why?" repeated Brian.

"Your papers!" demanded the officer.

Brian pulled his papers out of his back pocket and turned them over. "Why?" he persisted.

Sheldon discreetly shook his head.

The officer stared at Brian with contempt. He looked just as out of place in his American equipment as did his men, but his face was simply mean and cruel.

"We have the proper authority. You can see our papers are in order," said Brian.

"You will obey my instructions and hold your questions." The officer spoke quietly but his eyes were black hard rocks. A few times in Brian's life he had met someone he immediately disliked with a passion and who immediately felt the same way about him. Brian instantly hated the officer and stared back in contempt.

"Khmer Rouge were seen in the area," said Sheldon. "I'm sure the captain only means to protect us."

Brian looked to Sheldon and was sure the statement was meant as a distraction before anything harmful could result between him and the officer. Sheldon nodded for Brian to sit down. Reluctantly, Brian took the chair next to the captain.

The officer flipped through Brian's passport with an arrogant twist of each page. When he had finished leafing through it, he held onto the booklet and glanced at the women at the next table. They did not look at him, nor did they speak to one another. Avoiding the officer's glare, the old woman lowered her head which caught his attention and antagonized him. The old man stepped out of the doorway but stopped when he saw the officer was watching his family. Trying to look uninterested with those at the next table, the young woman gently bounced her baby up and down and nervously glanced down the street. The officer said something to them, and the old woman glanced up with a flash of fear in her eyes. Standing, the officer made his voice more demanding. The young woman looked up at him trying to smile as she answered. The officer shouted and the old woman's shoulders lowered as if he had cracked a whip over her back. Brian glanced at the old man and found he was frozen with his own fear. The baby began to cry and the mother spoke rapidly as she tried to satisfy the inquiries shouted at her. The officer's body became tense and he stepped towards her. His questions were now coming too fast for anyone to have answered. Brian glanced at the old man again whose expression plead for help. Whatever they were hiding was about to cost them dearly. "When will the road be cleared?" asked Sheldon in a much louder voice than the officer's. For an instant Brian's eyes fixed to Sheldon's, as he knew Sheldon had acted on behalf of the family. The insolence in Sheldon's voice spun the officer around.

"You may go when I say!"

"Fine, but why don't you at least find out what's happening?"

"I have sent men!" the officer shouted. "Everyone will wait!" He started to turn back to the women's table.

"If they do return." Sheldon roped the officer's attention and pulled him back. The captain slapped Brian's papers to the table and glared at Sheldon. The expression on Sheldon's face was strong but not defiant. "It is very important that we get there as soon as possible. You've already caused considerable delay and we have an important meeting."

"No one travels the road! If you wish to return to the highway, go!" the officer yelled. "But this road is not used! You are interfering with my efforts when you question my authority." All of the officer's anger concentrated on Sheldon's blue eyes, and Brian thought Sheldon had crossed over the safety line. The officer wanted to harm them.

"I'm not questioning your authority," said Sheldon coolly.

The captain looked back and forth between Brian and Sheldon with a calculating malice and then hurriedly walked away and entered the building to take a seat with the Australians. The women sat with their heads lowered, Sheldon drank from his beer as if nothing had happened, and the old man disappeared inside.

"Now what?" Brian smiled.

"We wait."

Although hours passed, the women never looked at them, but the old man kept a supply of cold beers on their table and his eyes twinkled with gratitude each time he set them down. The light was beginning to fade. Brian's stomachache was becoming almost unbearable as he was now experiencing sharp pains that came without warning. He tried not to let Sheldon notice and told himself that it would soon pass, but he couldn't help flinching when the pain cut through him.

"Maybe we should have stayed on the highway," Sheldon said aloud to himself.

The women began glancing inside the building as if they wanted to go in, but the captain and the Australians didn't show any sign of leaving.

"What's the matter with you?" Sheldon asked noticing one of the spasms.

"Nothing. I'm fine."

Sheldon watched him and another of the pains grabbed at Brian.

"The hell you are. What is it? You're pale." Sheldon reached over the table and touched Brian's forehead. "Christ, you're burning up! When did this start?"

"It's nothing. I'll be fine." Brian didn't want anything to interfere with the assignment. "It's just a stomachache. Really."

The old man came up behind them and Sheldon spoke with him in broken Cambodian.

"Come on," said Sheldon as he stood up. "He has a place where you can lay down." Sheldon dropped some money on the table, and the old man quickly picked it up and stuffed in into his pocket. "We aren't going anywhere for a long time anyway."

"If I could just rest for awhile, I'd be fine," Brian said, following the old man and Sheldon inside.

As they walked by the officer, his eyes followed Sheldon with a festering anger.

"Where are you going, mate?" one of the Australians asked Sheldon.

"We're going to rest for awhile," Sheldon replied without slowing his step or looking in the Australian's direction. Wanting only to lie down, Brian hurried past them. In the back of the building was a kitchen area with many cupboards, a small sink, and a large flat wood stove. Off to one side was a small room, and as they walked into it the old man pulled back a blanket that hung in the doorway. Other than mattresses lying on the floor, the room was empty.

"This will be fine," Sheldon said aloud to himself. Brian removed the cameras from over his head and gently dropped them to a mattress. Sheldon spoke to their host in Cambodian and then the blanket fell across the doorway. As Brian stretched out, there was another of the sharp pains. It helped to lie flat on his back. The ceiling was cracked around an empty light socket and smelled like herbs. It had probably been a storage room that had been converted into a sleeping area for the security of the old man's family.

"Don't worry. I'll be all right and we'll get to Poipet." Brian tried to sound confident.

"I know." Sheldon sighed deeply as he lay down. "Things like this happen."

The aching pain continued and kept Brian from falling asleep but the sound of Sheldon's breathing became slow and low. For a long time Brian lay listening to Sheldon and watching the one small opaque window in the room steadily grow darker. He thought of his home in the States. It would still be cold there this time of year. The sky would be an ugly gray, and his friends would be complaining about how tired they were of winter. It was strange to think he had ended up sick in the old man's backroom. Things certainly weren't happening as he had expected. He thought of Callie and how she might be home now. He thought of how she made the city seem clean and the discomfort of the heat bearable and unimportant. She somehow brought out the best in everything and made any frustration seem like a small inconvenience. He thought of the bleached-out village on the Mediterranean again and wondered if Sheldon was right.

Another sharp pain sliced through him and instantly she seemed far away. He told himself to think of something besides the pain, but it was nearly impossible. He tried to think of the two of them on the balcony at home. Then, from the other room, he heard voices and the sound of chairs around the Australian's table pushing across the wood floor tipping over and bouncing. The voices faded off as if they were going outside. Brian glanced over at Sheldon and tried to listen for something that would justify waking him. In a few moments, he heard the sound of the army vehicle starting and driving away. He sat up and reached out to touch Sheldon just as the old man came through the blanket and excitedly spoke in Cambodian. Startled, Sheldon raised up and looked at Brian and the old man with a confused half-awake expression.

"What's going on?" he demanded of Brian.

"I don't know. I can't understand him, but I think the soldiers are leaving," said Brian.

Standing up, Sheldon questioned the old man and as they spoke his voice became excited. Whatever they were discussing upset Sheldon so Brian stood up next to him and tried to listen as if he would understand.

"We have to get out of here," Sheldon said, glancing at Brian and pushing by the old man. "Now!"

"What is it?" Brian was confused, but the pain prevented him from moving with any speed.

"Come on!" Sheldon, already in the kitchen, called over his shoulder. Being lit by only one, small, kerosene table lamp, the kitchen was dark. "Khmers are on the other side of the bridge!"

Sheldon was already at the front of the door watching the bridge when Brian caught up to him. The old man's family sat huddled close together at a table against the wall. It was dark outside.

"Hold it," Sheldon said, extending an arm out to Brian. "Let's not just run out there."

"Where are they? I don't see anything!" said Brian, trying to look around Sheldon.

Sheldon was peering into the dark street. "Let's be sure before we start for the car."

The old man started jabbering and pushing both Sheldon and Brian towards the table. Sheldon glanced back and forth between the old man and the window, reluctantly taking a seat while asking him questions. With both hands on Brian's shoulders, the old man pushed him down into the chair next to Sheldon.

"What the hell are we doing?" demanded Brian. "Are we just going to sit here?! Christ's sake!"

"Shut up!" demanded Sheldon. "He thinks it's too late. We wouldn't make it to car." Sheldon was craning his neck as if he had seen something. The old man ran into the kitchen. Through a window Brian could see shadows running soundlessly in the street and across the square. Under the corrugated roof of the market stalls, one of the shadows soundlessly weaved its way between the tables.

"See 'em?" Brian breathlessly whispered, as he watched the cat-like figures fan across the town.

"Yeah," Sheldon mumbled. "Those sons of bitches that left us here! God damn them, God damn them!"

Returning with a small flag, Brian recognized from photos as the symbol of the Sihanouk regime, the old man, with his family's help, hurriedly hung it on the wall.

"Tell them not to put that up!" Brian insisted in near panic.

"Shut up," Sheldon demanded again. "God damn them!"

"I'm telling you, damn it! Don't put that flag up."

"Shut up!" Sheldon demanded in a panicked voice. "Where's the cameras?"

"To hell with the cameras. Sheldon, I'm telling you."

"We need them." Sheldon persisted, as he sprang to his feet and started to the back room.

"Forget 'em!" Brian called after him.

Then, almost hypnotically, the dark figures spreading across the village held Brian's gaze. The figures moved with a single purpose as they came closer to the restaurant. Brian felt the chill of helplessness. Glancing at the old man's family he saw nervous smiles reflected back to him.

Running back to Brian the cameras banged together as Sheldon carried them in one hand.

"Put 'em on the table!" Sheldon exclaimed in a whisper as Brian took the cameras from him. Sheldon nervously glanced at the old man for reassurance. Just then, three men rushed into the room. Two pressed their backs to the walls, one pointing his rifle at the family and the other pointing

his at Brian and Sheldon. The third had the open
window to his back, so automatically he had dropped
to one knee in front of the table and pointed his gun at
Brian's head. Brian stopped breathing. The man's
eyes squinted in confusion. He was thinking of
shooting. Unable to move, Brian waited for the flash
from the muzzle. From the side, the old man started
rattling in panicked Cambodian. Without warning the
table flew as the soldier kicked it away. Before Brian
could raise his arm, a rifle butt smashed into his face.
He felt his body falling to the floor and sliding against
the wall. Brian's neck and jaw felt crushed and small
lights rushed in front of his eyes like tiny insects. For
what seemed a long time, he was unable to move.
Then, slowly he pushed forward to raise off the floor
just as a boot buried in his ribs and knocked the wind
out of him. He hit the wall again and in reflex his
knees tried to pull to his chest, but their movement
brought more kicks from the other men now standing
over him. Brian could hear the wild pleas of the old
man and then someone in the doorway shouted and
the kicking stopped. The voice shouted something
else, and the men around him pulled Brian to his feet.
Then, with a quick jerk, they turned Brian around and
pushed him and Sheldon back into the kitchen and
slammed them against the wall. Brian slid to the
floor, curled, and waited for the beating to begin
again. He could feel the presence of the men standing
over him, but they left him alone. He tried to rise up
to look for Sheldon, but the sole of a boot pinned his
head against the wall smashing both his ears until he
could feel them bleed. The same voice that had
shouted from the doorway gave another command and
the boot was removed and stepped back. Not wanting
any more, Brian hesitated and then looked up. In the
center of the room stood a small man wearing green

fatigues taken from either a dead or captured government soldier. He watched Brian from under the floppy brim of a once white cloth hat that had been worn in bad weather. His thin face had a gloating expression as he looked down at Brian. The other men in the room had positioned themselves off to the side and looked confused and unsure as to what to do with Brian and Sheldon. Tensely, they awaited orders from the man in the hat. Brian glanced over at Sheldon who sat with his back against the wall wiping the blood off of his face with his shirttail.

"Are you all right?" Brian asked.

One of the men shouted at him. Then the leader spoke to the guards before he turned and walked out. Two of the rebels followed him out while the last stepped back and pointed his rifle at Brian. "What are they saying?" mumbled Brian.

"They're going to kill us!" Sheldon murmured through the pool of blood in his mouth.

The guard shouted before Brian could answer. The fear in Brian stole his breath and he told himself that it would not happen, but he helplessly waited for the shot as the panic in him grew. From the other room came the sound of people rushing about, and Brian thought he heard the old man chattering away. With the sound of more men approaching the kitchen, Brian looked over at Sheldon and found Sheldon's expression was drawn. He was waiting for it to happen, too, and watched the guard with eyes filled with dismay. There was nothing to do but wait. The moments aged Sheldon's face and Brian thought he was going to be sick. Angrily he told himself that he wouldn't let them see his fear; he could at least do that. He demanded to himself that he think of something else, anything! The States. The cold weather in the States. Think of the States. God damn it, think! But he saw only the fear in Sheldon's eyes. Callie, she should be home by now. Think of Callie, he persisted. He tried to picture what she would be doing.

Two men came through the doorway with the arms of a third wrapped around their necks. The face of the man dragged between them was wrenched in pain. He had been wounded in the side, and was dripping blood across the floor. Without paying any attention to Brian or Sheldon, they laid the wounded man between them. Then came two men carrying a make-shift bamboo stretcher. The man who was on the stretcher had had his pants removed and torn up for bandages that now wrapped a stub just above his left ankle and a stub above his right knee. The once green cloth was now huge swollen red bulbs. Their leader in the old cap stuck his head through the doorway and gave an instruction while pointing beside Brian. Without looking back, the men carrying the stretcher walked over and placed it a few feet away from Brian, then swiftly turned and started out the door. The face of the man on the stretcher was expressionless; his dark, glassy eyes were open wide but stared off into nowhere. Brian had seen that look before in the eyes of deer he had hunted in the high Sierra. It had never bothered him then. It was merely a moment before the animal accepted that although it could still push blood through its splintered body and smell the fresh scent of pine needles, it was already dead. Everyone in the room knew the man was dead and waited for him to accept it.

More wounded were brought in and taken to the side room, but Brian couldn't look away from the eyes of the man on the stretcher. The man was dead, yet his chest kept rhythmically rising and falling, clinging to the next moment. Like the animals Brian had stood over on golden mornings in soundless forests, the man was alone. Brian forced himself to close his eyes and turn away. He raced images of home, Callie, and times that had been special to him through his mind, but mixed in with them was the image of himself lying against the wall with that look in his eyes. He wished he had never hunted. He glanced at Sheldon and knew they were both about to die. Brian tried to move towards Sheldon and instantly someone shouted and the men around him began to club him with the butts of their rifles. Brian tried to crawl into a ball but then came a painful crash to his head, a flash of bright light and then there was nothing.

CHAPTER TEN

The sound of people passing by was the first sound that Brian could make out through the daze that the beating had caused. Dry blood held his eyelids shut. His head throbbed unmercifully and his back was in terrible pain. Then came the noise of the cupboards being opened and pots and pans being angrily pushed onto the floor. Someone dragged a dry cloth across his eyes, and the dry blood scraped his eyelids open.

Once his eyes were opened, he could see Sheldon trying to help him. As his senses came back to him, he was surprised that they were alive, but he was unable to move from under a great weight pinning him to the floor. He watched helplessly as one of the rebels found hidden in a cupboard the dry fruit and canvas bag of rice the old man had so carefully hidden for his family.

Slowly the weight holding Brian to the floor began to decrease until he was able to sit up with Sheldon's help. Leaning against the wall Brian turned to Sheldon to speak. Sheldon quickly shook his head, "Don't say anything," he whispered. The two of them sat as still as possible. Brian had no idea how long he had been unconscious.

Trying to make themselves invisible, they sat without moving or speaking for a long time. Then the leader of the rebels walked into the room and after noticing them he approached them and knelt down beside Brian and inspected his wounds.

"Can anything be done for him?" Sheldon's voice sounded as though he hadn't meant to speak and the atmosphere tightened with fear.

The leader looked up with the expression of someone that had been intruded upon. "No," he said watching Brian.

The realization that the leader spoke English was a hope. The leader rose and started to turn. "We're journalists!" said Sheldon, jumping on the opportunity.

Angrily, the leader wheeled around. "I know what you are!" He gave a quick order to the room and one of the men closest to the doorway rushed out. An older man standing on the far side of the room strapped his rifle over his back and spoke. The man that had been sent out of the room returned and brought the cameras with him. The leader grabbed them from him and shook the cameras accusingly at Sheldon. "You are what I say you are!" he shouted. "*Espionner!*" he said in French. He took a step towards Sheldon, "Spies!" That's what you are." His expression was angry, but it was also antagonizing as if he was enjoying the confrontation. Sheldon settled back against the wall, and after a moment the leader accepted that he was not going to provoke any further arguments and tossed the cameras towards the man that brought them into the room.

Other rebels had placed a large kettle on the stove and were heating water. The leader opened his backpack and removed several small green bottles and while directing how much of the liquid should be poured into the kettle handed them to one of the men at the stove. Then he removed rolls of bandages from his pack and walked into the side room.

Brian glanced over at Sheldon. His forehead had wounds that looked very painful. "Are you all right?" Brian asked quietly. No one else heard him, or at least they didn't pay any attention.

"I'll be okay," Sheldon answered in a whisper. "How about you?"

Brian felt the pain of his lower back, and when he inhaled his ribs hurt. "All right."

The fire in the oven caught, and orange light danced on the walls. Brian could feel he was about to pass out again. In an effort to fight it off he forced himself to memorize what was around him. For the first time Brian really looked at his captors. There were nine of them in the kitchen, and he was sure there were more in the outer room. They were making themselves comfortable on the floor or sitting on the counters. Their weapons were an international assortment. Several carried sub-machine guns that had long half-moon clips jammed into the magazines. Brian recognized them from radio photos as Russian weapons. On the back of one man was a harness holding four black tubes with rocket fins at one end. The man unhooked the harness and propped it against the wall. On the black cylinders there was white Chinese lettering. Each man had something that looked like a cotton towel wrapped around his neck and tied in a knot. Some were undoing the knots and spreading the towels out to lie on, other than their weapons it was their only piece of equipment. Brian thought of how out-of-place and over-weighted the government troops had looked with their American equipment. The rebels simply had their towels. All were unshaven and dirty. Like their leader, some wore captured green fatigues and army field boots. The rest had on civilian clothes and rubber sandals. They looked ragged and poor, but unlike the government troops their expressions were rigid and strong like steel. Countless battles against a better equipped but not superior enemy, and living in the jungle heat and monsoon rain had given them a confidence that the government soldiers lacked. Other than their leader, all of them wore bandanas around their heads, and in the waving firelight they cast shadows on the wall of a gypsy army.

The man that had thrown their table over and initiated the beatings sat quietly with his back against the wall closest to the doorway. He was relaxed and peacefully smoked the brown stub of an old cigarette.

Quietly the rebel leader walked through the doorway and stopped to glance over his troops. The men lying on the floor looked up to him like hunting dogs anticipating a command. The leader said something in a quiet voice and the men relaxed and laid their heads down. The water in the kettle began to boil. The leader began speaking in Cambodian but intermittently would slip off into French.

The men scattered around the room watched their leader with trust and respect. Their leader gracefully maneuvered his way through three languages exposing himself as an educated man, yet he had joined rice paddy farmers in a bitter and endless war. He was the type of person that the ruling regime catered to and held out to the world as the resource that would defeat the rebels. Yet he had turned his back on all that and had taken up arms with the lower classes, he lived with them in the jungles, fought with them in the muddy rainy season, and, if need be, their faces showed they believed he would die with them.

The man on the stretcher next to Brian exploded with the shrieking scream of pain. The horror of the sound pressed Brian's back against the wall. As the screams continued he was surprised that no one came to the man. Looking around the room Brian found the faces of the rebels looking at him instead of their comrade. Looking back to the wounded man Brian found a face of torment. Lifting his head the veins in his neck popped out, and his mouth hung open as he reached out for Brian. For an instant Brian couldn't pull himself away from the wall, and the man's eyes made him feel ugly for hesitating. The men in the room watched Brian silently, expecting something from him. Not knowing if he was correct, Brian felt the stare of his captors criticizing his failure to move. Sheepishly Brian slowly reached out towards the man's hand. He glanced between the hand and his captors half expecting his gesture would instigate another beating, but fearing one if he did nothing. The man grabbed Brian's hand and squeezed it like a vise.

"Easy," Brian said painfully pulling himself to his knees over the man.

The man's eyes were locked to Brian's. Brian realized the man was missing an arm and was bleeding profusely. Brian thought of how he and Sheldon would undoubtedly be the next to die.

"What do you think you're doing?" demanded Sheldon in a whispered hiss.

"Deep breathe, take a deep breath. Just watch my eyes." Brian placed the palm of his hand on the man's forehead, and the tense muscles in the man's neck relaxed and he laid his head down. "Just concentrate on my eyes and listen to the sound of my voice. You don't have to understand what I'm saying." The man's eyelids slowly closed and opened. "It won't hurt long. Just listen to the sound of my voice." For a long moment there was nothing else in the world but the contract between their eyes. It made no difference to the man that the face above him was a stranger. His expression calmed, and then his eyes glazed and he released a deep breath. The stub of his missing arm stopped jerking, and then all life poured out the eyes until they were dark little holes.

At first Brian didn't want to let go. He stared into the eyes and wondered what the man's name was and if he had a family, if he had been a peasant farmer or a city merchant, what had been so personal to make him join the fight, and, more than anything, if it had been worth it. How could anything have been worth it, thought Brian.

Feeling the eyes of everyone in the room, Brian pulled the man's hand from his and sat back against the wall. Everyone, including Sheldon was staring at him. He thought one of the rebels would spring forward and beat him again for tainting their comrade's last moments with a Westerner's touch. But their stern faces watched Brian with confused expressions. Then the leader quietly gave an order, and the man caring for their wounded moved to the stove and picked up a kettle to take into the side room while two men carried the dead man out.

Brian thought to himself that no matter how obvious it is that death is close at hand, and impatient, no one can be completely prepared to watch it at work. The fact that it had been one of their captors didn't make it any easier. One minute he had been alive and the next he was dead. Nothing had changed for the better or the worse. He simply died, and the world and everyone in it continued without him as if he had been meaningless. The only apparent impact of his death was that it had left the room less crowded and a little nervous.

It had taken time for the men on the floor to go to sleep. The firelight had flickered among them and lit their faces with the realization that time was passing, and whatever they were waiting for was late.

Sheldon had sat down with his back to the wall and fallen asleep. One rebel across from him sat with his legs folded and his rifle cradled in his arms. His eyes were heavy and fighting to close. The leader sat on the floor across from Brian with his back against the wall. Brian watched the leader who with the last of his men now asleep seemed to breathe easier. He stared at those on the floor, and then pulled one knee up and bridged his arm between it and his forehead. He was very tired and unconcerned with the fact that strangers were among them. The leader was a small man and had a slim and intelligent face. Brian guessed that before becoming a guerilla he was probably a teacher or a bureaucrat in charge of some small government agency.

The pain in Brian made any position uncomfortable, so he shifted his weight often. He didn't want to sleep. He was afraid they would be killed in their sleep. When he looked up, he found the leader was watching him with alert and suspicious eyes.

"I know better than to try," Brian whispered.

The leader didn't answer but pulled something next to him closer. Then he picked up one of the cameras. Turning it in his hand he looked at it with familiarity. He opened the back of the camera and removed the yellow film canister. Brian was relieved to see that only three inches of film trailed out of the canister, and therefore it couldn't have been the one they used crossing the border. The leader picked up a second camera. Brian's mouth began to dry up as he watched the case snap open and the camera slip out.

The back popped open, but the embers in the fire were dying and he couldn't see if it was the one he had used. Without thinking, he leaned forward to see if all the refugee shots were being fumbled in the fingers of the leader. The leader noticed his movements and looked up. A smirk spread across his face and he picked up the last camera.

"Don't," Brian said quietly.

The leader looked up and watched Brian with indignant eyes. "You still think you can tell ..."

"Please," Brian interrupted. His voice held the disheartened tone of someone watching waste. "It's only of the refugees on the road..."

The leader sat quietly staring at Brian. "Are you so sure you will have the chance to use them?"

Brian hadn't thought before speaking. He only thought of the photos' destruction. "There is nothing of benefit in their destruction, or you killing us," he added faintly.

"There is always benefit in killing one's enemies." The soft pronunciation of the English words had a rock hard sound to them and forced a part of Brian to give up and despair, but there was also something in the leader's voice that attracted him and made Brian feel that the man across from him was taunting a conversation. It was confusing and dangerous. Then, glancing around the room, he wondered if the men on the floor had failed to meet a basic need of the commander. He couldn't have jeopardized his command by encouraging questioning by those sleeping around him. Brian told himself again that it was dangerous, but the thought that familiarity might make it more difficult to order them killed encouraged him.

"We're journalists, and if anything, Western journalists have helped your cause."

The leader's face wrinkled in disbelief. "You exploit my people," he said, holding the camera at Brian. "Yet you say you've helped us. You've helped us like the French did. You've helped yourself to us. You've raped my people." The leader's voice was firm but intrigued. "What is in your cameras but the loss of the dignity of my country?"

"We only report what's happening," Brian defended.

"You sell newspapers. Nothing more." The leader's back came off the wall, and he leaned towards Brian. "If the American people were for our war so would be your papers. You write what is expected, not the truth." The leader's glasses flashed in the faint light.

"We report, that's all!" Brian nervously paused. "We've only watched your war."

"This war isn't our creation. It's the last seizure of a body originally infected by European exploitation and then reinforced by American imperialism." The leader's voice was still not angry. It was a canned speech he had given too often. So it sounded hollow. The firelight danced across his face and reflected off his glasses while he waited for Brian's reply with curiosity.

"The French colonies may have been an injustice," Brian gently reeled in the conversation.

"Your country uses its military might to install puppet regimes like Lon Nol. As long as they follow the desires of your government, they can operate as corruptly and viciously as they desire. In this way, your country establishes its empire." The leader paused and glanced around the room. "We must not wake the men." The leader looked back to him with an anxious expression. Brian told himself to relax, to be calm.

"One of the reasons the United States has supported Lon Nol was to protect Thailand from the threats made by your party, and North Vietnam."

"Our only concern is to rid our country of Lon Nol and his reactionary gang," The leader was still using hollow, simplified statements that held no conviction.

"And then what?" Brian asked through his swollen lips.

"The liberation forces of Cambodia will form an independent sovereign nation, to work for the development of a true socialism, which will aim at serving the people. Under such leadership the people will strive for more productivity and organize in the rural areas for the rapid industrial development."

For a moment Brian thought he would lose consciousness from the pain. "Do you really believe all that?" He had spoken without thinking and immediately regretted it. The pain had kept him from thinking clearly.

The leader's voice was smooth, and for the first time sounded original. "Americans pride themselves on how they have fought for their freedom. Yet you refuse to recognize any other people's right to do the same! When I was young I was taught to respect your country but it's a lie. You think you're better than Asians and that they don't deserve the same things."

"No, that's not true." Brian couldn't remain conscious. He was losing.

All at once the leader was pouring something mixed in water into his mouth. "Drink!" The bitter taste rushed through his sinuses and snapped his head clean. The leader hesitated and grabbed Brian's face in a strong hand. "You think you're better than me!"

"Are you going to kill us?" asked Brian directly.

The leader hesitated and stared at Brian. "Why do you assume I will make the decision?" The leader's voice was cold, making Brian's hope slip away.

"Tonight I held the hand of a man and watched him die." Brian paused, "I'm not assuming anything. I just don't want to join him."

Responsibility and sadness spread over the leader's suspicious face, and he watched Brian closely. "Did you think that would save you?"

Brian hesitated not knowing what to say. He told himself he had moved too quickly and lost the opportunity.

"Maybe you journalists do have a worth," the leader paused and Brian's heart raced. "But that doesn't mean you or your friend will see the sun rise," he added with the return of his stern expression. The leader reached over and woke one of the men that had been asleep. He gave him instructions that caused the man to sit up and turn to Brian. Then without looking at Brian, the leader lay down and closed his eyes. "The morning will bring your answer."

Brian stayed wake for a long time after the change in guards. His pain continued increasing until at some unremembered point he had fallen off to sleep. The sound of everyone moving woke him, and he glanced around not realizing where he was at first. Sheldon was sitting up watching the men helping their wounded out. All of the rebels were up and hurriedly moving in and out of the room. Brian could barely move as he's body was stiff and racked with pain. He watched the activity as if he really wasn't there. The fire was completely out now, and with only the shrouded glow of kerosene lamps it was hard to see.

"What is it, 4:30?" asked Sheldon.

Brian didn't answer.

Sheldon continued watching the last of the wounded carried out. Two of the rebels stood in front of them and watched with serious dark eyes. Brian's first impulse was to rush the doorway but he knew that even if he made it to the outer room, he would get no further.

"I overheard them. Their scouts have returned. The government troops are on their way to re-take the town," said Sheldon in a hollow voice.

Brian's stomach weakened, and he felt as if he were going to be sick again. He felt the stare of the men from across the room and, with it, the first rush of panic. Then he thought of the man that had died. "You've already been afraid," he told himself.

The noise in the room stopped, and Brian opened his eyes to find the leader was standing in front of him and looking directly at him. Brian tried to listen for any sound from outside. The leader said something in Cambodian and the words stopped Brian's breath. The two guards still in the room slung their weapons over their shoulders and hurried out. From outside came the far away rattle of automatic gunfire. The leader's tired eyes were fixed to Brian's for a long moment, and then they slowly blinked twice. "My family thanks you," said the leader who then turned and walked out.

Disbelieving that it could be over, Brian sat motionless.

"What the hell was he talking about?" Sheldon nervously demanded. "I was certain ..."

"I have no idea," said Brian shaking his head. He was afraid to think it was over, afraid that at any minute one of the rebels would run back into the room firing. Slowly he began to push himself to his feet. It was growing light outside and he didn't know what to do next. He had been so certain that he would not see the morning that its approach was disconcerting. Intermittent gunfire echoed from far off and then came the rattle of an automatic weapon closer to them. Realizing that Sheldon was at his side, Brian turned to him.

Sheldon smiled, "Do you believe it? Holy Christ, I can't believe it! He just left us!"

Brian wrapped an arm around his shoulder and started out the door.

"Wait. It's still too dark." Sheldon held Brian back. "Go out there now, and both sides will shoot you."

Brian wanted to watch the sunrise. He wanted to see it, to feel it on his face, and to watch the world come alive with the things he had previously taken for granted. From where they stood, he could smell the morning, and he realized that he had never appreciated just how clean and fresh mornings are. There were too many things he had taken for granted, that he had ignored as unimportant. Then he noticed that on one of the tables in front of him lay the cameras. Brian walked to the cameras and picked them up. "I almost hope they get away," he said aloud to himself. When he turned around, Sheldon's expression was one of frustration and disbelief, but Brian did hope they would make it, or at least the leader. From even further away came the sound of gunfire but now it came in rapid procession. Another battle had begun.

CHAPTER ELEVEN

The golden morning broke into what soon would be another white-hot day and the sounds of battle were replaced with the rumble of army trucks coming down the roads towards the town. Brian and Sheldon sat at one of the tables outside.

Sheldon looked at him with a questioning expression. "You look terrible. I don't think you can go on."

The second and third truck passed them and Brian didn't answer. Within moments, the town was filled with army vehicles parked around the square. Not knowing what was really expected of them, the government troops milled about the town. Brian couldn't help but smile at the sight of so many men being diverted from the needs of a retreating army to engage a handful of wounded guerillas. "They really over estimated what they were up against," he said sure that the rebels were far into the jungle by now.

Sheldon glanced over the square and smiled. "They can't afford to lose a town so close to the highway." He paused and looked at Brian with a concerned expression. "You should start back." Brian was beginning to be relieved to hear that Sheldon did not want him to continue to Poipet. He knew he was hurt, and he wasn't sure how long he could last.

In a group of soldiers across the square, Brian noticed two foreigners that looked like the Australians. "Isn't that ..." The sound of Sheldon's chair pushing away from the table interrupted Brian, and the angry expression on Sheldon's face answered the question. He stood up and started to cross the street. "Come on!" said Sheldon.

Reluctantly, Brian started after him. The night had been long and hard, and he didn't want any more trouble. Instinctively Brian glanced down the road for traffic and saw something that made him stop. "Hang on, Sheldon." Sheldon kept going. "Wait!"

The tone of Brian's voice made Sheldon stop on the other side of the street. "What is it?"

"I'm not sure," Brian answered without looking at Sheldon. Down the road off to one side of the bridge, a group of soldiers were circled around what looked like someone kneeling.

"I think it's the old man," Brian said as he started for the group. Sheldon followed a few feet behind him. As they approached, Brian could see that on the far side of the bridge there was another group of soldiers looking down at something in a patch of tule grass. One of the men in the first group moved to one side and gave Brian a clear view of the man surrounded by the soldiers. Brian stopped not wanting to believe what he saw. The man on his knees had his hands tied behind him and a copper electrical wire was tied around the neck. At the end of the wire was a stick. The soldiers were yelling questions at the man, and when he would not answer, the stick would be turned and the wire would tighten and cut deeper into his throat. Blood was oozing down his neck and chest and his bloodshot eyes bulged from their sockets.

"Is it the old man?" Sheldon asked, not having had as clear a view.

"No," Brian answered as he moved closer. "It's the rebel leader." The soldiers around the leader smiled and laughed in his tormented face, and the same officer that had left Brian and Sheldon without a warning the night before delighted in screaming questions at him. When there was no response from the leader, the officer kicked him between the legs and when the leader buckled, the man holding the stick violently jerked upward. A band of thick torn flesh rolled up the leader's throat. His eyes squeezed shut, and his head vibrated with the pain. He could not scream out. The soldiers became confused and jabbered excitedly to one another. They had done too much damage. Blood gushed from the leader, and the man with the stick tried to frantically unwind the wire, but as he did more flesh curled up the leader's throat. When it was obvious that he would soon be dead, the officer violently screamed questions.

Through the corner of his eye, Brian noticed the Australians walk up. The officer bent down in front of the leader and continued his screaming interrogation. The leader still refused to make any effort to answer, and angrily the officer made a gesture behind him towards his holster. Then he grabbed the leader by the chin and shook his head. Still there was no effort to answer. The officer rose up and stepped back.

"He's going to do it," Sheldon said quietly. "The camera. Brian! The camera." Sheldon's voice began to grow excited. "He's going to do it. Get the shot!"

Without thinking what he was doing Brian quickly grabbed one of the cameras around his neck.

The officer reached back and unsnapped his holster at the same time Brian unsnapped the camera case.

"Hurry, hurry!" Sheldon excitedly demanded.

Just as the officer pulled his pistol out, Brian raised the camera to his eye twisting in the range dial. Through the view finder the leader's face came into focus. Something inside Brian said "Now" and he pressed the button just as the back of the leader's head exploded. The leader dropped out of the viewfinder and the small glass window filled with canal water and became an ugly brown square.

"Did you get it?" exclaimed an Australian voice.

Brian didn't lower the camera until Sheldon reached over and gently pushed his arm down. He looked at Sheldon's blue eyes, but they were empty and cold like the feeling inside him. Some of the soldiers began to walk away, but most stood over the body and quietly laughed and spoke to each other. Brian looked down at the black box that hung from his neck and heard the leader's voice say again, "What is in your cameras, but the loss of the dignity of my country." For a moment he didn't feel. He just stared at the bloody corpse as if he were watching from far away. Then without saying anything, Brian began walking towards the soldiers, with each step his body becoming tenser.

"What are you doing?" Sheldon hurriedly moved alongside him.

"I'm going to get a statement," Brian answered sarcastically. I'm going to interview that son of a bitch!"

"Ease up, Brian. We're getting out of here now!" Sheldon said, taking hold of Brian's arm. Without stopping Brian twisted free. "Brian. I'm telling you! Damn it, do what I say!" Sheldon's voice was more frightened than angry and Brian ignored him.

The soldiers stopped talking and stared at him.

"Brian." Sheldon grabbed him again and made him stop. "This isn't the way." His voice was low so the soldiers wouldn't hear. "You have it. You've got the picture."

"So what!" Brian's anger exploded on Sheldon. "What the hell is that going to do?"

"What the hell are you going to do?" Sheldon paused and returned Brian's angry glare. "You're a writer. Do your job!" For a moment they stared into each other's eyes and then Brian glanced at the soldiers. Words in a newspaper thousands of miles away just weren't enough. Sheldon watched him with an expression that melted from anger to puzzlement. "What else can we do?"

"Can you just accept this?" Brian demanded looking at the corpse. "Is it that easy for you?"

"No." Sheldon paused and quietly sighed. "I've seen this before. It's what happens afterwards. Do your job. You have to deal with it! These men are losing the war!"

"Maybe they deserve to!"

"A few hours ago that could have been us. He intended to kill us!" Sheldon paused, shaking his head. "Don't lose it now."

There was no arguing with Sheldon's eyes. They held the clear reflection of reality, and reluctantly Brian accepted that they were as helpless now as they had been the night before. The officer was anxiously waiting the confrontation. He wanted it to happen. "He tried for us last night," said Sheldon, tilting his head towards the officer. "Don't play into him."

From behind them came the sound of a truck's engine and then the blare of its horn. Sheldon pulled Brian out of the way, and the truck drove over the bridge, pulled alongside the canal, and stopped. Men climbed out of the back of the truck carrying what looked like long, black, plastic bags. For a moment Brian's attention was diverted back to the officer as the Australians began to respectfully interview him. The officer happily explained in English that the dead man had been a relatively unimportant local leader of the Khmer Rouge forces. Brian didn't want to listen to the officer and turned his attention back to the truck.

Sheldon wasn't listening either but was watching the soldiers on the truck. Without taking his eyes off of them he released Brian's arm and pulled a camera over Brian's head.

"Is this one loaded?" he asked as he started across the bridge. Brian hesitated from following Sheldon. "Yeah. It's ready to go."

Sheldon reached the far side first and stopped to look down at something in the grass. The soldiers were laying out the bags on the canal bank, and as he walked up beside Sheldon, Brian realized that they were body bags.

"The rebels put up a fight. I ..." The words died in Brian's throat when he looked down and found that in the grass was the old man and his family. The young woman was lying on her side holding the baby to her breast. For an instant, he thought they were alive; the baby was cradled so close and gently to the mother. But the mother had been shot many times in the back, and some of the bullets had passed through her chest and ripped through the infant.

"Oh Jesus!" Brian anxiously turned around and looked down the canal. "Sweet Jesus." From beside him the camera's automatic wind hissed as Sheldon snapped off one picture after another. "Those bastards!" Brian exclaimed, glancing back to the officer.

Sheldon spoke to the soldiers in Cambodian and then to Brian. "That's why the rebels were here last night. These people were evidently his family." Sheldon hesitated. "That's why we're here now. He had come for his family, and they must have told him we had tried to help them."

"Damn it, Sheldon. That old man and his family saved our lives!"

"I know that," Sheldon said with a confused voice and then paused and watched Brian as they moved to the middle of the bridge. "I didn't want to see anything happen to them either."

"That son of a bitch!" Brian yelled out.

"Relax," insisted Sheldon.

"Relax!" exclaimed Brian. "Can you relax? Is that what your precious experience has done for you? Are you really that …?"

Sheldon grabbed Brian and turned him so they faced one another. "Listen, I'm not sure what you thought this job would be, but you're in the middle of it now! If you can't take it the first time out, say so. But don't get us both killed!" Sheldon's eyes squinted and the muscles in his face were tense. "And don't you ever attack my character."

For a long moment the two men stared at one another. They wanted to blame each other. They wanted to release a rage that was caught inside them.

Two soldiers began to carry one of the body bags towards the truck. Then Brian sighed, "I can't believe this son of a bitch, but you're right." He paused and Sheldon's blue eyes lost their anger. "It's just such a cruel waste."

"We're even," Sheldon said with a nervous smile. "It's been a hard trip. You're sick. We're lucky to be alive. Let's just get you the hell out of here."

At the other end of the bridge a group of officers stood over the leader's body while the Australians continued to question the man that had killed him.

"Don't say anything or ask any questions," Sheldon insisted as he handed the camera back to Brian.

Brian didn't say a word as they passed, nor did he look at the corpse. From behind them came the sound of the old man's body being thrown onto the back of the truck.

When they reached the highway Sheldon maneuvered the car in and out of the waiting crowd. It had grown during the night and had forced him to drive off the pavement and bounce along the shoulder of the road. It took much longer to travel to the border than it had to drive into Cambodia, and when they finally reached the checkpoint, the search of their car had been longer and slower than the day before. By the time they made it to the open road on the Thai side, it was mid-day, and when they reached the train station Brian began to feel hot. The train ride was smooth and that helped. Seeing that Brian was in pain, Sheldon spoke only when it was necessary and accepted Brian's harsh and impatient replies as merely Brian's irritation with his own discomfort. Unable to escape from it, Brian had tried to ignore the pain by taking out a small pad of paper and writing an account of the night with the rebels.

In the late afternoon the train slowly pulled into the station in Bangkok. Brian wasn't sure what time it was and was too sick to care. He only wanted to get home. Sheldon took his notes from him and promised to review the story that evening. It was painful to walk from the train through the station and out to the street where the taxis waited, but he had insisted Sheldon leave him on his own. He wanted to hurry home.

As he expected, the ride through the city was wild and jostled Brian in torment. The heat of the day was a predatory animal devouring what little strength he had left. He could only watch as the city passed outside his window while he prayed that she would be home.

When the cab reached the wharf, there were too many people returning from a long day at Saturday Market to drive down the soi. Brian paid the driver by handing him a handful of crumpled bills and started for home without waiting for his change. As he slowly moved through the people on the wharf, they watched him with concern. Several approached him and tried to help, but concentrating on home and repeatedly reassuring himself that Callie would be there and everything would be all right, he pushed past their offers.

Halfway up the stairs he had to stop to catch his breath. Putting his back against the wall he cradled his face in his hands. He had never had a headache like this. It increased with each breath and pushed his brain into a corner. His palms felt wet, and, lowering them, he realized he was drenched in sweat. As best as he could, Brian pushed himself up the remaining steps. Reaching the door he fumbled for the hidden key. Finally unlocking the door, he left it standing open and went in calling for Callie. When there was no answer, he desperately made his way to the bathroom. A cold shower, if he could only stay on his feet long enough for a cold shower, he thought. His eyes blurred and his stomach felt weak. Barely recognizing the white and drawn reflection in the mirror above the sink, he turned on the cold tap and splashed water on his face. His mouth was a cotton ball.

Just like that, his weak stomach tore in pain as if he had been kicked between the legs. Groaning he dropped to his knees and vomited continuously until he had no strength.

The last violent eruption pushed him to the floor where he lay unable to move.

Brian was not sure how long he had lain there when he heard the sound of Callie's panicked voice and felt her pulling at his arm.

"Please, darling. Please get up. Try!" The tile floor was cool on his face. He didn't want to move. "You must help me," she said pulling his arm around her neck and struggling to bring him to his feet. He moaned and weakly pushed up with his free arm. Standing for only a second Brian felt the pain race from between his legs to the small of his back. He buckled and the two of them almost fell.

"I'll get help." She was crying. "But you must help me get you to bed."

They stumbled together until he felt her turning him and as gently as possible dropping him on his back to the bed.

"I'll be back as soon as I get help. Just as soon as I can!" She held his face in the palms of her hands and kissed his forehead several times. Through the haze he could make out the cross on her necklace swinging and reflecting light in his eyes. He then heard her running out of the apartment, and then the door slammed closed.

When he woke, the room was dark and there was the sound of soft voices in the hallway.

"Callie," he murmured.

The voices stopped and someone quietly rushed into the room.

"Yes, darling?" Her voice was soft. The panic gone.

"What happened?" he whispered, wanting to go back to sleep. He felt her gently remove what felt like a washcloth from his forehead.

"You're sick, darling. Very sick. But the doctor is here now, and you will be fine in a few days." He made out the sound of her dipping the cloth into something on the nightstand and then wringing it out. It felt very cool when she replaced it across his forehead.

"The doctor gave you a shot and he will leave some medicine. I'll be back soon." Her lips were soft and cool when she kissed his cheek. She then slipped out of the room, and the quiet voices started again in the hall. In a moment he heard the click of their door latch, and immediately she was back. The bed springs squeaked as she gently sat alongside him. Nervously she pressed the washcloth and then the sheet as if reassuring herself that he was there. "You will be better soon, in a few days."

"Come to bed," he said, trying to open his eyes, but they were still blurred and hurt.

Her fingertips moved alongside his cheek and down his neck. "I'll sleep in the other room, darling. You'll rest better.

"No."

There was no sound or movement from her.

"Please."

She slowly stood up and moved around the room. He thought he heard her undressing and then on the other side of the bed the sheet pulled back and she slipped in beside him. Her body was cool against his. She nuzzled her cheek on his shoulder and he could smell her hair. He was no longer frightened and fell asleep.

CHAPTER TWELVE

Brian hated the late afternoon. The sun was at its hottest point and everything hard and uncomfortable in the world settled down on the day. It had been sixteen days since he returned from Cambodia. The mornings and the evenings were better now, and he was no longer walking bent and fused like an old Chinaman. Sitting under the canvas shade, he watched the river from the balcony. The fishing canoes would be returning soon, and with them would come excited voices and a frenzy of entertainment to mark the beginning of sunset, and shortly thereafter would come Song Per Song, and then Callie. During the first week of his recovery, Callie had stayed home with him, but by the time he was well enough to get out of bed for short periods of time she had to return to work. The thought that he was to stay home another five days seemed unnecessary and over cautious. He had been pumped full of antibiotics and given the shotgun diagnosis of acute Diverticulitis. It was all very general, and the doctor warned it could flare up again, and repeatedly warned that the intestinal infection could be a killer. For the first eight days, he had made daily visits to check in on Brian, but he never stayed long and each time left in a serious mood. On his last house call, he told Brian he could not return to work until next week and that if he overextended himself before then he would most probably suffer a severe relapse. However, that was all theoretical, for Callie wouldn't let him do anything but lie in bed or sit on the balcony. She was very serious about following the doctor's instructions. Although Brian grumbled and acted irritated with her pampering, she was really a very good nurse, and he missed it when she was not there. Each day, shortly after she had left for work, he would begin to grow restless. He tried to write letters back to the States, but he really didn't have anything to say to the people he had left behind. They wouldn't understand and it seemed pointless to try to explain. His confidence that he could deliver a message through his writing was gone. Each day of his recovery he spent thinking about the murder of the mother and child. How could anyone understand that waste, that crime? America didn't want to know about things like that, and neither did he. Seeing it had made it too real. It was no longer a subject to write newspaper articles about.

Although a new baseball season was starting in the States even the sports page of the Bangkok Post was dull and uninteresting. From the lack of anything better to do, Brian had fallen into the habit of using the mornings to write down notes about what he had seen and done since his arrival. It passed the time and seemed like a sensible thing to do. Maybe someday there would be a use for the notes, maybe a book. Usually by the time he finished, it was late enough to eat the lunch Callie had left for him. It was invariably the same type of soup and two pieces of dry toast. He hadn't regained his appetite, but he would finish the soup to avoid one of Callie's short but serious talks on how important it was for him to eat. The toast was out of the question. Thai bread was much too sweet and smelled like it had been stored too long. Every morning she stubbornly prepared it and every afternoon he stubbornly ignored it. It was a game they played. By expecting him to eat something she knew he wouldn't, she could count on him to finish the soup, and by eating the soup, Brian could count on Callie making more toast the next morning.

Today his frustration had finally caught up with him, and he had won the game by dumping both the soup and the toast. He knew it was a childish thing to do but it was also defiant and that helped him more than the food.

Days ago Callie brought home a stack of books from the American library and Brian had made an honest attempt to read one. He had found that the problem with reading anything longer than a news article was that it put him to sleep, and he was tired of sleeping. The war news was all bad. In a strange way he was thankful for his trip across the border. There was a certain freedom in the realization that it was so big that he could do nothing about it and that it had been foolish to ever think he could. Undoubtedly, Sheldon was disappointed in him and would never allow him to cover anything of importance. That thought bothered Brian so he tried to think about other things.

The first dot on the water that would eventually transform into a fishing canoe appeared. It was a long way off, but it meant that the day was ending and the sun would soon lose its ferocity. Most of the boats would come from the South so he watched in that direction, but there were four palm trees at the South end of the wharf that blocked part of the view. Two of them were old and tall with their palms brown and bent. The two young trees were only half the size, but their green palms proudly reached up like many fingered green hands.

By the time there were many dots on the water, Callie turned the corner and started down the soi. She was walking quickly with someone and the wave she usually gave Brian did not come. Whoever the man was with her was Thai and young. Brian could not get a good look at him and he became concerned when the man took hold of Callie's arm and stopped her. They appeared to be arguing, and Brian stood up to go to them when the conversation abruptly ended and the young man walked away. Expecting Callie to be upstairs before he could finish in the kitchen, Brian went inside and poured himself a glass of ice water. With water being the only thing he was allowed to drink, Callie had tried to add a little something to it by slicing up lemons and floating them on the surface of the pitcher. It made the water taste especially clean. As Brian walked back to the balcony, he was surprised to find that Callie had followed the man and was engaged in another argument. Brian couldn't imagine what the two of them could be discussing with such heat and he strained for a better view. Immediately Brian felt a shock. It was only a glimpse and Brian told himself that he had to be mistaken, but the young man looked like Sonthi Chovat. Brian stepped to the balcony rail, but the conversation ended and the young man turned and started back towards the river. Brian told himself it couldn't be the same man Sheldon had pointed out at the airport, not the same young man they had tried to follow.

When Callie reached the courtyard gate, she looked up. Her expression wasn't one of surprise, but it was clear that she hadn't realized he was on the balcony and it took a moment longer than seemed natural for her smile.

"How are you feeling?" she asked as she approached the entry door.

"Much better. In fact, so much better that I may go back to work tomorrow."

"You mustn't hurry it, Brian. If you do, you'll end up flat on your back again."

Brian turned and walked inside as Callie went through the door below him. When he opened the apartment door, she was halfway up the stairs.

"I really think you should wait until next week. The doctor wouldn't approve," she said, reaching the landing and then stepping into the apartment.

Brian wanted to ask Callie who had been with her, but he told himself to wait. From her expression, she seemed preoccupied with some other thought.

"Five more days isn't that long and it could make all the difference."

"Why don't you shower and change." Brian reached out and took a small brown bag cradled in Callie's arm. The bag was bulging with pear shapes.

"Ripe mangoes," she smiled. "Be a dear and put them in the sink." She turned and walked down the hall while Brian started for the kitchen with the fruit. "Did you eat your lunch?"

"Every bit of it," he said just loud enough for her to hear.

"Even the toast?"

Brian could tell by the sound of her voice that she had stopped and turned around. "Sure," he said without looking back.

"I talked to the Prince today." Callie's voice sounded far off as she moved into the bedroom. "He

and Sheldon want to stop by this evening to see you."
She paused. "I thought you didn't like that bread?"

Brian didn't answer.

While Callie was in the shower, Brian washed the yellow fruit and put it in a wooden bowl. Ripe mangoes were soft and tasted like peaches, but Brian preferred to eat them while they were still green and hard. Sprinkling a little salt on them made them taste like green apples. Before she finished, he sat down on the couch and tried again to start one of the books she had brought from the library, but he couldn't stop thinking about the young man. Callie was aware of Brian's interest in Chovat, and if she knew him it was not like her to keep it from him. He felt bad for even thinking she would make that mistake, but the possible consequence kept nagging at him. Setting the book down on the couch, he told himself it was ridiculous to allow his imagination to run away. He decided not to say anything until she had a chance to tell him. If she didn't, he could casually ask who it had been. It must have been someone else, someone who looked like Chovat. Callie knew a lot of young men through her job. It had to have been someone else. Callie was liberal minded, but Chovat was a radical and she would never associate with anyone like that. Brian told himself that it had been a long day. He removed a pencil from behind his ear and stared at its point while he turned it between his fingers. He wanted to tell himself that all Thais looked alike, but they didn't and he began to worry again.

"Now that's a deep thought," Callie said entering the room.

Looking toward the hall Brian found that Callie was watching him. Her hair was damp from the shower and she had on a baggy pullover cotton top.

"What is?"

"Whatever you're thinking." She smiled and started toward him. "Such a serious young man, but very handsome." Callie lay down on the couch and put her head in his lap. "Especially when you're lost somewhere in your own thoughts." She slipped her hand inside his shirt and gently rubbed his chest. "You know that though." She relaxed and closed her eyes for a moment. The noise from the wharf was increasing as the canoes arrived. It was a happy sound that made the day seem peaceful. "Do you ever wonder who you would be with if we hadn't met?"

"I wouldn't be with anyone," he replied.

"That's nice of you to say, but you would be." The brush of her hand felt good, and the position she was in pulled her top out of place. Her thighs looked soft and inviting.

"No," said Brian, thinking how long it had been since they had been together.

"Someone would have found you. I did. It probably would have been a Eurasian girl." Callie lifted her head and her hand stopped rubbing his chest. "Have you ever seen one?"

"Would I know the difference if I had?"

"Oh yes. They're all very beautiful. Half-European and half-Asian. They have long, shiny, black hair, but Caucasian features with round blue eyes and olive skin." You see a lot of them in Chiangmai," she added, putting her head back down and resuming the massage.

"Where's Chiangmai?"

"It's a town about five hundred miles north of here up in the Teak Forest. It has to be the most beautiful area in the country, and the women are very intimidating to the rest of us." Callie closed her eyes and looked as though she could fall asleep.

"Was it a hard day?" he asked.

"No. You're just comfortable. They wanted me to leave for the Province tomorrow, but I told them I couldn't leave you. Do you feel up to having Sheldon and the Prince over?"

"I feel up to a lot of things."

Callie opened her eyes and gave him a smile that meant she was going to ignore his innuendo. "You shaved today," she said, reaching up with her free hand and touching his face.

"I couldn't stand it anymore."

"You must be feeling better," she laughed.

"Much," he smiled.

Callie rose up and sat alongside him. "What would you like for dinner?"

"Don't tell me you are going to finally allow me a real meal!" he laughed.

"I'd better feed you something substantial before you get carried away. Besides, wouldn't you like a change?"

"Of course. I'm floating as it is."

"What do you think you could handle?"

Brian smiled.

"For dinner, Brian!" She laughed and stood up. "You're not well enough for that."

"In that case, I'll settle for some Kobe beef. I'll even walk down and buy it."

"You'll do no such thing." She insisted.

"That doctor doesn't know what he's talking about," he complained. "Soup and toast! How is anyone supposed to get well on that?"

"He has been very good to us."

"That doesn't make him a good doctor."

"He's gotten you well. I don't think you realize just how sick you were."

Brian smiled. "If you admit I'm well ..." He reached out for her.

"You're not that well!" she laughed and stepped back. "I'll make something that won't be too much for you."

"Kobe beef," he insisted.

"Vegetables," she smiled.

"Beef."

"Do you want to get sick again?" She was trying to act serious.

Brian smiled and watched her as she began to prepare their dinner. She was really very good to him, and the thought that she would hide anything from him now seemed ridiculous.

For dinner they had summer salad and vegetables, and after they had finished she talked Brian into playing several games of backgammon. To keep things interesting, they played for coins and Callie always won and delighted in teasing him by stacking the change in tidy little rows and stopping to count her winnings every so often.

"Do you want to play one more time?" she chuckled at the end of their last match.

"No," Brian said standing up from the table and walking into the front room. "Tell me more about Chiangmai."

"*Chiangmai.*" She re-pronounced the words, "*Mai*, Brian as in My God, you can't pronounce Thai words!" They both laughed. "Do you want to play again?"

"No, I'd prefer to play cards with Song per Song." Brian hesitated to look out the balcony. "I wonder why he didn't come up today?"

"You've grown close to him," smiled Callie.

"No. I simply prefer cards."

"You're just a poor loser."

"I'm just out of change."

She laughed and closed the board to follow Brian. "Chiangmai is the second largest city in the country, but that's really deceptive because it is much smaller than Bangkok and it's cooler. There is a small town considered a part of Chiangmai, but it is actually higher up in the Teak Forest. It's a very special place."

"It sounds like somewhere we should go," said Brian as they sat down on the couch. Callie lay down across him again.

"Do the Eurasian women have you curious?"

With the evening breeze coming across the river and in through the balcony doors, the fans made the room cool and relaxing. On one of the small tables the pages of a magazine snapped back and forth with the movement of air. Brian sat contentedly stroking Callie's hair. "No, I don't believe they're any prettier than you." He was thinking about the young man again. "I've never seen a Teak Forest. I imagine them as cool dark places with trees that have smooth bark."

"They are magical," Callie yawned and gave him a smile. "There is a place north of Chiangmai. It's higher in the mountains and near villages that have a yearly festival. The farmers and the hill tribes come to celebrate. Maybe we could go up there next week." She was excited.

"Celebrate what?"

"The moon, the Camburin flower, each other. It's just one big celebration."

"I can't miss any more work," said Brian, uninterested.

Callie laid her head back down, and she lost the excitement. "I know it was just a thought."

"Besides, after telling me about the Eurasians, taking you would be like taking sand to the beach," teased Brian.

"Oh, Brian," she complained sadly and closed her eyes. "I'm sure you would be disappointed in me if you saw one of them."

"No I wouldn't. I was only teasing." Callie lay still and Brian felt as though he had offended her. "I didn't mean that. It was a bad joke."

"You are happy here?" She asked, opening her eyes. "You don't regret moving in with me, do you?"

"Not at all. I'm very happy with you, and those girls could never distract me."

"Then why didn't you want to move in? Did you think it wouldn't be as good?"

"I was an ass."

"But you aren't an ass anymore, are you darling." Her smile was playful. "Or at least you're a happy ass."

They both laughed and when they were about to stop Callie began to laugh even harder. "Sand at the beach!" What a terrible thing to say!" She reached up and pulled the hair on his chest.

Savoring the last moment of the comfortable evening, he began to wonder again who she had been talking to and if it could have been Chovat. Brian glanced out the window, but before he could ask the question he saw the lanky figure of the Prince walking down the soi. Turning to look again he saw the Prince and Sheldon were about to reach the courtyard. "They're here."

Callie sat up. "There goes a good time. I was hoping the Prince would come alone. The poor Prince. I hate the way Sheldon treats him."

"They're best friends," replied Brian. "Sometimes you really dislike Sheldon, don't you?"

"Sometimes he's a conceited, vicious man who mistakenly thinks he knows a lot about this country."

"You make him nervous."

"Me?"

"He is worse around you. Maybe he thinks he's impressing you."

"You're making this up. It has nothing to do with me." Callie stood up. "I don't like the man. The way he treats Thais is ugly."

"Well, he thinks a lot of you. I think he would like to see himself with you," Brian teasingly laughed.

"I have to change," she said, starting for the bedroom and ignoring his comment.

CHAPTER THIRTEEN

After Brian let the Prince and Sheldon in, they stopped long enough in the kitchen to pick up the two chairs and to get each of them a beer. Then Brian led them out onto the balcony where they placed the chairs in a circle under the shade. Sheldon acted very friendly, and then he and the Prince looked Brian over and decided that he was merely finding a way to avoid work and laughingly accused him of having other women up while Callie was not there. The conversation quickly turned to the war news and how grim things were becoming in both Cambodia and Vietnam. Sheldon reminded them that he had predicted Vietnam would become active since the world ignored the war in Cambodia.

The Prince was enjoying his beer and avoiding the conversation. Instead he stood up and walked to the rail to watch over the wharf. By now all of the boats were in and the wharf was wildly alive. Brian was glad that the Prince was there and wanted to laugh and talk about unimportant things with him.

"President Thieu has hard times ahead. South Vietnam could fall," said Sheldon with a casual attitude. He glanced at Brian and then looked over at the Prince. Sheldon was eating one of the mangos and the juice was dripping on his shirt. Seeing that the Prince was watching the fishermen, Sheldon puffed out a chuckle. "What's he doing? Surveying his kingdom? He is so damn ridiculous. History is in the making and he could care less. He would rather watch the slope heads fish."

Hoping that he hadn't heard, Brian quickly looked at the Prince, and when he didn't turn around Brian told himself not to repeat the insult by a confrontation with Sheldon. "What's happened? What's going on in Vietnam?" Brian asked, looking at Sheldon and thinking with some embarrassment how fortunate it was that Callie had not heard him.

"Thieu's planned withdrawal from the Highlands turned into a retreat, the retreat turned into a rout, the rout turned into a slaughter. The end result is that the South lost one third of its territory." Sheldon looked at Brian with a serious expression. "Today it was fighting for peace, but by tomorrow South Vietnam will be fighting for survival." Brian could tell that Sheldon was really in an exceptionally good mood and just wanted to rattle the Prince.

"Hello everyone," said Callie as she walked onto the balcony. "Now that's enough talk about the war. It's a nice evening and there's no point in spoiling it."

"Callie!" exclaimed the Prince as he happily hurried to hug her.

"I agree," said Sheldon, under his breath. He raised his beer. "Let's talk about younger days and wilder ways, women in short skirts and long nights."

Brian smiled and wondered if Sheldon had been drinking.

Callie and the Prince were behind Brian, but the smell of the perfume she had put on made Brian glance over his shoulder. She had changed into a white skirt and sun blouse that didn't cover her small stomach and she had done something to her hair that made it look very fresh. It amazed Brian how she could all at once change her look.

"We must get Brian well enough to bring you out with us," laughed the Prince. "Without you, we haven't been having much of a time." The Prince laughed loudly and hugged her again.

"Did all of you get something to drink?" she asked, glancing at Sheldon's hand.

In one way or the other each answered yes but Callie was too busy glancing around Brian's chair to pay any attention. When she was satisfied that he was following the doctor's instructions and drinking only ice water, she looked up and smiled at him.

"I'm fine," Brian said, knowing what she was looking for.

Callie gave the Prince a warm smile as she sat down between him and Brian.

"You look very nice," said Sheldon.

"She always does," answered Brian.

"Thank you Sheldon, but Brian was just saying he was going to replace me with a Eurasian girl." Callie looked very sincere and everyone turned to look at Brian sternly until Callie chuckled. The Prince made a noise that sounded a little like a laugh. "The sickness has affected his head."

Brian nodded to the Prince. "She is leaving out quite a bit. In fact, an entire conversation."

"I was telling Brian about Chiangmai."

"Haven't you been there Brian!" exclaimed the Prince.

"No. Callie was just talking about ..."

"Oh, you must!" The Prince interrupted in excitement and stood up. "Wars or no wars, you have to visit Chaingmai. There's no other place like it. You can see a small war anywhere but Chaingmai is special."

Sheldon and Brian began to laugh.

"I am very serious about this," announced the Prince. "If you left my country without seeing it you might as well have never have come to Thailand." Callie reached back and took hold of the Prince's hand. "I was telling him we should go up next week for the Festival."

"Splendid. The two of you go for the festival, and when you return Brian will be completely well. Better than he has ever been."

"I've missed too much work as it is. We'll have to go some other time," said Brian.

"Nonsense!" asserted the Prince.

"Excuse me," Callie interrupted as she stood up. "I'm going to make some tea. Can I get anything for the rest of you?"

"I think everyone's fine," Brian answered. "How about you, Prince. Are you ready?"

"I'm fine. Thank you." The Prince was anxious to continue.

"Then I'll be just a moment," said Callie as she stepped to Brian and leaned close to him. She smelled good and Brian didn't listen as the Prince started talking again. "How are you feeling?" she asked.

"I'm okay."

"Would you like anything?"

Brian smiled. Callie wanted to laugh but the Prince was exhorting the charms of Chiangmai, "I already told you no!" she whispered.

"I've heard enough about Chiangmai," announced Sheldon. His stern voice caught both Brian and the Prince by surprise. "With all the important changes that are taking place in your world, it's unbelievable that all you can talk about is a

peasant's festival. When are you going to wake up!
You irritate the hell out of me!"

For a long moment, the Prince stared at him in
brewing silence. "You have no idea what it is for me
to watch what is happening!" he finally said in a low
and powerful voice. "You are nothing but a spectator
who criticizes and acts superior." Brian could not
believe that the man he knew as a mild party boy
could be so strong. Sheldon's face was shocked and
he remained silent.

"Where is America now? It made promises
and insisted on fighting the communist, but when it
could not win, it ran away and left those that had
believed its promises to stand up to the last storm. A
storm that is just beginning! A storm that will spread
over my country and all Asia. It will change my
world, but not yours! I cannot stop it. I must bend
with the storm.   I and my country must survive it
because it is on us, but you can leave, and leave your
storm to us!" The Prince's eyes were piercing and
Brian was stunned by his strength.

"Wait a God damned minute," demanded
Sheldon. "I've never once mislead anyone and I've
never done anything to harm you or your country."

"You cannot say that men in your job do not
form world opinion!" exclaimed the Prince in
interruption.

"I can say that." Sheldon spoke quietly but
with a superior air that seemed meant to needle the
Prince.

"We report on what others are doing, which
may or may not form world opinion. We simply get
the facts."

The Prince's face took on a frustrated
expression.

"What the Prince is trying to say," Brian interrupted, "is that we don't bother to tell the world the good side of a country." Brian wasn't sure where he was going but he wasn't going to allow Sheldon to spear with the Prince any further. "At least we haven't in this part of the world." Sheldon looked at Brian with surprise. "Hell, we have the world believing that damn near every Asian is a communist wearing black pajamas and delighting in the killing of American eighteen-year-olds."

"Exactly my point," the Prince proclaimed.

"I'm not arguing that, Sport." Sheldon didn't appreciate Brian's defense of the Prince. "We report on the newsworthy."

"Sure we do, Sheldon, but that's the Prince's point. We decide what is worthy enough to be the news."

Sheldon's expression became smug and Brian told himself to be careful. "Are you saying that we cover the wars," Sheldon intentionally emphasized the plural, "because as journalists we have decided they are newsworthy?"

"Of course not. But that's only a half-truth. We can't expect the world to care about another country's war if we don't write about the people it affects, and if we write things that only separate Americans from the war, we are shaping things. In that way we form world opinion as much by what we don't write as what we do."

Sheldon glanced timidly between them. He wanted to argue, to be right, but even he had to accept the obvious truth. Sheldon was buckling. Brian continued with a smile. "For example, I've never heard of Chiangmai until just today. Now maybe this festival is newsworthy, maybe it's not. But we won't have anyone there to even check. That's what the

Prince is saying.   How can we expect anyone in America to care about what's happening here when all they read about Asia is war news." Brian realized that Callie had returned and taken her seat next to him. She was watching him as if she knew what he was thinking. It made him feel warm and happy. "Hell America had to be drug into World War II."

Sheldon leaned forward resting his arms on his knees and dangling the beer bottle from his fingertips, swinging it back and forth like a pendulum. He was thinking about something, and Brian hoped that the evening could take on a happier atmosphere. When Sheldon looked up, he glanced at everyone and realized they were expecting him to say something.

"You're right," he said to Brian with an uninterested swing of the bottle in his direction.

The Prince was still intensely staring at Sheldon. It was obvious that he wanted to say more but was forcing himself to remain quiet.

"Don't give yourself a heart attack, old man," said Sheldon with a glance at the Prince. Sheldon stood up and started for the doors. "I've heard a lot about your tea. Would you mind if I tried some?"

"Of course not." Callie said as she started to stand.

"I'll find it. Just sit down."   Sheldon disappeared inside and the atmosphere became more relaxed and everyone quietly watched the river.

"Are you all right Prince?" asked Brian.

The Prince looked at Brian with intelligent but angry eyes. Then he nodded and turned his attention to the river, leaving Brian to wonder if he really knew the Prince.

When Sheldon stepped onto the balcony, the Prince quietly took his seat.

"This is delicious," Sheldon announced after a sip of the tea.

"It will also slip up and hammer you if you're not careful," replied Brian without taking his eyes off of the Prince. With the fishermen working below him, the Prince turned to watch over their efforts. Brian felt proud of him and liked him even more. He looked taller and sat very straight.

The sunset had been particularly beautiful. The clouds that hung on the far horizon hid the sun for a moment, but just before it dropped out of sight it escaped from beneath them burning with the deep, orange glow of flames that licked at the clouds and lit the sky on fire. The darkness that followed closed the balcony off from the rest of the world and left it a small island of light surrounded by a black velvet curtain. Sheldon and the Prince drank one glass of tea after another, and Callie, feeling secure, ignored her normal limit and happily allowed herself the freedom to slightly overindulge. It was one of those marvelously intoxicated evenings that come only when a small group of people spark into a spontaneous glow of warmth and friendship. The Prince had forgotten Sheldon's intentional needling and both laughed a little too loudly. The wharf was deserted and quiet, and there wasn't much traffic crossing the bridge. Brian was tired but he didn't want the night to end. Callie had turned on the old radio, and the American station quietly played familiar songs in the background. Sheldon was laughing but he turned to Brian and for an instant seemed somewhat concerned. "We should be going soon."

"It's still early," Brian encouraged. "Besides, if you go Callie will make me play backgammon again, and she's already taken me to the cleaners."

"He is a very poor loser," Callie laughed.

Sheldon watched Brian. "Are you sure you feel well enough? You look tired."

"I'm fine," Brian hesitated. "Maybe a little tired, but I have all day tomorrow to rest."

"You're sure?" asked Callie.

"I'm fine. Everyone stop worrying about me," Brian laughed. "Hell, tomorrow all of you can come by and watch me lie around and sleep."

"Do you know where I'd like to go?" Callie unexpectedly asked. "I'd like to go to the Sea Palace."

The Prince's expression went blank, and he looked at Sheldon and Brian, not believing what he had heard. For an instant no one said anything so Callie excitedly glanced between all of them.

"That's a men's club," answered the Prince nervously,

Callie looked around at each of them with a smirk. "I know exactly what it is."

"Then why would you want to go there?" Brian asked.

"I don't know. I've heard the Prince mention it and I'm curious."

"Well just forget it."

"Prince will take me!" she laughed.

The Prince pressed back in his chair. "They won't let women like you in."

"Why? All I want to do is look around." Callie was serious and that made the rest of them laugh. "Well, what is it like?" she insisted.

"It's just a large room with a lot of women sitting behind a glass wall," announced Brian. "And it isn't a place for you to be in!"

Callie looked at Brian with one raised eyebrow and a half smile. "Behind a glass window? And just how do you know?"

"Oh, come on!" Brian scoffed. "I went in there once." Her smile became a disbelieving grin. "They have a restaurant and bar. I've been inside it for a drink."

"And...."

"And nothing."

"Is it all plush and gaudy?"

"No." Brian wasn't convincing.

"Well, is it decorated in red?"

"It has red carpets." Brian pointed a finger at her. "Now if I was there for a woman, would I remember the carpet?"

Callie laughed and shook her head. "What does your memory of a red carpet have to do with it?"

"Well, I wasn't there for that."

"Callie," interrupted Sheldon. "Brian is much took egotistical to make it a simple business transaction."

"I'm not sure if you're trying to help me or insult me," laughed Brian.

"It would offend you to pay," laughed Sheldon.

"I'm too young to pay."

"You have too much ego." Sheldon leaned back in his chair and sipped from his tea and stared at Brian with a cocky expression. Then Sheldon slowly reached into one of his shirt pockets and pulled out a folded piece of paper. "This is the copy I saved for you." He hesitated, before handing it to Brian. "This is your first big one. It will never seem quite as important again." As he held out his hand Callie reached across while she looked at Brian for permission and took the slip of paper from Sheldon. Sheldon reached back in his pocket for a cigarette. "Read it aloud so the Prince can hear it," said Sheldon. "I put together an editorial from your notes. I didn't rewrite any part of it. I simply cleaned it up and sent it out over the wire," explained Sheldon.

"Did any papers pick it up?" Brian asked in a shocked voice.

Callie slowly started to read to the circle of chairs. Her voice was serious but as she moved down the column it also became delicate. She made the words sound strong yet gentle and everyone including Brian listened intently. Callie's voice added something to the words and made Brian feel as if he were listening to someone else's work. They brought out vivid pictures of sleeping rebels watched over by their tired leader. Of the old man shuffling in and out of his dilapidated restaurant. Of the happy and chubby smile of the baby. Of the loneliness of the dying man on the stretcher. The blood stained tule grass and the photograph of the leader's head exploding. Occasionally, Callie would hesitate and glance up at Brian, and each time she did, the soft light in her eyes grew stronger. After she started the last column she stopped and looked up at Brian. Her eyes now sparkled with the light. Then she looked at the Prince and then at Sheldon and started the column again.

Now that I have seen a small part of a small war, this writer can safely say there has never been a wrong side to any war and there never will be.

Wars are never fought for the wrong reasons. People go to war for all the right reasons. To protect their homes and families. To throw off an unbearable oppressor. To fight for an ideal more important than their lives. When we remember these acts by others we call them noble and courageous.

To show our respect and gratitude we annually pay homage to the blessed dead by having our old soldiers dust off their medals and march among waving flags to the sound of slightly offbeat drums. Boys watch the passing of heroes, and, being children, spend their youths half hoping to join the parade. They look at even old soldiers and see strength and honor and men who were right. We all need to believe in something, and the music of a parade is something we can keep time to so we believe in it. Yet once we have marched off with it we find the enemy believes just as strongly, and each can equally justify acts of brutality against a vicious enemy. The parade is a trick done with mirrors. From one angle we see patriotism and glory, and from the other we see quiet desperation and meaningless death. The catch is to know which is a reflection and which is an illusion. Having seen only a moment of such brutality, I realize the pen is indeed mightier than the sword. For the side that wins a war will write its history and it will be the side that was right.

We should at least be honest with ourselves and, more importantly, to the boys watching the parade. Whisper in one's ear, lives are not given in wars, they are stolen."

Callie looked up with a soft tranquil expression. Her eyes were filled with intimacy. "May I keep this?"

"Yes," said Brian a little embarrassed by her enthusiasm.

Callie looked to the Prince and smiled. "I knew it."

The Prince was touched by the article and without speaking further they communicated something between themselves and then the Prince glanced at Brian. "Yes," he said quietly and smiled.

"Knew what?" Brian asked glancing between them. His question broke the string between Callie and the Prince, and she turned to him unleashing her enthusiasm. "Just that you're a good man." She was quickly hugging Brian, and when she stepped back she hesitated and brushed at his hair. "Who will be an important writer someday."

"It was a good piece Brian," said Sheldon. The tea was catching up to him, and he was slouching comfortably in his chair. "You've sold your first article."

Brian looked around savoring the moment. Lights of a boat appeared far down river, and while enjoying the feeling of success and thinking of the man on the stretcher Brian watched the reflection dance on the water. The lack of any conversation finally distracted Brian and he looked back to the circle to find that all were lost in their own easy thoughts. There was an air about each of them that heralded the end of the night, but none of them wanted to be the one to bring it up.

"Sheldon, do you ever wish you were just a reporter again?"

Sheldon looked at Brian with the memories of thousands of stories flashing across the years and over his face. "I'm over the hill," he said without regret. "They were good days, though." He stood up, stretched, and stepped to the rail. For a moment he looked out over the river. "I was good." Then he smiled back at Brian, "better than you'll ever be."

Brian knew that Sheldon wasn't teasing, but remembering their capture, he couldn't help but return the smile. "You still have a few good moves," Brian paused. "But not many."

"A few," Sheldon laughed, nodding his head.

Brian didn't want the night to end, and in an effort to keep it alive he asked Sheldon how he had first met Godfrey. It was a story he had heard before, but Sheldon liked to talk about those times, and he hoped it would postpone the end. Happily Sheldon started. Those were the old days when even wars seemed less complicated and foreign correspondents were a small group of writers that traveled over the globe with the ease of walking from one room to another. Most of them had never gone to college and certainly didn't consider themselves political scientists or sociologists. They were simply reporters and slightly mavericks that either couldn't or wouldn't settle down to newspaper jobs stateside. He told them of hard-to-get stories they had managed and how when Godfrey was about Brian's age and just starting, Sheldon had taken him under his wing. Together they had covered a number of big stories and a countless number of small ones. Laughingly he told them of one wild excursion after another in cities with strange sounding names in Europe, the Mid East, and Asia. They had been all over the world together. Either assigned to the same bureau or managing to cross paths. Callie delighted in the humorous side of the stories and Sheldon went on with them until he had to reluctantly accept that it was getting too late for Brian.

"What made you become a reporter?" Callie asked with a knowing smile that the story would be interesting.

"We should be going. Brian looks exhausted," said Sheldon, not really wanting to leave.

"No. I'd like to know." Brian smiled with anticipation.

Sheldon hesitated and thought about it. "My father and I never really got along. He had a farm in Kansas." Sheldon smiled. "I never cared for farming, but I liked to shoot pool. In fact, I liked it so much that I would get off of the school bus and walk down to the pool hall."

"How old were you?" asked Brian.

"Oh, about the sixth grade, so I must have been about eleven or twelve." Sheldon wanted to laugh. "Anyway, one afternoon I was coming out of the pool hall when my old man's pick-up slowly rolled by." He laughingly emphasized slowly rolled. "When he stopped and asked me what I was doing uptown, I told him the teacher had sent me in for fertilizer." They all laughed. "You see, it was a small farming town and as a class project the teacher was having us raise some row crops near the school. So, on the spur of the moment and under pressure, it sounded good to me." Sheldon paused and he looked happy with the memory. "Well, the old man told me to climb in the truck, that I shouldn't have to carry a bag of fertilizer all the way back to school and that the teacher shouldn't have asked me to. Now, he knew I was lying, but he made me buy the fertilizer. All the way back to school I tried to come up with some way out of it, but when we pulled up, he jumped out and slung the bag over my shoulder and gave me a look I'll never forget."

"You went inside with it?" laughed Callie.

"I was frightened! I didn't know what else to do but to follow him in. There I was, bag of bull-shit on my shoulder listening to my teacher politely explaining that the bag wasn't the only thing full of it!" Sheldon was laughing too hard to continue and paused to catch his breath. "Of course the class thought it was funny, but the old man didn't see any humor in it at all. He took me home and beat me with his belt until his arm gave out. That night my mother rubbed salve on my butt and back. I remember how she cried and how damn much it hurt when she touched me. Right then I knew I hated him, that I would leave as soon as I could." Sheldon stopped and thought. "It's funny how you can think something when you're that young and it will stay with you." He shook the thought off and continued. "Later when I was sixteen, my father bought a new blue Ford tractor. About three o'clock one morning I was out in the field plowing. We had a dry well boarded up out there, but I forgot where it was."

Knowing where the story and the tractor were going, Brian and Callie began laughing.

"All of a sudden, BANG! One of the back wheels crashed through the boards and the front of that tractor came straight up. Well, that was it for farming and me. I left it sitting out there and went back inside the house to sleep. Three o'clock in the morning, Jesus Christ!" Sheldon paused. "I was sitting on the edge of my bed when my old man came in and asked what I as doing. When I told him, he just stood there staring at me. He couldn't believe it. Then he asked me what the lights in the field were." Sheldon jokingly mocked the anger in his father's voice. "That's my tractor? That's my new tractor and you drove it into the old well?" Right then and there I told him to take his tractor and his farm and ..." Sheldon abruptly stopped and looked at Callie, and his bashful look made them laugh even harder. "My mother's brother was an editor of a small newspaper upstate. I had never thought of that kind of work but my mother stepped between the old man and me before one of us killed the other, and for the first time in her life she stood up to him. She sent me to live with my uncle and I began my newspaper career. It wasn't great work, but it was a lot better than farming. Four years later the Korean War broke out, and I went to work for the military news service, *The Stars and Stripes*, as a war correspondent."

Although everyone was still laughing Sheldon was calm and his expression became a fond smile for a private thought.

"Is she still alive Sheldon?" Callie asked softly. The laughter of the Prince and Brian rapidly faded off, and Brian looked at the Prince expecting to find an expression of familiarity, but the Prince did not know the answer.

"No." Sheldon paused and sipped at the last of his tea. "She died years ago. I wanted to go home for her funeral but there wasn't any point. The old man and I probably would have just fought." Sheldon gave Callie a warm smile and finished his tea. "But she was a good mother." The gentleness of Sheldon's mood surprised Brian. He had resented Sheldon's ability to brush off the deaths they had witnessed in Cambodia, but he now realized those had been outside of Sheldon. His years of seeing such tragedy had made him hardened to it out of necessity. Sheldon's eyes turned to Brian where they rested in contemplation of some thought. Then he glanced to Callie and back to Brian.

"I think you should cover Chiangmai."

"What?" asked Brian not understanding the change in subject.

"I want you to do a story on the Festival."

Callie looked at Brian with an excited and surprised smile. "Maybe it is something we should cover," Sheldon continued, "and if it is, you're still fresh enough to see it for what it is."

"You've just had too much to drink," laughed Brian. He was sure that Sheldon was simply feeling good and wanted to do something out of character.

"Well, that may be true, but it has nothing to do with the assignment. I want you to go and take Callie with you, but you bring me back a story with a flavor of its own that the people in the States will read."

"Tomorrow you'll change your mind," smiled Brian.

"We're going to cover the Festival," Sheldon said in a committed tone. "If you don't want the assignment someone else can go."

"No, I want it."

"Then it's settled." Sheldon started towards Brian. "We have to be going. It's late and we've stayed too long as it is." He shook Brian's hand in a very businesslike manner and turned to Callie. "Thank you for the nice evening and for introducing me to this special brew of yours." He smiled.

Callie stood up and gave him an unexpected hug and kissed his cheek. "You're more than welcome. It's been good for Brian to see both of you." Sheldon's hesitation to touch Callie and then his smile showed he was pleasantly surprised with the affection.

With Brian obviously tired, they all insisted that he not see them to the door and remain in his chair. Callie walked them out holding hands with the Prince and telling him that Brian would soon be well enough for all of them to go out again. While the final farewells took place, Brian sat watching the dark form of the river. He was very tired, but their guests had left him with the gentle feeling of security and he didn't want to go to sleep yet. Callie laughingly told them goodnight again and then the latch clicked. The sound of it at once reminded Brian that he had not asked her about Chovat, and the secure warm feeling disappeared.

"Oh, Brian. Isn't it wonderful?" She hurriedly walked up beside him leaned down and hugged him. "You're going to love Chiangmai. I know you can't appreciate just how lucky we are but after you've seen it you will." She sat down on his lap. "There is one thing I want us to do."

"What?" Her excitement made Brian smile.

"I want to take the night train."

"That's fine. It makes no difference."

"It does! There is something I want you to see just as the sun comes up, and if we take that train we'll get there a little before dawn."

"Goodnight!" the Prince called up to them from the soi. Brian waved and the tall silhouette waved back. When he looked back to Callie he found that the atmosphere of the evening and the pleasure of the tea still sparkled in her eyes. She was watching with a smile and he knew she no longer thought he was too sick.

Callie took him by the hand and they walked inside. They left the balcony doors open for fresh air, turned off the light, and started down the hall in the dark.

"Brian," Callie asked over her shoulder as she led the way, "What were you really doing in the Sea Palace?"

CHAPTER FOURTEEN

It turned out that Sheldon's generosity had been inspired by Callie's tea, but he was too stubborn to admit it by completely canceling the assignment. Instead, he limited it to three nights and acted as if that was his intention all along. The prospect of spending one of the nights in a train was enough to make Brian want to call it off, but Callie was much too excited to disappoint, so he was unsuccessful in trying to talk her into leaving in the morning. When that failed, he and Song Per Song made an afternoon out of going to the station to purchase the tickets. It was his first attempt to actually leave the apartment and it proved to be more than he was ready to handle but he swore Song Per Song to secrecy.

A long line of taxicabs were waiting to pull up in front of the station and unload, so Brian paid the driver off and unloaded their luggage, then he and Callie hurried along on foot. The sidewalk was crowded with people greeting one another or saying goodbye, but Callie was happy and quickly slipped between the people pulling Brian behind. When they passed the last of the cabs and were about to turn and walk into the station, Brian noticed a monk and a peasant woman sitting side by side. They sat out of the way with their backs against the wall. The woman was selling fruit and the monk was collecting handouts. Alongside the woman was a row of newspaper vending machines and Brian turned towards them. "I'm going to buy a paper," he said letting go of Callie's hand.

"Please hurry."

Brian smiled over his shoulder at Callie's impatience. "We've plenty of time."

"I know, but please."

"It doesn't leave for forty-five minutes." Brian found a machine with the English headline of the Bangkok Post and fed the proper coins into the slot. "How many times have you been to Chiangmai?" he laughed, as he pulled on the machine's door.

"Don't make fun of me. You wouldn't like it if I wasn't the type to get excited."

The door still wouldn't open. He jerked several times on the handle and the machine began to rock on its legs. "These things never work," he sourly complained.

"Don't tip it over!" Callie laughed and touched his shoulder. "There's a magazine stand inside."

"All right." He reluctantly turned away from the machine, but before picking up the suitcase, he sorted out some coins and while holding them out in his palm, Brian selected a mango from the woman's basket. The woman glanced several times between the coins and Brian's face and then picked out her change with a blue-veined hand. Her coolie hat lowered to hide her face and the pocket in which she stored her money.

"A newspaperman that can't buy a paper." Brian grabbed the handle of the suitcase and started for the doors. As he stepped next to the monk, he set

the mango in the holy man's bowl.   Graciously the
monk put the palms of his hands together and nodded
a slow bow.   Brian stepped towards the door, but
Callie wasn't beside him so he stopped and turned
around.   She was standing in front of the monk with a
smile on her face.

"What is it?"

She didn't answer.

"What's wrong?   I thought you were in a
hurry."

After hesitating a moment longer, Callie took
hold of his hand and rushed them along.   "I am.   If we
hurry we'll have a better choice of seats."

"Why were you looking at me like that?"

She smiled up at him.   "You just surprise me
sometimes."

"What are you talking about?"

A wall of noise and confusion encircled them
as they stepped inside the station. "Never mind me."
She continued to smile.

The railroad was run by the State and was
punctual, modern and air-conditioned in first class.
Callie's impatience had worked in their favor and had
given them the opportunity to select both the seats and
the sleeping compartment they wanted.   After the train
had been on the move for several hours, it reached the
vast central plain North of Bangkok.   Richly fertile
and wet, the landscape that passed by the window was
green and giving.   With a young crop just breaking the
water's surface, rice paddies stretched to the horizon
and created an emerald earth with mirrored flashes of
blue.   It was the rice bowl of Asia, and it was filled
with farmers tending their paddies.   The farmers

didn't wear black or brown like those in the city. Instead they had on washed-out blues and yellows, earth tones, and oranges. There wasn't one pointed coolie hat among them. Instead their coolie hats were broad like stovepipes.

"Look at this." Callie nodded out the window. In the center of a rice paddy was a muscular water buffalo, and on its black back sat a young boy. Their window flashed past the figures but not before Brian could see that the boy watched the train with an open mouth. Just as Brian was about to look away, the stooped figures of peasants knee-deep in water, zipped by. Instantly, there was a second line of peasants. All had a large clay jar strapped to their waists and the skeleton of a basket in their hands. They were carrying the baskets upside down, and ignored the train too quickly stab the baskets in the water.

"What are they doing?" Brian asked.

"Fishing."

"With those baskets? But the fish can swim right through them," said Brian shaking his head.

That's the idea," replied Callie. "If they're small enough to get away they don't want them.

Their window flashed passed the scene. Then came another rice paddy and still more fishermen. One of the fishermen reached down shoulder deep through the center of his basket and lifted out by the tail a twisting fish and dropped it into the clay jar.

"They make it look easy," he smiled at Callie.

"If you don't mind getting wet when you fish."

"You should see me trout fishing," Brian laughed. A smaller group of peasants came into sight and all had something in their baskets.

"In America you spent a lot of time in the outdoors, didn't you?" she asked.

"I used to like to fish and hunt," Brian answered, as he waited for the next group of peasants. "But I don't think I'd like hunting any more."

"Why?"

Brian turned to her, thinking of the man on the stretcher. "Oh, I don't know. It just doesn't interest me." There was only the landscape passing outside. "Let's go to the Club Car and have something cold to drink."

"The doctor didn't think you should have any coffee or liquor yet," Callie objected, and looked at him with a serious expression.

"I don't want liquor. Besides, I'm hungry and I know you are by now."

"There were too many things to do this morning and I was too excited to eat." Callie stood up and they started down the aisle. She took hold of his hand. "I'm glad you don't think you'd like hunting anymore. It seems like an awfully sad sport."

What Brian called the Club Car was actually the diner. It had rows of tables alongside the windows and a small bar in one corner. Each table was covered with a white tablecloth and red napkins to match the flower arrangements next to the windows and the curtains that were pulled-back out of the way. It was crowded but very pleasant and relatively quiet. Callie was finishing her meal so Brian glanced out the window and opened the newspaper he had bought in the station.

"You must be getting tired of me. We look like an old married couple with you hiding behind that paper."

Brian looked over the top of the newspaper and smiled. "I want to see what's going on in the world." When he turned to the war articles, the one that caught his attention was a small column with the headline, "Fighting Near Poipet." The article briefly explained that the siege was steadily creeping down on the town in a battle for dominance of the highway that ran through Poipet. The fight was now clearly turning in the favor of the rebel forces, which meant that thousands of refugees would soon be helpless. The war they had sought to avoid would soon squeeze the town into a panic-stricken anthill. Out of the refugee camps now forming on the Thai side of the border came stories of savage mass murders. People spoke of how entire villages including children and pregnant women were tortured and killed by Khmer Rouge forces. It was too reminiscent of Nazi Germany to believe, so most papers weren't printing the stories. Most refugees hadn't actually seen any killings, just the corpses that were left in piles.

On the other side of the paper, Callie began to clatter and tap her fork on the china plate. Brian lowered the paper, and she tried to look as if it had been unintentional.

"Are you bored?" he asked.

"Oh, don't mind me," she glanced at the window. "You enjoy your paper and relax."

"I'll read it later." He folded it up and sat it on the chair next to him.

The steward walked up to the table and Brian paid for their meal. He was a young man and proud of his white coat and when Brian handed him his tip he grinned and cleared off the table to hurry away. "He's probably new," Brian smiled. "I don't think he's used to tips."

"That's because Thais don't expect tips unless they're working around foreigners. What would you like to do now?" asked Callie.

"Let's just sit here and watch the scenery."

"I have a better idea." Callie reached into her purse and pulled out the small book of Thai words and phrases.

"I don't want to study that now."

"It's a good time for it."

"Everyone I want to talk to tonight understands English."

"That's not the point. It's the effort. In the States you expect people to at least try to speak English." She opened the book. "Now the important thing to remember is that the language has five tones and each can change the meaning of a word."

"I think I need a drink."

"It's not so bad. Now, just try." She handed the book to him. On the left margin was the Thai phrase and on the right was the English definition. "Start anywhere and I'll help you with the tone."

"*Cop kun*, thank you." He didn't want to do the lesson and his voice was sarcastic. "*Kun poot len*," Brian laughed. "You must be joking. I can't do this."

"Speak in a normal, conversational voice. Generally, vowels follow English pronunciations: "a" as in father, "e" as in extra."

"I'll never learn this."

"Yes you will. Just try."

"*Leo sai*. Turn left. *Leo kwah*. Turn right."

"Better!"

"*Pom yoo tee.*, Where am I? *Pom Rak Kun*, I love you." Surprised by the definition, Brian stopped and looked at Callie. He had never said that to her. She was looking down in a strained effort to be a detached teacher.

"Go on," Callie said without hesitation.

Then Brian realized neither of them had said it to the other. For an awkward moment, he paused wondering if they did love each other.

"Go on," repeated Callie.

The language lesson had gone on until the shadows of sunsets slid over the countryside. Brian and Callie were sitting on the east side of the car so the distorted shadow of the train raced along outside their window as the day approached its end. The Thai couples were amusing to watch, for they all tried not to show any open affection for their companion, but some of them were not very good at the pretense and gave themselves away with the simple, little things lovers do for each other. They were like children who thought they were being discreetly clever but were really quite obvious.

On the horizon the hazy silhouette of mountains could be made out, and as they looked across the car and out the other windows there was another mountain range, but it was closer and less difficult to see.

"We'll be starting up soon," Callie said with increasing anticipation.

"They don't look very high. More like hills than mountains," said Brian.

"I think around six thousand feet."

Brian glanced out the window. The mountains were rapidly closing in around them. Midway between the train and the mountains was a group of buildings. One of the roofs was a round dome that funneled into a spiral and then into a sharp point. "What's that place?"

"It's a Wat." Callie glanced out the window. "A Buddhist monastery. The building that looks like a needle is called a *Chedi*, pronounced [*jay-de*]." She glanced at Brian, and he smiled at her determination.

"You'll learn," she laughed. "The sphere usually contains a vault where they store religious articles."

"They're impressive. They take their religion seriously," said Brian, as he tried to get a better view.

"Very. That's one reason why the Thais are such nice people. Except for the belief in the afterlife, Buddhism is very similar to Christianity. Only it's much more benign."

"What's that largest building?" asked Brian.

"That's the *Bot*, pronounced [*boat*]. It's the most important building in the temple ground. You might say it's the cathedral. They're very beautiful inside, but the reason the monasteries are so important is because they are also the basic schools. Most children, particularly outside the cities, receive most of their education in monasteries. The monks teach them." For an instant the train bogged down as it started up the grade. "You're going to love the mountains," she said quietly with a smile as she reached across the table and laid her hand on Brian's.

The train wound through the mountains, and the teak forest reached down from the hills to form a dark curtain on the other side of the window. They left on a dim reading lamp and a small fan that blew air up and down the length of the bed. Their sleeping compartment was air-conditioned, and the fan felt good and made them pull the sheet up over them. It was a small room with bunk beds that pulled away from the wall. Each bed was really only large enough for one person, but they were satisfied with locking into place the lower level and climbing into it together. It was peaceful, lying close to Callie and listening to the rhythmic click of the tracks. She rolled over onto her side and gently touched Brian's forehead with her fingertips to trace his profile. "Do you remember the Royal tea when we met?" she asked.

"Uh huh," Brian answered lazily. He was very comfortable.

"I knew right then what you were like."

"How could you have known anything about me? We only spoke for a moment?"

"I mean before we ever talked I knew." She began to laugh, and the sound of it made him laugh along with her. "You were standing under the trees and looked like a little boy a long way from home and out of place. Lost at the circus." She put her hand under the sheet and laid it on the inside of his leg. "I couldn't help but feel sorry for you."

"Sorry for me!" Brian exclaimed.

"I've been in the same spot. New to a country and out of place. It's hard not to care for someone like that."

Brian laughed, "Well, I admit I wasn't quite sure of myself."

Callie kissed his cheek. "That was what was attractive about you. The way you watched everyone and tried to fit in. You weren't like most Westerners. You didn't look down on the Thais." Callie glanced at him with a raised eyebrow. "Well at least not as much as most do."

"I thought they were eccentric," said Brian.

"Well, that's patience of a sort. You're not a patient person, but you're not closed-minded either. You changed and accepted things for what they are." She paused and smiled with the thought. "Like today when you bought food for the monk. You wouldn't have done that a few months ago, but today you didn't even think about what you were doing."

"Why is that so important to you?" Brian felt self-conscious.

"It's simply nice to see. It makes me care for you a little more."

Brian kissed her.

"Let's not make love, darling. I want you to just hold me." She removed her hand from his leg and brushed at his hair.

"All right." He was disappointed.

"You don't mind do you?"

"No."

"I just feel like being close to you," she said.

"I understand." They lay quietly for a moment while the small fan's breeze passed over them several times. Callie moved her head to look at him. "We can if you want to."

"No. Let's just listen to the tracks." He brushed the hair off her cheek.

"I want to." She put her hand back on his leg.

When Brian opened his eyes he was lying on his side, facing the window.

"We're almost there!" Callie exclaimed in a voice to wake him. She was already out of bed. "Hurry so we can catch one of the cabs that will be waiting. There won't be many." It was still dark outside. Brian rolled over and sleepily watched Callie tuck her blouse into her skirt. The compartment was cool and the bed comfortable. He pulled the sheet up to his neck. He didn't want to get up. "We only have ten to fifteen minutes," she encouraged.

"I'll be up."

Callie began to hurriedly pack their things into the suitcase. Lying across the foot of the bed were the clothes she had left out for him to wear. The things he had worn the night before were already packed away. Callie looked into the small mirror and brushed a hand back through her hair to let it loosely fall at its own will. Then she turned to him with an excited smile. "Please, Brian."

He let out a deep breath and pulled the sheet back.

As Brian and Callie made their way down the corridor towards the exit, the train came to a jerking stop. Other than the porter they were the only ones in the hallway, but as they moved past the compartments the sounds of early morning movements, coughs, and voices came from the other side of the doors. The door of the last sleeping compartment was half open, and as they passed Brian heard the click of a suitcase being closed. The porter took hold of Callie's arm and helped her step off of the train. He smiled at Brian and nodded. The platform was deserted, and looking into the windows of a stationhouse, Brian wished he could find a cup of coffee.

"This way," Callie said, taking hold of his hand and leading him toward the side of the building.

There was a small gate with a tired looking railroad employee waiting to check through the arriving passengers. As Callie hurried Brian past the man, he glanced at their one bag and then stared at Callie. The sound of the other passengers stepping off the metal steps on the side of the cars made Brian look over his shoulder. The other passengers were sluggish as they came off the train and would not be competing with them for a cab.

"What's the rush? No one's going to beat us to the taxis." complained Brian.

"Don't be cranky. We have to get there before the sun comes up."

"Where?"

"It's a surprise." They turned the corner, and in front of the station there were four taxis waiting. "You'll feel better in a moment."

"I'd like to a slow down and wake up."

"Please don't be a little crank."

They reached the first cab and Callie opened the back door and slid in. By the time Brian closed the door behind him, Callie had already given instructions to the driver. Following her orders, the driver sped off before a single other passenger had reached the street.

The road that led into town forked, and they took the prong that curved up into the countryside. Callie was sitting close to Brian with a hand holding tightly to his knee. As the car wound up the small road, she kept glancing over her shoulder as if they were being pursued. With a thud, the car turned onto a dirt road and accelerated to make it up a hill. At the crest of the hill, the car pulled over and came to an abrupt stop.

Brian looked to Callie in question, but she was already sliding out the other door.

"Is this it?"

"Yes."

The door closed behind her and Brian stepped out. Looking around he couldn't see that there was anything but a flat area that looked like a lawn. The night breeze moved about them and the air was fresh and smelled like a forest.

"What's here?" Brian asked, trying to decide what the hurry had been.

"Pay the driver. He'll drop off our bag and check us into the hotel." The horizon was starting to show light.

"You don't want him to wait?" Brian asked over the roof of the cab.

"No. We'll be here for a while and it's a short walk. Please darling."

"Okay, okay." Brian walked around to the driver's window and paid the fare along with a generous tip to insure that their bag would make it to the hotel. Before Brian could turn around, Callie took him by the hand and led him out onto the lawn. The headlights of the car turned around and started down the hill.

"What is this place?"

"You'll see," she said squeezing his hand.

"What's the secret?" he insisted.

"It's not anymore. Not now that you're here." Callie was smiling, and Brian could see by her expression this was important to her. "This has been my private spot, and I want you to see it without any preconceptions." She turned his shoulders towards the horizon. "Just look at the sun." Callie stepped behind him. The horizon grew lighter and he started to glance back at her. "Don't turn around!"

Brian tried to look behind them, having caught a glimpse of the dark outlines of buildings. His curiosity was getting the best of him. The sky faded from black and on its far edge the dark forms of the far away rain clouds appeared. Then a thin line of red cut across the horizon. Rising out of the grasslands below him, the first arch of the sun drifted slowly upwards. The line of red became a wider line of orange, then a band of yellow. As the sun rose toward the clouds, their edges became gold and silver, and for an instant all the colors washed together and then suddenly there was a fresh blue sky. He was standing on the top tier of a layered plateau. Far in the distance were the endless flat lands, green and glistening with rice paddies and reflecting the blue sky. The rolling hills, covered in the dark teak forest, rolled up the plateau to surround him. In clearings in the forest were bright patches of violet opium poppies. Below him was a sleepy little town with roofs of orange and yellow tiles. A large, green park dotted with shade trees bordered the north side of the town. Disappearing in and out of the trees a stream laced down the mountains and wound through the park like a blue ribbon. The train was now quietly snaking its way through the mountains. From the town the forest marched up the road that had brought them there. The trees circled around him and he was standing in a garden. He turned around, and when he did, his breath died in his chest. Behind Callie was a monastery, and its immense spiral dome was layered with gold. It reflected the morning sunlight into his eyes, and he realized that all the roofs were covered with tiles of copper and gold. Stone steps led up to a wall that surrounded the compound. On both sides of the gates stood forty-foot figures of sentinels. They had the bodies of men but the faces of animals and the ears of wolves. Their helmets funneled into sharp points, and their uniforms were made of jade and gold. The tops of busy trees popped up from beyond the wall, and located near them were large, gold, lace umbrellas.

"This can't be real," he said aloud to himself.

"It's real." Callie was watching him with a radiant expression while the breeze played in her hair. The serenity and beauty of the place had settled on her and given her something Brian didn't recognize.

"Its name is *DoiSuthep*," she smiled. "My temple of dawn."

"It's magnificent," his words hung above him in wonder. "But how did ..."

"Now do you understand why we had to see it at dawn?"

"Yes."

She was proud of her temple and delighted in his appreciation of it. "Legend has it that after a great battle a conquering army stood right where you are, but they were so moved by it that they couldn't bring themselves to plunder the monastery and returned home empty handed."

"You always believe the best about people," he laughed.

She stepped towards him and put her arms around his waist. "It's still here. No one's plundered it!"

The morning was in her hair, and all that was about them collected in her eyes and reached into him, as one would gently wake a sleeping child. There was no point in trying to deny it any longer. "I love you, Callie."

"I know," she said quietly with warmth and understanding. "I've known it for a long time." He pulled her to him and held her close. "I love you, Brian, and you mustn't worry about us anymore."

CHAPTER FIFTEEN

The walk back to the hotel had been pleasant. The town had the same seasons as Bangkok but not the heat, and that alone made it a garden spot. The hotel was on the north side of the town and faced the park. It was set out away from the other buildings and looked Indonesian with a long, covered porch lined with oversized white wicker chairs. When they arrived, the other guests were moving about the lobby with the energy of people that had just awoke, but Brian and Callie were tired and checked in and went up to their room for a morning nap. The window in the room did not have a glass pane. Instead there was a tall set of shutters that made it shadowy inside when closed and allowed the flow of air.

Brian was asleep on the bed and he began to dream of elephants. His mind's eye saw them wandering across dusty plains in Africa and performing in circuses. The noise of their trumpeting grew louder and louder until it opened his eyes, and he realized it wasn't a dream at all but a sound coming through the window. Callie rose up at the same time and looked at Brian with a groggy expression.

"Did you hear that?" Brian asked, as he hurriedly stepped to the window.

"Hear what? I felt you get up."

"Don't be so sleepy. Listen, listen," he insisted. Several of the animals trumpeted. "That! Elephants!"

Callie smiled but she didn't look surprised.

"You knew!" Brian jerked the shutters open. On the far edge of the park, there was a cloud of dust and through it he could see the animals. "There must be more than thirty down there!"

"It's a very special festival this year." Callie's voice was happy. "Usually they hold the round-up far to the southeast, at Surin."

"Round-up," Brian laughed disbelievingly.

"Somewhat." She chuckled. "Every year in November there is a gathering of the elephants."

"Wild ones?"

"No! The ones used for draft animals. In Surin the round-up is huge, more like two hundred elephants." She stood up and started for the window. "Up here they won't have as many, but during the Camburin festival they bring them in from the hills. Those animals are used in the lumber industry." She stepped alongside Brian and looked out the window. "In the teak forests they use them to lift the trees that have been cut down."

"What the hell are they going to do with them here?" laughed Brian.

"The lumber camps compete with one another in games. Besides, it's more Thai logic," Callie smiled. "The men want to leave work and come to the festival, and if the elephants aren't here, what point is there?"

"This is craziness!" Brian was excited. "What else haven't you told me?" Across the park people were beginning to erect canopies to set up an open air market.

"I promise you'll never forget this trip," she said taking hold of his arm.

Brian had insisted that they hurry down to watch the elephants and had barely allowed Callie enough time to wash her face and find her shoes. To protect the landscape, the elephants were kept beyond the park on a brown field that lay between it and the forest. The crowds watching the games were pushed tightly together in a ring that surrounded the field. It was made up of tourists from the cities and peasants from villages, but they laughed and pointed at the animals like children. Eventually, Brian found a thin spot in the spectators and managed to weave Callie to the front. The people around them kept glancing up at Brian in curiosity, but they all smiled and tried to make room for them. A small peasant boy on the shoulders of his father stared at Brian and ignored the elephants.

"It looks like we're the only foreigners here!"

"I'm sure we are." Callie tilted her head back and smiled mischievously.

The field was divided into different areas for the different events. Down the length of the field, they held races. Six elephants at a time would pound their way to the end of the track trumpeting wildly as their jockeys bounced on their necks among flapping ears. The elephants liked to run, and it was surprising how fast they were, but it really didn't matter who won the race because each elephant believed it had. Each raised its trunk towards the clouds and declared itself champion with wild happy trumpeting. The men that rode the elephants wore colored armbands and controlled the animals with the tap of small sticks.

Directly in front of Callie a tug-a-war was going on. Each camp would select its strongest elephant and it would compete against the men of another camp. One elephant against seventy or eighty men seemed like a fairly even match until the rider touched the animal's head with the stick, and the line of men were dragged on their heels across a chalk line. When Brian was about to suggest they move on to the next event, another lumber camp produced its entry. It was larger than the other elephants, but its tusks were yellowed and one was broken and very short.

"That's a big boy," laughed Callie. "But he looks much older than the others."

"He's probably done this so many times he knows how to cheat," smiled Brian.

"Elephants don't cheat."

"No, elephants don't forget," Brian insisted.

The men waiting for the challenge took hold of the rope while the other end was tied to their opponent. As the men positioned themselves, the elephant turned its head and looked at the crowd.

"He's looking at us!" exclaimed Callie.

Brian laughed "Maybe he's never seen foreigners either!"

"I'm telling you he is! Look at him, his eyes are on us!"

"I take it you're rooting for the elephant," laughed Brian.

"With all those men! The poor old thing will probably die," she laughed.

When all appeared ready, the rider tapped the side of the elephant's head to make it pay attention to the men in front of it. Then the first man on the rope yelled, and the rope jerked off the ground and stretched tightly in the air. The stick touched the elephant again, and it began to move backwards. On its third step, it seemed to step down on soft earth that wouldn't support it, and its front leg buckled.

"Oh!" Callie clenched Brian's arm. Seeing that the elephant was in trouble, the first impulse of the men on the rope was to pull harder, and they leaned back off balance. The elephant's trunk rose with a trumpet, and it stepped backwards with a jerk of the rope, and then it stepped forward. The slack in the rope caused the men to fall backwards and when they hit the ground the animal without delay dragged them across the chalk line. The spectators laughed and cheered.

The defeated men jumped to their feet and circled the elephant to shout insults.

"I told you he would cheat," laughed Brian, as he turned to Callie and nudged her in the direction of the other events.

"He didn't cheat! He out-smarted them!"

"That's called Sand Bagging," chuckled Brian, as the argument behind increased, the men yelling and the elephant trumpeting.

After they had circled the field and watched the elephants parade, charge, compete in lifting contests, and give rides to those that were courageous enough to climb aboard, Brian and Callie made their way to the open air market and to a fruit stand. A boy stood behind the table collecting money and dipping paper cups into bowls that contained a thick, yellow liquid. Behind the boy his family sat on the ground, cutting an assortment of fruit and mashing the pulp into one mixture. When it was Brian and Callie's turn, the boy glanced up, and seeing the two of them, he hesitated and smiled. As they walked away with the concoction, Brian looked down at the cup in suspicion. When he raised it to his lips, it smelled odd, but it tasted rich and fibrous and left his mouth feeling clean and wholesome. They wandered into the park and watched the merchants putting up their stands. The afternoon was pleasant and the noise of the spectators and elephants faded away. Coming to a bridge that spanned a stream they crossed over to the other side and followed it toward the mountains. Callie reached out and took hold of Brian's hand. It was placid and soothing, and he was glad that he was in love with her. He admired her and more importantly he liked her.

"Have you ever been in love before?" he asked with a glance.

Callie watched him before answering. "I've thought I was, but now I'm not sure."

"Did you like them?"

"You're a silly darling," she laughed.

"No, I'm not. You can love without liking the person."

"That would be terrible!"

"I think most people are like that," said Brian.

"I don't want to talk about people I've known before."

"I don't want to talk about any one specifically. I just asked a question."

"It's much too nice a day to think of such things. Besides I've never cared for anyone like I do you." Brian smiled at her serious expression.

They continued towards the mountains, but he knew she wouldn't leave it at that. She walked along looking down with concern. "You like me don't you?"

"Yes. I like you very much."

She was smiling again. Brian let go of her hand and put his arm around her shoulder.

They walked up into the trees, and the width of the stream swelled until it cut into the rocky sides of the mountains, and the dirt path became a floor of stone. The forest came down to meet the stream, and trees grew out of the rocks on the water's edge. Beneath the water's surface, smooth, black rocks glistened in the sunlight. A covey of small red and white birds exploded from a tree and startled Callie. When they reached a flat spot, a shallow pool created a small waterfall. In the pool floated green, fragile pads the size of dinner plates. From the center of the pads extended long stems, and on the end of some of the stems were pink blossoms.

"What are those?" Brian nodded at the pool.

"Lotuses."

"I'll be," he smiled. "I never really believed I'd see one. I mean, people mention lotus blossoms when they talk about this part of the world, but you don't pay any attention and you don't think of them as real."

"They grow everywhere here, in ponds, lakes, flooded fields. For centuries they have been offerings to Buddhist monks during religious festivals. The lotus even has its own festival at the end of the Buddhist lent."

"Is this festival for the Camburin flower religious?"

Callie smiled and looked up at him. "In a way. Come on. Just a little farther up, there's a much nicer waterfall."

As they moved along the embankment, the sound of a waterfall slowly grew in strength until it became a loud crash. The stream cut sharply to the left, and then through the trees Brian could see the white water dropping down a stone staircase. Pulling Callie along, he cut through the trees and came out in front of the pool the waterfall fed. Because they stood so close to it, the sound of the fall was now a roar. Looking down, they saw a series of falls that twisted and turned their way through the trees down the mountain.

"It's beautiful," said Brian in amazement. "It looks like it's pouring out of the trees!"

Callie had let go of his hand. He turned to where she was standing on a rock slab that trailed down into the pool. Her expression was excited as she looked up at the mountains and turned in a circle to consume the scenery. She was too involved to notice him walk to her and when she turned in his direction, Brian stopped her by putting a hand upon each side of her head. Her hair was soft to the touch and her eyes were electric. The gentlest of smiles appeared on her face and she kissed him and then laid her head on his chest. "We should have brought our swimsuits," she said.

Brian looked at the inviting pool and then turned back to her and began to unbutton her blouse. She stepped back with a bewildered smile. "What are you doing?"

"I'm taking your clothes off."

She pushed his hands away. "You can't do that. Someone could come up here." Brian stepped closer and loosened another button.

"Brian," she insisted.

"No one's going to come up here," he replied.

"If they do?"

"If they do," he interrupted, "we'll be in the water. They won't be able to see us."

"No. This is crazy."

"What's so crazy about it?" He removed his shoes and pulled his shirt over his head. Callie began to laugh and glanced over his shoulder. "You wouldn't dare." Brian unbuckled his belt.

"All right, I believe you." She reached for his hands but he turned sideways.

"Brian!"

"I'm going swimming and if anyone comes, that's their problem." His pants dropped to the ground and the belt buckle clattered on the rock.

Callie laughed wildly as he ran down the slab and dove into the pool. On impact his body flinched with the sudden cold. Under water, the roar of the waterfall was a deep rumble. Coming to the surface his body tingled. He shook the water from his hair and waved Callie in. "Come in. No one is going to catch us." She was still laughing. "It's perfect!" he insisted.

"I'd die if someone came up here."

"No one will."

Callie slowly looked around the mountains while she coyly unbuttoned her blouse.

"Oh come on. There's no one up there."

"I am," she answered in a doubting voice. Callie stepped to the water's edge and modestly unhooked and dropped her skirt. The blouse was quickly on top of it, and she splashed into the pool.

"It's cold!" she shouted at Brian accusingly.

"Only for a second. Then it will feel good."

Callie swam to Brian and put her arms around his neck. Her naked body pressed up against his and she smiled. "We're crazy to do this."

"It feels good to be crazy. Besides," he laughed, "if any Thais come along, we'll just tell them it's an American tradition." He pulled her tight. "Every American has skinny dipped."

"Now that we're in here, how are we going to dry off?"

"We'll lie on the rocks like a couple of turtles."

"I'm not lying up there naked!"

"Oh," Brian pushed her head below the surface. Callie came up with shiny straight hair. Then laughingly she put her arms around his neck again and kissed him.

They floated on their backs and watched white clouds slowly drift across a lazy blue sky. The mountains around them were serene and private and so thick with trees that it formed a green wall. They stayed in the water for a long time and then baked themselves dry by lying on the rocks. Callie said she wanted to go back to the hotel and clean up before the evening festival, so she began to dress. Brian had put his pants on when he realized she was not beside him. Looking back, he found she was kneeling on the rock staring at him. She was beautiful, and her eyes were excited with the thought of him. Brian let his pants fall to the ground and he kneeled beside her and took her in his arms. With a long kiss, he laid her back on the rock, and in the warm sun he made love to her with the roar of the waterfall hiding their sounds.

Afterwards, they reluctantly dressed and started down the mountain.

"I wish we could stay a week," she said whimsically.

"It hasn't even started. Don't think about leaving."

"I know. It doesn't matter how long I stay here. I still hate to leave."

"Don't think about it." Brian took her hand, and they allowed the slope of the mountain to trot them towards the hotel.

CHAPTER SIXTEEN

The preparations for the festival had been promptly completed, and more people than the town could normally boast of, filled the park. Many of them had undoubtedly arrived during the day from Bangkok, for they dressed in Western styles. They had cameras hanging from their necks, and Brian watched them with the annoyed eye of a resident watching the influx of tourists. Striped canvas shades, large colorful umbrellas, thatched roofs and pointed tents were promptly erected over concession stands that sprang up everywhere like weeds. Smoke from open fires curled into the sky and the air was filled with tantalizing smells. A strange mixture of different types of music and the suppressed excitement of hundreds waiting for darkness electrified the air. At the first stand there was a small, blue tarp and under it was a man with a baby elephant that had a black-faced monkey sitting on it. A long line of tourists laughingly waited to take a picture with the animals. The owner stood quietly beside the elephant, smiling at the easy money stretching out in a line in front of him. The elephant tried to touch and smell the people with its trunk as they positioned themselves around him, and the monkey blinked and shrieked away from attempts to pet him. From there, a maze lay before Brian and Callie, and they started into it with high expectations.

There was no order to the concession stands. One could be devoted to dried fruit, while the next could be a silversmith hammering a design into an ornate vase, or a woodcarver cutting and polishing teak into bowls. Callie and Brian stopped to watch a man making paper parasols. His stand was polka-dotted with the bright colors of the open umbrellas he had finished. The one he was working on in his lap was sky blue, and he was carefully painting delicate white flowers with red centers on it. Further down, a kite maker advertised by flying his wares above his stand. Kites of every color hovered above his temporary shop, and his young son thrilled the crowd by diving at them with a kite. In front of one stand there were small wooden boxes, and on top of the boxes were live jungle squirrels. Although you couldn't see how it was done they had to have been tied to the boxes for they didn't try to escape and laid calmly. Their backs were black fir but their sides and under-bellies were sable. They were cute, little things with black eyes, and it made Callie sad when she explained they were a delicacy and would end up in someone's pot. Funny looking birds, with long bright feathers, peaked out at the people from under large baskets. There were masks, head pieces, bronzeware, silverware, enamel pottery, lacquerware, snake skins, jewelry, fat gunnysacks of vegetables and every other conceivable luxury and commodity one could wish to buy. Unlike the markets in Bangkok, there was no barking at the potential buyers from eager merchants. The atmosphere was light and contagiously happy.

Coming to a large open space between two stands, they stopped to see what was attracting the attention of the crowd. Under a large umbrella, a small boy squatted beside a young man. In front of them someone lay under a red cotton sheet. The young man was talking to the crowd and the boy was fidgeting with a wooden bowl.

"What's going on?" Brian asked Callie.

Callie laughed. "The person under the sheet is dead."

"What?" said Brian in a tone of disbelief.

"They're saying he is and that they are going to bring him back to life."

"Okay," Brian now laughed. "A revival meeting of sorts. The one under the sheet recovers and the little kid collects contributions from the crowd. The guy dies again and in the half hour is brought back to life in front of a new group. Let's keep going."

"No, wait. Let's see how he does this."

For a long time the young man waved at the crowd and over the body while rattling away something Brian was uninterested in listening to. Then he went into a chant and circled a hand over the body. Expecting the dead actor to throw back the sheet Brian only half-watched. The chant continued and the tone of the would-be savior became high pitched. As Brian was about to look away, the sheet began to move, but it wasn't rolling off it was rising up. The body smoothly rose in the air to stop and float at the waist of the now standing sorcerer. The spectators applauded and the small boy ran to them to fill the bowl. There was nothing under the body and the umbrella overhead wasn't bowed or stressed from hidden wires that could be lifting the body.

"What the hell?" Brian said aloud of himself.

"Magic!" Callie applauded.

"It's a good trick. Do you see any wires?"

"Nothing. It's magic!" She took hold of Brian's arm and smiled. There were too many people in front of Callie and Brian, so the boy didn't attempt to collect from them but hurried around those in the front of the circle. The sorcerer chanted again and the body drifted back to the earth. With the body on the ground, the young man quickly jerked off the sheet and snapped it in the air. Then he held out a hand to the boy it had covered and helped him to his feet. The revived boy acted groggy and then emotionally hugged the sorcerer. The crowd applauded again and the little boy hurried about with his bowl collecting more change.

"So much for magic, let's have something to eat," said Brian shaking, his head.

"You're such a skeptic," Callie mocked, as they started on their way.

Going from one concession to another, they sampled fruits, vegetables, and a wide variety of smoked fish and meat. Callie found a stand where they sold a rice wine drink and bought two bottles. Wandering through the maze they sipped on the one she had opened until they were tired and decided to rest by finding a comfortable place on the lawn. The grass was sprinkled with people eating dinner or just peacefully enjoying the company of one another. There really wasn't a sunset. The sun just dropped behind the mountains and the sky anxiously became dark. The first evening stars appeared bright in a happy sky. Across the park, colorful streams of paper Chinese lanterns glowed, and more and more people wandered out of the market place to relax in front of one of the many stages. At the far end of the park, closest to the forest, there were modest tents and make-shift thatched shades. Whispers of smoke rose from in front of each, and the sound of a flute and muffled drums mingled over the tents. One man had walked away from the tents and stood looking down on the park while he played his flute. He wore a white square hat. His shirt was dark-colored and baggy. A blue skirt hung to his knees and under the skirt he wore on black pants with blue rings at the ankles. At his side hung a tasseled sash with many red balls at the end.

"Those people up there are the Mau tribes," Callie said, noticing Brian's interest. "We'll go up there later, but right now they're just beginning to celebrate."

"Just exactly what are they celebrating?"

"I'd rather wait and let you see it."

"All right." He lay back and listened to the sound of the flute. The market place was nearly empty now. Looking at the park and its flower gardens, he thought of the Prince. Brian told himself that he would have to remember to thank his friend for insisting that they go to the festival. The atmosphere truly was different than anything he had experienced before. It was peaceful and satisfying, and it made the world a better place for Brian just to know it existed.

"Brian look at this."

He rolled over in Callie's direction, and, seeing the moon, he sat up in wonder. The flute player was still on the knoll playing, but the moon had risen directly behind him as if called by his music. It was an enormous orange circle and the flute player stood in the middle while he danced and played. "I've never seen anything like it! It's huge!" said Brian in disbelief. "Why would it be so big here?"

"More magic," she laughed.

Slowly the light of the moon became bright white, and the musician became a dark silhouette that danced to the whimsical music he made for the heavens. "It is magic," smiled Brian. He looked back to Callie and found that the moon-light sparkled in her eyes.

Dim footlights of the stage closest to them turned on and a curtain was drawn back. Frozen in position with bent arms and bowed legs were Siamese dancers wearing bright costumes and pointed hats that looked like the spiral towers of a temple. The exotic sound of Thai music began from alongside the stage, and in perfect unison the dancers came to life and moved together in seductive rhythm. The dance was like a walking ballet, and it told a story. Through the corner of his eye, he noticed a group of people sitting down, and Callie put a hand on his leg. Looking in their direction, he watched the women in the group take their places. They were Eurasian and absolutely gorgeous. One of them then noticed Brian and smiled, but before he could return the gesture Callie squeezed his leg and her fingernails dug in. The woman looked up to the stage and then glanced back to Brian still smiling.

Many of the other stages were now active. On one, two men performed a sword duel. Light flashed off the blades as the dancers acted out a fierce battle that was as graceful as the women's seductive moves on the first stage. On another there was a magic show that involved fiery explosions. The Chinese lanterns were now colorful bright dots in the night, but the real intrigue lay at the top of the knoll. The flute player had been joined by other musicians, and although Brian could no longer hear them, he could imagine their sound as they danced in the moonlight. Callie watched the show in front of her, but Brian watched

the sparks from the fires on the knoll. Shadows
drifted about the flames and called to him in whispers
of smoke. Flares of orange light lashed out at the
night and lit mysterious Asian faces. The park was
festive, but there was magic on the knoll.

Unable to wait any longer, Brian took Callie
by the hand and led her up the hill. As they were
reaching the crest, Brian looked back over his
shoulder. The stages were puddles of white light and
those upon them were marionettes worked by strings
hidden in the dark. The music from the stage could be
heard, but now the flute player and his companions
controlled the night air. Off to the left the large
shadows of the elephants stood quietly. With the next
step Brian and Callie could see the tips of jumping
flames and then the fire and everyone that was around
it. With the glow revealing Brian and Callie's
presence and reflecting off their white faces, a
hesitation traced through the air and mixed with the
sweet smell of burning opium. The music and
dancing continued, but the elders that had been
singing were not as loud and watched the newcomers
suspiciously. Brian looked at Callie and hoped that
she was about to say something to relax their hosts
and to save the moment, but before she could a man in
an orange robe started towards them.

"*S'bai dee roo?*" called the man as he stepped
around the last of the elders. It was a young monk,
and he smiled happily at them and seemed pleased
that they were there. Both Brian and Callie pressed
the palms of their hands together and nodded a bow.
"*S'bai dee, Lop kum,*" they answered at the same time.

"American?"

"Yes," Brian announced happily. The timidity
of the celebrants had disappeared with the monk's
acknowledgment.

"Good, I talk some American. Come sit."
Brian and Callie walked with the monk towards
another fire. "I see you at the temple today."

"Yes," Callie answered.

"I wanted my husband to see Doi Suthep at
dawn." The use of the term husband caused Brian to
glance at Callie. Acting as if she hadn't noticed his
reaction, Callie didn't return the glance, but she
couldn't keep from smiling.

"That when it meant to be seen," nodded the
monk. The monk turned his attention to Brian. "Have
seen many of our holy grounds?"

"Actually no." Brian felt self-conscious. "I'm
sure they're all as beautiful."

The monk gave him a puzzled look.

They had reached a group of people sitting in
a circle, and the monk extended an open palm.
"Please take with us ..."

Callie interrupted with a sudden burst of Thai,
and the monk relaxed into his own language. He
began nodding his head and laughing with Callie. The
monk looked at Brian with a smile. "Please no be
offended by my smile." The monk was sincere as if
addressing an important problem.

"Of course not!" Brian laughed and touched
the monk's shoulder. The monk liked the friendly
gesture and Brian instantly liked the young holy man.

"I no finding fault. You honored our temple,
for it glowed with the light of affection and yearning.
I smiled, for as you so looked at our temple your wife
looked upon you." Brian turned to Callie in surprise
and found that the flames flashed upon her face.

"It is a wonderful thing," the monk spoke
slowly and carefully so as to pronounce the word
correctly. "It is Buddha's most precious gift for a man

and woman to take from one another. Through affection he remains with us."

"Have you been in the monastery long?" asked Callie, with the ring of embarrassment in her voice.

"For less than one year. I hope to take the vows of priesthood at *Doi Suthep* and to remain in these hills with these people." The monk looked around the circle. "I have been a poor host." Happily he began to name each person in the circle and as he did each nodded and smiled. Then he asked their names and the process began again. One of the young men in the circle handed both of them a wooden bowl with a muddy liquid in it. Brian looked at Callie with no idea of what was expected of him. He wasn't sure if the bowl was for drinking or washing.

"It's a drink for the festival," the monk explained. "The hill people make it from wood."

"Wood?" Brian glanced at Callie and then back to the monk. "You mean like worm wood?"

The monk didn't understand and looked at Callie.

"It's an alcohol, Darling."

In front of everyone except the monk, there was a bowl, and the absence of one made Brian hesitate.

"As a monk and future priest I cannot drink this spirit. Meo are devout in many ways but they make the drink." Brian reluctantly raised the bowl and drank from it. The liquid burned as he swallowed, but the terrible taste he expected was not there. The faces around the fire were pleased with the acceptance of their generosity. Brian held out the remaining bottle of rice wine, and it was graciously accepted, but tested with the same doubt he had shown.

A few feet from the fire, there was a sleeping shelter which was really nothing more than a thatched roof to use in case of rain. From the roof hung several cross bows and tubes filled with short arrows. The Meo hill tribesmen were hunters and their weapons were proudly displayed. Working as an interpreter, the monk asked questions about the capital and what life in Bangkok was like. The eyes of the young mountain people anchored into Brian and Callie as they listened in disbelief. The simplest things amazed them, and they looked at one another with puzzled expressions. They were not interested in the war, and Brian avoided the subject.

"You must understand," said the monk, "that coming to this festival is the closest most of these people will ever come to the world outside. They are born, raised and die in these mountains. The life beyond is strange to them."

"I'm sure it seems no more exotic to them than they appear to me," answered Brian.

"Many of them have only heard of Westerners. You are the first and last some will ever see. They live separately from the rest of the country and follow their own traditions and customs."

Callie touched Brian's arm and leaned toward him. "One of the high points in their lives is coming to the festival and seeing people from the city."

"Then why do they stay up here? Why don't they go into the market or at least down to the park at night?"

Callie and the monk looked at one another, both with faint-hearted smiles. "There are several reasons for the festival," began the monk. "The people below have come for their own reasons and they look upon the hill tribes as outsiders."

"Even here there is prejudice," added Callie. "The hill tribes are generally thought of as backwards and ignorant,"

The monk nodded. "Our country is small and made up of many differences. Meos wish only to be left alone to live as they always have. But, come! Tonight is joyous, and there are things for you to see."

With the monk leading them, they moved in between the fires, listening to the elders sing while the young danced and whirled to the music. The fact that Westerners were among them was its own delight and reason for keeping the bowls filled. The expectation in the air intensified with the start of every new song. The hill tribesmen were building up to something, and although Brian didn't know what it was they happily insisted on him being a part of it and dragged him into their dances to laugh and sing. Callie and the monk avoided being so caught up and remained on the edge of the fires where they talked in serious tones until Brian finally escaped from the heartbeat of the encampment and joined them out off breath.

"You've found a new profession," Callie laughed.

"It must be the altitude," panted Brian. "Or this mud." Brian glanced at his empty cup. "This stuff is strong." Someone surprisingly appeared but only paused long enough to fill his cup before disappearing into the crowd.

"We have fortune told," exclaimed the monk as he led them towards another fire. Around its glow a group of old men sat watching the dancers. The monk introduced Brian and Callie to them, and when it was explained that they were Americans, the old men's eyes twinkled with interest. There was one ancient man that the rest showed respect to, and when the monk used the old man's name there was a title at the end. Brian wasn't sure, but he believed the old man was a shaman of some sort. The monk touched Brian to indicate he should sit down, and when he did, Brian's bowl was topped off again. Those around the old man listened intently as he asked Brian questions in broken English. The elder was proud of the fact that he could speak the foreign language, and although it was difficult to understand him, Brian tried to act as if the old man used it perfectly. He was most interested in Bangkok but wanted to know about the war. The old man listened with a serious expression as Brian spoke. Callie and the monk had stepped aside to finish whatever it was they had been discussing. The old man picked up a bamboo tube that was filled with sticks, and after shaking it, he dumped them on the ground. All those around the circle craned forward to see how the sticks had fallen. The music was building to its conclusion, and those that waited for the old man's prediction seemed anxious. The old man looked up and stared at Brian for a long, uncomfortable moment. Slowly, he explained that the sticks can sometimes be wrong and that nothing was infallible. Then he told Brian that he would find many successes in his life, and pleasure, but not pleasure alone. The sticks foretold of darkness which could mean danger.

The music abruptly stopped, and then the flute player that had called out the moon hit a single high note that he held for a long time. Everyone in the encampment came to their feet and Callie was quickly at Brian's side. Without asking any questions, Brian moved with the flow of people to the edge of the forest where the hill tribesmen lit torches. The rest of the musicians broke into a melody that was mellow and beckoning, and the torches formed a line of swaying singing people. Brian anxiously felt as though they kept something from his Western eyes, hidden in the darkness beyond the torches' glow. Callie put her arm through his, and the world outside of that place was as far away as the moon and much less important. "What's this about?" he asked looking at Callie.

"They're about to search for the Camburin flower." She pulled up against him. "Once a year, on the night of the big moon, the Camburin flower blooms in the forest. If you find it and hold it in your hand without crushing its petals it's a panacea to life. You will live happy and healthy, and death will be allowed to come for you only in your sleep. The dust from the petals gives the holder protection and perfection in his life and true happiness."

"You sound like you believe in this," whispered Brian.

"Look around you." The expressions of those around them were soft and hopeful. "Even if a Camburin flower is never found it does exist, at least for this night in their faces. Tonight nothing can harm them, not poverty, not war; they're absolutely safe and content." Brian looked at her face shadowed in the torchlight and found all the mystery of the festival. The melody of the song slowed and then became more of a hum. The old shaman was standing with his back to the forest until he was satisfied that the people were ready. Then he turned and started into the trees. Callie pulled Brian's arm to tell him not to follow as the line of torches moved away from them. The monk stopped and looked back at them in expectation. "We've taken enough from these people," said Callie. An affectionate smile spread across the monk's face and he stepped back to them and placed a hand on each of their shoulders. "May Buddha bless this night, this place, and the two of you." He turned and set out to join his people.

Brian and Callie had watched the torches disappear one by one before walking down the knoll. Although the festival below was still being celebrated, it seemed unimportant, as they both thought of the search that was taking place in the forest, so they avoided it by taking a path along the edge of the park. The park was lined with trees which were blooming tiny pink and white blossoms that floated silently to the ground. When they were nearly to the hotel, the path crossed a small, wooden bridge. They stopped midway across it and looked back at the festival. A string of Chinese lanterns spanned over the bridge, and Callie turned Brian so that the light was in his face. Some of the blossoms had caught in her hair and delicately rested there as if placed by hand. Thinking that there must also be blossoms in his hair, he raised a hand to brush them away.

"Don't," Callie caught his hand. "Leave them." She paused and studied him with an amazed and happy gaze. "You're beautiful," she barely whispered.

Brian quietly laughed. "Men aren't beautiful." Her eyes moved about his face and hair, and then she gently reached up and touched one of the blossoms. "You are." With the touch she all of a sudden looked worried. "You'll always love me, won't you, Darling?"

"Of course I will. You don't need to worry about that."

"People say that at first, but sometimes they stop. I've seen it happen."

"It won't happen to us."

"We won't let it happen, will we," She insisted.

"No."

"Oh, that's right darling. Let's be wonderfully different! I couldn't bear it if you did stop! But if you do, you'll tell me, won't you?"

"I never will."

"But if you do."

"Yes, I'll tell you."

"Hiding things from each other is terrible. It puts things between you."

"We won't do that."

She watched him for a moment and then stepped between his arms. "I don't want you to ever stop. Just don't stop."

"I promise," he said.

"You can't promise that. No one can." Her expression changed and balanced between fear and pain. "Do you love me?"

"Of course I do."

"Then come with me!" She turned to lead him off.

Brian pulled her back. "Where are you going?"

"Please! If you love me, come with me. I can't explain."

Her desperation outweighed Brian's hesitation and he allowed her to lead him off.

Callie nervously guided him back to the monastery. Once there, she took him to the temple.

"We have to remove our shoes."

Brian did as she requested and they stepped through the door. Slowly, the lights ahead of them took shape and appeared to be flickering candles. There were large round pillars in front of them that rose towards the roof and disappeared into the darkness.

"It's so dark I can't see yet."

"Just don't let go of my hand," she whispered. As they approached the pillars, the sweet smell of burning incense and the sound of muffled chanting drifted about them. When they reached the pillars, Callie turned and guided them across the floor. Looking through the spaces between the pillars, Brian could see that the floor dropped away to a lower level. Covering the floor was well over a hundred monks. Their knees bent under them, and their holy foreheads lowered to the ground. When a certain tone of the chant was hit, their orange-robed backs would rise in unison. The chant would continue until a different note bent their backs down. Above them, long chords dropped out of the darkness and cradled pots of burning oil. On the altar a two-story, golden figure of a smiling Buddha sat watching over the ritual. Around the Buddha were hundreds of tiny candles and piles of countless flowers. On each side of the deity facing one another were two smaller gold Buddhas, and these had the palms of their hands pressed together in prayer. The candlelight hung about the statutes in an orange and iridescent glow. Callie turned again to carefully maneuver down three steps onto the main floor. Hugging the wall they made their way to the front and sat down on their knees in front of the altar. A humming note was struck and the monks rose. Across the floor, one of the monks looked up and was surprised to see them. He was young and willowy with long pointed eyebrows. He smiled and continued his chant. Callie placed her palms together and gave the monk a graceful bow. Awkwardly, Brian copied her, and when he rose the young monk's smile became wide and warm. The chanting faces echoed mystery and reverence off the walls to swirl and blend together in the darkness over Brian's head. The chants came in waves, and like the ocean, its underlying power was crowned by delicate but frenzied foam. He turned to Callie and found that an aura of orange candlelight surrounded her white face. The dark sanctity of her eyes caressed him, and for the first time in his life he was home. Callie held her hand out in front of her towards the Buddha and placed his hand on top of hers. Then taking a flower lei from her neck, she tied their wrists together.

"I will never leave you, Brian. I will always love you and belong to you." Her voice was a gentle whisper. "We could be no more married, if you can say the same."

For a moment Brian could only watch her face with the candlelight dancing in her eyes. Then he gently repeated the vow.

CHAPTER SEVENTEEN

When Brian and Callie returned to Bangkok, they found the city tense with the rumor of war and the expectations of invasion. It was not the Khmer Rouge the Thais feared but the North Vietnamese. Thailand had backed the U.S. and allowed bombers to fly from its airbases to attack the North. Now the air was filled with the fear of retribution.

It was never openly spoken of, but it was common knowledge that the refugee camps along the border were becoming enclaves for modern day war lords. Officers that had deserted from the government forces of Cambodia had crossed into Thailand and found that the Thai government was willing to remain silent and share authority of the camps with men that could organize and control the masses. It was rumored that the camps were becoming training grounds for a new group called Khmer Serei, and their professed ambition was to liberate Cambodia of all Khmer Rouge. An ongoing civil war was promised as the country of Cambodia slipped deeper into the darkness.

Sheldon was sure that any noble or patriotic image of a Khmer Serei was superficial, and that the camps were nothing more than pest holes for smugglers and black marketers. The people in the camps were chips in a corrupt game. The International Red Cross and other humanitarian organizations which supplied food or medical provisions to the camps did so according to the number of refugees each held. No one spoke of it publicly, but it was rumored that very little of the supplies were used in the camps. Instead they formed a stock pile of goods to be sold on the black market throughout Asia. The world was uninterested in the human side of the war. Commerce and military support were the issues, not the people that made it possible for the corruption in the camps to exist. Like unwanted relatives they were provided for, but not cared about.

Brian's story on the festival had not been picked up by one paper in the States, but it had been received well by the English language papers in Asia. The Bangkok Post had heralded it as an inspired report that captured the heart of old Siam. For Brian, Chiangmai had put something in perspective. There would inevitably be wars and hunger, but what he cared about was himself and Callie. To get caught up in the troubles of others was foolish. It was all too big and cumbersome to do anything about. The important thing was not to be swept away by things you could not change. He was happy with Callie.

Callie's trips into the provinces had been restricted to the northwest towards the Burma border. He was lonely when she was gone, but as long as she stayed away from Cambodia, she would be safe. Anymore, it seemed as though they had very little time alone, as friends of hers were constantly showing up or telephoning. The government's paranoia had caused it to push the cultural bureau's work. The more the peasants saw the government trying to help them, the less likely the spirit of revolution would cross over the border with the refugees. It was plastic politics and a nuisance because it took her away from him, but it was a sign of the nervous times.

Brian came into the office late and milled about drinking coffee. With the air evacuation from the Cambodian capital underway, one could expect a story at the International Airport, and Brian was on his way there, but first he wanted to arrange a dinner with Sheldon and the Prince. Callie was going to be at the cultural bureau late, and he wasn't in the mood to spend the evening alone.

He was about to pour another cup of coffee when one of the Thai staff rushed up to Brian. She was Sheldon's personal secretary and treated everyone, including Brian, as subordinates, but this time she looked nervous as she approached.

"Mr. Brian, no one else here. You take call!"

"What call?"

"Man from Cambodia!"

"Cambodia! Who?"

She grabbed Brian by the arm. "You come, take call, no one else here."

"Okay, okay." Brian followed after her.

"You come!" she demanded, as she pulled him towards the telephone. Brian was sure it was a mistake as telephone communication with Cambodia was nearly impossible. Undoubtedly, it was someone that had mentioned the country but was certainly not calling from there. With an explosion of nerves, she thrust the receiver into Brian's face. "Godfrey!"

"What!" Brian exclaimed, grabbing the receiver.

"Hello!"

"Hello, this is Godfrey." It was a bad connection, and the voice cutting through the static was hollow. "Listen, you're evidently the only American there, so take this message and make certain Sheldon gets it."

"Right," exclaimed Brian.

"Only Sheldon."

"I understand."

"Uraiwan dead. No lead as to crossings...."

"Wait, wait. Let me get a pencil." Throwing open a desk drawer, Brian slapped a pad of paper to the desk and began writing. "All right, go on."

"I am headed for P. Penh. Estimate twenty days before complete collapse. Have you got all that?"

"Yes, are you giving up on the crossings?"

"What?"

"Are you giving up on the crossings?" Brian yelled into the receiver. There was a long pause on the other end.

"Who is this?"

"Brian. Sheldon's been having me monitor you."

"Brian!" Godfrey interrupted. "I wasn't sure for a moment. I'm looking forward to meeting you. Have you got the message?"

"Yes. How'd you get this call through?"

"Luck and bribery," the voice laughed. "I'm not giving up, but the government's about had it. I want to cover the fall of the capital. Tell Sheldon that the crossings are true, that I've seen one. The story is now on your side of the border, and once the government goes, all hell is going to break loose. Tell Sheldon." The static drowned the voice out.

"What? I couldn't hear you!"

"Tell Sheldon it's only going to get worse. I'll pick up from our side when I leave here."

"Do you need anything?"

"Nothing you could get through. Do you have the message?"

"Yes."

"I have to give up the phone now. There's others waiting."

"Good luck."

"Always." The receiver clicked dead. Brian hung up and finished writing the message out. When he read it through, he was excited. He felt as though he had stumbled into a secret about something important, and it made his blood hot for more. After putting the note on Sheldon's desk, Brian decided not to wait any longer and started for the airport. On his way out the door, Sheldon's secretary hurried after him calling his name.

"You go to American Embassy."

"What for?"

"Students protest."

"They do that all the time. I'm going to the airport." She was trying to be helpful out of gratitude for his assistance with the call, but the students were restless with the times and marched daily.

"No. This story, communist students, this be good story."

She smiled as if telling him a secret. Brian watched her for a moment and decided she knew more about hot leads than anyone in the office. "All right, I'll go there before I go to the airport."

"No!" she took hold of his arm and squeezed. "This where to go." Her eyes were insistent. "This where to go." Her voice was low, and she nodded her head. Brian watched her with the thought that she was saying more than she wanted.

"Are you that sure?" he asked.

She nodded in confidence with raised eye
brows.

Brian caught a cab for the Embassy, telling
himself that if she was wrong, he could go on to the
airport. It would be easy to get a story there as the
evacuees from Phnom Penh were off loaded from
airplanes. They were the fortunate people, the upper
class citizenry of Phnom Penh that could buy or bribe
their way out by air.

The American Embassy was located on the
Boulevard Wit Thayu, but Brian had known the traffic
would be bad so he had the cabby drop him at Soi
Ruam Rudi. The soi circled around the back of the
embassy and made it an easy walk. When he was
directly behind the embassy, he could hear the
protestors chanting and yelling, and it made him pick
up his pace. Located on the soi was the Arab
Embassy, and its staff members were huddled together
on the balcony where they could look over the brick
wall of the American compound and across its garden
to the demonstrators on the far side. The noise was
too loud and the Arabs were too concerned for it to be
just another march. Brian wound up the remaining
film in the camera, and while jogging down the soi,
loaded a fresh roll. Turning the corner onto Wit
Thayu, he ran into a long line of honking cars. The
students had blocked off the boulevard in front of the
embassy and had stopped traffic for blocks. Without
hesitating, he continued to run back up the street
towards the waving signs and chanting. On this side
of the embassy, the brick wall was replaced with a
black wrought iron fence, and as he neared the

protestors, U.S. Marines in battle dress arose on the other side of the fence. With the leather soles of his shoes skidding across the sidewalk and coming to a stop, Brian clicked off two quick shots of a black-faced Marine that looked frightened behind his young grimace.

"Don't go down there!" the Marine called after Brian as he rushed on. So as not to attract any more attention than necessary, he slowed to a fast walk. The drivers of the cars were panicky and looked from side to side with frightened expressions, trying to find a way out of the jam. Now close, the chanting became a violent tide of "U.S. war mongers!" The first car in line timidly beeped its horn, and three protestors exploded onto its hood with pounding fists. Brian could barely hear the whirl of the camera's automatic wind as he fired off shots in rapid succession. He wasn't sure exactly what he was aiming at but focused and pressed. Without stopping he moved into the crowd. Bouncing off the shoulders of the protestors, he snapped off shots as he was carried away in the torrent. With the screams enclosing around him, Brian lowered the camera and looked for high ground. He couldn't see any other journalists; if they were there, they were out on the edge, so he excitedly whirled off more exclusive shots. Forcing his way between the enraged activists, he pushed across the driveway of the embassy and put his back to the brick column of the gate. All at once, the crowd was lifting someone onto the top of the column opposite Brian. Realizing who it was, Brian lowered the camera with a smirk. After all the searching, Chovat was right in front of him. From the perch, he screamed obscenities in both English and Thai at the Marines. In an even angrier burst, he pivoted to the crowd and led them in their chant.

Brian raised the camera and whirled off shots of the radical. "Sheldon will be so happy to see you!" said Brian to himself. Over the top of the crowd, Brian could see the brown uniforms of Thai police waiting behind barricades. Along side them were fire trucks with their hoses unwound and ready to be used against the crowd. Chovat's fury shot sparks into the explosive mass in an effort to ignite a riot. Fumbling with a new roll of film, Brian looked for a way out. Chovat's face wrinkled into a scream, and those closest to him attached the American Eagle emblem attached to the pillar he stood on. Two of the Marines stepped towards the gate but were instantly ordered back into position. The American eagle clung to the bricks and was bent and maimed but would not release.

In a flash, Brian's back was slammed into the corner of the bricks, and hands flashed out of the crowd and wrestled for the camera. Without thinking, he punched at the only pair of eyes he could see in the crowd and they disappeared. Shoving the others out of the way, he started edging along the fence, but before he could slip away, someone in the crowd pushed him sideways into the fence. His shoulder jammed into the iron pickets and he lost his footing. Brian yelled in pain as his shoulder wrenched under his weight. There was a flash of silver from a knife blade, and then a brown hand blocked it before it could strike. From behind him someone pulled Brian to his feet and freed him from the pickets. The man holding the knife had a bloody cut at the corner of one eye from Brian's blow. In shock Brian caught his breath as he recognized the man that had stopped the knife from finding Brian was Chovat. Brian watched in disbelief as the two Thai men bitterly argued. Chovat turned to Brian and stared at him with eyes that oozed hatred like puss from an open sore. "Go, go!" he yelled. The man with the knife reached behind Chovat and shoved his hand into Brian's face. Chovat spun around and slapped the man. Their argument erupted again, but this time in the barrage from Chovat came a word that sounded like the French town of Calais. "Go!" Chovat screamed at Brian. The hands holding Brian released and pushed him forward through the crowd. It was Callie. In Chovat's accent it had sounded different but it was Callie! Brian knew that was what Chovat had said and he was angry. Angry with the repeated question in his mind, why use Callie's name?"

Once Brian was safely out of the crowd, he crossed the street and hurried down to the corner away from the police. Passing a recessed doorway, he stepped into it and leaned with his back against the wall. He tried to convince himself that he was imagining things, but he knew he wasn't. He couldn't accept that Chovat knew Callie, even though he remembered seeing them on the wharf. Angry at himself for not confronting her, he tried to think of an excuse for her. In an instant the poisonous eyes of Chovat had made two things clear to Brian. The first was that Chovat was dangerous, and the second was that Callie and Chovat had a connection. Brian waited, certain that as the crowd continued to work itself into a riot, Chovat would slink from the danger. The crowd burned the American President in effigy, and began to throw beer bottles at the Marines which forced the police into action. With an inflated admiration, Brian watched his young countrymen stand unshaken before the tremendous crowd. He was proud of the Marines and of the tormented eagle that still refused to let go of the embassy wall. At the same moment, the fire hoses were turned on and the police assaulted the crowd. Chovat and three of his followers slipped out of the mass and ran along the fence. Brian didn't follow until they were half a block away and secure enough to stop running. Staying on the opposite side of the street, he dogged them a few blocks into an old section of the city that was lined with warehouses. They met another young Thai and disappeared into one of the buildings. Brian passed the warehouse and stepped into a deserted soi that was catty-corner from the building. On the warehouse's wall was a metal sign with the Thai government symbol. It would soon be dark and that meant the camera would be useless. He was too far away to use a flash, and if he did he would give away his position, so there could be no photos. He sat down with his back against the wall and waited for something to happen. There were windows just above the truck doors of the warehouse, and in his impatience Brian tried to figure out a way to reach them without being seen. Through the windows, he could see the green, canvas tops of large trucks. He sat alone with the consuming question of how Callie and Chovat were connected. He couldn't imagine what possible excuse there could be.

After Brian had been there for over an hour, the sound of an approaching car brought him to his feet. A taxi pulled up in front of the warehouse and stopped facing Brian. The figures in the cab went through the motions of paying the driver, and then the door closest to the warehouse opened. Brian's heart stopped as he disbelievingly watched the tall figure of the Prince step from the vehicle. The Prince waited by the car door, and Brian heard himself mumble "No."

Desperation swelled in his chest and then crashed as Callie stepped from the car. Watching her,

Brian felt empty and alone, and then defiantly he stepped out into the street. Pushing the door closed, the Prince looked up and saw him. He took hold of Callie's arm while saying something, and then she looked up in shock. Except for the cab pulling away, the world stood still and they stared at each other with frightened faces. The taxi stopped alongside Brian. Reaching for the door handle, he made himself look away.

"Brian!" Callie called to him.

He ignored her and opened the door.

"Brian!" she screamed in a voice that was breaking up in panic.

"Go!" he ordered as he slammed the door.

CHAPTER EIGHTEEN

Brian went to the Erawan Hotel and sat in the dark bar thinking no one would look for him there. He wanted to get drunk, but he just stared at the glass and tried to sort through the images spinning in his head. She might have been meeting Chovat for an innocent reason, but like a dull ache his self-interrogation often came to the same conclusion. All the phone calls and visits she had been getting had something to do with the hateful young man. He couldn't imagine how to explain it to Sheldon, and then he realized he never could tell him. He was angry at everyone, including himself for not confronting her when he saw her with Chovat on the wharf. How could he have been so stupid?

Then with a great pain, he asked himself if she had lied about loving him. Frustrated, Brian threw a wad of crumbled bills on the table and left the dark bar.

Nomadically, Brian wandered home along the river. What to say and how to say it were insurmountable questions. Maybe she was frightened enough to stay away, and he could simply collect his things and disappear. That was the way to handle it. Just to step out of her life and leave Sheldon and

Godfrey to their own discoveries. Maybe the end of the war would finish the whole thing, and no one would ever know of his stupidity. Maybe no one would ever know how foolish he had been and how easy it had been for her to lie to him. He told himself that it would not benefit him for the deception of the Prince and Callie to be dragged into the light. Yet his anger wanted him to be the one to bring them down.

When he reached their soi, lights from the inside of their apartment lit the balcony. The doors were open and the drapes moved with the breeze. Brian waited for a moment, but no one came out onto the balcony, so he hurried on in the hope that she was not home.

Standing at their door, he hesitated and then unlocked it and stepped in. Callie was sitting in the overstuffed chair that faced the doorway. Her expression was pensive and she stared at him while he slowly closed the door. The click of the latch seemed loud and Brian stood motionless watching her.

"What is it you think you know?" she spoke in a subordinate voice.

"That I'm not nearly as good at this job as I thought." He walked into the room and sat on the couch across from her. "That what we've been looking for has been in my bed the entire time. What I don't know is just why you're involved. But I know you are."

Callie timidly looked down. "Are you asking me as a reporter or as my lover?"

"Damn it, don't play that on me! I'm asking! The man you're supposed to love."

"I do. I do love you, Brian. That has nothing to do with it."

Brian took a deep breath and told himself to calm down. "It has everything to do with it. Isn't that why the Prince introduced us? Tell me the truth for once! I'm not going to Sheldon. I want to know for myself."

Callie looked ashamed and glanced away.

"Tell me! It's my life you've been playing with! I can't tell anyone without destroying my own career. You're safe!"

She watched him with frightened eyes. "Sheldon never talked about Godfrey, in detail in front of the Prince, at least not until you started asking questions. When he assigned you to monitor Godfrey the Prince had the idea that we should meet." Brian sighed a heartless laugh and then the room was silent.

"I always thought he was harmless, a fool. It seems he's anything but," said Brian weakly.

"Try to understand."

"Understand!" demanded Brian. "What the hell am I supposed to understand? That you've used me and lied to me. That someone who's supposed to be my friend isn't. That the woman who's supposed to love me doesn't. It's not hard to understand!"

"I told you it has nothing to do with how I feel about you." She moved to the couch and sat alongside him. "Remember when the Prince introduced us? Remember how after we talked I started to leave? There was something about you that made me want to run. I didn't want to do it to you." She reached out to touch his face. "I ..."

"Right!" Brian stood up before she could touch him and walked to the balcony doors. "But you stopped yourself, and you've done nothing since then but make sure you had me." He turned to her. "That wasn't necessary, not to the point you brought it."

"Believe me I know how you feel." She began to cry. "I'm sorry. I didn't mean for this to happen. Believe me I know how you feel."

"No you don't, people say that, but you don't know!" He stepped towards her. He wanted to grab her and shake the betrayal from her. To pull the lies out and crush them beneath his feet. "I never knew enough to help you! Do you realize what you have done for nothing?!"

"You have a right to be angry, but know what you're angry about." She stood up. "Is it because I've kept something from you or is it because you don't believe I love you? You have to ask yourself that because they are two different things!"

"If you loved me, why didn't you tell me? Why didn't you come to me?!"

Callie didn't speak and her silence hurt. Brian let out a deep breath and turned to the window. He waved his arm through the drapes and looked out across the river. "Why do I feel that I've done something wrong?"

"You haven't," she answered quietly.

"Damn it, I know that!" he exclaimed. "You're the one that has lied and cheated! You're the one that's to blame!" He paused and stared at her in anger while he told himself to calm down. "You still haven't told me how you're involved, or exactly what it is you're involved in."

The room remained silent and that in itself hurt. "You may not trust me, but you owe me at least that!" He demanded.

"I can supply the transportation."

Brian nodded with a quiet but sarcastic chuckle. "The bureau's trucks." He said aloud to himself. A boat with blue lights was on the river. "Damn it!" He lashed out at himself in frustration. "I should have known. I should have sensed it. It's perfect. It's so simple that it's perfect! You have all the necessary papers to travel freely, access to trucks, and if you were stopped you'd have a built-in alibi. Hell, the government put you out there!" Feeling depressed he paused. "You really are what Godfrey's been looking for." He let the drapes fall and turned to her. "All those trips to the provinces, you haven't been on the Burma border?"

"No," she said quietly.

"And lately all those phone calls and visitors."

"They're involved."

Brian nodded, "And you've been using any information I had?"

"Yes." She sounded insecure and paused. "A newspaper story would have destroyed everything." She stepped towards him to offer an explanation. "At the beginning we thought it would be easier to learn things through you. What town Godfrey was in, the name of his sources. It was just to keep us safe. It was never that I was to get personally involved with you. That just happened, and I've been terrified you would find out! You haven't betrayed anything. As it turned out you didn't know enough to help us! You don't have to feel used; I was with you because I love you!"

Brian felt embarrassed and ashamed. The words, "You didn't know enough to help." rang in his ears, and it made him feel only more foolish. Brian all of a sudden felt tired and walked over and sat down in one of the chairs. He rubbed his forehead with the palm of his hand.

"What do you intend to do?" she said in a fragile voice.

"What can I do? Break a story that could put you in prison."

"I meant about us."

Brian rested his head back against the chair, and his hand slid over his mouth. He stared at her for a moment and then dropped his hand. "I came for my things. I thought you'd still be out, and we could avoid any unpleasantness."

"You can't do that. You're not going to throw us away!" Her voice cracked but her expression was firm. "I won't let you!"

"You've already thrown it away! You used me!" He stood up and angrily moved to her.

"How, by helping people that would die otherwise?"

"Thousands are coming across every day." He insisted. His anger tightened his muscles and demanded vengeance.

"And thousands more are dying." She stood up in front of him with a committed voice and expression.

He wanted her to beg his forgiveness. "I don't care about anyone right now but me and you!" He angrily pointed back and forth between them. "The two of us, not the world."

"You don't mean that."

"The hell I don't!"

"They're victims, Brian, without us."

"The whole damn world is a victim. The Cambodians, the Khmer Rouge, the North Vietnamese, the South Vietnamese, the Americans. They've done nothing but victimize each other, and for what! A political scrap!" Brian bitterly shook his head, "Even so we didn't have to be victims, we could have made it!" His anger exploded, "But you were nothing better than a whore!" The accusation erupted from Brian with pleasure. He wanted to hurt her, to crush her in his hands. He grabbed her by her shoulders and shook her hard. "What have you done to us!" He pushed her away. For a moment he just stared at her. "You made us both victims."

The strength in Callie's face crumbled and left her looking small and alone. She sat and stared at the floor. When she finally looked up, her expression was composed, but she looked lost.

"We only lose if you let us. There's no doubt that you should be angry, but I don't think you truly doubt my love. I was deceitful, and I would have gone on being. I cared for you too much to risk telling you. Maybe that's wrong but look at what's happening! At first I told myself that you'd be reassigned and we would end. We're not talking about me cheating on you. I was involved in this long before we met, and it's important, Brian!" She paused. "The funny thing is that we probably never would have met if I hadn't been." Callie glanced away, "If I really believed you'd leave me, I'd go out of my mind."

"Nothing's that simple anymore."

"Don't hang on to principles that don't belong here. Let go, please!"

"We're not talking about just refugees. If we were, it would be easier for me to accept!" shouted Brian. "The people you're with are radicals. They are capable of anything, and if you think they're ..."

"I don't know what they've done, and neither do you," she interrupted. "The only thing worth talking about is the lives that are being saved." Callie's face lit up with insistence. "It doesn't make any difference if others condemn me, but you mustn't. You're passing judgment without seeing them! No one will help them. The world doesn't even acknowledge them. What we manage is only a trickle, but everyone we save is one more! One more that won't have his life swept away like trash, one more that has a chance to hide in a crowd and continue living. What's wrong with that?"

"If you believe there's nothing wrong with it, why didn't you tell me?!"

"I was afraid! I was afraid of this. I've wanted to. God how I've wanted to. In Chiangmai the monk told me I had to but I ..."

"The monk?" Brian interrupted in disbelief. "Don't tell me!"

Callie lost heart and settled back. "We asked him to help us." She looked lost and watched him with an expression that waited for the worst. "Stay Brian. Help me," she asked quietly.

He was tired and couldn't think straight and looking at her only confused him. Part of him wanted to storm out, but the rest of him wanted to sleep, to turn off his mind and pretend he didn't know. "What do you expect from me?" he asked in a tired voice.

"Only to be here." She tried to smile.

Brian let out a deep breath and watched the moving drapes. When he looked back, her expression held hope. "Let go, Callie. It would be better for everyone."

With an intense stare, she slowly shook her head. "I can't," she whispered.

"And I can't give up everything I believe in. Principles can't be worn like a coat; they can't be taken on and off! If I stayed we'd both lose. We would destroy each other."

The strength in Brian's voice tore at Callie, and all hope disappeared from her face. The desperation in her eyes made him resent her. The resentment built into guilt and the guilt made him resent her even more. "You caused this, not me!"

"Is that what it's come down to Brian, which one of us is at fault? I didn't think one of us could be without the other."

He stared at her not knowing what to say. He wanted to remain angry, but he felt it fading and leaving only depression.

"Let it alone for tonight." She sat very still and barely spoke above a whisper. "Stay with me tonight."

There was an instant when he wanted to say yes, and then the impulse turned his anger and frustration in on him. "What's going to change? What's going to be different in the morning? We'll wake up the same people with the same problem, only it will be harder!"

"For who?" she exploded. "Harder for you to stay angry, harder for you to blind yourself!" She wanted to cry but forced it down. "I don't deserve that!"

"Deserve! After what you've done!"

"Yes! I don't deserve to be left like some bar girl you've finished with." There was nothing left to hold her together, and like a dry twig, her strength snapped and she broke apart. "Not like that. Don't leave me like that. I feel cheap enough."

Unexpectedly, there wasn't any satisfaction in seeing her hurt. It only caused him more pain. He wanted out; he wanted to quietly leave and forget her, but it was too complicated to be that easy. They had been too close and he had loved her too much. If he hadn't, he might have seen what was happening before it was too late. Brian told himself to be strong, that she had brought it on herself.

"All right! It's over. It's done. You're finished with it no matter what else happens. You're through with all this!"

"Brian, please," she said, desperately trying to control herself. Wiping her eyes she caught her breath. "Help me."

"I am. You're out of this. They've taken advantage of you, but it's finished! You didn't realize what they were. You were foolish and they used you!"

"You're not thinking. You're letting your feelings and pride get in the way," she pled.

"I'm giving us a clean chance. They're dangerous and you're done with them."

"People are people! How many times do I have to say it? All the titles you put on them can't change that."

"Who do you think you're dealing with? You're so damn naïve!"

"No, you don't understand." She stepped forward with commitment. "What we're doing is worthwhile; it's the most worthwhile thing you could ever do. We need you."

"You don't seem to understand," he demanded. "I'm not becoming involved. You're getting out!" he shouted.

"Brian, too many people are coming across the border for Thailand to handle it alone. The United Stated will have to get involved."

"Are you crazy?! I'm trying to put this behind us. I'm sure you thought you were doing the right thing, but it's over!"

She stared at him and then began to glance around the room. Each time her eyes came back, they held a little more strength. She could see he was on the edge, but to back away from his one demand was unthinkable. "Brian, think about what you're doing, what you're saying."

He controlled himself and spoke quietly. "There's no other way." He stepped towards her. "Walk away from it. You've done enough!"

"I won't ever ask you about Godfrey again. We'll find another way. The Prince can get the information from Sheldon, or we'll do something else." Abruptly Callie stopped herself. The futility of either persuading the other stepped between them like a cruel and silent stranger. Brian wanted to stop it, but they had come too far.

"You're in it too deep," he heard himself say. "You won't stop."

"You could change. Help me," she begged.

"No," Brian said trying to smile. "I couldn't." Reluctantly, and with the last hope of shaking her free of him, he removed the door key from his pocket. With a click that seemed to echo across the room, he placed it on the table nearest him. Her eyes darted to the key and then back to his. "I'll send for my things."

She nodded with a quiver and swallowed sharply.

CHAPTER NINTEEN

The next day Brian was exhausted. He had spent the night at the Erawan Hotel, and he hadn't been able to sleep. Without Callie next to him, the bed had been terribly empty. Unsuccessfully, he had tried to convince himself he would be fine without her and that he was lucky it was over. Finally, he had found some consolation in the thought that she must have been feeling even worse than he. On the way to the office, his mood changed a dozen times. First he was hurt, then angry with her, then angry with himself, but with each change, the one constant was his hatred for Chovat and the Prince. Somehow they must have forced Callie to become involved, and then her own conscious mislead her.

Throughout the morning, Brian had accomplished nothing and everyone including Sheldon kept their distance. He kept thinking that at any moment she would call or walk through the door, that she would plead for another chance and admit that he was right. Continuously he glanced at the clock, and each time that he did his mood became darker.

Sheldon skirted the corner of Brian's desk and dropped the photographs of the embassy under siege. Brian unenthusiastically glanced at the black and white proofs. "Newspapers", he said aloud in a disgusted and tired voice.

In the early morning hours, the heaviest rocket attack yet had been launched against Phnom Penh. Everyone in the office was rushing reports and radio photos between their desks. Hundreds had died, and the city had nearly collapsed under the surprise attack. Watching Sheldon, Brian felt ashamed at how easily he had been made a fool of by Callie. Again he looked up at the clock and seeing that it was noon he told himself to give up. She wasn't coming.

"That's enough!" He stood up and slammed his chair to the desk. With a defiant stride Brian maneuvered between those rushing away from Sheldon. "I want to talk to you," he demanded.

Sheldon kept working. "Just a second."

"Now!" Brian insisted. Sheldon looked up, too surprised to be angry. "I've had it. Either send me back to the States or reassign me."

Sheldon stared at Brian. "Well, this isn't the way to ask," he smirked. "Trouble in love land?"

"I'm not asking. One way or the other I don't care if it's Vietnam, Cambodia, or the States, but do it!" Brian turned and started for the door.

"Wait a God damned minute!" Sheldon called after him.

Brian spun around. "I'm on an airplane tomorrow, any direction you want to send me, but you send me!"

Everyone was watching, but Brian didn't pay any attention and stormed out. He was determined to be free of the whole damned thing. He was determined to be free of her.

At 4:00 in the afternoon, Tigers was practically empty, so Brian sat at one of the large tables by himself. The windows were at his back, but the blinds were drawn and the air conditioner was on high. At the bar sat three retired servicemen. Being away from the office helped, and he didn't feel so foolish when he was away from Sheldon. It was quiet but he was sure that before long the servicemen would begin to recount their brilliant and devoted careers. Their stories were consistently the same and eventually ended in drunken agreement that the military had given each of them a raw deal over some trivial infraction. Even though they were quiet now, Brian found them irritating, for he knew they would soon be drunk and loud.

There weren't any bar girls or waitresses working so the bartender kept an eye on Brian's glass, and when it was half-empty, he would automatically pour another beer and deliver it with toothless smile. Brian told himself that it was now out of his hands. Callie forced it and there was nothing he could do but drink and forget the entire matter. He consoled himself with the knowledge that he would never be used by anyone again. He was too smart for that now. No one would ever be able to use him again.

By the time the sunlight, slipping through the cracks in the blinds, turned to late afternoon gold the bar had filled up. The servicemen had been joined by other noisy patrons, and some of them glanced jealously at Brian's large table. He was beginning to feel the effects of the bartender's personal care and was about to waive him over for a refill when the door opened and Sheldon stepped in. Brian took a large drink from his beer and waited to be noticed. "Outstanding," he said aloud to himself. Sheldon was going to have a lot to say, and there was no point in Brian waving for his attention. When Sheldon finally spotted Brian and started for the table, Brian realized the Prince was with Sheldon. Moving towards the table, the Prince anxiously watched Brian from over Sheldon's shoulder.

"You want to tell me what this is all about?" demanded Sheldon as he and the Prince sat down.

"I'm getting out," said Brian staring at the Prince. "And just how are you doing Prince?" said Brian sarcastically.

"I ought to fire you and leave you stranded. It's what you deserve, you arrogant ass," interrupted Sheldon.

"Then do it." Brian couldn't take his eyes off the Prince.

"Can you believe this stupid son-of-a-bitch?! He doesn't appreciate a damn thing. When I was his age, I did what I was told and respected the authority of the people running things."

"Yeah, like becoming a farmer." Brian finished the last of his beer.

"What did you say?!" Sheldon was angry. "You're just looking for trouble."

"He didn't mean it the way it sounded." The Prince leaned into the table. "Let's have a cocktail and calm down."

Sheldon glanced back and forth between them, his steel blue eyes wanted a piece of Brian. He stood up. "You better get a hold of yourself." He turned and started toward the bar to order. All at once, the Prince leaned closer to Brian. "We've things to settle."

"I don't have anything to say to you, and you don't have anything I want to hear."

The charade was over and with a confident expression the Prince watched him with determined eyes. "You're going to listen," he said firmly.

Sheldon glanced back at them. Brian waited until he was farther away. "I don't want you here, so don't push me. You'll regret it. Believe me!"

"We need your help."

"Go to hell!"

"I don't think you realize."

"Don't push it!"

The Prince leaned back and glanced around the room. The light from outside was fading. When he turned back he wasn't the same man Brian had been close to. He was desperate. They stared at one another with the Prince searching for an opening and with Brian determined not go give him one.

"Brian, you don't understand."

"No, you don't seem to understand. It doesn't matter. It's done," insisted Brian in a voice meant to end the conversation.

"Of course it matters. What you think of me is unimportant, but she matters, and she could be arrested if you ..."

"I don't believe you're suddenly worried about what happens to her. You've used her! Nothing you say will change that. Not now," interrupted Brian "And don't tell me you're really worried about me putting her in jail! You bastard, the only thing you care about is yourself!" The Prince's expression relaxed which caused Brian to dislike him more. "It's all about you, isn't it?! I couldn't do anything to harm Callie, even if part of me wants to!"

"Then you shouldn't be afraid to listen."

"You son of a bitch, I should kick your Asian ass!"

"You're not thinking about what's at stake. Hundreds of people."

"I know exactly."

The Prince glanced away to check on Sheldon's progress. Following his eyes, Brian watched as Sheldon ordered and joked with the men at the bar. "Have you seen her?" Brian couldn't help asking.

The Prince watched him for a moment and then smiled. 'Yes, early this morning."

"Did she send you? Be honest if that's possible."

"No. When I left her, she had no idea I would see you."

Brian was disappointed. It would have been comforting to think she was trying to reach him. As he thought more about her, his anger grew. "Then Chovat must have put you up to this errand."

The Prince looked at him with a puzzled expression. "What do you mean?"

"Don't hand me that crap. You can go back and tell him that you're all safe. I'm just going to get the hell out of this country. You can have it and everyone in it."

"No one sent me. I came for you on my own, and we don't have much time." Brian glanced at the bar. Sheldon was rolling dice. "You shouldn't be so unreasonable. Try to be a little more understanding. It's no one's fault. There is no one to blame."

"I can think of two...beginning with you."

"Then it's as much your fault," the Prince accused with a raised brow.

"You're damn right it is. I should have seen it happening."

"If you'd been willing to accept what's around you, we could have told you," insisted the Prince.

"I'm sure you would have done that," Brian mocked.

Anger flickered in the Prince's eyes, but he quickly controlled himself. His face took on a curious look. "What are you really angry about? That Callie's involved, or that she kept something from you?" He leaned back in his chair, "or that you weren't cleaver enough to see it?"

Brian's anger rushed through his veins and his arms tingled with the desire to reach across the table. A dice cup slammed to the bar, and Brian turned to see Sheldon lose a round of drinks to the men on the stools. Laughing, Sheldon paid and collected the drinks for the Prince and Brian.

"I just had an idea. Maybe I can work a deal with the government. I'll tell 'em what I know in exchange for Callie's exit visa. Then they could put the rest of you bastards in jail." Brian smiled and finished his beer.

Surprisingly, the Prince's expression remained controlled as he watched Sheldon's approach. When Sheldon was about to the table, the Prince reached out and helped him with the glasses.

"Thanks, old buddy," Sheldon smiled. "Gin and tonic for you, two beers for us, and three shots."

"What are these?" asked Brian as one of the small doses was set in front of him.

"A touch of home." Sheldon wasn't quite so irritated. "Maybe it'll straighten you out."

"He's only homesick. He'll feel better soon," the Prince added and raised the shot to his face and smelled. "What is this?" He was securely back in his performance of the harmless rogue and his mastery of the role made Brian rage.

"Whiskey." Sheldon didn't sit down.

With a weak attempt at a smile, Brian picked up his shot glass.

"American whiskey is too expensive to drink all afternoon." The Prince watched Brian closely.

"We only need a couple," said Sheldon. "You can only take a few of these."

The Prince took a sip and his face instantly distorted as the liquor burned its way down.

"No!" Brian rebuked. "You can't play with it. You have to do it like this." He snapped up his glass and popped it down. His eyes squinted as the whiskey bit into him. The Prince swiftly did the same, but this time his face didn't wrinkle.

"Brian and I were just deciding what he should do," said the Prince.

"It's done!" exclaimed Sheldon. "But understand this! I know what all this is about."

"What are you talking about?" Brian looked at the Prince as Sheldon sat down on the edge of the empty chair. Brian's heart raced with the thought that Sheldon knew about Callie.

"You told me any direction I wanted to send you. Well, you got your wish, big shot, but you better do one hell of a job." Shaking his head Sheldon turned towards the Prince. "It won't be long before he's wishing he was back here drinking with us."

"Where?" Brian anxiously asked.

"Cambodia. I'll send you in on one of the supply planes out of U-tapao. When you arrive at Pochentong Airport go directly to the American Embassy. Don't go wandering around the city. When Godfrey finds you, do exactly as he tells you." Sheldon started to turn to the Prince but hastily looked back. "And you tell him that he has authority to fire you on the spot if you get out of line! And one last thing, I know you must have argued with Ms.

Wonderful, and that's where you found all this bullshit to make demands on me. But don't think you can back out when she makes up with you! No way, buddy boy! You think you can make demands on me because of a tiff with her, you're out of your mind and more importantly, you're out of my hair!"

"That's fine with me," Brian answered with his mind racing through images of the besieged capital. He was out. She was no longer a part of his life, and no one would ever know how stupid he had been.

When he looked across the table the cold eyes of the Prince made him feel guilty and stole from him any feeling of relief. "When do I go?"

"Tomorrow. You're the one who set the time." Sheldon fumbled with his empty shot glass. "That's not bad whiskey."

"I'm not complaining." Brian said as he stared at the Prince. "I'll need to pack," he insisted "and a chance to tell Callie." He would have to go tonight for his things.

Sheldon picked up his beer and took a long drink. Then he paused and smiled at Brian. "I already told her. She stopped by the office. You see, even with your attitude I take care of you. This way, she thinks it's my idea, and it won't be so messy for you."

Brian quickly felt sober. She must have realized he was serious and tried to fix things before something like this could happen. He began to wonder how she was taking the news and stopped listening to Sheldon.

"I hope you find your story in Cambodia." The Prince's voice brought Brian's attention back to the table. His eyes were making a point. "Be careful."

Brian's relief was short lived. The Prince had known before him that Sheldon was sending him, and he had probably told Callie to try and stop him. Brian turned a confident expression to the serious face. "You can bet I will be."

"I doubt it." Sheldon took another long drink which nearly emptied his bottle of beer.

"What's the matter, don't you think I can?" Brian looked at Sheldon. Who knows? Maybe I can break the story about all these crossings from that side of the border."

"I think we should have another of these." Sheldon tapped his shot glass to the table.

"I agree and I'll pay if you'll order," said the Prince as he pulled out neatly folded bills from his pocket.

"Oh no." Brian reached across the table and pushed Sheldon's hand away. He wanted to be alone with the Prince but he wanted to insult him first. "If we're going to do this let's play by the rules we're used to." He tossed out some bills from the small pile he had left on the table. "That's what the Prince is used to, letting other people pay the price." Sheldon gave Brian a strange look and started for the bar without the money. Brian watched him until Sheldon was too far away to hear and then he pounced on the Prince. "You never give up! I know now what you're after. You don't care about me or Callie. You just want me to protect you once I'm there!" The Prince still watched him with confidence. "Well I'm not being used anymore."

The Prince's expression became stern. "I've used our friendship and her feelings for you, but we've had little choice. I didn't find pleasure in it but it was necessary." Brian stared at the Prince and for an instant the strength in the Asian face faltered. "No one pushed anything on her, and whatever I am doesn't justify what you're doing to her."

"What am I doing!" demanded Brian. "I'm not the one who screwed things up."

"She did what she had to; you're a brash young man. No matter how she would have told you, the result would have been the same. You tell yourself you've been betrayed, but Callie was the one that believed in you. She saw you beginning to understand and had faith that you were strong enough to look beyond yourself."

"There is only one question I want answered from you. Are you a communist? Or more importantly is she?"

The Prince laughingly scoffed as if the question were ridiculous. "Would it make you feel better if she was?"

"Answer me!"

"Callie's beliefs are her own. She acts according to her own conscience."

"Answer the question."

"I asked her for help and she agreed. There was never any discussion about her politics. I can tell you that she believes in this." The Prince sipped from his gin and tonic, his eyes searching for a crack in Brian's stern expression. "You'd feel much worse if she'd been anything less than totally committed."

Brian didn't like looking at him and glanced away. "How'd you get involved?"

The Prince hesitated while his eyes watched Brian with distrust. He glanced towards the bar to be sure no one could hear them and then reluctantly his expression gave his answer.

"You?" Brian chuckled insultingly. "No, you're no communist. You're too damned selfish."

"The changes that must come to my country won't be made by revolution, not in the way you mean. It will take much less."

"That doesn't answer my question."

The Prince sipped at his drink. He was deciding how much to say and being careful not to become drunk. "I was asked for help." He ventured a real smile and it made him seem vulnerable.

"I'm sure you were, Comrade." Brian returned the smile with an arrogant grin. "And I bet you came cheap. All that Chovat had to do was buy you a few cocktails and make you feel important. How much did he have to spend before you'd dirty the lives of your friends?" Brian held up his beer to the now intense eyes. "Here's to the Prince, a man who measures friendship by free drinks and does business by bribery and lies." Ever so slightly, the Prince tilted his head back, and his cheek muscles tightened. "Oh, now don't look so noble. You'll drink with anyone who's willing to buy. I've seen you do it enough times."

The Prince sat very still, his eyes now very small and piercing. Brian knew that he had hurt him, and it felt good. Their hatred for each other formed a bridge between their eyes, and Brian remembered the snake pit in the border village.

A light flickered in the eyes of the Prince and a vicious smirk slid across his lips. "Callie is a beautiful woman."

The pleasure disappeared and Brian's hand squeezed around the beer glass. The Prince's expression melted into the stare of an intrusive stranger and made Brian twinge with self-consciousness.

The Prince looked over at Sheldon in contemplation. "Maybe we don't need you."

Brian's hand fired across the table grabbing the Prince, "You son of a bitch!" The people at the closest table were half out of their chairs. Brian's free hand was shaking and he wanted to smash the glass into the smirk. "You act like a pimp and I'll kick your ass right now."

"A foreigner that hits a Thai goes to jail." The Prince's voice was tauntingly calm. "You'll never make your airplane." Through the corner of his eye, Brian could see other people were beginning to watch. The Prince looked satisfied and in control. "You won't be able to tell Sheldon why this happened, and he would never send anyone so impulsive to cover the war."

The shaking in Brian's hand traveled up his arm and into his neck. More than anything he wanted to feel the arrogant face breaking under his fist. The Prince waited as if he wanted it to happen.

One at a time, Brian forced his fingers to loosen from the lapel. His arms slowly pulled back across the table. "You'd like me to." Brian sat back in his chair.

The Prince watched him angrily. "You're a weak and intimidated man. You've set out to hurt her for being something you know she's not."

"It's principles," Brian answered in a hollow voice.

"If it's principles, you've already abandoned them! If she means that much to you, isn't it worth trying to understand? You're thinking with your pride and running from the responsibility of having to choose!" The Prince paused, his eyes burning with anger. "That makes her feelings for you a waste, and you'll leave here with nothing. Run! Take your pride and leave her with us." His expression twisted as if he had smelled something repulsive. "What good is there in a principle which is valued more than life?"

"Don't sit there and try and sound like some God damned humanitarian. It doesn't matter to you what or who is used as long as you get what you want."

The eyes of the Prince lost their sharp edge but not their strength. Raising his glass he studied Brian from over the rim. The sound of Sheldon's approaching laugh made Brian turn away.

"I don't follow Chovat." The Prince's voice was cold and pointed. "I'm the one Godfrey wants." His eyes were stones, hard and sharp.

Brian stared at the eyes and told himself not to believe, that it was a lie meant to confuse him. "You're a liar," he hatefully exclaimed. "You're protecting Chovat or someone else."

The proud expression of the Prince displayed the truth. "Am I? Your eyes believe me. You don't want it to be true because it means you are even less perceptive than you thought. That's what you hate. That and the idea that something besides you could be so important to her."

Three shot glasses clattered together spilling some of the whiskey onto the table. "That's enough dice for tonight," Sheldon announced. "Let's drink these and let Brian go take care of things."

Still not accepting what he had been told, Brian reached for one of the glasses and without waiting for companions quickly drank his.

"I think it's too hot tonight for American whiskey," said the Prince. For the first time in a long while, the name of "America" made Brian lonely. He watched the bubbles rising in the last of Sheldon's beer and tried to think of home.

Sheldon slid his empty shot glass across the table. "It's always too hot."

Feeling small and cheap, Brian watched Sheldon. Then he turned to the Prince and stared into his black eyes, and for a frozen moment he imaged dark huddled figures waiting on the border.

The walk back to the apartment had been almost refreshing, but the thought of what was waiting had kept Brian from fully enjoying the breeze off the river and the warm friendly feeling of being almost drunk. He was nearly to the top of the stairs when he remembered he no longer had a key. Embarrassed with the thought of knocking, he reached for the doorknob and was surprised to find it unlocked. That's just like her, Callie is too trusting. He opened the door, irritated with Sheldon for telling her and found his suitcases were waiting next to the door. The sight of them and the fact that she had accepted his departure hurt. Hearing him, Callie stepped out from the kitchen with a plastic pail she used to water the plants. She looked tired, and by her hair, he thought she'd been lying down. For a moment she looked at him but then turned and tilted the spout into the first pot. She glanced at him but quickly turned back to the plant. "These poor things have gotten so dry. I've neglected them."

"I want to talk to you."

She stopped pouring but she didn't immediately turn around. When she did, her face was expressionless, and her eyes avoided his by nervously moving about the room. "I already know. I saw Sheldon this afternoon." Her voice tried to sound gentle and reassuring. "He mentioned that he needed someone else in Phnom Penh and was sending you."

Brian was truly angry with Sheldon. He had made things harder to say than they already were.

"It's wonderful, Brian. I know how long you've wanted an important assignment." She stood very still holding the pail with both hands.

"I," he started but then stopped himself.

"You'll do fine," she said. "You're a much better writer than you think." Callie paused and looked down. "I'm so very sorry about last night. It was all for nothing. We didn't have to go through that. It would have ended anyway, but it wouldn't have been us doing it. It wouldn't have been so ugly."

"Stop this."

Her courage was shaken and she turned to the next plant. "I've packed your things for you."

"Look at me, Callie."

Her back tightened and then quivered. He knew she was trying not to cry. "Will you stay with me until it's time?" He didn't answer, and when he didn't she turned to him. As discreetly as possible, she wiped her eyes and then with the last of her courage waited.

"You're better at this then I am. You're stronger," said Brian quietly.

"I've had more time to worry about it." Her expression was wrapped in anticipation and fear. She wanted it over with and at the same time dreaded its coming. She was alone, and Brian told himself just to do it.

"It's over Callie. I've backed out." Her expression wavered in confusion. "I turned it down." Her eyes now locked to his, and her lips parted, but the sound came from the ticking of the clock.

"But you said …" she paused confused.

"It doesn't matter. Maybe it never really did," he said. Slowly, Callie's expression changed. Her lips wanted to smile while her eyes wanted to cry. Brian's chest tightened and it was hard to speak. "When it came to it, I couldn't leave you." The pail hit the floor, and all at once she was in his arms, her face pressed into his chest. She was trying to speak, but she could only cry. Brian tightened his hold against her shaking body and gently raised her head. At first when he tried to speak he had no voice. "We're going to be all right." Callie broke into a sob and buried her face in his chest. Her breath was warm and moist on his skin. From the beginning, she had been a storm in his life, and he had failed to take his own warning. Now it was too late, or he was too lost.

CHAPTER TWENTY

Brian and Callie hurried down the street. It was difficult for her to keep up with his anxious pace. Brian reached over and took the small duffle bag off her shoulder. It was very light, but it was a nuisance to her. "What's in here?" he asked.

"Things we'll need." With the bag gone, she took hold of his hand. "Sheldon wasn't very pleasant to you today, was he?"

"No. He'll go on sending me out on hack stories and being an ass until he's satisfied with the punishment." Brian smiled at her. She was wearing shorts and a flowered blouse. "I'm afraid I've disappointed him. The way he sees it, after all my complaining, when it came time to go on my own I didn't have the guts."

Her expression changed and she looked sad.

"I want this. I can't be half in and half out," said Brian.

Her hand squeezed his. "Not all of them will want you."

"That's something they'll have to get over." He wanted to get her mind off their plan. It was dangerous and she was having second thoughts. "Have you ever noticed that no matter what city you're in, if you go into the bad side of town, all the people are too fat or too skinny." He gestured towards two men sitting in a doorway where there was one of each.

"That's because they can't afford to eat right."

Brian smiled at her and from her expression she wasn't sure why. "You always see the best in people." He said with a laugh and hurried on. "But you take things much too seriously."

When they reached the corner, Brian turned towards the warehouse, but Callie stopped him. "I didn't set out to do this to your life." She spoke in a nervous tone that caused him to pause.

"This is my decision," he reassured her.

She tried to smile and they went on. "Chovat is the one that'll cause trouble," she said quietly.

"Let me worry about Chovat." Brian tried to sound confident to reassure her but he was worried.

"The Prince will know how to handle him," said Callie aloud to herself without conviction.

In the corner of one of the large truck doors was a small entrance door. Brian glanced across the street where he had hidden when he had followed Chovat to the warehouse. Then he quickly reached to open the door. He didn't want to think about what he was doing. Stepping inside, they let the door close on its own. The only light was from the windows at the top of the roll-up doors. The garage was shadowy and the smooth cement floor looked wet. Parked in front of them were five huge American Army transport trucks. The trucks were painted dark green and looked new. Even the floor beneath the trucks was clean.

"They're already here, aren't they?" he asked with the feeling that they were being watched.

"Yes." Callie began to lead him between two of the trucks. Except for the sound of their own footsteps, the garage was dead silent. The tall canvas canopies that arced above the truck's beds blocked out the sunlight and left the back of the garage dark. Brian watched the sides of the canvas for movement. He had the feeling that once they were behind the trucks, men would jump down from the beds and cut them off from the door.

"Your equipment's good," said Brian trying not to sound nervous.

Callie flashed back at him a mischievous grin. "America has been very generous."

As they walked past the trucks, no one came out of the black holes of the cargo beds. Callie was taking him to a small office at the back of the garage. Its door was closed, but through the opaque window in its center came the yellow glow of a desk lamp. In front of the lamp stood the dark outline of men watching them. When Callie reached for the door, she glanced back at him with the same regret she had outside. Brian put his hand on the middle of her back and lightly pressed her forward. She opened the door and the stale odor of cigarette smoke rushed out. When they stepped, inside someone pushed the door closed behind them and the small room became crowded with Chovat's hate. The light reflected off stern, young Thai faces standing in front of them. Brian tried to keep his face expressionless. Knowing that the Prince was at the center of the organization didn't lessen his contempt for the hard face of Chovat.

Chovat took a step forward and began arguing with Callie in Thai, his hand gesturing accusingly at Brian. The other Thais became nervous and listened intensely to Callie's replies. The one smoking took rapid puffs of his cigarette and engulfed his moon-shaped face in a cloud. There were five of them, and they were all dressed in dark clothes that made them look more like peasants than university students.

"He is here to help!" Callie insistently broke into English.

"We never agreed to bring him here. That was never agreed!" shouted Chovat.

Brian was impressed at how well Chovat spoke English. He stepped closer to Callie. "The Prince knows."

Chovat's eyes darted to Brian. He knew it was a lie but the others relaxed and no longer sensing their paranoid strength, Chovat had to reluctantly allow things to ease.

"He never informed us." Chovat stared at Brian.

Callie nodded hello to the others. "He'll be here soon." She stepped around Chovat to look at what was spread over the desk. With the others gathering around her, Brian tried to convince Chovat with a labored friendly expression but Chovat was not taken in and didn't bother with the pretense.

"Darling, you should understand this." Feeling Chovat's eyes moving with him, Brian stepped around the desk and leaned over Callie's shoulder. On the desk was a detailed map of one small area of the border. "This is where we have to be by late tonight."

"What are these black areas?" Brian pointed to one of four black squares.

"We call them stations. They're safe areas where ..."

"No more!" Chovat exploded in interruption. As Brian was turning towards him, Chovat rushed to the desk and jerked the map from under Callie's hands.

"We tell him nothing until the Prince arrives." Rolling up the map into a long tube, Chovat stared at Brian.

"Hand that back," Callie ordered in a quiet but forceful voice. Both Chovat and Brian glanced at her. She had never looked so strong.

"He's a foreigner, an outsider. He doesn't belong here!" Chovat snapped with contempt. The small room was quiet for a moment.

"So am I," Callie held out her hand. "And he is mine." Chovat's eyes slowly moved between her and his comrades. From outside came the sound of the small door being closed. The moon-faced boy was immediately at the windows of the office door and when the others stepped up behind him Chovat defiantly slapped the tube to the desk.

"Now we'll see what has been agreed," announced Chovat.

Callie took hold of Brian's hand.

Recognizing whoever it was that had entered, the moon-faced boy hurriedly swung the door open and went out to meet the newcomer. When voices started outside the office, Callie looked up at Brian. "It's the Prince." Chovat was reluctant to leave them alone, but he moved towards the door anxious to question their leader. Surprisingly, the Prince was not wearing his brown suit but was dressed like the others in dark clothing.

Seeing Brian, the Prince raised his hand in a friendly gesture. He had obviously already been told Brian was there. "Are the trucks ready?" he asked Chovat.

"Yes, but what of him?"

The Prince looked at Brian and then Callie. "He'll do as he's told."

"We never agreed to bring him here!" insisted Chovat.

"You were never asked to agree," snapped the Prince. "Now open the doors and start the trucks."

Chovat was embarrassed by the scolding and angrily moved towards the door, He spun around. "She was showing him the map."

"Go," demanded the Prince.

Chovat hesitated but then hurried out. He yelled something at the others and after a moment came the sound of pulleys lifting the truck doors. Brian stood in shock. He never would have believed the Prince to be a self-confident leader with the ability to control others. The Prince moved to the desk and picked up the map.

"I didn't realize you were coming this trip." Callie's voice was nervous.

"He's right. We didn't agree that Brian would come," said the Prince.

Brian stepped closer to the light. "She didn't have any choice. You can't expect me to wait at home."

The Prince watched him for a moment. There was still a strong resentment in Brian, and he didn't try to hide it. When he looked at Callie, a smile touched the corners of the Prince's mouth. "Come along." He started out to the rumbling trucks. "The three of us can ride together."

It was well after midnight when the noisy little caravan turned off the highway onto a dirt road. The red tail lights of the truck in front looked blurred to Brian. He was tired and stiff from sitting so long, but the details he learned from listening to the Prince and

Callie astounded him and left him feeling even more foolish for being so gullible, while at the same time he couldn't help feeling a twinge of pride as he learned some of their secrets. They were organized and clever.

The Prince had selected from information provided by Callie three villages in the north for the ultimate destination of this trip. Each village would receive a truckload of refugees. What had been intended by the United States government to be aid to the remote villages of Thailand would be used as inducement for their acceptance of the refugees. Callie was the one that had traveled to the forgotten hamlets and discovered what the villages needs were. Water purifiers, tools, medicines, whatever their vulnerable spot was, she would tantalize them with the availability of change. All they had to do was supply shelter and food until their guests were able to care for themselves and removed to assimilate into the Thai landscape with new identities. Cambodia and Thailand shared much the same culture and religion which made assimilation relatively easy, but there was no guaranty that once the refugees and suppliers were dropped and the trucks disappeared into the night that the homeless were not driven off. Callie didn't like to talk about that and relied upon what she called the warm and natural spirit of the Thai people. The more fortunate Cambodians were the educated or those believed to have been of importance in the old Sihanouk regime. Those people weren't left in villages but were brought back to Bangkok. The capital of Thailand was a world of both the seen and unseen. Its black market was as large as it legitimate economy, but more imaginative and powerful. The necessary papers could be bought if the holder of them could speak the language and could produce enough money for the bribe. Although the Prince didn't come right out and say it, he hinted that if the person was, or could be made to appear important enough, there might exist ways to continue their exodus into other countries. Carrying the conversation a little further than he had meant to, there was evidently a middle man that worked between the Prince and the American Embassy that helped with the identity papers.

Brian couldn't help imagining the headline: "Corruption in the U.S. Embassy Discovered."

As they came closer to the border, the atmosphere became tense and Callie explained. The guides, as she called them, were resourceful Cambodians that held off their own escape to organize and run the stations on the Cambodian side of the border. The pick-up spots were planned in advance but sometimes were not accessible. On either side of the border a patrol could wander too close which would cause them to abort the night operation and cause days of delay while a new pick-up spot was arranged.

As they drew closer to the border, the Prince explained that although the Royal Thai army was a danger to them, the real threat was from the B.P.P., which was short for the Border Patrol Police. Their name was a misnomer, for they weren't police at all but a militaristic body freed from the authority of the army. They were well-trained, well-equipped, and brutal. They had absolutely no pity for the Cambodians and were fast becoming no less capable of atrocities than the Khmer Rouge. The benefit of Callie's authority would be lost with the B.P.P., even if they were caught before making the pick-up. With the dashboard instruments giving off a dim, green glow, the Prince explained that at first the Border

Patrol merely forced any Cambodians it caught trying
to slip across the border back into their own country.
However, that game of cat and mouse had not lasted
long before it became the practice of the Border Patrol
to first collect whatever money and valuables the
refugees had with the promise of letting them through
only to force them back into Cambodia after taking
their valuables. This purely economic approach to
their position of power had not lasted long before the
Border Patrol grew tired of chasing the same people
back across the border night after night. That was
when the killing began. Once they had collected the
valuables from the Cambodians, they would simply
shoot them down. Some of the B.P.P. had become
bored with even that and had become sadistically
creative. Anymore it was not unheard of for these
elite Thai military men to put the refugees in trucks
and transport them to an area known to be mined,
then at gunpoint unload them to force them to start
back into Cambodia by way of the mine field. As
Brian became fully disgusted with the stories, the
Prince artfully reminded him that America was just
beginning to accept refugees, while Thailand had
officially allowed in thousands. The border was a
barbaric region soaked in blood and corruption. The
people trying to get in had little or no hope, so they
hid between the vengeful Cambodian Khmer Rouge
and B.P.P. and prayed for the sound of a small group
of trucks.

As they traveled, the road became so bad that
they had come to a near stop, and still the supplies that
would be used to bribe villages rattled and slammed
together. When they topped the crest of a small hill,
Brian noticed that the lights came from one of the
resettlement camps. The refugees that were allowed
in through the highway check points were taken to

these camps. Yet what they found was not sanctuary but holding pens corruptly run by officers of the Cambodian army that had deserted to become businessmen of the worst sort. As the Prince put it, they were dirty capitalists who were ingenious at making a profit from the misery of others. Even with such conditions, the camps would have been ideal places to deposit their passengers, but the camp commanders would never risk their affluent positions by quartering the very people the Thais were insisting be kept out.

After the lights of the camp had disappeared far behind them, the truck in front of them slowed. The Prince had been expecting it and pulled to a stop with squeaking brakes. "We'll be here for awhile." He turned off the lights and motor. Brian opened the door and stepped out. There was a breeze, and as he turned to help Callie down it moved through the back of his sweaty shirt and made him shiver.

"Thank you, Darling," Callie whispered as her feet touched the ground. "We've things to do. Come along." She reached back into the truck and grabbed the duffle bag and something else that Brian couldn't see. Callie started for the back of the truck, and the moon-faced boy passed them at a jog. Brian turned and watched him disappear down the road.

"Where's he going?" Brian asked.

"We're not far from the border now. He'll go ahead to be sure there isn't a patrol waiting." Stepping around the back of the truck, Chovat was covering the headlights of the truck he was driving. Glancing over his shoulder, he gave Brian a hard look. Callie handed Brian two small discs. "Clip these over the tail lights." The discs had slits in the center to allow just enough light for the truck behind theirs to see when to brake. When they had finished, Callie picked up the bag and started around the side of the truck. "Change into these."

"What?"

"Put these on." Callie handed him a roll of black clothing as she began to undress. Removing her flowered blouse her white skin looked soft in the light of the quarter room. "Don't let anyone know who you are or what you are. Talk as little as possible. Just get them in the trucks." Callie handed him a pair of shoes. They were black Chinese slippers.

Holding his shoes in his hands, Brian looked at them and laughed quietly. "We're going to drive up in these noisy monsters, but you want me to walk softly." It seemed like a useless precaution, but he began to pull off his shirt. The drivers of the other trucks began closing their doors. There was enough light to see that the road was lined on both sides by jungle and dog-legged to the right not far ahead. Putting on the dark clothes, Brian felt alone. It was too late to stop, but he thought of America and of his family. If they knew what he was doing, they would never understand. He was leaving all that he knew and took for granted behind, and even if there was no other choice, it was hard. Callie stopped buttoning her shirt and took hold of his hand. Her face was soft and comforting. She seemed to know what he was feeling, and she wanted to make it easier. Brian told himself it would be alright but he wasn't convinced. Callie put a scarf around her head to cover her hair. Brian told himself she was his corner of the world, and he watched her as if his stare could place everything on hold and they could exist in the moment and not take the next step.

In front of their truck came the sound of excited voices. The moon-faced boy had returned and something was wrong. Brian and Callie started towards them stuffing their street clothes into the duffle bag. "I'm not wearing these silly things." Brian held the slippers out to her.

"Put them on in the truck!" she insisted.

The Prince was leaning against the front of the truck listening to the report. Brian and Callie stepped along side him. "What is it?" Callie interrupted. Chovat and the others ran up from behind.

"Tracks, the army or border patrol had been through here tonight," the Prince answered quietly.

The moon-faced boy kept explaining. "What direction?" Brian's voice joined in the excitement.

"North," answered the Prince while gesturing for the boy to stop. "There is an open area just ahead with a small stream running through it. Tubtim says that there are many sets of tank tracks in the soft mud."

"Must be personal carriers." said Brian under his breath.

Chovat stepped into the conversation. "If the mud is soft, they came through tonight. We will have to come back." He turned and started for his truck.

"Wait!" ordered the Prince. Callie began questioning Tubtim in Thai. Impatiently Chovat stepped back to them and waited for her to finish. "He can't say whether they are going north or south," she reassured, "and it could have been hours ago."

"I don't like it," insisted Chovat. "We must postpone."

The Prince watched the strength in Callie's face. The depth of her commitment reflected at all of them. All except Chovat were watching her.

"What do you say?" the Prince surprisingly asked Brian.

Brian watched Callie with a smile. "We should go on."

"This is reckless!" Chovat exclaimed before breaking into Thai.

"Quiet!" The Prince glanced between Brian and Callie and then turned to the still panting Tubtim.

"We're too close to turn back," Callie quietly encouraged. There was a moment of silence when no one knew what direction would be ordered.

The Prince turned and hurried toward the truck. "We go on."

When the first truck in line reached the meadow, it hesitated like an animal reluctant to move into the open. The slits in its brake light caps stayed on longer than Brian expected. The idling of their motor was a deep constant throb that measured time slowly.

"Come on," the Prince mumbled to himself. Callie reached over and with a tight grip took hold of Brian's knee. One by one the brakes of the other trucks squealed to a stop. Brian, Callie and the Prince glanced at one another.

"If the B.P.P. is out there, they know we're here," announced Brian. "God damn it! Just go!" In a flash the brake lights disappeared and the lead truck started slowly across the meadow. The Prince didn't hesitate but popped the clutch and stayed on the tailgate of the truck in front of them. Looking in both directions, they couldn't see any sign of danger, but Brian had the chilling thought that maybe the B.P.P. was waiting for all five of the rumbling trucks to enter the clearing. At the midway point, the first truck dropped down an embankment and splashed into three feet of water before starting up the other side. Again the Prince didn't hesitate, and the front of their truck rose and then dropped over the embankment and into the water.

"Some stream," Brian said aloud, as the splash came through the window. Before the first truck was clear of the opposite bank, its brake lights flashed. "Don't stop!" exclaimed Brian, but it was too late. The Prince had jammed his foot into the peddle. The truck ahead of them accelerated and splattered their windshield with mud. "Hit it!" Brian demanded. The Prince popped the clutch, but their truck didn't move. With one move, Brian opened the door and jumped thigh deep into the water. Splashing toward the back of the truck his arm wind milled to the truck dropping down the embankment. "Don't stop," ordered Brian. Chovat accelerated and slammed into the tailgate. The front wheels of Prince and Callie's truck caught and began to pull it forward. The engines roared, and then like a muddy cow the truck lumbered out of the hole. The first truck was still spinning mud into the air and was beginning to slide sideways. "Easy!" Brian yelled as he splashed towards it. Reaching the water's edge he stepped on something slimy and fell forward. The wheels pelted his face with mud. Slipping and sliding, he managed to pull himself alongside the truck. "Not so much gas! Ease up. It'll grab!" The engine slowed and the wheels found enough solid ground to pull the truck forward. The last two trucks splashed in and out of the water. Crab walking up the slippery embankment on all fours, Brian reached the crest and began running to the still moving trucks.

In the confusion, Brian's truck had ended up first in line and they had stopped farther into the jungle than he had hoped. By the time he reached for the passenger door, he was winded from the run in the heavy wet clothes. Jumping in alongside Callie water splashed onto her face. The Prince reached across Callie and slapped Brian's leg. "Good job! You see you've already helped us!" The Prince laughed and Callie squeezed Brian's hand as the truck sped forward.

Outside Brian's window, a hundred yards away, was Cambodia. It seemed dark and dead on that side of the jungle. The trucks capped headlights allowed only a slice of light through to illuminate only a small part of the road. The chuckholes in the road made the lights jump about in an erratic motion. Jungle growth loomed in and out of the lights and seemed to be choking off the passageway. Unseen branches snapped and banged on the side of the truck, and the Prince slowed again. By the tense atmosphere in the cab, Brian was sure they were almost there. The road made a sharp turn to the right and the jungle pulled away. The truck stopped and the Prince turned off the lights. At first it was pitch black until the quarter moon's light slowly became enough to see by. Down the road was another, smaller clearing. The Prince waited until all the trucks had stopped and doused their headlights. Then he flashed theirs twice. There was no return signal. The Prince glanced at them in concern before repeating the flash. Again there was no reply. Taking a deep breath, the Prince turned to Brian. "They should be there." He repeated the signal a third time. Still no answer came.

"Maybe the B.P.P. did go north," whispered Callie.

Brian leaned out the window. There was no way of turning around without first driving into the clearing. The Prince flashed the lights twice. When still no reply came he looked at Brian not knowing what to do.

"Has this ever happened before?" asked Brian. Callie and the Prince shook their heads. "Wait a second and try again." Brian opened the door and stepped out onto the running board. The men in the other trucks were nervously leaning out their windows. "Once more Prince." The lights flashed. From the far end of the clearing, a pinhead of light blinked twice at Brian. "There we are," he said sliding back in with relief. Callie grabbed his leg and her fingernails cut into his skin. The Prince was out of his seat, vainly trying to look out the muddy window.

"What's wrong?" Brian asked holding his breath.

"That's not the right signal," Callie weakly answered.

"What?"

"They should double ours. It should have been four return flashes."

The Prince sat back down, and Brian leaned around Callie to see him. "You can't back out of here!"

"I don't know what to do. Maybe it's a mistake." The Prince was shaken and glanced around them as if expecting to see troops surrounding them.

"Try it again. Flash three times."

The Prince hesitated nervously. "Do it," insisted Brian.

The Prince did it, and when the reply came Callie slowly counted six return blinks. Melting into his seat the Prince started the truck.

"Wait a minute." Brian reached across Callie's lap and kept the Prince from putting it in gear. "If the Border Patrol is as well trained as you say, that signal wouldn't be hard to figure out."

The Prince turned to look down in the meadow. "We will send someone down on foot."

"No." Callie surprisingly interrupted. "If the others knew the signal was off, we couldn't stop them from trying to back out of here. If it is a trap, they'd be on us before we could find a place to turn around anyway." She glanced between them.

"We haven't any choice," Brian said. "We're either worrying over nothing, or its too late."

She looked down into the meadow and her grip on Brian's leg tightened. "How could we have picked this spot?"

CHAPTER TWENTY-ONE

They had allowed the meadow to remain dark and empty, knowing that on the opposite side was either life longing for itself or a trap ready to snap shut. When Brian could no longer stand the indecision, he stepped into their circle and glanced at his companions. It was too dark to see their faces but he knew their fear. "We need to cross." No one responded. "I'll go if no one else will." He spoke in a strong, quiet voice.

"I'll go with you," Callie promptly responded.

"No," he insisted. "Only one needs to go!"

"I've done this type of thing before. You haven't."

"Tubtim will go with me," Brian announced confidently. He could not see the round face of his acquaintance, but everyone could sense the surprise of Tubtim.

"I can move faster," Callie insisted.

"He and I are going," said Brian starting down the hill into the meadow. "If it's safe, I'll give you six rapid flashes."

Without confidence, Tubtim began to follow. He nervously glanced back at his companions as if expecting them to stop him, but no one did as he and Brian disappeared into the darkness.

As Brian and Tubtim made their way across the meadow, they moved very close to each other and flinched at any noise the other made. Repeatedly, Brian questioned why he was there. If only he had been able to convince Callie it was not their problem. As they moved closer to the far side of the meadow, his thoughts focused on the refugees that might be waiting. He resented them and wished they had stayed in Cambodia. It was their country and a problem they had created. He wanted to be back in Bangkok with Callie.

"You think we go far enough?" whispered Tubtim. "Maybe we wait to see if they come rest way?"

Brian hesitated. "No, we'll go on." He tried to sound reassuring. "Let's finish this." He tried to hide his fear.

Tubtim's fear now weighted him down and caused him to lag slightly behind Brian. The night closed in around them as they moved closer to the black wall which was the jungle in front of them. Instinctively, Brian felt his body bending closer to the ground and his heart pounding in his chest. All of a sudden there was the sound of a rifle bolt locking into place. Both of them froze and the air was electric with Tubtim's panic. "Tell them we're here to pick up," Brian whispered.

"What if B.P.P.?" Tubtim whispered in panic.

"Tell them!"

Tubtim rapidly began to translate into the darkness. When he had finished the night remained silent.

"Again!" ordered Brian.

Tubtim had just started to speak, when a voice cut through the night. Instantly they were surrounded by silhouettes holding weapons, but unlike Brian's visit to the border town, these weapons were held in the air and hands began to touch his shoulder and gently move him towards the jungle.

Clearly their presence was appreciated and relief spread among everyone. When they reached the tree line, they were guided onto a path and led a short distance before they were abruptly stopped. Not knowing what was expected of them, Brian paused. The dark figures around him spoke quietly. By the tone of their voices, he knew they expected him to reply with instructions, but he had no idea what they were asking. Glancing for Tubtim he began to notice dark shapes huddled close to the ground moving towards him.

"They have many for us tonight," Tubtim whispered.

For a moment Brian watched the huddled shapes. Then he turned and moved back to the meadow and began to flash the signal. The trucks were quickly across the meadow and stopped in a line. From behind him the jungle came to life as women and children ran for the trucks. Right away the Prince was in the middle of the excitement giving orders and reassurances. Callie rushed to Brian's side and gathered two small confused children in her arms. "Thank God you're safe!" Callie exclaimed, as she turned to rush the children to a truck.

Brian was caught in the excitement and began to usher people towards the trucks. Reaching the back of a truck, he promptly began to lift people up and into the cargo bed. The sound of the first full truck starting its engine and pulling away excited the night. More people rushed from the trees, and the second truck started its engine and began to pull away. Looking over his shoulder, Brian could see that there were too many people to take them all.

"Some will have to stay behind," he shouted into the air. The crowd continued to press towards the trucks. Without warning the world came to a standstill as everyone heard the first sound of metal grinding against metal. At the same moment everyone realized it was the trucks of the B.P.P. troop carriers.

"Pull away! Pull away!" the Prince ordered. The truck Brian was filling started its engine and jumped forward. Hands desperately grabbed at the tailgate that was closing.

"Callie!" Brian screamed in confusion as he glanced in every direction.

"Brian!" Callie was in the back of the truck surrounded by crying children and desperate parents.

Brian began to run for the truck, but with his first step he collided with one of the small figures that had been caught in the confusion. The sound of an elderly woman's voice rang out as she hit the ground. Spotlights danced through the night from the B.P.P. troop carriers. Those that hadn't made it into the trucks rushed past Brian to disappear into the trees. Brian glanced between the truck that carried Callie and the old woman on the ground. The spotlights danced across the ground near them. Brian wanted to run for the truck. He could still reach it. He told himself to run, but felt himself reaching for the old woman. Pulling her to her feet while grabbing the small bundle of belongings next to her, Brian pulled her towards the trees as the spotlight chased behind them. Just as the light was about to catch them, Brian pushed her into the dense jungle. The light moved over their heads as the sound of the trucks disappeared into the night. Realizing what he had done, his heart sank as he lay in disbelief.

The next morning the sun hammered on the earth. Under the canopy of the jungle, Brian and his new companions were safe from direct sunlight but not the stifling heat. The air was thick and moldy and filled with the buzz of tiny insects. Occasionally one could hear the scream of a monkey high in the trees or the call of an unseen bird. Sweat rolled down his face and burned Brian's eyes. The world smelled of decay and rot, and the only human sound was that of the occasional slap at an insect or sigh of discomfort.

The old woman lay close beside him as she had all night. They had been lucky. The B.P.P. hadn't tried to catch them, which only made Brian worry that the trucks were the target. His fears of Callie being caught or killed had prevented him from sleeping. He tried to convince himself that the trucks had made it safely through, but each time he was nearly convinced, another wave of panic would break over him and pull him down into despair.

He desperately needed to put his mind somewhere else, and without thinking he began to unwrap the small bundle lying between him and the old woman. Unfolding the corners of the bundle revealed a silk scarf. Unfolding the scarf Brian was amazed to find precious stones of assorted types and sizes. Brian glanced at the old woman sleeping beside him, and for the first time noticed that although her clothing was dirty, she was well dressed and certainly of the upper class. Looking back to the treasure, he noticed that several pieces of jewelry were missing stones. The prongs which had held the gems had been intentionally pried apart to free the stones.

"You must have used them to bring you this far," Brian said aloud to himself as he looked down at the old woman. Amongst her belongings was a bent photograph. Picking it up, Brian realized that it must have been of her family. Standing in a garden, in front of a beautiful home, was the old woman. Surrounded by children and grand children, she proudly smiled and bathed in the warmth and love of her family. Brian glanced at her again. She looked almost non-existent lying alone beside him. Never in her life could she have imagined herself in such a place with such a person. There was a letter beneath the photo and although he could not read it, Brian suspected it must have been written by one of her children. Maybe one had made it into Thailand and sent word back for her to follow.

The old woman quietly awoke and gently watched Brian sorting through her things. She slowly rose up and took the letter and the photo from his lap. Embarrassed at his intrusion, Brian sheepishly turned his attention to her. In her eyes tears pooled as she began to turn away. Realizing that she assumed she was being robbed, Brian gently took hold of her arm to turn her attention towards him. Then he quickly folded her belongings and tied the bundle closed. As he handed it back to her she became confused and reluctantly reached for the bundle with an ancient hand. Then, seeing he had meant her no harm, she leaned her head against his shoulder and began to quietly cry. Her emotion brought the attention of those around them. Glancing from one face to the next, they all seemed surprised by his honesty and touched by her tears. Then he came to the face of one person that watched his every move and whose black eyes glared in hatred. Chovat had been left behind also.

Brian looked back to the old woman. "We'll get out tonight. They'll come back for us tonight," he said trying to comfort the old woman and himself. Then he began to worry about Callie again.

The day passed slowly. The jungle was suffocating and Brian longed to see the sky, but he knew to move out from under the thick growth was too dangerous. Throughout the day he felt the eyes of Chovat. Although he was exhausted, there was no hope of sleep. The jungle sucked the energy out of him, but heat, insects, and Chovat's eyes kept him awake.

The old woman became talkative even though they did not speak each other's language. One by one she pointed at each figure in the photograph and repeated the person's name until Brian could recite them all. Once the names were established, she proudly presented each of her own children by calling their names while gesturing as if she were rocking a baby. As the day continued, she explained which members of her family had made it out of Cambodia by calling their name then pointing towards Thailand. At mid day Brian was surprised to find those resting nearby had prepared a meal, by each person contributing what little he had. There could be no fire, for the smoke would be seen; but when the dried fish and fruit were ready, he was the first to be presented with a meal. Wrapped in a large green leaf, they had given him the largest portion. Their generosity took him by surprise and embarrassed him. They had little and from the looks of them had barely survived for some time now. He felt ashamed at his well-fed appearance, but they insisted upon his having more than an equal small share. For the fist time he paid close attention to the faces around him. They all stared at him with hope shining in their eyes. Brian knew none of them might make it across the border alive, but they watched him with misplaced confidence. Most of them were women and children. Brian began to notice the toys the children had to play with, and towels and diapers and small little things of every sort that only a mother would remember to pack and weight herself down carrying. Unlike the refugees he had seen on the border with Sheldon, these people were not panicked. They watched him with wide gentle eyes that looked at him with their last hope. They were no longer faceless numbers to be argued about over cocktails in Bangkok with Sheldon. Their past political affiliations were now meaningless. They were simply people trying to stay alive. For the first time, Brian truly understood Callie. Her betrayal of him had been for the faces that now watched him, and for the first time in his life he felt his own small value.

As night approached, Brian was unable to hide his anticipation. Anxiously he began to move towards the meadow and with him went the old woman and close behind was Chovat. As darkness began to slip across the land, Chovat's presence closed in on Brian. Whenever he looked for Chovat, he found the dark eyes fixed on him. The stars steadily took the night like spectators to the approach of something dangerous.

"Maybe they're not coming," said Chovat from directly behind Brian.

Startled, Brian swiftly turned to face the voice. Chovat's expression was stern as he reached down and separated the old woman from Brian. Before Brian could say anything, Chovat was standing close to him. He stank of sweat.

"She'll come," said Brian sharply.

"It may take a week. We don't know. As far as we know they may not come at all. Maybe they got caught," smirked Chovat.

"I said she'll come, and she will."

"If she doesn't come back, what will you do?" Chovat clearly enjoyed the torture of his argument.

Brian stared sternly at Chovat. "Then I'll go find her," said Brian as he placed his hand on Chovat's chest and pushed him back. Chovat slapped his hand away. Brian quickly pushed him again. "She'll come, and until then stay away from me!" Brian reached out and took the old woman's hand. Then he led her away to a place where they could watch the meadow and wait.

Time became the enemy. The refugees quietly huddled around Brian. They were attracted to him like lost ships towards a light. They seldom moved or made a sound. They had come so far and clearly had suffered a dangerous journey. Brian did not want them to know he was unsure of their rescue, and he shrank from their misplaced hope in him. Occasionally, one of the babies would begin to cry, and the mother would disappear with the child into the jungle only to return when the baby had calmed down. There was no grumbling or complaining. Brian wanted to complain and the urge shamed him so he stretched out his legs to lie down and look at the stars. Frustration was building in him, and he wanted to be angry, but glancing at those lying quietly nearby caused him to hang on to what composure he still had. Remarkably, the old woman patted his hand and smiled at him as if she could read his very thoughts. She was motherly and tender even though she was exhausted. She looked so fragile that he was frightened for a moment that she would not make it through the night. Then he scolded himself for doubting her. Of course she would make it. She had made it this far; of course she would reach safety. Brian felt close to her and wondered if her children were busy searching for her, or if they assumed she was one of the many dead in Cambodia. Instantly, Brian had a thought that lifted his spirits. He would personally find the old woman's family and get her to them. That would be worth doing he told himself. He could imagine her expression upon first seeing her surviving children. "That will be a sight," he quietly said aloud to himself as he glanced down at the old woman. Then looking at the figures that lay around him, he felt foolish for having ever thought himself better than them. There was strength in each of them that he didn't have and as the night continued his admiration for them grew.

For several hours Brian lightly napped, but his anticipation and Chovat's presence prevented him from being able to truly sleep. As the hours slowly lingered on, his anxiety ate away at him. He tried to convince himself that Callie was safe, but as the night passed without a sign of her, he could not control his worst thoughts. He knew she wasn't dead. He told himself he would feel it if she were dead. He would know it if she died. But the night was passing, and if she did not come, it was because she could not.

Looking down at the old woman's light breath, he was amazed at how fragile she was and yet how far she had come. Glancing over the sleeping figures of her companions, Brian began to plan for the next day. He would have to organize the armed scouts into leaders for foraging groups. The jungle would supply them with food of some sort, and fresh water would have to be found.

Then silently Brian laughed at himself. The scouts knew more about the jungle and how to survive in it then he could ever learn. He was the least equipped to organize or lead anyone.

Suddenly, people nearby began to rise up and peer into the night. Brian strained to hear what had caught their attention. From far away came the rumble of trucks. The armed guards ran up and down the line instructing the people to remain quiet and still. Their orders went unheeded as each of the refugees was determined not to be left behind again. Eagerly each person collected their meager belongings and positioned themselves to be the first to the trucks. Brian watched for the first glimpse of the trucks. Then, from the far side of the meadow, came the small slits of light from behind the capped headlights of Callie's trucks. Excited, Brian rose to watch as the trucks signaled and the scouts on his side of the meadow replied. His heart raced. "Thank God!" he said aloud. When he looked down to the old woman, she did not move. Brian melted to his knees and held her in his arms. "I told you she would come." He could barely speak. The rumble of the trucks grew closer. "I am sorry, I am sorry," he kept repeating, as he rocked the lifeless old woman in his arms.

CHAPTER TWENTY-TWO

In the weeks that followed his meeting the old woman, Brian's need to be involved grew with each trip he made to the border.

The round faced Tubtim tried to avoid being teamed with Brian, but more often than not, his efforts failed, and he found himself being included in things he had not volunteered for.

Sheldon had steadily grown frustrated and suspicious at Brian's increasing unavailability until Brian finally left the Bureau under the excuse that he wanted to go independent. Sheldon had seen it as a personal insult and accused Callie of pulling Brian's teeth and making him less than a man. The Prince managed to keep them fairly informed on the efforts to break the story of the smuggling of refugees, but as the war in Cambodia neared an end, the number of refugees increased beyond the official census, and more and more people were searching for an answer. Brian was continually trying to increase the number of people they could bring to safety. There was a vast pool of refugees regularly waiting, and time was running out. Everyone knew that once the war was over, the Khmer Rouge would close the border completely and the slaughterhouse would have no exit.

Brian had also begun to attempt to chronicle the consistent and unending rumors of the terrible things taking place in Cambodia. If you weren't killed immediately by the Khmers, you were forced into slave labor camps where food could be obtained only from the guards. If one were to forage in the abundant countryside for even a piece of fruit, he would be killed. The Khmer Rouge was classifying people in towns as "new people" and systematically killing them. A rural uneducated populous was to be the only remaining base to the new regime.

Hurrying home at the end of the day, Brian rushed through the crowd on the dock. Song Per Song called his name, but Brian gave him only a quick wave and continued home. He was anxious to speak to Callie and the Prince about his new plan. The possibilities were endless. No longer would they need to bribe villages in the north to take in and hide small numbers of refugees. It was simple and something they should have done to begin with. Seeing that Callie and the Prince were waiting for him on the balcony, he hurried on.

"Brian! How could you ignore Song Per Song that way?" said Callie from the balcony as Brian came through the gate.

Brian glanced back at the small boy trying to make his way through the crowd. "I've something important to explain." Brian hurried in the door.

When Brian appeared on the balcony, the Prince was clearly anxious to hear his plan, but Callie was more interested in the slow approach of Song Per Song. "You don't spend much time with him anymore," she said accusingly.

For a moment Brian didn't understand whom she was referring to, until he looked back towards the river. "I've something important to tell you. I believe we can start bringing in as many people as we can possibly move."

Both Callie and the Prince looked at him as if he was being ridiculous. Then Callie moved towards him. "Brian, I know you want to help, but we have been doing this a long time."

"I'm serious," interrupted Brian. "We start bringing them in and dumping them in the camps."

The Prince and Callie looked at each other in disappointment.

"I'm serious," insisted Brian. "We can do it."

The Prince put a hand on his shoulder. "That will never work my friend ..."

Brian stepped away to interrupt the Prince. "Everything has changed today. I confirmed it at the embassy."

"Embassy?" asked Callie.

"Yes, the U.S. Embassy. Today the United States agreed to immediately start processing and transporting refugees to the States!"

For a moment, the Prince and Callie looked at each other without speaking. "Are you sure?" she asked.

"Absolutely."

"Then that means ..."

"It means an entire bureaucratic system will have to be set up, with bureaucrats from the States and Thailand running the operation."

"Or the U.S. Army!" said the Prince.

"Either way, it will be a huge, confused operation. At least for a considerable time," smiled Brian.

"But how do we get them in the camps? They'll never be accepted." said Callie.

Brian smiled at each of them. Song Per Song quietly walked onto the balcony without looking at Brian. "You want to play cards?" Brian asked Song Per Song. The child shrugged his shoulders, but his eyes lit up with excitement.

"It just won't work," Callie insisted.

Toying with their interest Brian hesitated.

"Brian!" she exclaimed.

"The U.S. plans on working out of the most populated camps, at least at first, and the first thing they will do is bring in a huge amount of supplies, to the largest camps, to feed and care for the population."

Callie's expression did not change.

"We know the camps are corrupt, so we show them how to increase their profits. It's perfect black market financing." Brian smiled, but Callie still didn't seem to understand. "The number of refugees in each camp shifts from a burden to a positive." he added, but neither she nor the Prince understood. "The more refugees you have, the more supplies from America, the more food, the more clothing, and the more medicine! That gives those corrupt bastards running the camps incentive to increase their numbers! Now the more people they have, the more merchandise for the black market!" Brian smiled. "And as the U.S. moves refugees out, we become the means to repopulate the camp, which keeps the supplies coming that turns into money, which grows with every refugee we can supply!"

Callie shook her head. "I don't like it. We're ..."

"You will! We'll increase the number of people we bring across tenfold!" exclaimed the Prince excitedly.

Callie still had a confused expression. "But we will be making it possible for those parasites to use those poor souls! And once they are in those pest holes, they won't get their food or medicine or anything else. Those camp commanders will starve them to death."

Brian put his arm around her shoulder and spoke softly. "But they'll be safe, even if they are hungry."

The balcony became quiet as both Callie and the Prince thought about the possibilities.

"The people themselves become the bribe," Callie said aloud to herself.

Brian relaxed and confidently sat down and began to shuffle the playing cards while Song Per Song discreetly watched with the hint of a smile.

Within three days and with the help of the U.S. Embassy, Brian had narrowed the potential camps down to the one suspected of being the most corrupt.

Chovat had been the antagonist to Brian's plan. He had argued every possible problem that might arise. Finally, he stated that it simply should not be followed because it was Brian's plan. He accused Brian of taking control of their operation simply because he was a Westerner and found it offensive to take instructions from Asians. When the others agreed to try the plan, Chovat angrily stormed out of the meeting.

The next morning, Brian, Callie, and the Prince rented a car and set out for the camp. The excitement Brian experienced with the thought of the possible increase in refugees carried him through most of the day before the heat and frustration of getting lost wore him down. The difficulty in finding their destination increased with darkness and prevented them from reaching their goal until dark.

As they approached the camp, its pale, blue electric lights illuminated the wire fence that prevented the Cambodians from leaving the facility. Around the fence were stationed armed guards that aimed their weapons at their vehicle as it came to a stop in front of the gate.

"Friendly group," said Brian, as he watched the slow approach of a guard.

"Real humanitarians," Callie replied accusingly under her breath.

The guard shouted something at them, and the Prince immediately took control and went into a lengthy explanation in Thai language which Brian could not understand. Slowly the other guard's skepticism improved, and they stepped to the vehicle to listen in amusement over the debate.

"What's so entertaining?" Brian quietly asked Callie.

"He's trying to convince them that if they don't allow us to see the commander now that they'll find themselves in deep trouble by morning."

"How's he doing?"

"Not very well."

Overhearing their discussion, the Prince erupted into a demanding tone of voice which made all of the guards clearly nervous.

Then, reluctantly, the guards moved to the gate, and, looking at one another with a confused expression, they began to open the barricade.

"As soon as you can, drive through," the Prince explained in a nervous voice. "I don't know how long this will last."

Before the gate had opened more than a few feet, Brian speedily drove the car towards the gate which caused the guards to quickly push it open. Before anyone could protest, the car was through and approaching the only structure which looked as though it was somewhat permanent. Once through the initial barrier, there was an endless sea of tents and poorly constructed shanties that stretched to the night's horizon. The glow from small orange fires dotted the ground. The air was thick with the grotesque smell of a huge open sewer. The figures of individuals that loomed up in the headlights were nothing more than skeletons who watched their approach without expression.

"My God!" gasped Callie. "This was what I was talking about Brian! How can we be part of this? How can we bring people to a place like this?"

Brian set his determination and fixed his attention on the large building they were now stopping in front of. "One step at a time, but whatever you do, trust me for just a little longer." Brian turned and stared into Callie's eyes. "I know what I'm doing; I just know this will work." Callie wasn't convinced and her eyes began to slowly pull away. "Trust me!" he said.

All at once, there were new guards around their car, only these were more determined and all of them pointed their weapons at them. These guards were older and better dressed. The one giving orders seemed better trained, and those he was ordering responded hurriedly.

"We have to get out of the car," said the Prince nervously. "These fellows are mean. I'm afraid I might have made a mistake."

"We'll be all right," insisted Brian, as he opened the door and stepped from the vehicle. The Prince and Callie were directly herded to Brian, and then they were all pushed towards the building. Upon entering the building, Brian paused in awe. Every manner of valuable one could conceive was in the warehouse. There were chandeliers, rugs, furniture, one well-conditioned English Jaguar and mounds and mounds of clothing. The guards began to push them through the building towards a light at the far end. As they continued their winding course through the stockpile of confiscated belongings, Brian's disgust welled up in his chest. Watching from side to side, he noticed stacked boxes reaching nearly to the ceiling of the warehouse. Each box had printed across it CARE.

When they reached the end of the building, they were escorted through a small door into an office and combined living quarters. The lighting was very dim, but Brian could make out two figures on the far side of the room. Callie and the Prince stepped close to Brian and attempted to peer through the poor light.

"These are the people you advised me of?" said an unfamiliar voice. The other figure whispered an answer.

"Well, they aren't quite what I expected from your description. Except your right about her. She is very pretty."

The voice was clearly Asian but it spoke perfect English. Certain that he was in front of the camp commander, Brian took one step forward. "Are you Dang?"

"I am, and you are Brian."

The shock of hearing his own name resounded in his ears. Brian swiftly glanced at Callie and the Prince, but their expressions were as shocked as his. The second voice began to whisper again. Brian asked, "How did you know my name? Who is that with you?"

"You are not here to interrogate me," answered Dang.

Brian was confused and didn't know how to approach the challenge. He hesitated, and with his hesitation, indecision began to take hold of him. "We came here to do business with you…"

"I know exactly why you are here," interrupted Dang.

"I don't understand. We didn't even know we were coming here until yesterday…." The words died in the air as Brian realized who the other figure was. He glanced at Callie and the Prince, but they had not made the connection. "Since we only decided yesterday where we were going, it must be one of us. Is that you Chovat?"

Dang began to laugh as if a practical joke had been caught before completed. "My little game has ended much too quickly. But in any case it was amusing for a moment."

"As I was saying, we've come a long way to do business with you," said Brian as he glanced at Callie and the Prince. "But we didn't expect Chovat, one of our own, to have already made the trip. Did the two of you already know each other?"

"Unfortunately not. This young man approached us this afternoon with a very interesting proposal. He also told us that you would be arriving shortly behind him." Dang reached out and turned the control of a gaslight which grew in intensity until the room was illuminated. Dang was a large, sweaty, fat man reclining behind a large hammered brass table. The sweat rolled off his black hair and down his unshaven face. He smiled at Brian menacingly from a mouth that needed dental work. Beside him was the skinny figure of Chovat. With an expression of distain, Chovat stared at Brian and then glanced at the Prince as though he was proud of his deception.

"You had no business coming here on your own, Chovat," said Brian in a firm voice.

"And you may not speak to my new associate in that tone!" said Dang angrily. "He has come to me with a most worthwhile business proposition. One that he told me you would claim as your own, but he in fact is the man who can help me."

Brian focused his stare on Chovat who began to lose his confident expression. "Is that right?" Brian smiled. "We must be discussing two separate matters. I would suggest that you offer us something to eat and something cold to drink so that we can discuss real business."

Chovat erupted into a demanding voice with both hands flaying at the air.

The Prince leaned close to Brian. "Chovat wants you removed immediately."

Dang obviously found the eruption entertaining as he glanced between Brian and Chovat. Brian's confidence began to return as he watched the increasing tirade of Chovat. Callie reached down, and as indiscreetly as possible, took hold of Brian's hand. Dang saw Callie's movement and watched intensely. Slowly Dang raised his hand towards Chovat and began to motion for him to sit down. Reluctantly, Chovat followed the instruction. Then Dang turned his attention again to Brian. He stared at him for what seemed a long period of time. "No, no, I think I will do business with Chovat. He and I understand one another, and I doubt if I could ever say that about you."

Brian was right away frightened that he had brought them into danger. The personal belongings stacked in the building clearly established that Dang was just as corrupt and ruthless as rumored. If Dang was not going to work with them, Brian was scared that he might not want any outsiders to know and understand the operation he and Chovat were going to put together. Callie and the Prince looked at Brian in confusion and worry.

"Ask Chovat how he will bring the U.S. supplies to this camp!" said Brian.

"Oh, we've discussed that thoroughly. I believe all camps will soon be receiving American support." Dang spoke with confidence and Chovat relaxed next to him.

"Undoubtedly," Brian said as he nodded. "Our information about you has indeed been mistaken. I was under the impression that you were an educated business man. But, if you wish to remain less profitable than the other camp commanders, so be it." Brian turned towards his companions. "I'm sorry for bringing you here. We'll do better tomorrow." Brian began to move as if he expected to be allowed to walk back to their vehicle.

"What are you saying?" asked Dang from behind.

Brian turned around with as much authority as he could find. "How do you expect him to be of any real benefit to you," said Brian pointing to Chovat. "There is nothing he can do to convince any of the Americans that will be coming, that your camp deserves or should receive the greatest amount of supplies. I can do that, and whoever I do it for, will make much more money than Chovat will bring to you."

Dang's interest was clearly peaked, and Chovat was worried. Dang took a step towards Brian. "How would you do this?"

"Did Chovat tell you I'm a journalist? That what I write about will influence the aid which will come to the camps. I'm the one that can make you famous. I can make this camp the one that has to receive the greatest amount of supplies. In short, I'm the one that can help you." Brian's voice was strong and confident even though he was shaking inside. "And we have the trucks to bring the people to you. Chovat doesn't have anything."

Dang looked between Brian and Chovat as he considered the possibilities. The air was thick with indecision and suspicion. Then Dang turned towards Brian with a warm smile. "Maybe I have been too quick to make a decision. Sit here with me, and we will have something to eat and drink and you can describe for me in detail how you can help me." Dang shouted orders at his Cambodian guards, who immediately scurried around the room collecting pillows for everyone to sit on. Then, one hurried off undoubtedly to order the preparation of food.

"I am the one who should receive the benefits you have mentioned. My camp is extremely large, much larger than the others. I try to be an endless mountain of generosity to my countrymen, but there is little to give," said Dang with a sad expression.

"We've seen your generosity," said Callie. "This warehouse is filled with your generosity, and the scarecrows we saw in your camp make it quite clear just how generous you are!"

Dang glared at Callie angrily. "Women do not speak in that manner to me." He turned his attention angrily to Brian. "You will not allow her to interrupt us."

"Of course not," Brian said, putting a hand on Callie's lap as they sat down. "But she is in fact quite right. After all, there will be inspections of the camp. There will have to be some limits set. A minimum standard on how anyone in this camp is treated or this opportunity to make a great deal of money will not last."

Dang sprang to his feet. The beads of sweat on his face bubbled and dripped off his chin as he angrily stared at Brian and Callie. "You will not tell me how to run this camp!" he yelled.

"I would never do that," answered Brian quickly. "But, if we are going to accomplish what we want, then there must be better treatment of those left in your care. It's simply a matter of making you a greater profit."

Dang's interest was re-kindled, but he stood motionless for a moment considering the possibilities. Questioning his authority slowly gave way to his greed. Chovat could no longer remain composed and jumped to his feet to once again attempt to dissuade Dang. The two began an intense conversation until they had reached some type of agreement. Reluctantly, Chovat took his seat again beside Dang as large plates of food were brought into the room and placed on the brass table between them.

"We have the trucks and governmental approval to transport in this area. We have the people to bring you who will drastically increase the amount of aid you receive. Those same trucks can transport those supplies back to Bangkok to be sold on the black market. Chovat has no trucks."

"Neither do you!" announced Dang. "The woman provides them."

"Yes, but she will not provide anything unless I say so."

Dang glanced at Callie's face.

"And only I can fix a problem you have," Brian continued. "No one but me can take you from a suspected criminal and make you a respected and honored protector of the refugees. I can do this by writing about it in the newspapers in Bangkok, and with my connections and those stories, I can eventually provide you with an exit visa that can take you and your wealth to the States."

Dang's expression was serious and he listened closely to every word.

"But if you want to do business with Chovat, ask yourself the question, how will he protect you from the changes the government will want to make now that the U.S. is going to be involved? How long will it be before you're replaced? As soon as they drive into this place, they'll throw a net over you." Brian glanced at the food in front of Dang. "You can eat everything in front of you right now or you can share a little of that meal with others and eat well the rest of your life." Brian paused and the room was silent.

Dang stared at him in deep concentration.

"Unless your image is changed quickly, you will go from commanding the camp to living in one of those filthy tents outside." Brian paused. "Chovat can not help you."

Dang's eyes darted between Brian's and the table.

"The authorities will have to replace you."

Dang glanced at Chovat.

Brian smiled, "No, Dang, you'll do business with us, because you're smart and that's the smart move."

CHAPTER TWENTY-THREE

In the next month they moved more people across the border than they had been able to manage for the last three months. Seeing the huge profit to be made, Dang had excitedly arranged for the bribing of the Border Patrol which now avoided their pick-up points. The camp was brimming with the newly arrived. The supplies from the United States were arriving with the white, smiling faces of U.S. Bureaucrats who were foolish enough to believe they were in control. With each shipment, Dang's greed for more increased as did his dislike for Americans. Brian was following through on a string of articles on the camp. The local papers couldn't get enough on the refugees and the strong but compassionate ex-patriot named Dang that did more for them than anyone could expect. It was a joke between Callie and Brian at how defensive Dang became over his new public personality. None of it was true, but he would sit and read the articles over and over and insisted on reading them aloud to his men.

As the stockpile of supplies from the U.S. grew, so did the number of armed guards in the employ of Dang. A Frenchman that had served in the South Vietnamese Army, as a highly paid instructor, had come to work as the captain of the camp guards. He was a well-built, balding thirty-five year old that had been in Asia most of his life. He said his name was Jon Michael, but Brian suspected that was an alias. The Frenchman was a cold character that didn't show any emotion except for a sadistic smile when he was ordering the refugees about. There was something about the Frenchman that caused Brian to suspect that he was wanted by the police in more than one country and that he was more than capable of killing. His presence made Dang even more dangerous. He liked to drink too much, and he stared at Callie even in front of Brian.

After Chovat attempted to make his own deal with Dang, the Prince had insisted that Chovat was no longer to be involved with their group. At first it was a worry that his banishment might cause a mutiny within the group, but other than a short lived grumbling by some of the younger drivers, it went almost unnoticed. Chovat had been angered by his displacement, but he hastily went to work for Dang. The combination of Chovat and Dang didn't make sense to Brian. Although he had never cared for Chovat, he had believed him to be a dedicated revolutionary, not a common thief immersed in the black market. Dang gave Chovat the job of monitoring the moves of Brian and the others. Of most concern to Dang was whether they were taking refugees to any other camp. Consequently, with each day, Dang's greed grew. Chovat was given the use of one of Dang's old jeeps which would unexpectedly arrive at the pick-up station and follow the trucks back to the camp. Although Dang tried to hide it, he hated the improvements that Brian and Callie insisted be made to the camp. Dang was certain that the Americans would soon lose interest in the condition of the camp, and the wastefulness of caring for the refugees would end. Brian suspected that soon the camp would have its own trucks, and the need for theirs would disappear.

Brian told himself to stop worrying. They seldom made it back to Bangkok, and when they did, their balcony became a remote island where they could hide from the turmoil that had become their lives. Callie was busy watering her plants while Brian worked on his next article. It was peaceful, and watching her was more interesting than writing more lies about Dang, so he set his note pad down and contently watched her move about their home. Feeling his eyes, Callie glanced at him. "What are you doing?" she laughed.

"Watching you. Why don't you come over here and take a break."

"I'll be done soon."

"I think you should come over here."

Callie looked over her shoulder at him without stopping her watering. "Just what do you think you're going to do?" she teased with a coy expression.

"I intend to make passionate love to you." Brian stood and started towards her.

"Brian," she said moving away from him. "It's too early for us to go to bed," she teased and tempted with her bashful act.

"It's a perfect time."

She was wearing a light blue work shirt and white shorts. The supple curve of her neck was exposed, as she had tied her hair back to stay cool.

"Brian." She set the watering can down and walked backwards away from him. "Maybe later, after we've gone for a walk along the river." She laughed and moved faster as he approached, but before she could turn Brian caught her and pulled her into his arms.

"We can walk afterwards," he insisted with a smile and then kissed her. She relaxed into his arms and kissed him intensely for a long time.

"You're right, Darling. We can walk later." She took him by the hand and led him down the hall.

Lying quietly next to her, Brian watched the light in the room fade with the end of the day. There was no noise or commotion to deal with, just the movement of the cool sheet as it rose and fell with her breath.

"There's nowhere in the world I'd rather be," Brian said aloud, but he was speaking more to himself than to her.

"Really?" Callie rolled to her side to watch him. "I had to worry about you leaving for so long. That all seems so long ago. A lifetime ago." She reached out and traced his profile with her finger tip. "If anything now I'm a little jealous of you."

"What?" Brian chuckled and put an arm around her. His fingers stroked up and down the small of her back. "Are you serious?"

"Well, in a way, yes. Sometimes when I watch you at the camp, when I see how much everyone else depends on you and looks to you."

Brian turned to her. "Not really?"

"Sometimes," Callie's voice changed and took on a troubled quality. "Sometimes I wish we were just somewhere else, anywhere else, doing nothing but living." She paused and tried to smile. "You know Brian, the world won't let us alone. They don't want people to be happy." She lay down and rested her head on his shoulder. "Maybe I'm selfish, but sometimes I feel as though I've given you away, that you don't belong to me anymore."

"I'll always belong to you."

"Promise me a part of you will always be just mine."

"All of me."

"No, that's not realistic."   Her voice was insistent.   "You already belong to them; they need you. I just want to know that a part of you is just mine."

"Yes. Of course there is."

"Promise you'll never let it change."

"I promise," Brian said with a smile.

"No, promise! Tell me you promise."

"I promise Callie. I'll belong to you forever."

Callie watched him intensely to reassure herself. "I wish things could have been different." Then she kissed him passionately and they made love again.

When they were both just about to fall asleep, someone began pounding on their door.

"Who could that be?" Brian exclaimed in an irritated voice as he threw the sheet off.

"Darling, it's only 8:00. It's not the middle of the night."

"Oh." Brian was still irritated at the intrusion. "You're right. It felt as though it was much later."

Callie was already out of bed and dressing. "I told you we should have waited."

Brian reluctantly rolled out of bed. There was a second loud knock at the door. "We'll just start all over again later," he smiled.

and the voice of the Prince came. "Oh dear, he sounds angry." She hurried down the hall to let him in.

"Don't panic," Brian called after her. "It's probably nothing." Rushing to get dressed Brian, hurried after her. He was buttoning his pants as Callie opened the door and the Prince rushed in.

"What's wrong?" Brian asked with a smile.

"Tubtim is missing." The Prince's voice was angry. "Along with a truck and full load of..."

"When did this happen?" demanded Brian.

"Oh no," Callie sighed. "Oh, dear. Don't stand in the doorway and discuss this." She reached out and gently ushered the Prince away from the doorway.

"You're right," said the Prince as he glanced at their half-dressed condition.

"Now tell us what's happened," said Brian as the Prince took a seat on the couch.

"Last night Tubtim and two others left the pick-up station with a full truck. They never made it back to the camp, and no one can find a trace of them."

"They must have wandered into the Border Patrol that Dang hasn't bribed." There was disbelief in Brian's voice.

"No!" exclaimed the Prince. "Tubtim is a good boy. He's been with us from the start. He wouldn't make such a mistake."

"What else could it be?" asked Callie.

The room was silent, but the stare between Brian and the Prince communicated their shared fear.

"Chovat has something to do with this." Brian's voice was firm and angry. "I don't know how, but he's involved. I can feel it. Have you spoken to him?"

"I tried. But he isn't concerned with me. He's Dang's man now, and he won't be bothered with my questions."

"Have you spoken to Dang?"

"He only pays attention to you. He wouldn't even see me."

"Well, the son of a bitch will see us!" Brain turned to Callie. "Start packing. We're going back tonight, now in fact!"

"That's not all," interrupted the Prince. "I spoke with Sheldon today. Godfrey is back in Bangkok and Sheldon is angry with you."

"Me? What the hell for?"

"He told me that you owed him. I really didn't understand him, but he didn't want to tell me too much and I didn't want to make him more suspicious."

Brian hesitated but his concern was with the fate of Tubtim. "Sheldon's problem will have to wait."

"But what if Godfrey came back with descriptions of you from the other side of the border? What if he suspects you're…"

"To hell with his suspicions." Brian put his hand on the shoulder of the Prince and looked into his face with confidence. "What we do now is find Tubtim."

The Prince stared at him for a moment and then began to slowly nod his head. "Yes, he must be our first thought."

Brian released his shoulder and smiled. "We'll straighten this out."

The Prince's expression grew hard. "The time has come for us to remove our problem. Chovat is mine to deal with."

"What do you mean?" asked Callie.

"I mean to kill him before he can cause any greater problem."

"No!" Callie exclaimed. She took hold of Brian's hand and squeezed it hard. "We can't do something like that! We can't!"

"No one said we're going to." Brian tried to move Callie towards the bedroom. "Please just help me now. Tubtim needs our help."

"Brian we can't start killing people."

"We can!" exclaimed the Prince. "If that one has betrayed us, what would you have us to do? The next time it could be you or me or Brian!"

Callie's expression was near panic. "We don't know what's happened. Maybe Chovat had nothing to do with this. This is insane. We all got involved in this to help people, to do some good, to save lives for God's sake. Now you're talking about killing someone." She grabbed Brian's arm with both hands. "You can't let this happen. Promise me this won't happen!"

"We don't' even know…"

"Promise me Brian! We're not killers!" She looked to the Prince. "Chovat wouldn't do what you're thinking! No matter what he feels towards us, he wouldn't do that!"

"He's a risk to all of our lives," the Prince replied in a firm tone.

"No he's not, not really. There has to be another explanation of where Tubtim is."

"Are you willing to risk us all?" demanded the Prince.

The room was silent. Callie looked between the faces of the Prince and Brian until her eyes came to rest on Brian's face. "I don't believe he would do this, and I know you could never go along with killing him.   I could never forgive any of you if this happens."

Brian looked to the Prince. He knew that the stern face of his friend was probably right. Chovat was a danger to them, and he wanted to agree with the Prince for all of their safety.

"We don't touch Chovat. Callie's right. We concentrate on finding Tubtim and helping him."

"If we can," said the Prince unconvincingly.

It took them all night to reach the camp, but as the sun rose they drove through the gate. It was a different place from what it had been when they first saw it. No longer could one smell human waste or urine. Brian had forced Dang to provide facilities for the refugees, including home made showers. The shanties and huts were being replaced with tents because Brian insisted that more of the supplies from the U.S. be used in the camp. As the tents went up, so did the spirits of the recipients. They kept the dirt floors clean and swept, and they cooked enough food to fill the air with wonderful smells and no one any longer looked starved. In the middle of the camp was a large tent with a red cross stretching across its roof. This was the camp's new hospital, which was staffed by doctors and nurses that were refugees themselves. Callie had organized a group of women to oversee the orphans that were among them.   Brian had even organized a small police force among the refugees. Unlike the camp guards, they were unarmed except for a note pad and pen to take down the name of an offending party. The man was then turned over to a grievance board made up of camp residents who would pass judgment on the guilty and require them to perform the more distasteful jobs in the camp, such as latrine duty. It was fast becoming a well-organized and functioning tent city where people could survive in relative comfort if they could avoid the Frenchman and his armed guards.

Stopping the car next to Chovat's new living quarters, Brian focused his attention on two Thai Army Jeeps that were parked and guarded by Thai soldiers.

The Prince and Callie looked at Brian with concern.

"Maybe they're here because of Tubtim?" said Callie quietly.

"I hope not," replied Brian, as he turned towards the newly erected office and residence of Dang. "We may already be too late."

"Brian!" shouted the Frenchman from a distance. Brian turned to watch the captain of the guards hurry to him. "We need to speak before you go in."

"What's happening here?" Brian pointed to the Jeeps.

"Dang is very angry." The Frenchman turned to Brian and began to walk towards the row of tents. "They came in last night for an inspection."

"Inspection? Who came for an inspection?" Brian took hold of Callie's hand as they walked.

"Thai officials and Americans who are with the relief authority and some who are with the U.S. Embassy." The Frenchman raised his arm and circled it in the air. "They're going through everything!"

"What do they want?" Brian asked.

"The camp! I think they want the camp."

"What have you heard about Tubtim?" asked Brian.

The Frenchman looked confused. "What are you talking about?"

"Have they mentioned Tubtim?"

The Frenchman shook his head. "This has nothing to do with him."

"Are you sure?" Brian demanded.

The Frenchman stopped and looked at Brian coolly. He didn't like being spoken to in that tone of voice. The Frenchman's eyes were lifeless and threatening. "You better put your attention on helping Dang." There was a clear threat in his voice that made Callie squeeze Brian's hand.

The Prince stepped very close to the Frenchman. "He wants to know about Tubtim. We all do!"

The Frenchman hesitated, his eyes not wanting to leave Brian. "I don't know anything about Tubtim." He smirked, making it obvious that he was lying.

The anger in Brian grew to a rage. "I'll find him, and when I do…"

"Brian," interrupted Callie as she squeezed his hand again. "People are watching." She began to walk again which separated them from the Frenchman. "Please, Darling, that animal frightens me. Let's just find out what's going on."

"Follow me," said the Frenchman as he hurried past. "I'll take you to Dang, but I'm warning you. He's not pleased at this inspection."

As they followed the Frenchman, they stayed far enough behind so that he could not overhear their discussion. "The inspection must be because of Tubtim," said Callie.

"I don't know," answered Brian quietly. "None of this makes any sense." Brian glanced back at the Prince. "You don't think Sheldon gave us up do you?"

The Prince shook his head no.

As they walked, a buzz began around them as the refugees took notice of their presence. Commotion grew from behind them as a small crowd began to follow them. More and more people joined the crowd and people began to encircle them to put their hands together and bow respectfully.

"Farang!" shouted a young boy as they passed him. Then others began to repeat the phrase.

"What are they saying?" Brian asked the Prince.

"They don't know what to call you. They know you're a foreigner, but they don't know your name."

Brian realized that some of the faces around him looked familiar.

"They are thanking you," said Callie over the voices. She looked frightened and amazed at the same time. "You belong with them, but they can't have all of you." She reminded.

The crowd became too large to move through, and the call of "Farang" rose to the sky as more people ran towards them. Brian didn't know what to do. He looked between Callie and the Prince, astonished at what was happening. The Prince quietly began to join in the chant until he, too, was swept away with the excitement.

Brian looked at Callie for explanation, but the crowd had her surrounded and the people were touching her and bowing in front of her. The refugees recognized both of them and their gratitude was immense. Callie nervously bowed back at those bowing to her and tried to smile at the crowd, but she was uncomfortable with her fame.

"It's you, Callie!" yelled Brian over the crowd. "It's you!"

Callie smiled at him, "Look around you!" she called in a shaken voice.

The crowd around Brian was much larger than those around her. It was growing with each moment as the frenzy was magnetically pulling more people into the mass. Brian stared at the happy faces rejoicing in front of him and realized their celebration had little to do with him or Callie. They were celebrating life itself and their good fortune to have escaped the danger on the other side of the border.

Brian looked back to Callie and loved her even more for her modesty. She had been the heart that had saved so many, but she was uncomfortable with the recognition. For an instant he felt a little guilty for enjoying what was happening, but the power of it was too much to ignore.

"You're the one we're looking for," came a voice from near Brian. Slowly maneuvering through the wall of people came three Americans and two Thai officials. Behind them came Dang and the Frenchman. "They certainly know you," yelled one of the Americans.

Dang stepped close to Brian. "Yes. We are all very fond of our young American friend. Until he came, I was all they had," he shouted over the crowd but his eyes could not hide their anger.

The Americans began to shake Brian's hand and to introduce themselves, but Brian was unable to think of anything as he watched the crowd continue to grow and the chant became still louder. "Does this happen every time you arrive?" asked one of the Americans.

Brian turned to the man asking the question. He was wearing a clean, freshly pressed white shirt.

His short hair and horn-rimmed glasses made him look out of place.

"I said, does this happen every time?" His handshake was firm. "You can't tell me they read the few articles you've written, so just why are they so fond of you?" There was no question in the man's voice. "Would you like to explain that to us?"

Brian didn't know what to say. He felt trapped by the gratitude of the crowd around him. When he looked to Callie, her eyes were worried. There was no way to explain what was happening. It was too big to cover with a lie. The American's eyes were confident and bore into Brian.

Callie pushed her way next to Brian and took hold of his hand.

CHAPTER TWENTY-FOUR

Removing them from the crowd did not happen easily. The refugees wanted to see and touch them, and neither the Frenchman nor Dang himself could intimidate the crowd. Once they were removed to the living quarters of Dang, it was clear the Americans and Thai officials were not pleased by the opulence Dang surrounded himself with. Instead of attempting to downplay his living conditions, Dang openly went out of his way to show off his authority and abundance, in the mistaken belief it would impress.

"Where do you live?" asked one of the Americans of Brian.

"We live in an apartment in Bangkok. When we're here, we stay in one of the tents."

The American watched him distrusting. "Has the war been as fruitful for you?"

"The only thing it's brought us you've already seen," Callie answered without expression.

The man glanced between her and Brian.

"Please have a seat," Dang announced. "I'll have something prepared for us to eat."

"We're not hungry," Brian said as he stepped towards Dang. "What I would like to know is where Tubtim is?"

"Oh, he's about somewhere," Dang said as he waved his hand at Brian. "These gentlemen have been inspecting our camp, and I'm sure they would enjoy…"

"I need to know where Tubtim is," insisted Brian.

From over Dang's shoulder peered the Frenchman.

"I don't know where he is right now." Dang's eyes were angry, but he tried to hide the emotion. "There are thousands in the camp. How can I know where everyone is?"

"Is there some special concern for this individual," asked one of the Americans.

"Yes," replied Brian "He's a colleague of mine, an interpreter, and it's important that I find him right away."

"There are many here that can interpret for you," said Dang "What we need to do is to come to an understanding with these gentlemen." His eyes shot across the room at Brian. "These gentlemen have the crazy idea that this camp should be run by someone else."

"We are not criticizing anything, mind you," said the leader of the Americans. "My name is Paul Grady, and I'm responsible for the proper placement of supplies from the United States. It has been determined, by the Thai government and the United States, that it would insure better operation of the camps if they were overseen directly by the Thai government. After all, we are on Thai soil." He glanced accusingly at Dang and then Brian. "And we certainly want to see those for whom the supplies were intended receive them." Mr. Grady stepped towards Brian. "I must say, I've read the articles you've written on the camp, and I'm a little surprised at some of what I've seen."

"Such as the affection the people have for Brian?" said Callie defensively. "If for one moment you think Brian has done anything improper, then let's step outside again."

Mr. Grady stared at her for a moment. "No, I don't need to see that again." He looked back to Brian. "I understand what that is about, and I hoped an American wouldn't be involved in what troubles me today." Then he turned to Dang. "However, there are things that concern me about you. For instance, the armed guards you're utilizing. You, sir," he said gesturing to the Frenchman, "How do you come to be here and what is your function?"

"He's merely a training officer that has been teaching our guards how to do their jobs," interjected Dang.

"Yes, I'm sure." replied Mr. Grady disbelievingly.

Dang could barely hold back his anger. "If you will excuse me, I need to speak to Brian."

"Fine," said Mr. Grady accusingly.

Dang hurriedly took Brian by the arm and led him into another room. "You must stop this thing! This is a very bad thing!"

"Where's Tubtim?" asked Brian.

"That has nothing to do with our problems! These damned Americans think they can take this camp from me! You must help me!"

"What can I do?"

"This is your fault!" erupted Dang. "Before you came, no one wanted my camp. You tricked me with this American aid!"

"You're a rich man because of it."

Dang reached out and grabbed Brian's shirt. "You will stop this." He spoke in a desperate tone. "You will do it!"

"Where's Tubtim.   What happened last night?" insisted Brian.

"I don't know!   And that insect is of no concern now!"

"There's nothing I can do."   Brian glanced back into the main room.   "You've been planning to replace us with Chovat, but your timing stinks!"

"You'll regret this," hissed Dang.

Brian swiftly turned to him.   "I don't know what happened to Tubtim.   Maybe you had nothing to do with it, but I know Chovat did!   And I know you're finished here!   You'll be no more than one of the residents.   No more pockets to pick!   No one will guard you and protect you from the people you've raped."   Brian turned and started out.   "Hell, you'll be lucky if they don't kill you."

"Mr. Grady," said Brian as he entered the room.   "I'll be leaving now.   My friends and I will look for Tubtim elsewhere."   Brian glanced at the threatening scowl of the Frenchman.   "But if you ask me, the people outside of this room will be better off the sooner you bring in professionals to run the camp."   Brian hesitated, but he was unable to resist his desire.   "The warehouses in this camp are filled with contraband these men stole from the very people they were supposed to protect."   The room went silent. Brian looked at each face.   Only Callie was not surprised.   "I was about to expose them in my next article, but better you handle it."

"And where will you be?" asked Mr. Grady in an accusing voice.

"I'll be at home."   Smiling at Callie, he repeated their address and then they started out.

"I've questions for you!" demanded Mr. Grady.

"And I'll be happy to answer them," replied Brian as he glanced over his shoulder. Both Dang and Mr. Grady looked confused, and the Frenchman slipped out a back door.

Suddenly, they were outside and the Prince grabbed Brian's arm. "What have you done?!"

The Prince was shaking with anger. "We'll never be able to bring anyone here! They'll replace Dang today! All we worked for is over!"

"It already is!" answered Brian.

"Why!" demanded the Prince. "You hear people call to you and you go crazy! Your pride did this!"

"He knows because of the people!" Brian said as he grabbed the Prince by the arms. "It was finished when we arrived! As soon as he saw the crowd, how else would the refugees know us!" The Prince's eyes softened. "Before long everyone will know."

"There is no proof!" exclaimed the Prince.

Brian turned the Prince to face the tent city he had helped to create. "Of course there is."

They immediately returned to Bangkok. The ride back was slow and quiet as each of them tried to imagine what would happen next. What they had created had grown out of control and could now destroy them. Brian felt guilty, for his ambition had taken them down the road that lead to their being discovered. He had put them all in danger.

"It was worth it," said Callie.

"I'm to blame," answered Brian. "I'm the one that caused this."

For a moment no one spoke. "We took the risk together," answered the Prince. "To be caught by our own success is not such a bad thing," he smiled. "We could have been discovered in many ways. Tubtim could have informed."

"Tubtim." Brian tried to shake off his depression and focus on their missing comrade. "We have to find him!"

The car was silent again as each of them worried about the moon faced boy.

For the next two days every inquiry Brian made of Tubtim led nowhere.

There was nowhere left to turn but to the military itself. If they had Tubtim, Brian might be able to do something for the boy, but simply waiting would accomplish nothing. Leaving the house, he did not tell Callie where he was going. He knew she would worry and try to convince him not to go. Instead he told her he was going to a meeting with the Prince.

The sidewalk was crowded with government employees hurrying back to work. The smell of barbecuing beef sticks filled the air.

Brian stopped and stared at the large building that housed the offices of the Border Patrol Police. It was an ominous building, and he really did not want to enter its doors. If Tubtim had been caught, they would have tried to make him talk, and if he had, they might already be looking for him.

He was about to step off the curb and cross the street when he saw Sheldon exit the building with another man. For a moment Brian did not recognize Sheldon's companion and then realized that it was

Godfrey. At the same moment, Sheldon looked up and saw Brian. Sheldon froze in his tracks for a moment before rushing towards Brian with a confused Godfrey in tow.

"What the hell do you think you're doing here!" demanded Sheldon when he reached Brian. "Wave a cab quick!" he ordered to Godfrey. "What the hell have you done?" said Sheldon in disbelief. "They have one of your friends in there."

Brian's heart sank. "How is he?"

"Not good! But better than you'll be before this ends." A cab rolled up to a stop, and Sheldon pushed them all inside and ordered the cab back to Brian's apartment. "You're in it up to your ears now!"

"What do they know?" asked Brian in a voice that tried to hide his fear.

"They know a young American couple was bringing Cambodians in illegally. You son of a bitch! When did she get you involved? Why didn't you come to me?"

Brian glanced at Godfrey who watched him with distaste. "Why? So the two of you could write about it? I don't expect you to understand, but I did the right thing."

"The right thing was to do your job. Not become a part of it!"

Godfrey removed his safari hat and fanned his face. "When I think of all the work I put in," he said as he hesitated and shook his head at Brian. "I could kill you myself."

"Don't flatter yourself. You were never that close." Brian turned to Sheldon. "They don't actually know it's me. Not yet anyway, right?"

Sheldon hesitated and watched him in amazement. "That's only a reprieve. What we have to do is get you out of the country, and soon."

"I'm not sure I can do that," said Brian.

"Are you listening to me? You don't have any choice!" Sheldon insisted.

"That's where you're wrong," Brian glanced between them. "There's always a choice."

His companions looked at one another and the cab sped on.

When they arrived at the river, Sheldon told Godfrey to wait by the docks and keep an eye out for police cars. Looking at Godfrey, Brian couldn't help being disappointed. He was short, and although a good looking man, he no longer seemed admirable. He just seemed overly self-assured to the point of being conceited.

Into the courtyard they could see the surprise in Callie's and the Prince's expressions.

"Hello, my old friend," called the Prince happily from the balcony.

Sheldon did not respond. "How involved is he?" he asked Brian.

Brian didn't respond.

"Oh hell, up to his neck!" Sheldon shook his head.

Brian smiled. "Are you mad because we didn't let you in on it, or is it because you couldn't figure it out?"

Sheldon did not respond.

When they entered the apartment, there was an atmosphere of dread.

"Hello, Sheldon," said Callie as if calmly expecting bad news. Sheldon glanced at her but did not reply.

"The Border Patrol has Tubtim," announced Brian quietly.

"Oh, dear God," said Callie. Then she glanced between Brian and Sheldon, surprised that Brian would speak of it in front of Sheldon.

"He knows. He warned me."

Sheldon shook his head. "All of you, for Christ's sake. I need a drink." He started for the kitchen. "I hope some of that tea is still here."

Brian and Callie stared at each other without moving. The Prince slowly turned and walked onto the balcony.

"Has anyone seen him?" Callie finally asked.

"No."

"Then we don't know how he's been treated. Maybe ..."

"They know we're involved. They just don't have our names," interrupted Brian. "Sheldon believes we should leave the country right away," he hesitated. "But I'm not sure. I'm not sure what you'll want." Brian could sense that Sheldon had stepped back into the room.

"I have what I want," she paused. "Brian, I don't think we can do anymore. We've done all we can."

For a moment Brian didn't know what to say, so he tried to smile. "It's all falling apart so quickly, and it's my fault. I caused it!"

"You dumb ass, you're standing on sand! You don't have any choice anymore!" ordered Sheldon. "Forget what you've done to my reputation and yours. We're talking about a Thai prison for both of you!"

Callie walked to Brian and put her arms around him. She began to gently cry. "I'm so sorry; we've made such a mess of things. We can't stay now; they'll take you from me if we stay."

Brian imagined her again in a bleached-out Greek village, in a white dress near the sea. Everything was happening so fast, he didn't know what to say or do.

"For Christ's sake Brian, I should leave you in this mess! After all, you certainly weren't loyal to me," Sheldon said as he glanced at Callie and the Prince. "None of you were! You have to get out of the country now! This isn't a game. You're likely to spend the rest of your life in a Thai prison, or worse!"

"I appreciate what you're trying to do Sheldon, and I know I don't deserve your help."

"Screw that. With you, I can get you out today! We'll use Godfrey's exit visa. Callie will have to follow in a few days."

"I'm not leaving her!" insisted Brian.

"It will take two days to get her an exit visa," Sheldon exclaimed. "There's no other way."

"I won't go without her!"

"Please, Brian, everything will be fine you ..."

"No," interrupted Brian. "We go together."

"Are you still trying to save someone?" Sheldon chuckled sarcastically. "You don't' have the time! It would take days to get the visas. Don't be stupid!"

Brian looked at Callie. "We will leave together. As soon as things can be arranged."

"Brian, please do as he says," Callie pleaded.

"Together! We go together," he answered.

"If there is any sense left in both of you, you will listen to me." Sheldon said impatiently.

Brian turned to Sheldon. "Please try to understand that I appreciate what you're trying to do. I know you want to help us, and I know you think we let you down. But I can't go without her. I won't."

For a moment Sheldon stared quietly at Brian and then nodded. "Okay."

"What about the Prince?" asked Brian.

The Prince moved towards them, wanting to join in the conversation. "I'll be fine. I'll go north, and with my family ties, they'll be sure to overlook me. But there are other things you need to know. I was just telling Callie about it when you came."

"What now?" exclaimed Sheldon.

The Prince ignored him and continued. "Last night the border patrol showed up at the camp with a large force. They were there to arrest Dang."

"Dang?" shouted Sheldon. "Don't tell me you're involved with that cutthroat! When I read your articles about him, I just assumed you were stupid."

"We've had an arrangement with him for a short time," said Brian without looking at Sheldon. "Go on Prince."

"They arrested many of the camp guards. The ones they did not arrest were disbanded. But the Frenchman and Dang managed to get away. Remember Dang blames you for everything. He's convinced that he would still be in his camp if he hadn't listened to you or if you would have helped him with the inspectors."

Brian turned to Sheldon. "Was Chovat arrested with Tubtim?"

"Not that I heard."

The Prince looked to the floor and shook his head. "Chovat is with Dang and the Frenchman. I'm sure of that, and that's one more reason to worry. Chovat could bring them here."

"They're too busy saving their own skins," said Brian.

"You really don't know who you're dealing with," said Sheldon. "These guys can be dangerous people! Asians don't let an enemy get away!"

"That's not the worst of it," added the Prince. "The Border Patrol received bribes from Dang. There's no way for us to know who was involved, but they won't want to be exposed. They would be safe if they could get their hands on all of us. There's no way to know how much danger we're in because we don't know how high the corruption goes!"

Sheldon hesitated and then nodded. "And the American Relief Organization wants to speak to Brian."

"Why do they want to speak to Brian?" asked Callie in a near panic.

"Because they believe he must have known the things he was writing about Dang were not true. And if he knew, then he might have been a part of the corruption. After all, the stockpiles and supplies were there for everyone to see. So how did a reporter overlook them?"

Brian watched Callie closely. She was frightened but he didn't want her to see how frightened he was. "Sheldon's right. Someone will come. Maybe because they'll think we were part of the corruption, or maybe because they realized we brought the people across the border, or maybe to hide their own corruption, but they will come." Brian turned to Sheldon. "Whoever comes, it will go hard on us, and that's why we leave together."

Sheldon watched him for a moment and then accepted Brian's decision. "If you're going to leave together, we'll have to move right away. I'll arrange for the exit visas."

"Why would you do that for us? We lied to you for months," said Brian.

For a moment Sheldon did not speak. Instead he looked between Brian and Callie until the faintest of smiles hinted across his face. "I suppose in all of this, you're the ones who did the best thing. The rest of us just watched. Right or wrong, you did something about it. Besides, never would have thought you had the balls." Sheldon walked up to Brian and placed a hand on his shoulder and with a smile said, "Now we have to save them."

Callie walked to Sheldon, and put an arm around his waist. "Thank you. I'm sorry that we had to do things behind your back."

"We all had a choice." said Sheldon. "You made yours, Brian made his! I'll make mine, and once you're gone, things will go back to the way they were."

The room was silent and each of them knew it was untrue. Everything had changed, and for good or bad, they would never be the way they were.

CHAPTER TWENTY-FIVE

That night Callie made Brian the same meal she had prepared for their first night together. Both of them tried to act as if nothing was wrong, but they couldn't hide from each other the lost feeling that hung over their heads and filled the apartment. When they went to bed they held each other closely and spoke very little. Their world was no longer in their control but in control of events that had been put in motion by others.

"Do you think we made a difference?" asked Brian in a voice he didn't recognize as his own.

Callie sat up and looked at him in surprise. "Of course we did. Look at all you accomplished in a short time! There were so many of them!" Her voice was filled with love, maybe more love than she had ever shown before. She bent down and softly kissed him.

"I love you Callie, but I don't want this life to end. I don't want to leave." Brian turned to her. "Does that surprise you?"

"No," she smiled. "I've watched. You belong here as much as I do, maybe more."

Brian felt lonely. "I feel like we've been cheated. Now that we should be able to stay here in peace, we have to leave. We've helped others, but we've lost our home."

Callie laid her hand on his chest. "I'm your home. I'll make you happy, I promise. No matter what else ever happens in our lives, we have each other." She stroked his arm for comfort. "That's more than most ever have."

They lay quietly with the oscillating fan blowing air up and down their bodies. After a long time Callie's breathing changed, and she fell to sleep.

In the morning they decided it would be better if Brian went to the consulate for their exit visas, while Callie found Song Per Song to say goodbye. Brian couldn't bring himself to say goodbye to his gambling partner. He knew Song Per Song would blame him for taking Callie away.

It had taken most of the morning to get through the process of obtaining official permission to leave the country. Then he stopped by Sheldon's office to check if there was any more information on Tubtim. Brian hadn't said anything to Callie, but he felt guilty about Tubtim's fate.

Sheldon had been easily convinced that an article inquiring about Tubtim's fate might in fact save his life and be of interest to the readers that had been following Brian's articles. The only catch from Sheldon was to require Brian to ghostwrite the article that morning. Now that he had completed the effort, Brian felt much better about everything. When he returned to the apartment, he decided to relax before he started to pack. He was sure Callie would be home soon, and they could do it together. The day after tomorrow they would safely be on their way. He reassured himself that their luck would hold and they would escape.

Brian walked out onto the balcony with a cold, potent Thai beer. Sitting in one of the white wicker chairs, he was blinded by the reflected sunlight from the river. He reached up and pulled the canvas umbrella to an angle that would provide some shade. Thinking of all the things he had grown to like in the city, sitting on the balcony with Callie was what he would miss the most. He told himself they would find another balcony and another river. As long as she was with him they could make anywhere a home. As he drank the beer, he tried to think of where it would be best for them to live. The first stop would be Hong Kong, simply to get out of Thailand. From there they would decide what to do and where to begin a new life.

Brian thought of Song Per Song and wondered if the little guy would miss playing cards. He wasn't nearly as tough as he liked to act. In fact, he was a softhearted boy that craved affection and gave it freely. Brian smiled, thinking how jealous the little guy was of Callie, and he hoped he wasn't too hurt over her leaving Thailand. Then he thought of how Sheldon had volunteered to do whatever he could to help Brian find another job. It had shocked Brian to find that, after everything, Sheldon still thought of him as a friend.

Thinking of all he and Callie had been through together, he began to realize that as long as they were together they would be all right. Brian began to enjoy himself for the first time in a long time. Although there were still thousands on the border trying to get into the country, Brian told himself that now that the U.S. was involving itself in the operation of the camps things would improve. The U.S. might even become convinced to do something to stop the killing inside

Cambodia. In any case, change was on the horizon and things would improve.

Watching the crowd on the dock, Brian was able to pick out Callie by her blonde hair when she stepped out of Song Per Song's canoe. The sun happily sparkled off the water. She waved at Brian before reaching back and taking hold of a bag handed to her by Song Per Song. There was nothing in the world that could be as beautiful as Callie with the sun in her hair. She began to move through the crowd with Song Per Song in tow. Brian was excited over the happiness of Callie as she continued to wave at him. "Everything will be all right," he said aloud to himself.

Glancing at the crowd, Brian noticed a figure that for a moment looked like Chovat. Brian stood and walked to the rail as the figure began to move to intercept Callie. The sun off the river blinded Brian and he lost sight of the man. He told himself it was his imagination, that the warnings had made him paranoid. But still he searched the crowd for the man. When he could not find the figure, Brian turned his attention back to Callie. She was waving again and holding the small bag in the air. She was smiling.

Out of nowhere, Chovat was swiftly beside her. Before Brian could think there were three loud pops. The crowd screamed and scattered away from Callie as she fell to the ground. Brian heard his voice screaming, "NO!" as he jumped from the balcony. His ankle folded upon impact under his weight and would not hold his weight as he tried to run to her. When he was nearly there, he saw her try to raise herself, but she could not, and fell back into the large pool of blood growing beneath her. He forced his way through the crowd and fell to his knees beside her, but before he could touch Callie, there was a sigh of breath from her, and then she was gone. Brian froze, unable to breath or move. Then he realized that Song Per Song lay beside her dead. Brian reached out and pulled her to him and with his face buried in her hair he began to sob.

Two days later, Brian stood on a plateau and watched the sun rise off the temple that she loved so much. Below him was the sleepy town where they had stayed during the Festival of the Camburin Flower. He soaked up the sight of the endless flat lands far below the town and back to the forest that surrounded him. Far below him were the endless green and glistening rice paddies. Through the dark, teak forest he could see glimpses of the blue ribbon that was the stream they had swum in. The orange tile roofs of the town caught the morning sun and reflected it in all directions. He thought of the festival and the myth of the Camburin flower.

Then Brian turned and watched the sun shining from the high golden spirals of the temple. It really couldn't be happening. He really couldn't be there. He tried to tell himself that at any moment she would take his hand and they would walk to the hotel just as they had before. Then, one small black cloud drifted passed the golden spiral, then another and another until the air was filled with a plume of smoke that rose from the bed of flowers that covered her wrapped body. The fire roared from beneath her and the smoke grew black. Motionless, Brian watched as his love filtered across the sky beyond his touch. A hand reached out and touched his shoulder. Brian turned and looked into the face of the young monk they had met at the festival. The monk's eye held back tears which almost caused Brian to cry again. The roar from the fire grew still louder.

"Maybe we should go now?" asked Sheldon from behind him.

"Not yet," he replied in a hollow voice.

Someone else touched his shoulder and then stepped close enough to whisper, "Chovat will pay for this, I promise you," said the Prince.

Brian didn't respond. He turned and stared at the clouds of rising smoke.

"Brian, we can't do anything more," said Sheldon.

"The two of you go ahead. I'd prefer to walk back to the hotel."

"Are you sure?"

"Yes," he said without turning to look at them.

"All right, we'll wait for you there." Sheldon and the Prince turned and a moment later he heard the cab leave. Strangely, he felt more comfortable with them gone. It had all been a game life had played on them. They were not going to be allowed their happiness. Like the Camburin flower, their plans and hopes would never be found. He suddenly realized how alone he actually was. He belonged to a past that drifted away with the smoke above his head. For a long time, the young monk stood quietly beside him. Then the flames caught below the small, wrapped body of Song Per Song that lay next to her.

The fire now became a blazing inferno. He told himself she wasn't alone anymore and turned and started walking down the hill. He tried to console himself with the thought that she had saved so many. That she was a Camburin seed in each of those who survived and would remember her.

THE END